ICHIGOMASHIMARO

草莓 …… 軟糖（二）

...arasui

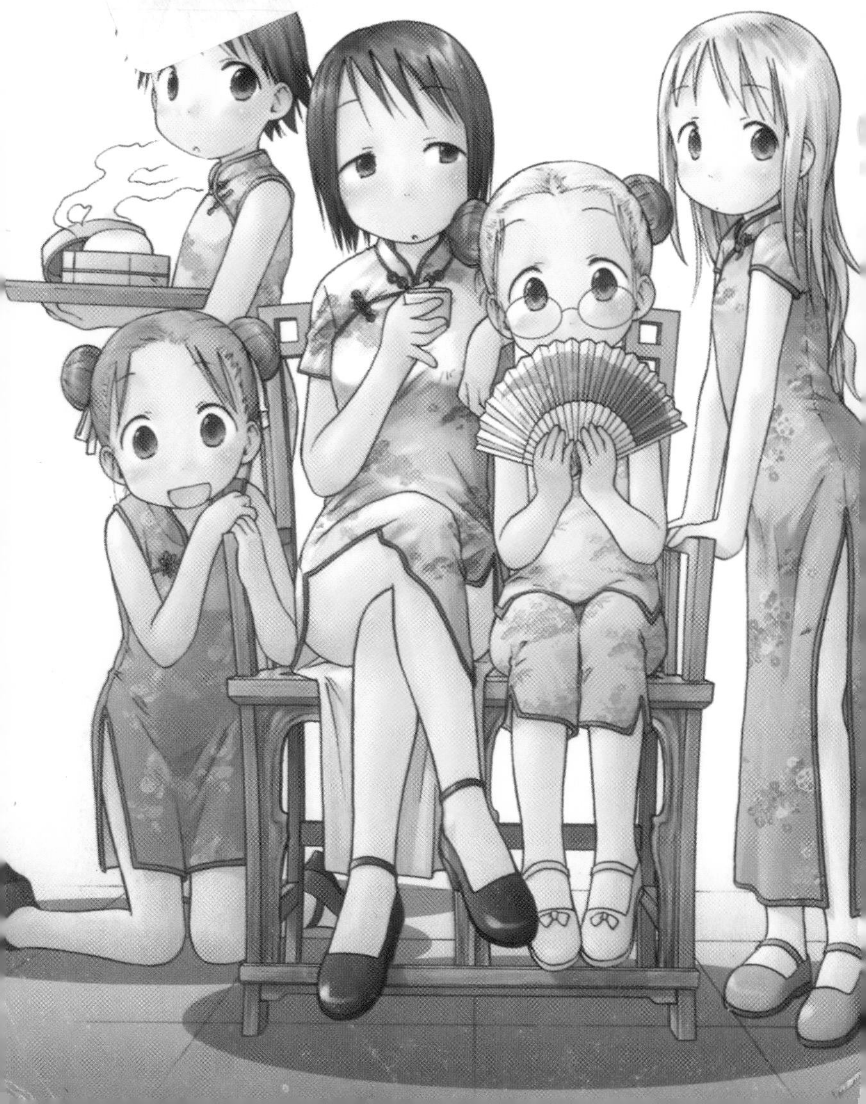

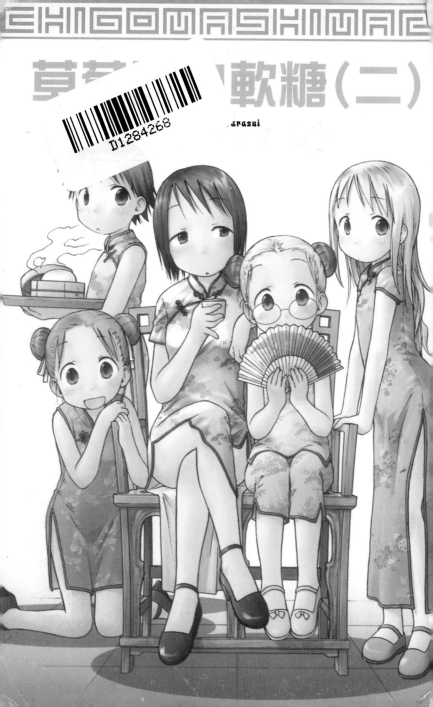

STRAWBERRY MARSHMALLOW

ICHIGO MASHIMARO

VOL. 2

BY Barasui

HAMBURG // LONDON // LOS ANGELES // TOKYO

Strawberry Marshmallow Vol 2
Created by Barasui

Translation - Emi Onishi
English Adaptation - Nathan Johnson
Retouch and Lettering - Jihye "Sophia" Hong
Graphic Designer - James Lee

Editor - Katherine Schilling
Digital Imaging Manager - Chris Buford
Pre-Production Supervisor - Erika Terriquez
Art Director - Anne Marie Horne
Production Manager - Elisabeth Brizzi
VP of Production - Ron Klamert
Editor-in-Chief - Rob Tokar
Publisher - Mike Kiley
President and C.O.O. - John Parker
C.E.O. and Chief Creative Officer - Stuart Levy

A  Manga

TOKYOPOP Inc.
5900 Wilshire Blvd. Suite 2000
Los Angeles, CA 90036

E-mail: info@TOKYOPOP.com
Come visit us online at www.TOKYOPOP.com

ISBN: 1-59816-495-3

First TOKYOPOP printing: November 2006
10 9 8 7 6 5 4 3 2 1
Printed in the USA

CUTE GIRLS ARE BACK IN TOWN

Nobue Ito

Age 16. The oldest of the bunch, and has as an irrepressible addiction to nicotine. When she's not puffing on a cig, she's teasing the girls through any means possible.

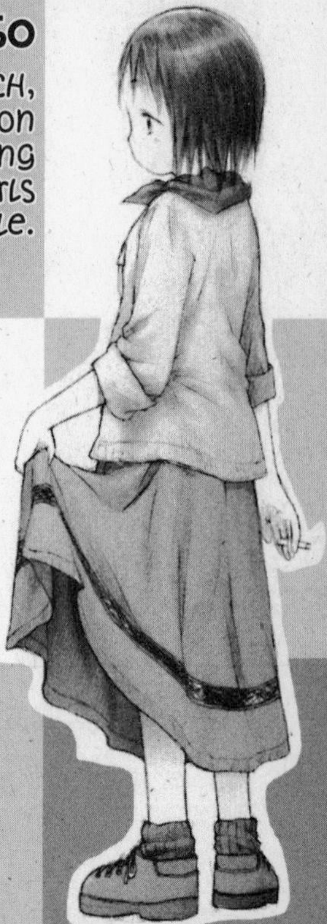

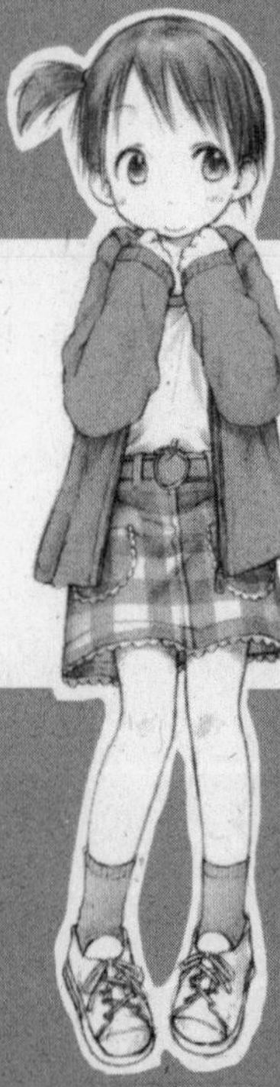

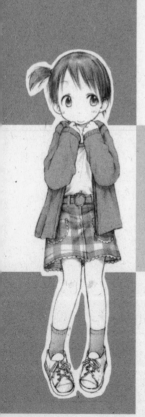

Chika Ito

Age 12. Nobue's little sister, and complete opposite. She tends to play the victim to the other girls' antics.

Miu Matsuoka

AGE 12. THE CUTEST OF THE CUTE, THIS SPAZZTASTIC BALL OF ENERGY LIVES NEXT DOOR TO CHIKA, AND WILL NEVER PASS UP THE OPPORTUNITY TO BRING A LITTLE MAYHEM TO THEIR LIVES.

Matsuri Sakuragi

AGE 11. ALSO KNOWN AS "MATS," MATSURI IS TIMID, A CRYBABY, AND COMPLETELY LOST WHEN IT COMES TO SPORTS. SHE'S ALSO OFTEN TEASED BY THE GIRLS FOR HER MYSTERIOUS WHITE HAIR.

John

MATSURI'S PET FERRET.

The Strawberry Marshmallow
Volume 2
Cartoon by Barasui

STRAWBERRY MARSHMALLOW

ICHIGO MASHIMARO

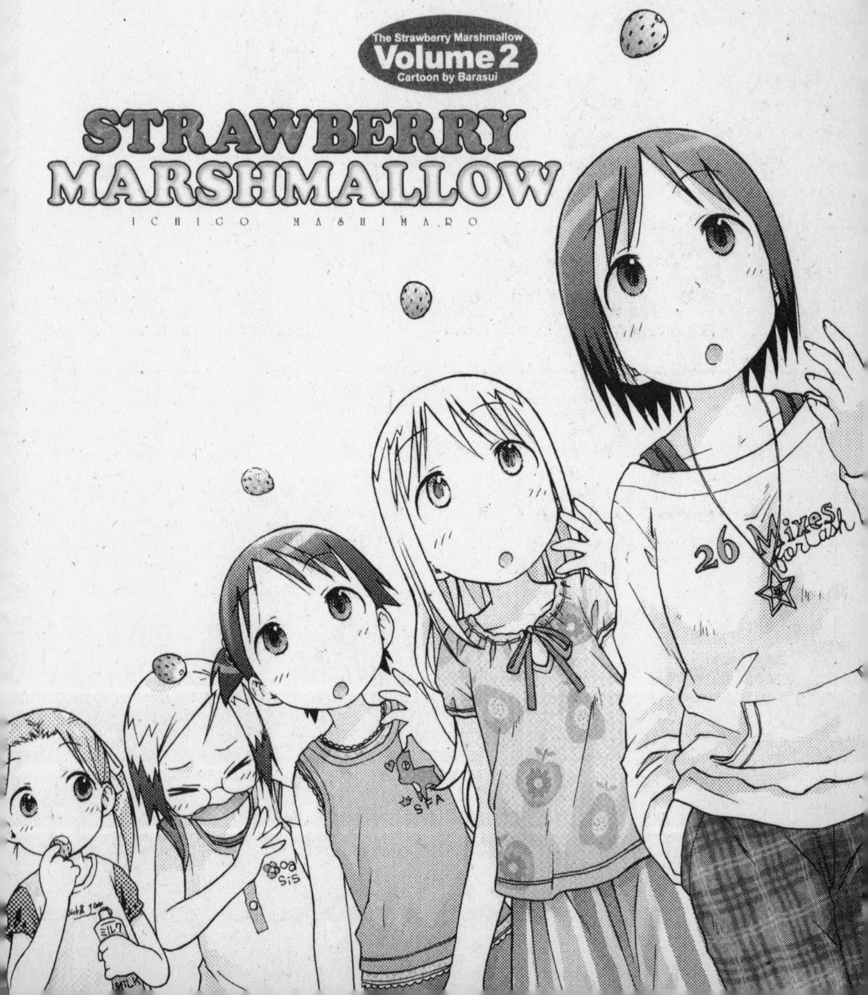

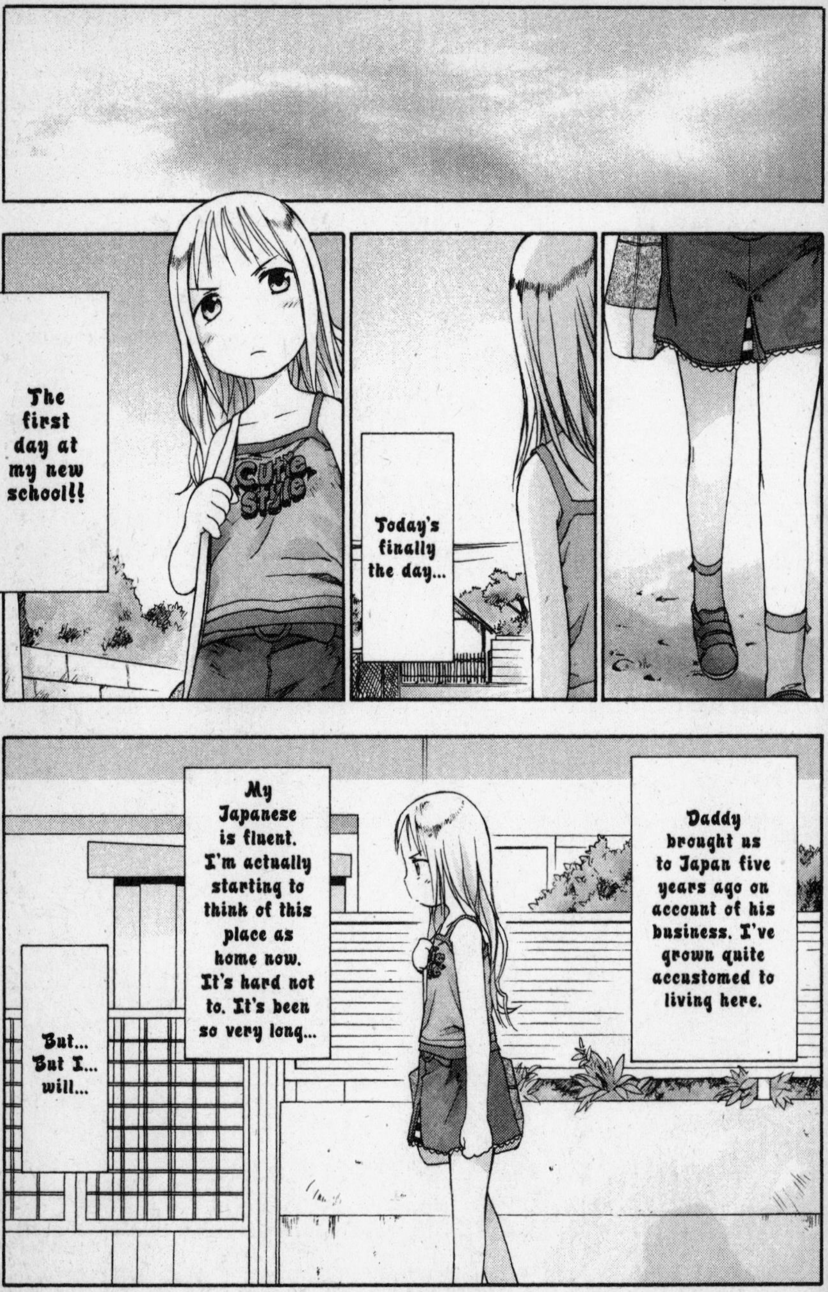
Today's finally the day...
The first day at my new school!!
Cutie Style
Daddy brought us to Japan five years ago on account of his business. I've grown quite accustomed to living here.
My Japanese is fluent. I'm actually starting to think of this place as home now. It's hard not to. It's been so very long...
But... But I... will...

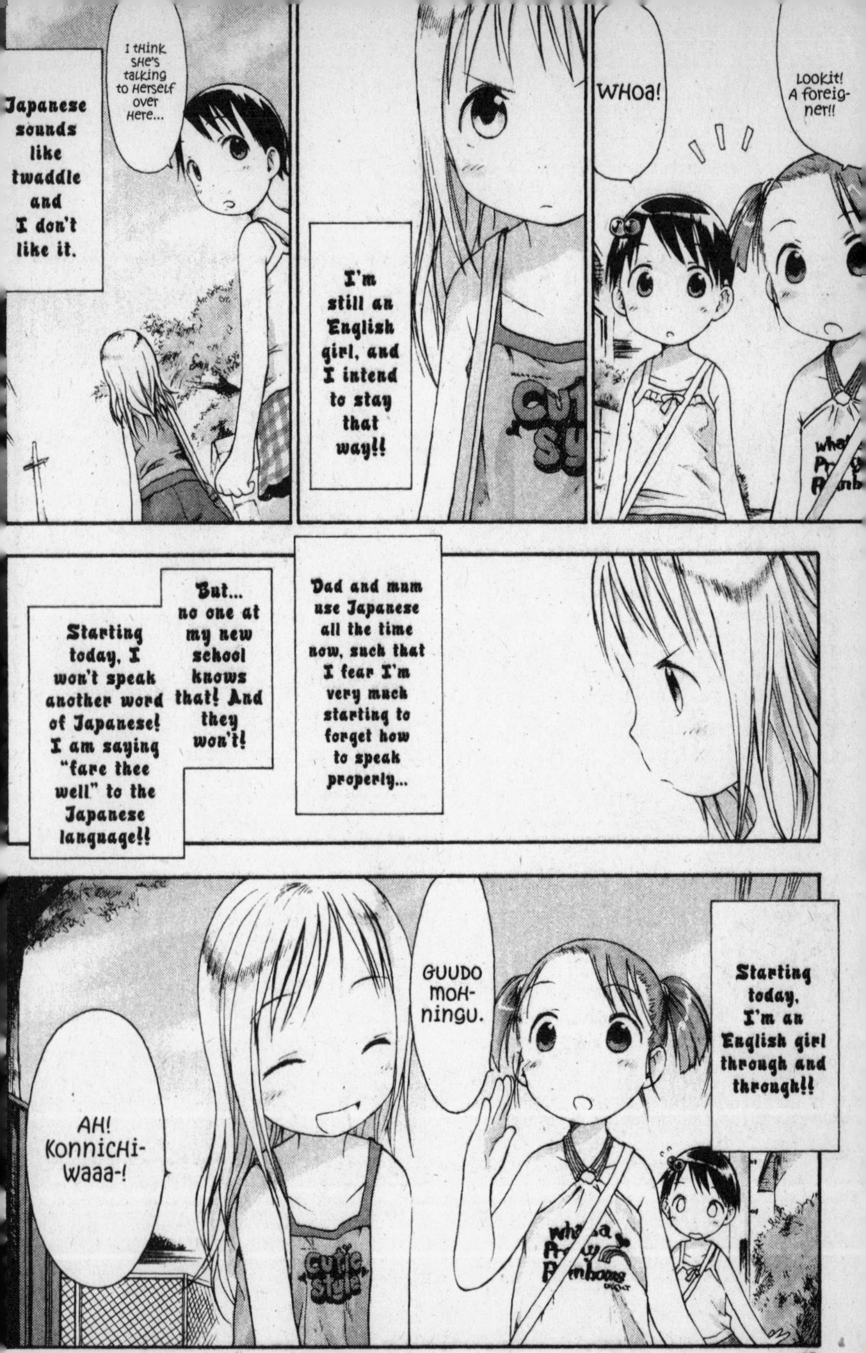
Lookit! A foreigner!!
WHOA!
I'm still an English girl, and I intend to stay that way!!
I think she's talking to herself over here...
Japanese sounds like twaddle and I don't like it.
Dad and mum use Japanese all the time now, such that I fear I'm very much starting to forget how to speak properly...
But... no one at my new school knows that! And they won't!
Starting today, I won't speak another word of Japanese! I am saying "fare thee well" to the Japanese language!!
Starting today, I'm an English girl through and through!!
GUUDO MOH-NINGU.
AH! KONNICHI-WAAA-!

episode. 11

ANA

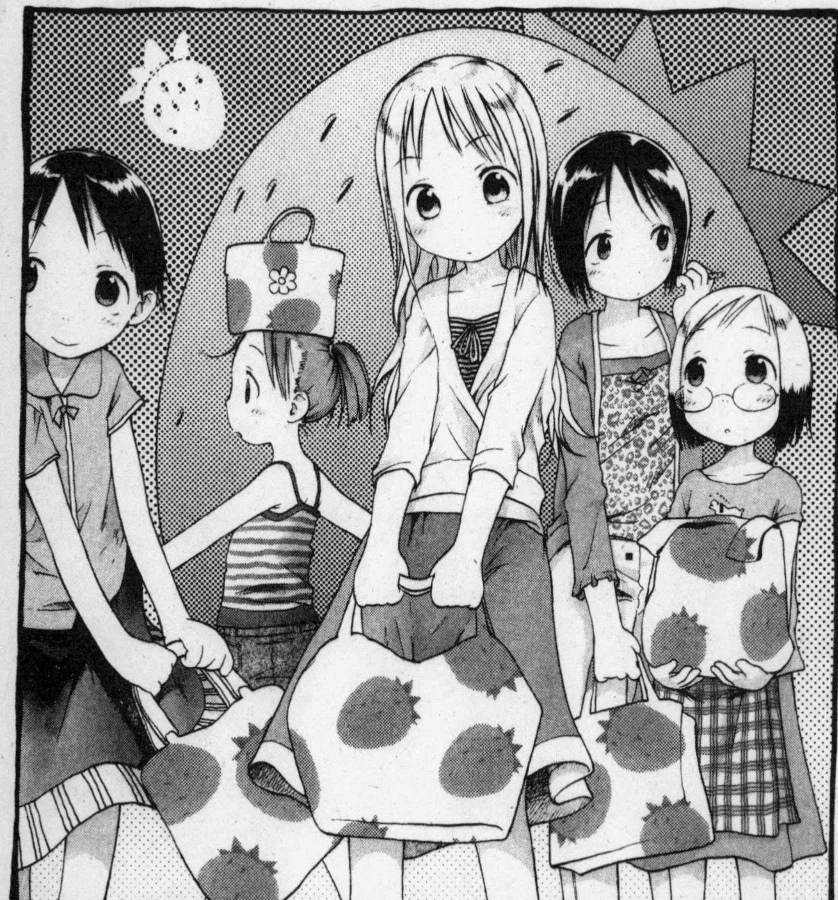

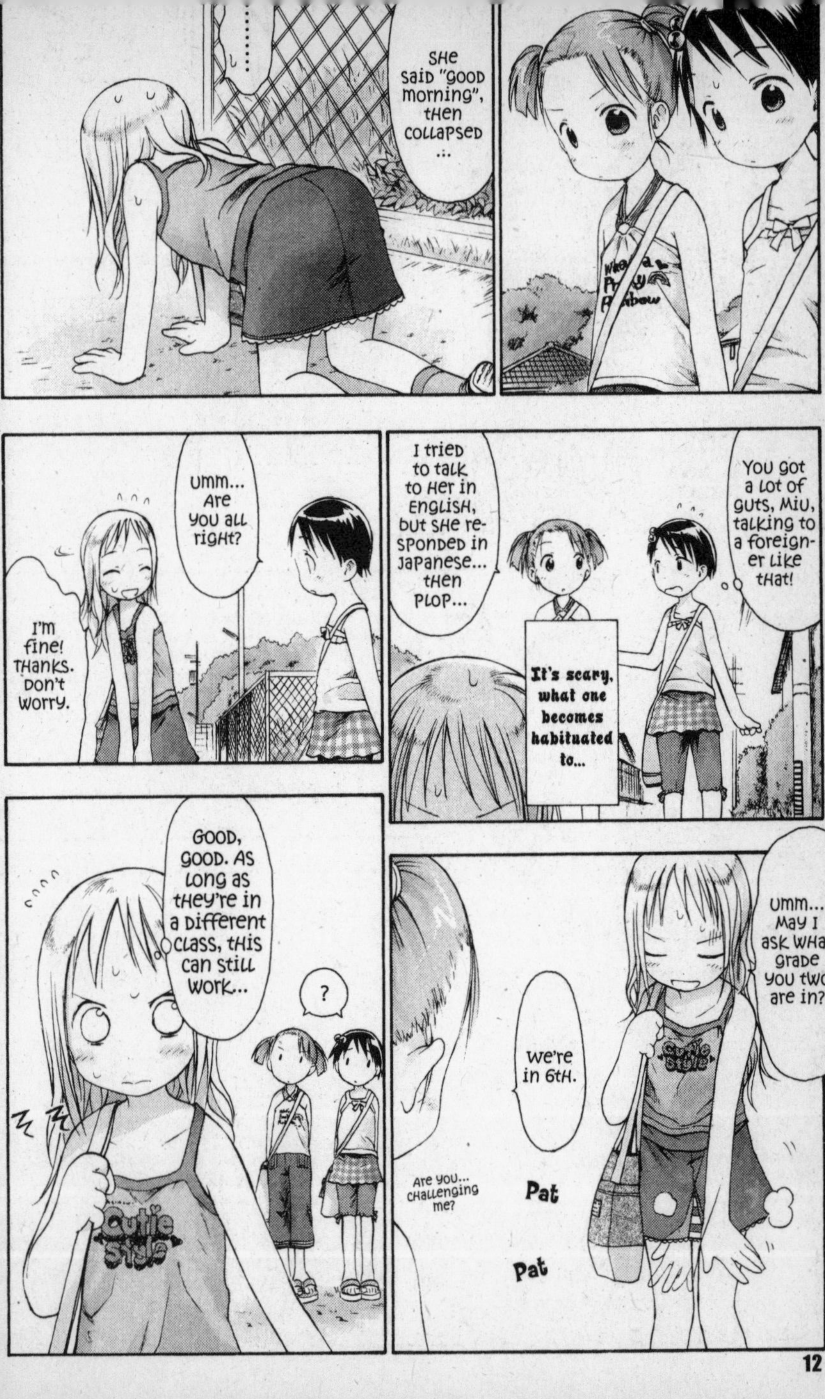
......
She said "Good morning", then collapsed ...
You got a lot of guts, Miu, talking to a foreigner like that!
I tried to talk to her in English, but she responded in Japanese... then plop...
It's scary, what one becomes habituated to...
Umm... Are you all right?
I'm fine! Thanks. Don't worry.
Umm... May I ask what grade you two are in?
We're in 6th.
Pat
Pat
Are you... challenging me?
Good, good. As long as they're in a different class, this can still work...
?

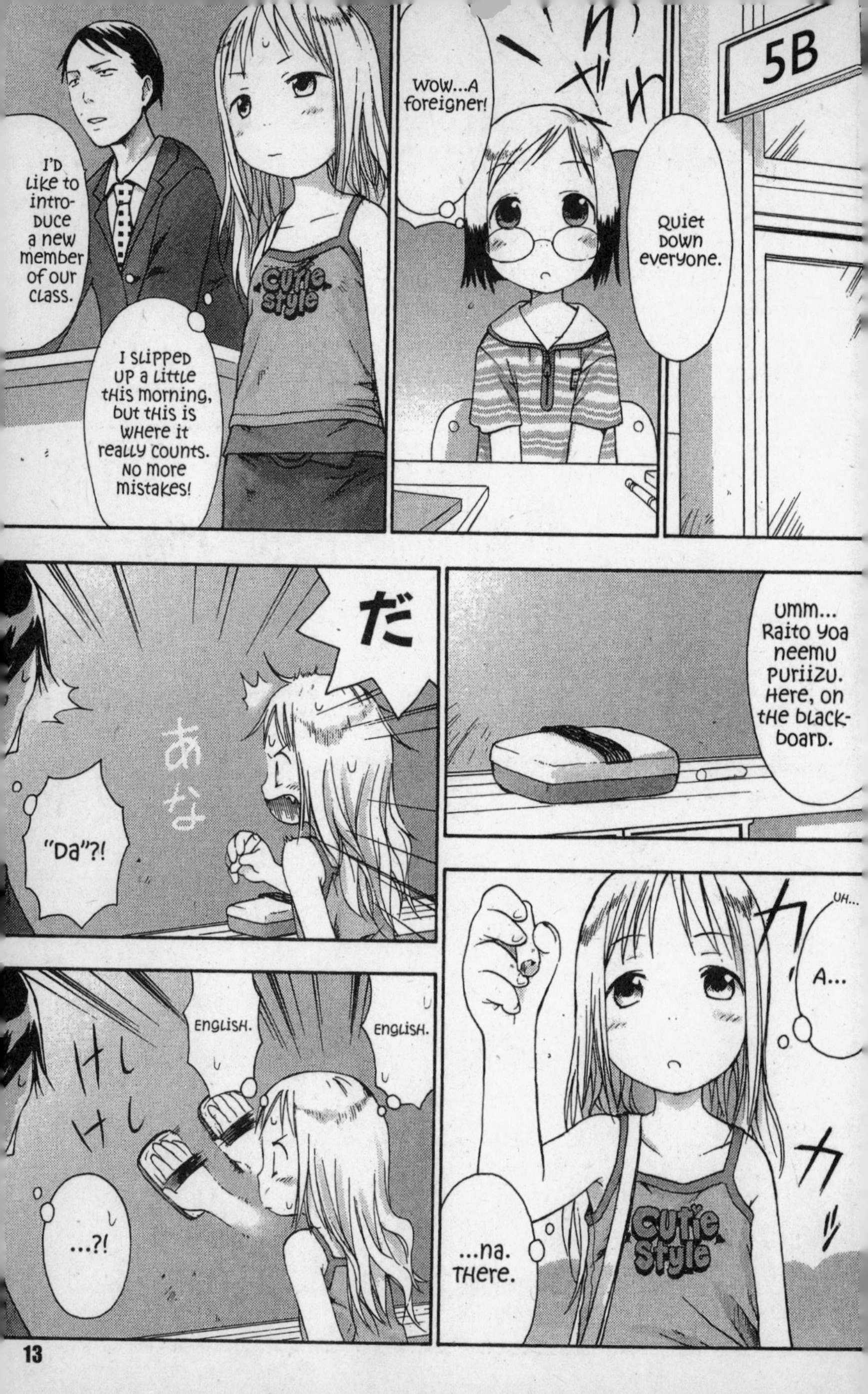
5B
ざわ ざわ
Quiet down everyone.
WOW...A foreigner!
I'D Like to intro-duce a new member of our class.
I slipped up a little this morning, but this is where it really counts. No more mistakes!
Umm... Raito yoa neemu puriizu. Here, on the black-board.
UH...
A...
カ
カ
...na. There.
だ
あな
"Da"?!
English.
English.
けし
けし
...?!

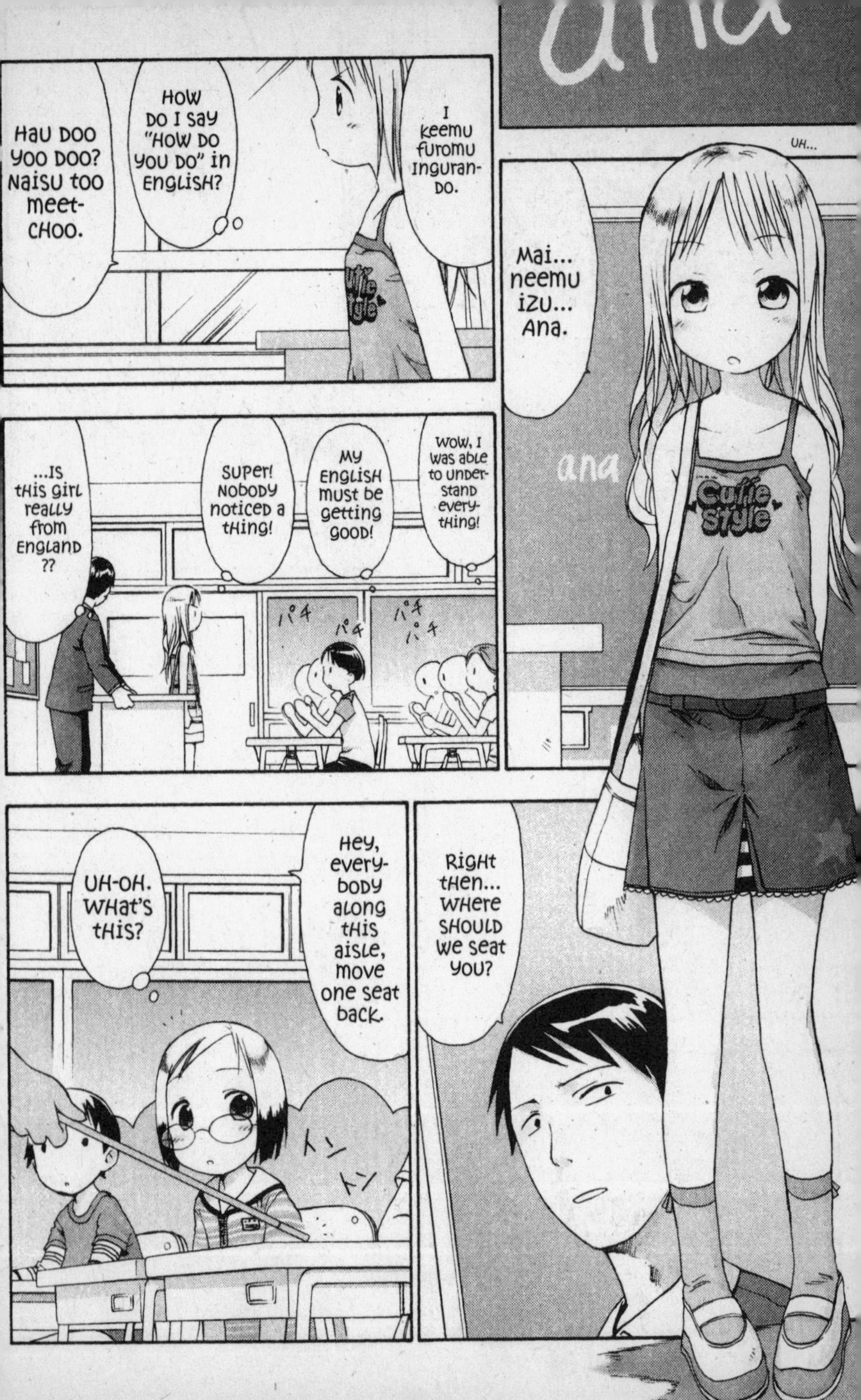
ana
UH...
Mai... neemu izu... Ana.
ana
I keemu furomu Inguran-do.
HOW DO I SAY "HOW DO YOU DO" IN ENGLISH?
HAU DOO YOO DOO? NAISU TOO MEET-CHOO.
WOW, I WAS ABLE TO UNDERSTAND EVERYTHING!
MY ENGLISH MUST BE GETTING GOOD!
SUPER! NOBODY NOTICED A THING!
...IS THIS GIRL REALLY FROM ENGLAND??
パチ パチ パチ パチ
RIGHT THEN... WHERE SHOULD WE SEAT YOU?
HEY, EVERYBODY ALONG THIS AISLE, MOVE ONE SEAT BACK.
UH-OH. WHAT'S THIS?
トン トン

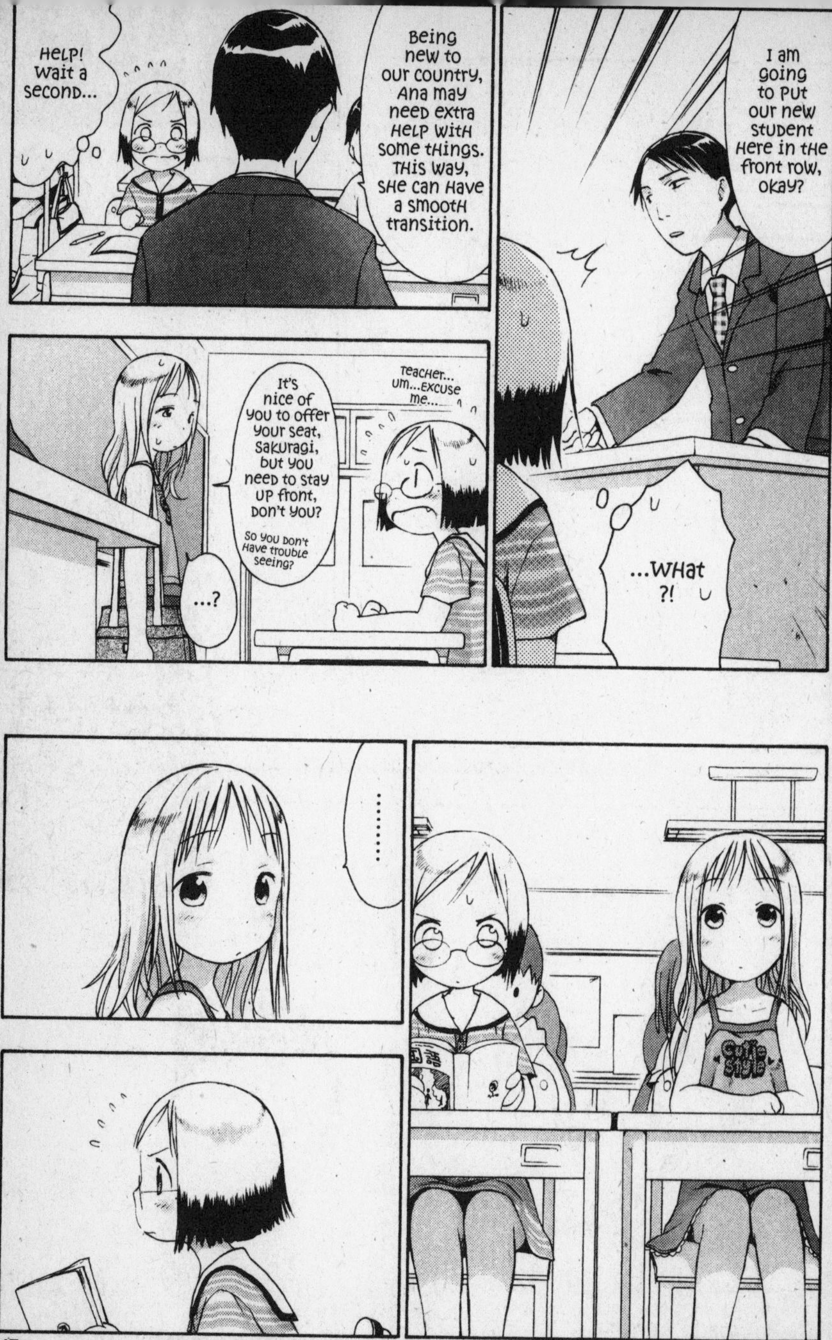
I am going to put our new student here in the front row, okay?
...What?!
Being new to our country, Ana may need extra help with some things. This way, she can have a smooth transition.
Help! Wait a second...
Teacher... um...excuse me...
It's nice of you to offer your seat, Sakuragi, but you need to stay up front, don't you?
So you don't have trouble seeing?
...?
......

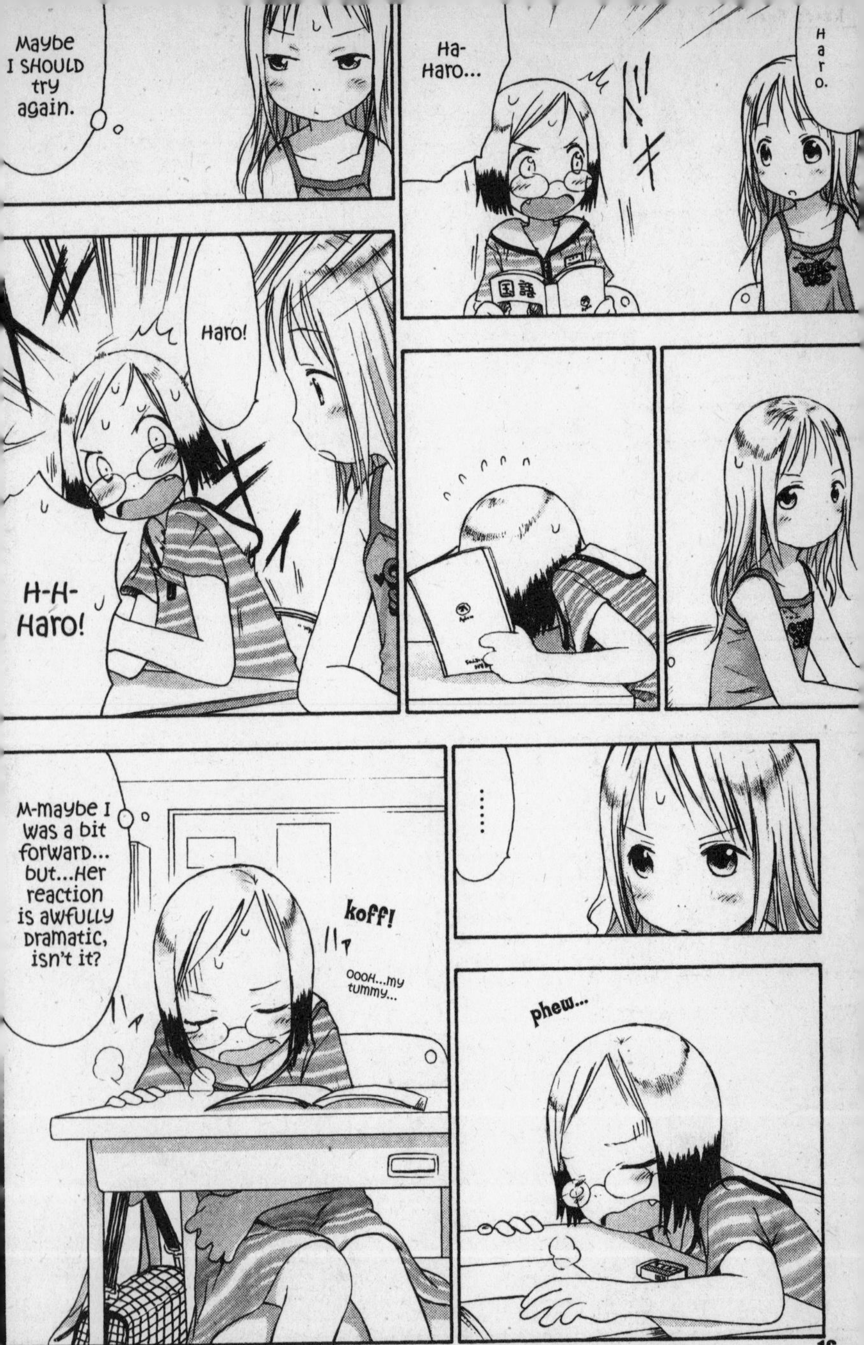
Haro.
Ha-Haro...
Maybe I SHOULD try again.
Haro!
H-H-Haro!
......
phew...
M-maybe I was a bit forward... but...Her reaction is awfully Dramatic, isn't it?
koff!
oooh...my tummy...

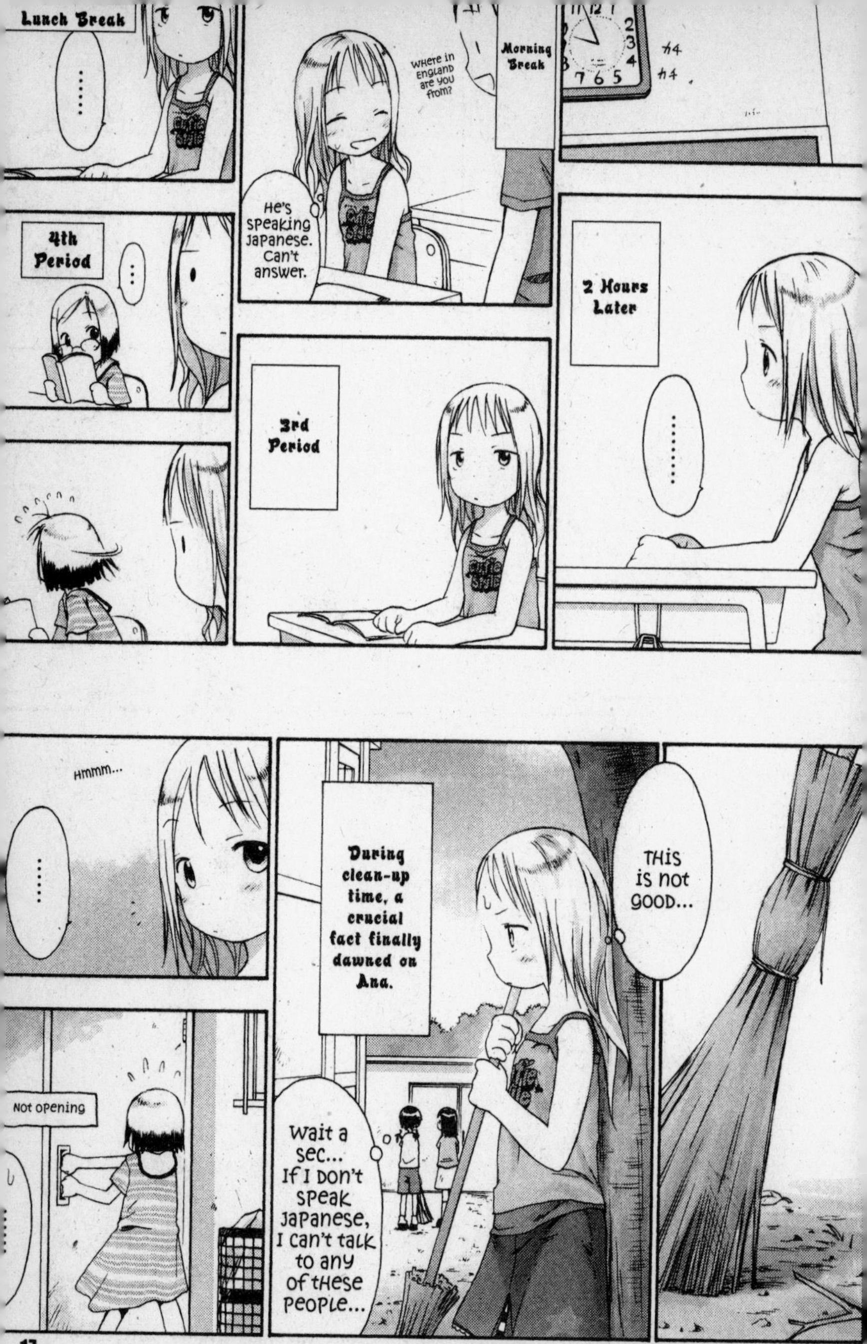
Morning Break
Where in England are you from?
He's speaking Japanese. Can't answer.
2 Hours Later
....
3rd Period
Lunch Break
......
4th Period
...
During clean-up time, a crucial fact finally dawned on Ana.
THIS is not good...
Wait a sec... If I don't speak Japanese, I can't talk to any of these people...
Hmmm...
......
Not opening

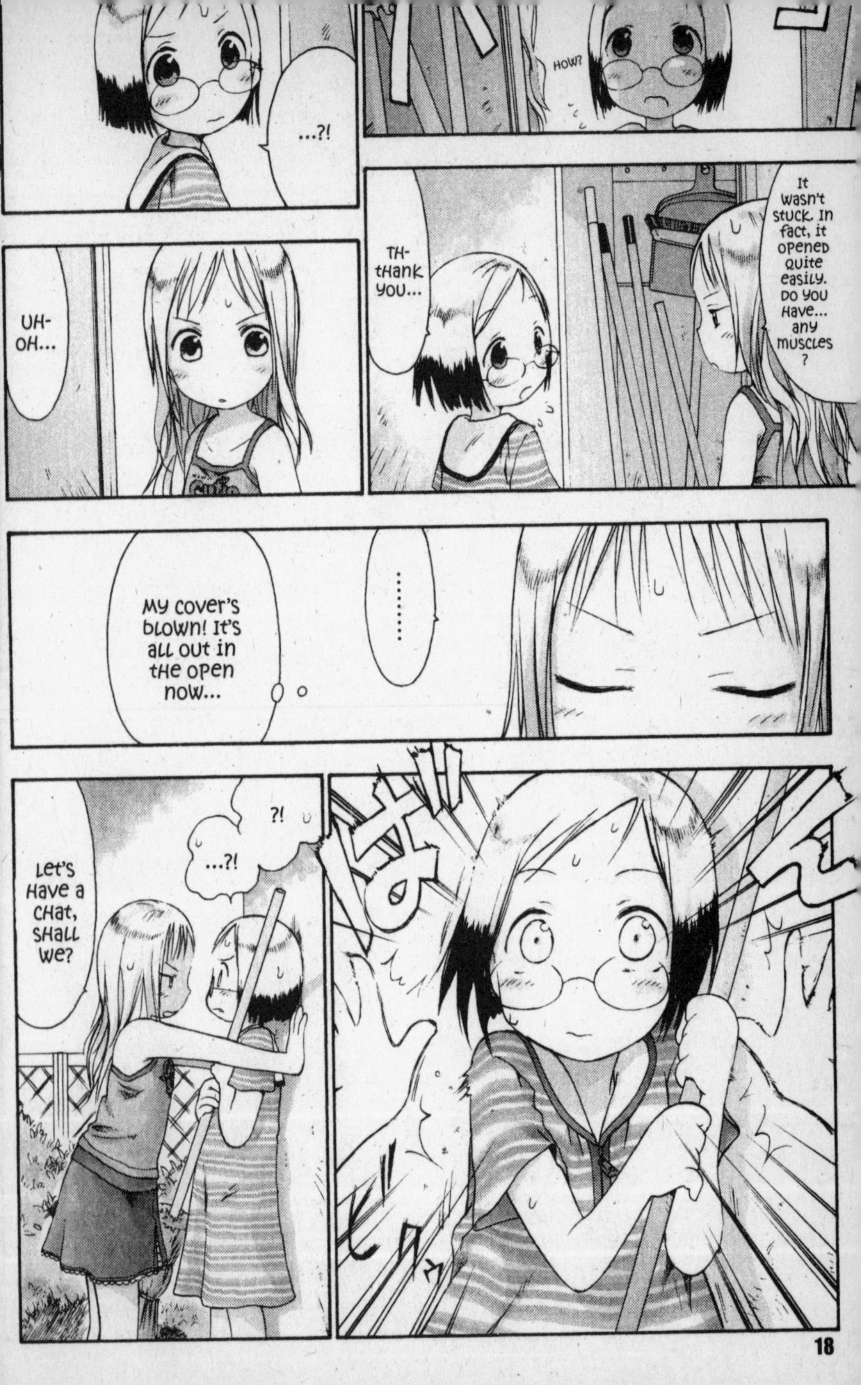
HOW?
...?!
It wasn't stuck. In fact, it opened quite easily. Do you have... any muscles?
TH-thank you...
UH-OH...
......
My cover's blown! It's all out in the open now...
?!
...?!
Let's have a chat, shall we?

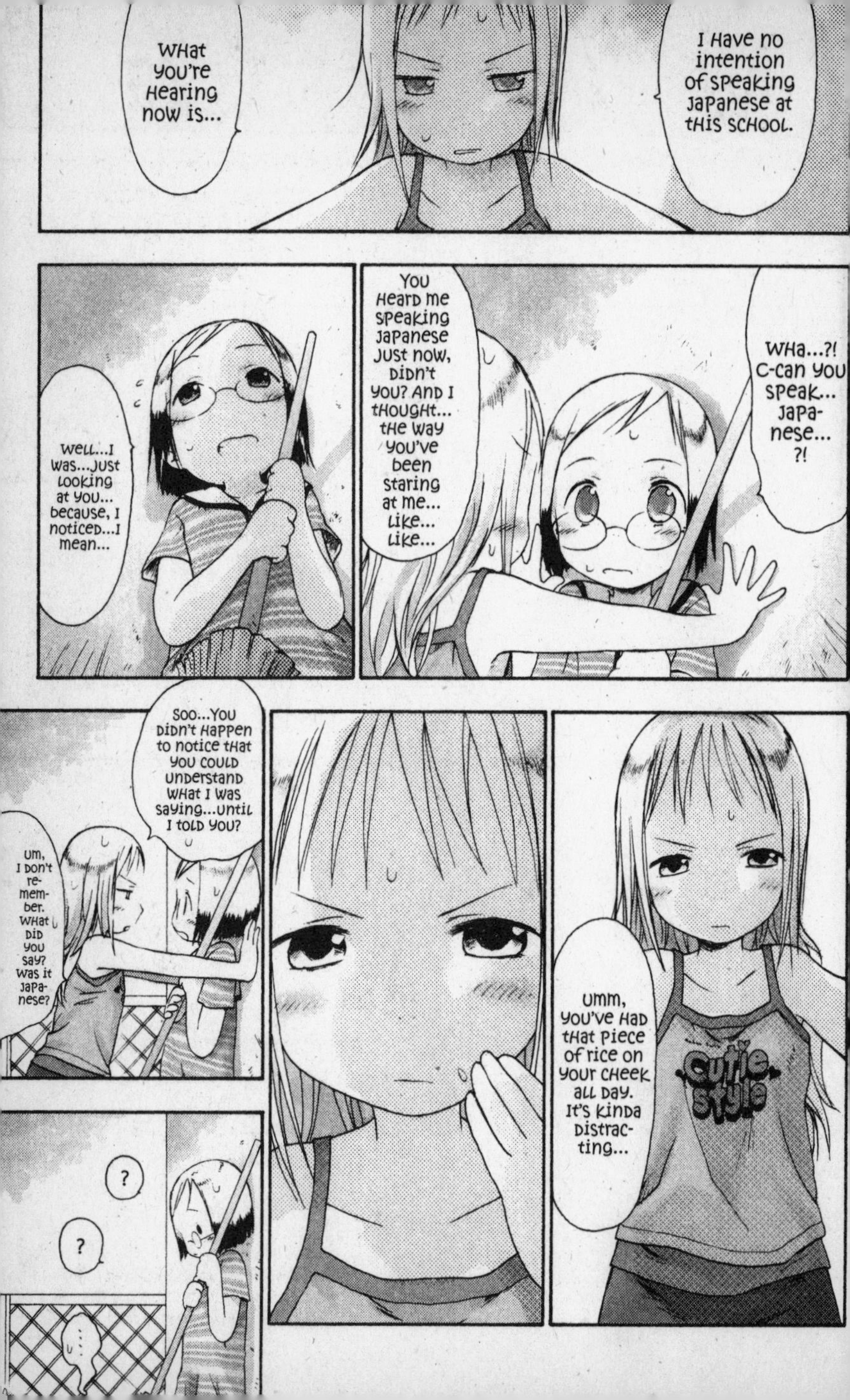
I have no intention of speaking Japanese at this school.
What you're hearing now is...
Wha...?! C-can you speak... Japa-nese...?!
You heard me speaking Japanese just now, didn't you? And I thought... the way you've been staring at me... like... like...
Well...I was...just looking at you... because, I noticed...I mean...
Umm, you've had that piece of rice on your cheek all day. It's kinda distrac-ting...
Soo...You didn't happen to notice that you could understand what I was saying...until I told you?
Um, I don't re-mem-ber. What did you say? Was it Japa-nese?
?
?
...

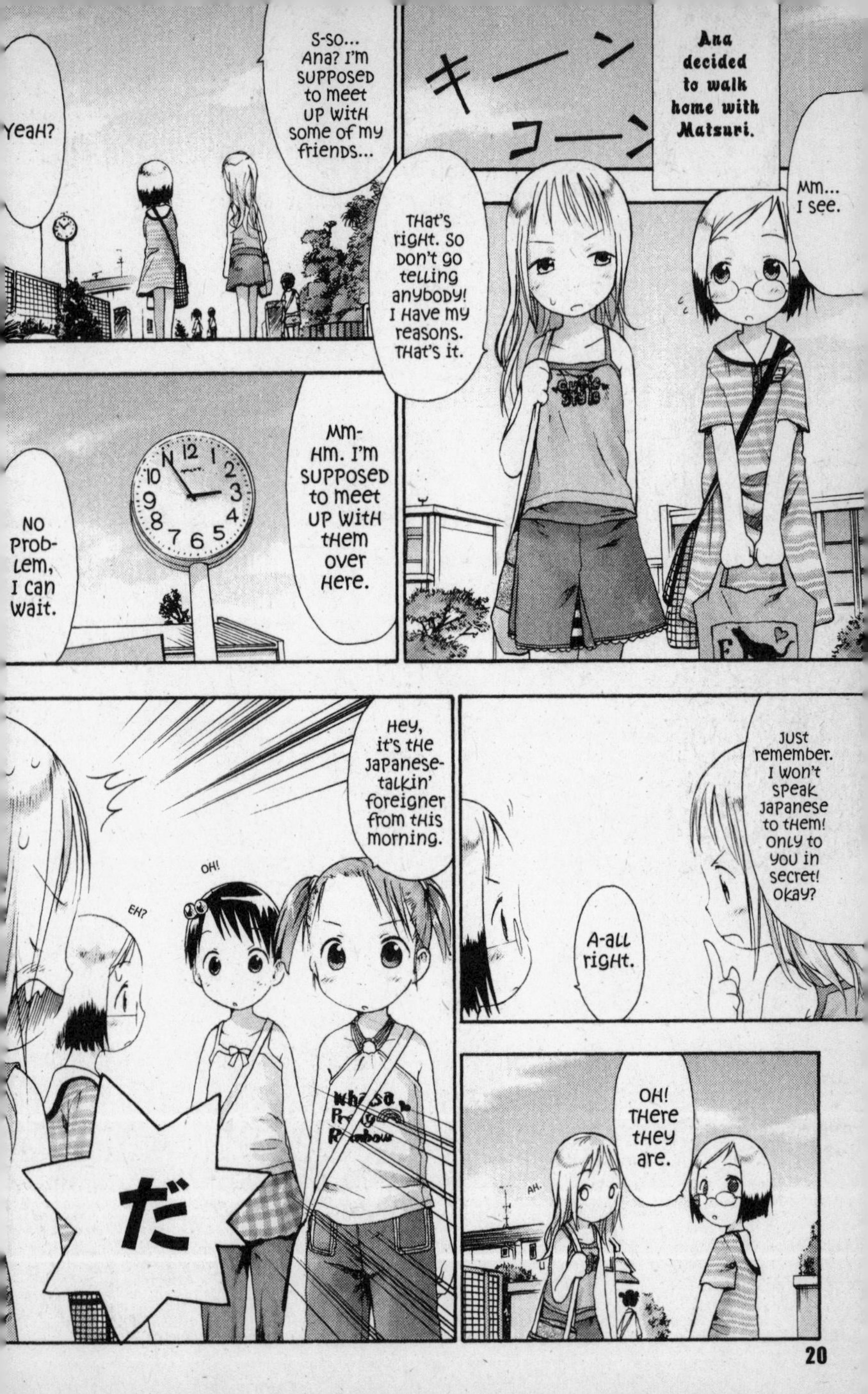
Ana decided to walk home with Matsuri.
キーン
コーン
Mm... I see.
That's right. So don't go telling anybody! I have my reasons. That's it.
S-so... Ana? I'm supposed to meet up with some of my friends...
Yeah?
Mm-hm. I'm supposed to meet up with them over here.
No prob-lem, I can wait.
Just remember. I won't speak Japanese to them! Only to you in secret! Okay?
A-all right.
Oh! There they are.
Ah.
Hey, it's the Japanese-talkin' foreigner from this morning.
Oh!
Eh?
だ

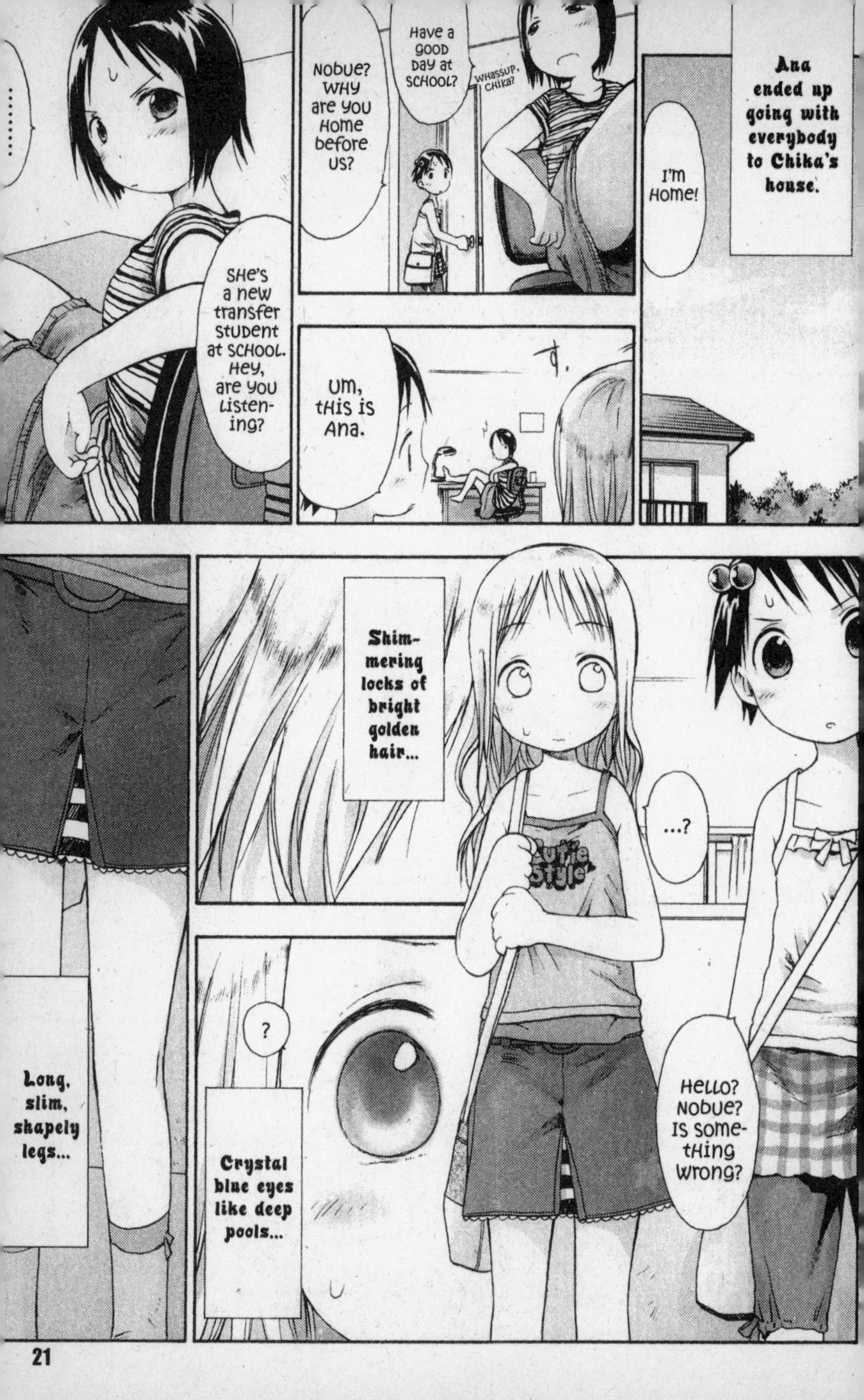
Ana ended up going with everybody to Chika's house.
I'm Home!
Whassup, Chika?
Have a good day at school?
Nobue? Why are you Home before us?
す
Um, tHis is Ana.
SHe's a new transfer student at SCHOOL. Hey, are you listen-ing?
......
Shim-mering locks of bright golden hair...
...?
Hello? Nobue? Is some-tHing wrong?
?
Crystal blue eyes like deep pools...
Long, slim, shapely legs...

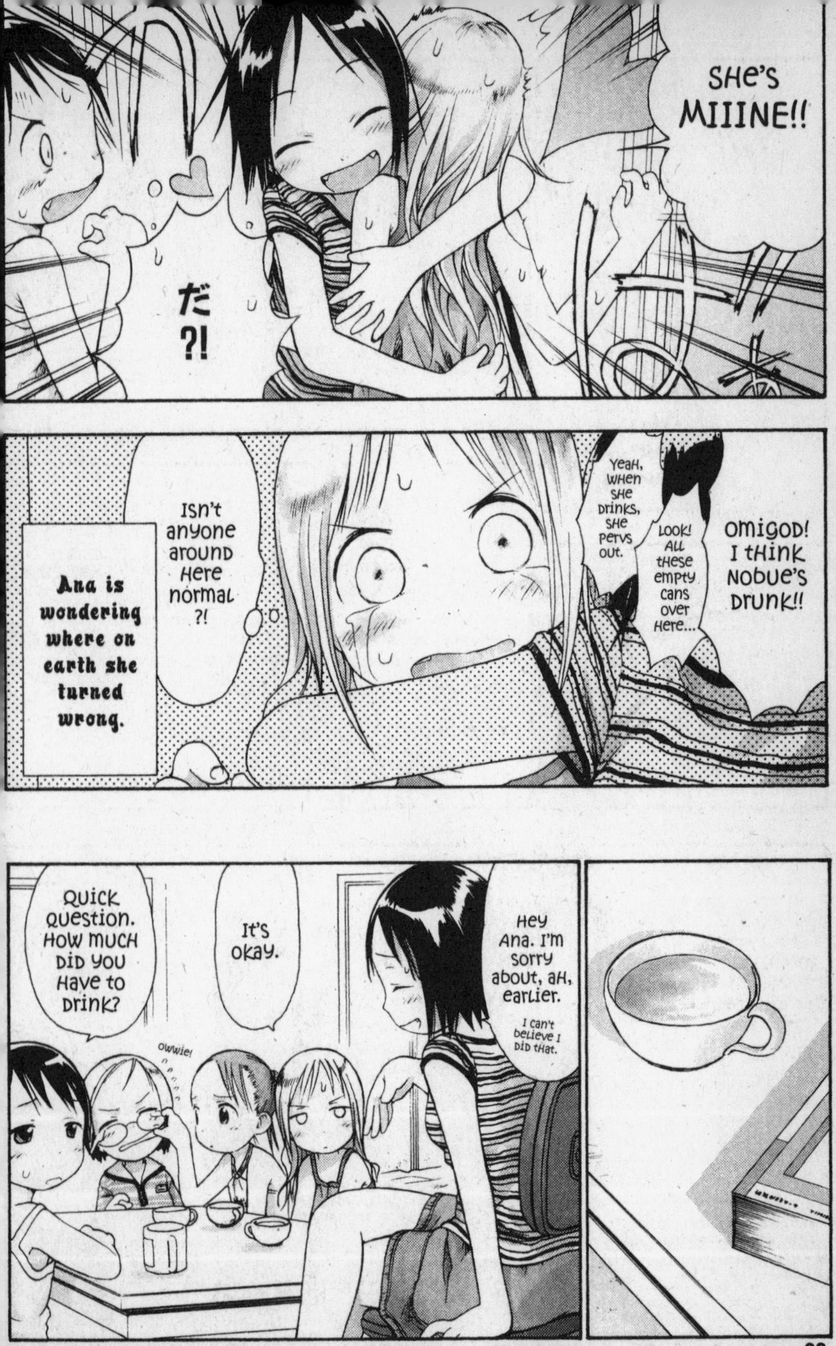
SHE'S MIIINE!!
だ ?!
OMIGOD! I think Nobue's drunk!!
LOOK! All these empty cans over here...
Yeah, when she drinks, she pervs out.
Isn't anyone around here normal ?!
Ana is wondering where on earth she turned wrong.
Hey Ana. I'm sorry about, ah, earlier.
I can't believe I did that.
It's okay.
Quick question. How much did you have to drink?
Owwie!

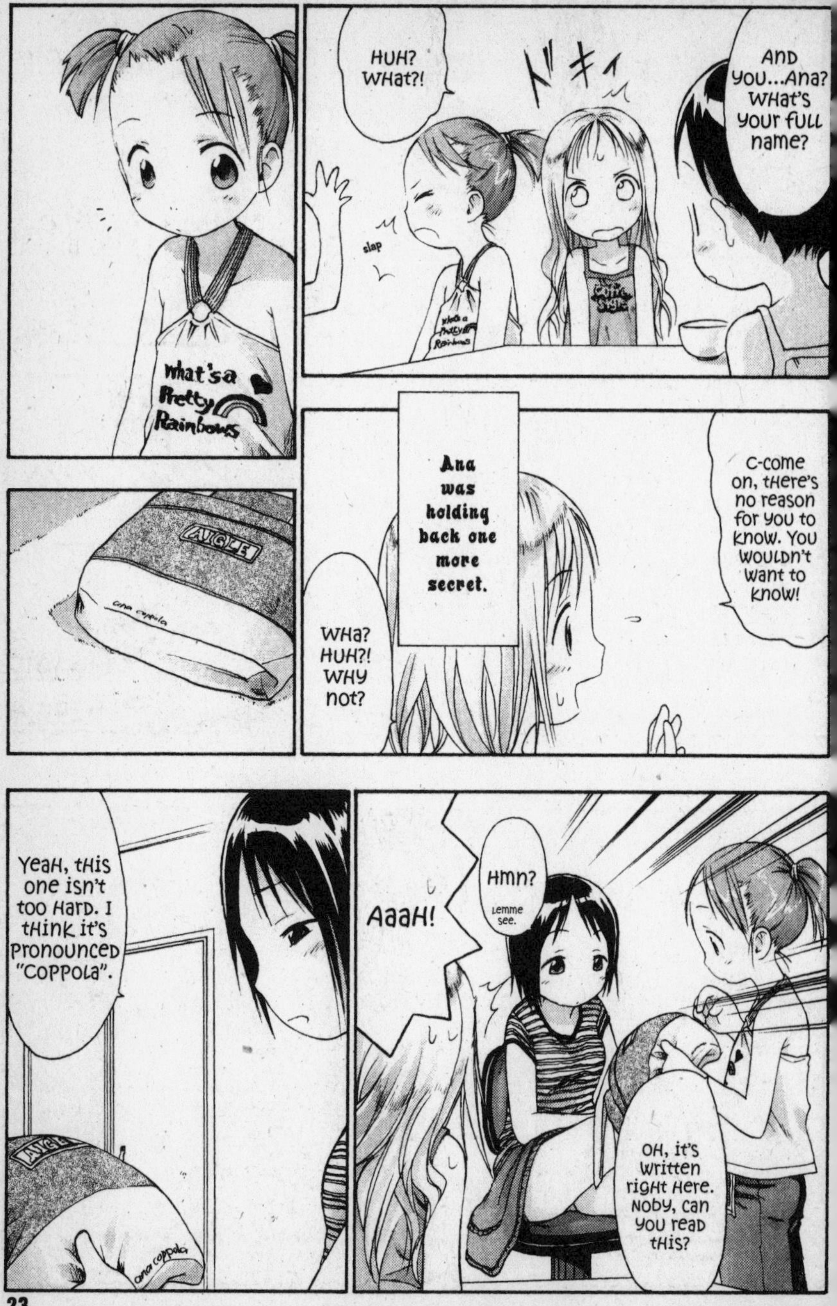
And you...Ana? What's your full name?
ドキィ
Huh? What?!
slap
What's a Pretty Rainbows
C-come on, there's no reason for you to know. You wouldn't want to know!
Ana was holding back one more secret.
Wha? Huh?! Why not?
AIGLE
ana coppola
Oh, it's written right here. Noby, can you read this?
Hmn?
Lemme see.
Aaah!
Yeah, this one isn't too hard. I think it's pronounced "Coppola".
AIGLE
ana coppola

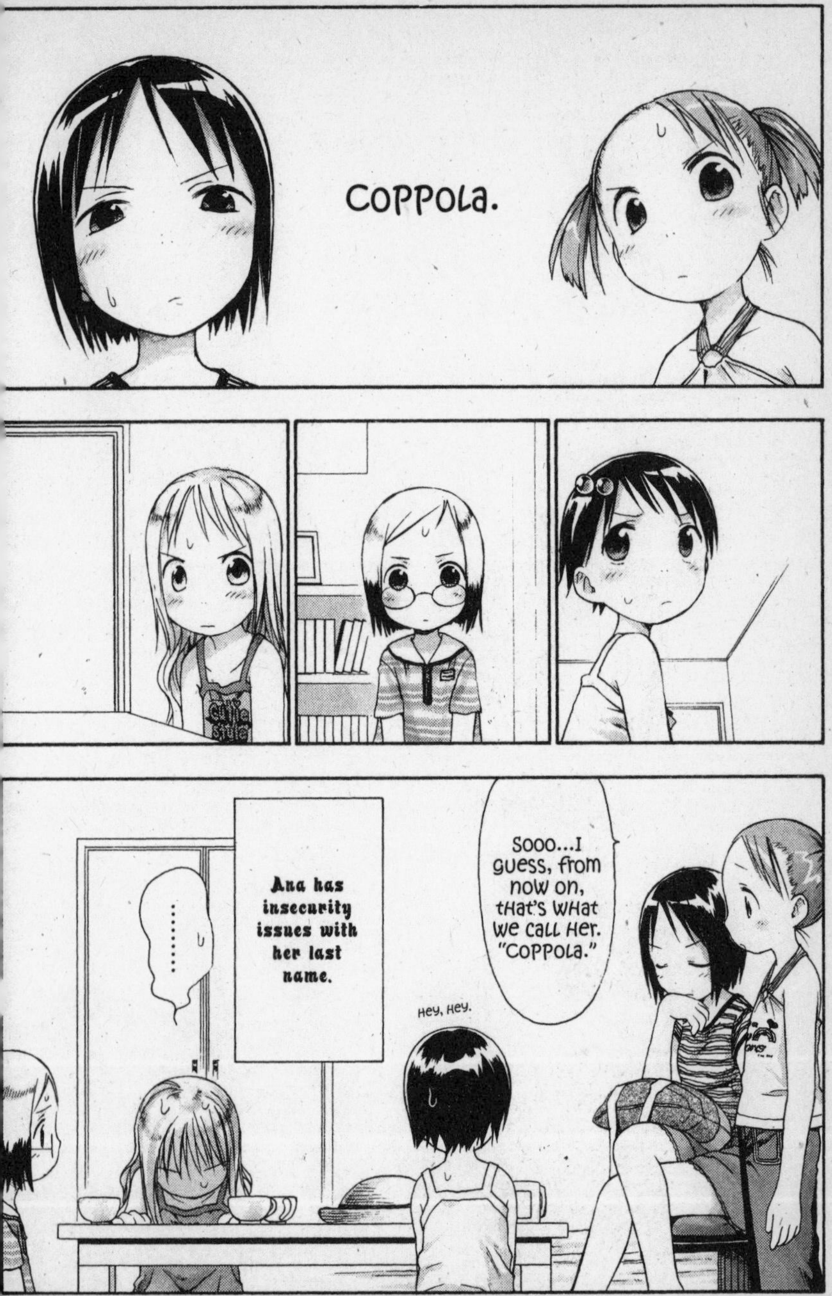
COPPOLA.
SOOO...I GUESS, FROM NOW ON, THAT'S WHAT WE CALL HER. "COPPOLA."
HEY, HEY.
Ana has insecurity issues with her last name.
....

HALLO WORK

nobue

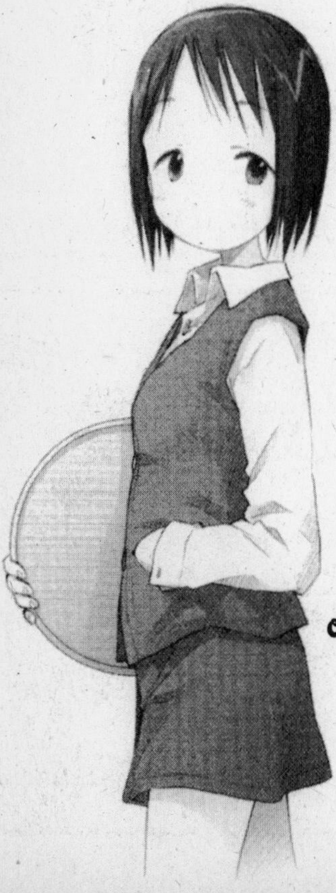

Office Lady

HALLO WORK

chika

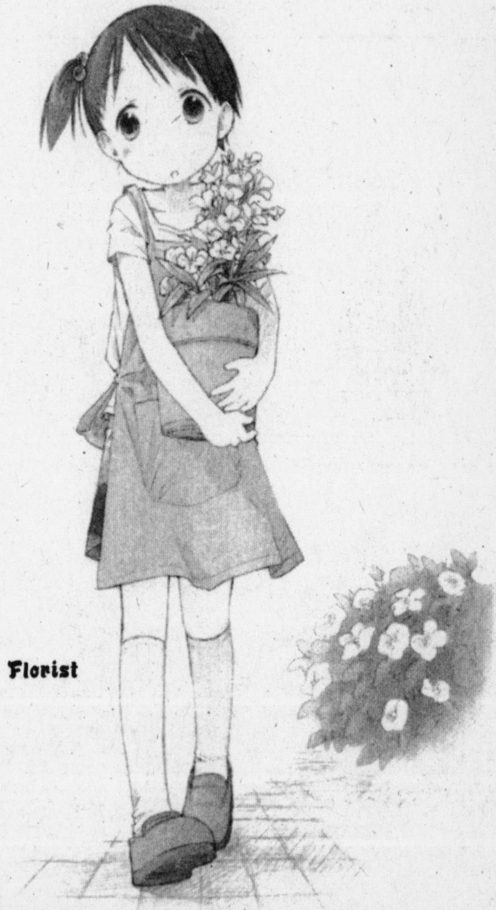
Florist

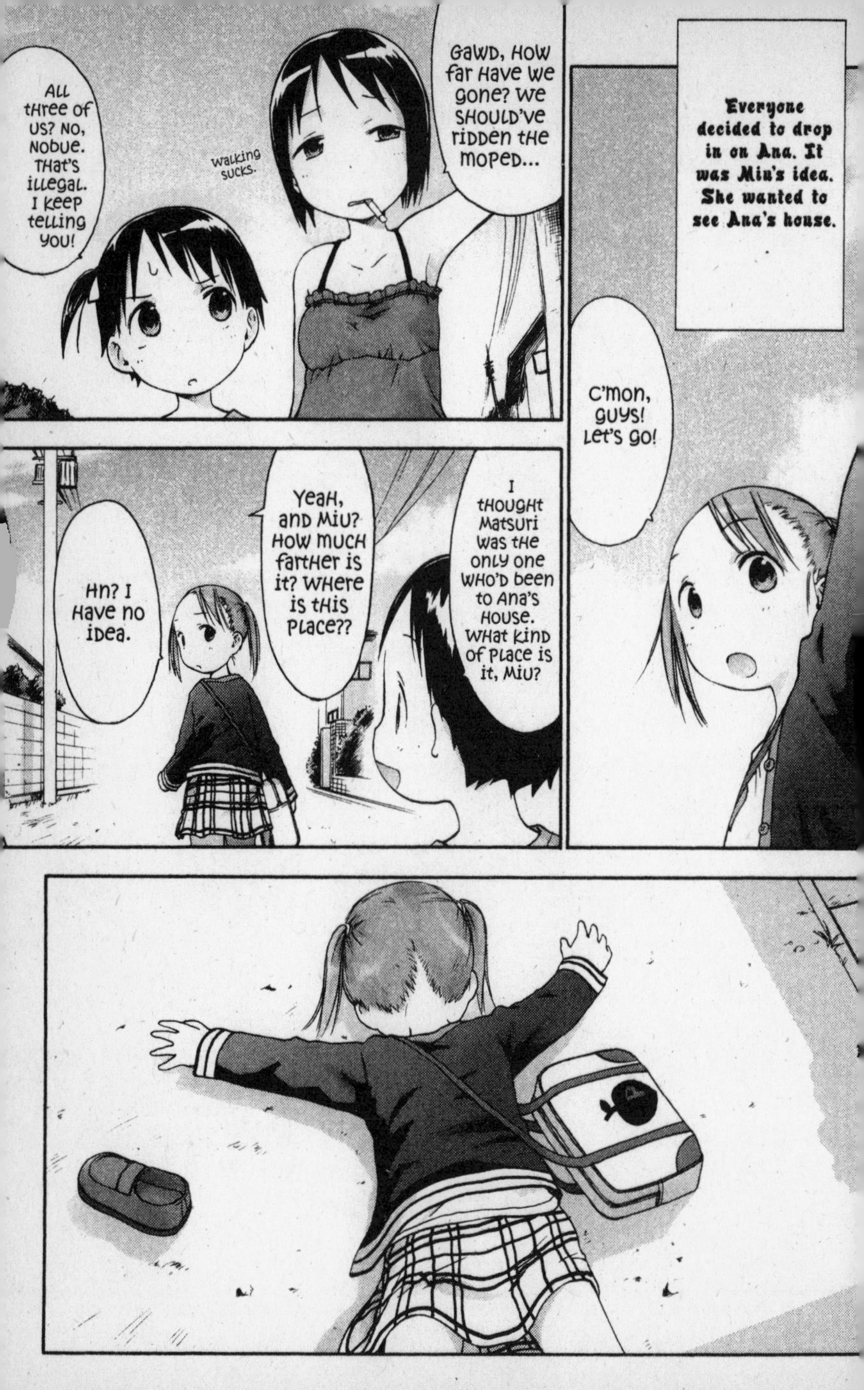
Everyone decided to drop in on Ana. It was Miu's idea. She wanted to see Ana's house.
C'mon, guys! Let's go!
Gawd, how far have we gone? We should've ridden the moped...
Walking sucks.
All three of us? No, Nobue. That's illegal. I keep telling you!
I thought Matsuri was the only one who'd been to Ana's house. What kind of place is it, Miu?
Yeah, and Miu? How much farther is it? Where is this place??
Hn? I have no idea.

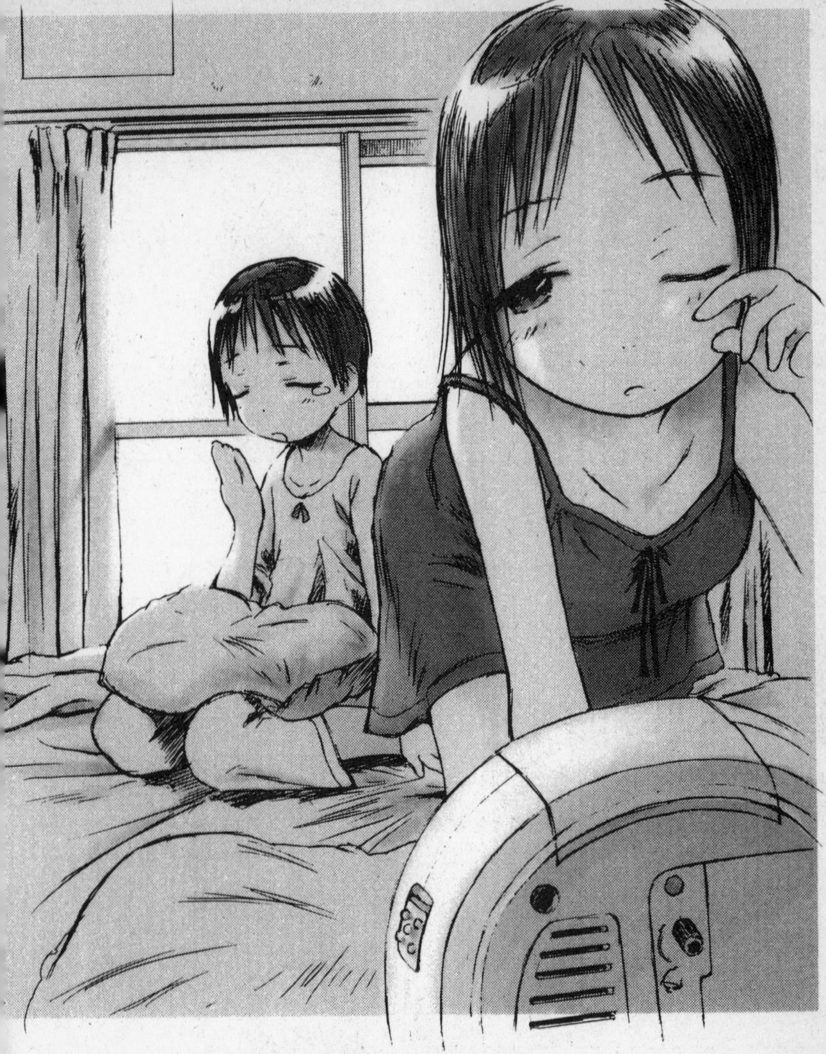

episode. **12**

ANA'S HOUSE

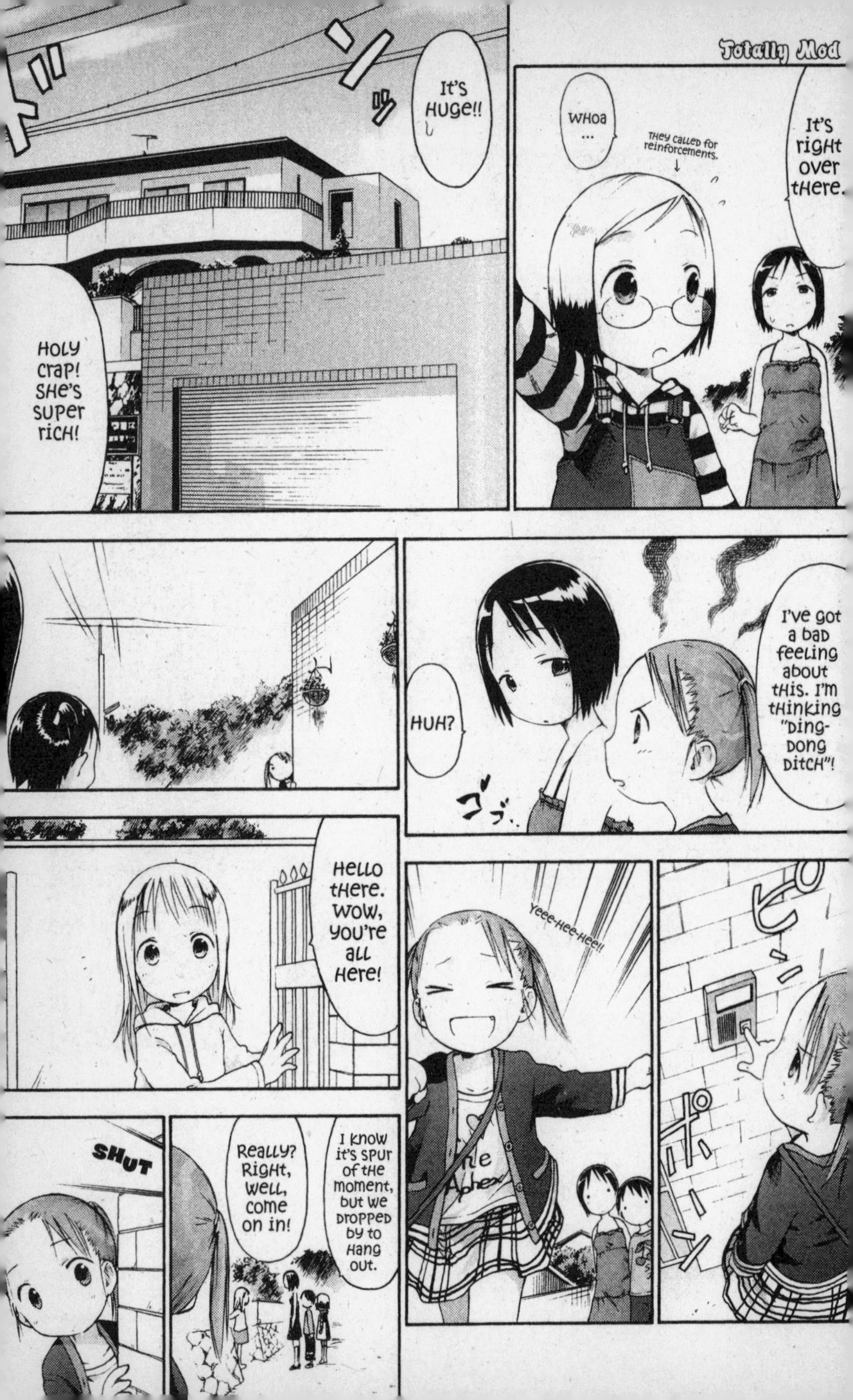
Totally Mod
It's right over there.
THEY called for reinforcements.
WHOA ...
It's HUGE!!
HOLY crap! SHE's super rich!
I've got a bad feeling about this. I'm thinking "Ding-Dong Ditch"!
HUH?
Yeee-hee-hee!!
Hello there. Wow, you're all here!
I know it's spur of the moment, but we dropped by to hang out.
Really? Right, well, come on in!
SHUT

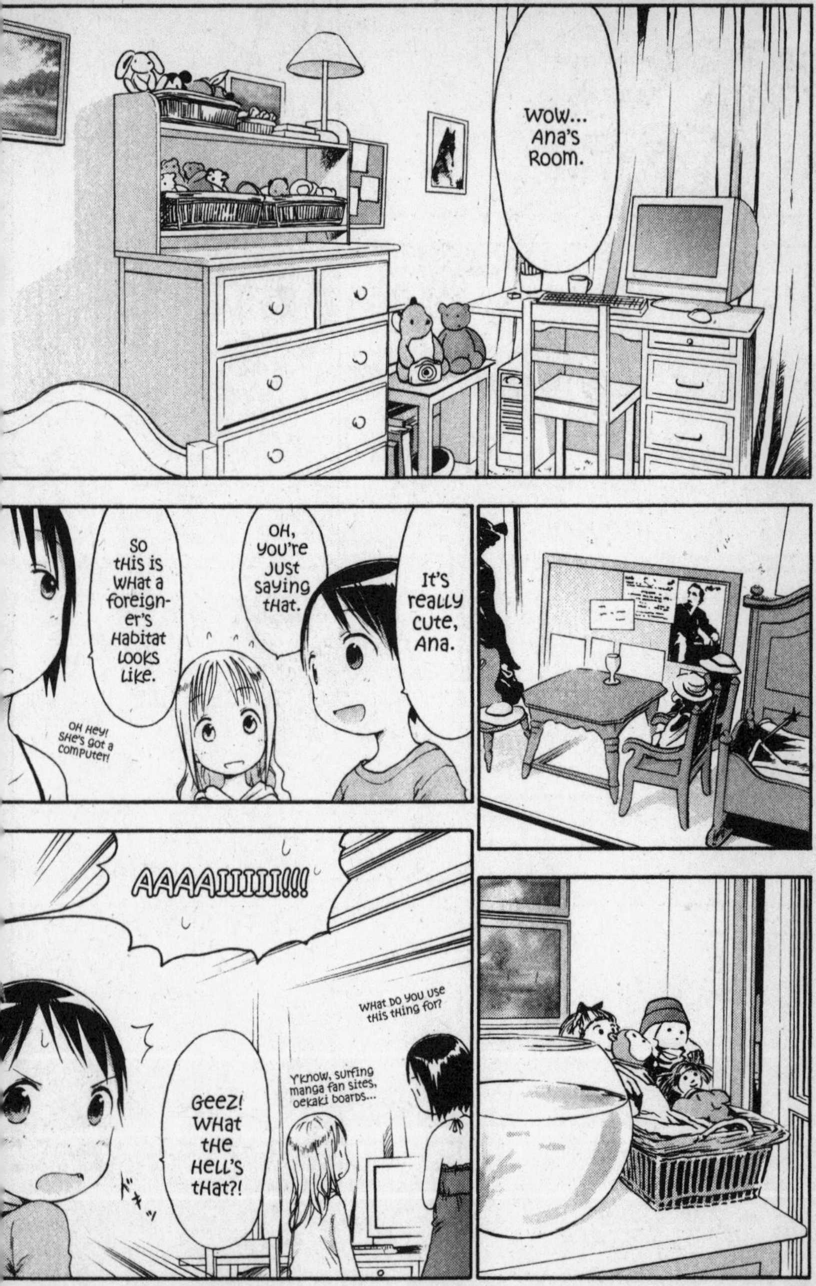
WOW... Ana's Room.
It's really cute, Ana.
OH, you're just saying that.
So this is what a foreigner's habitat looks like.
OH Hey! SHe's got a computer!
WHAT DO YOU USE tHIS tHING for?
Y'know, surfing manga fan sites, oekaki boarDS...
AAAAIIIII!!!
Geez! WHat tHe HeLL's tHat?!
ドキッ

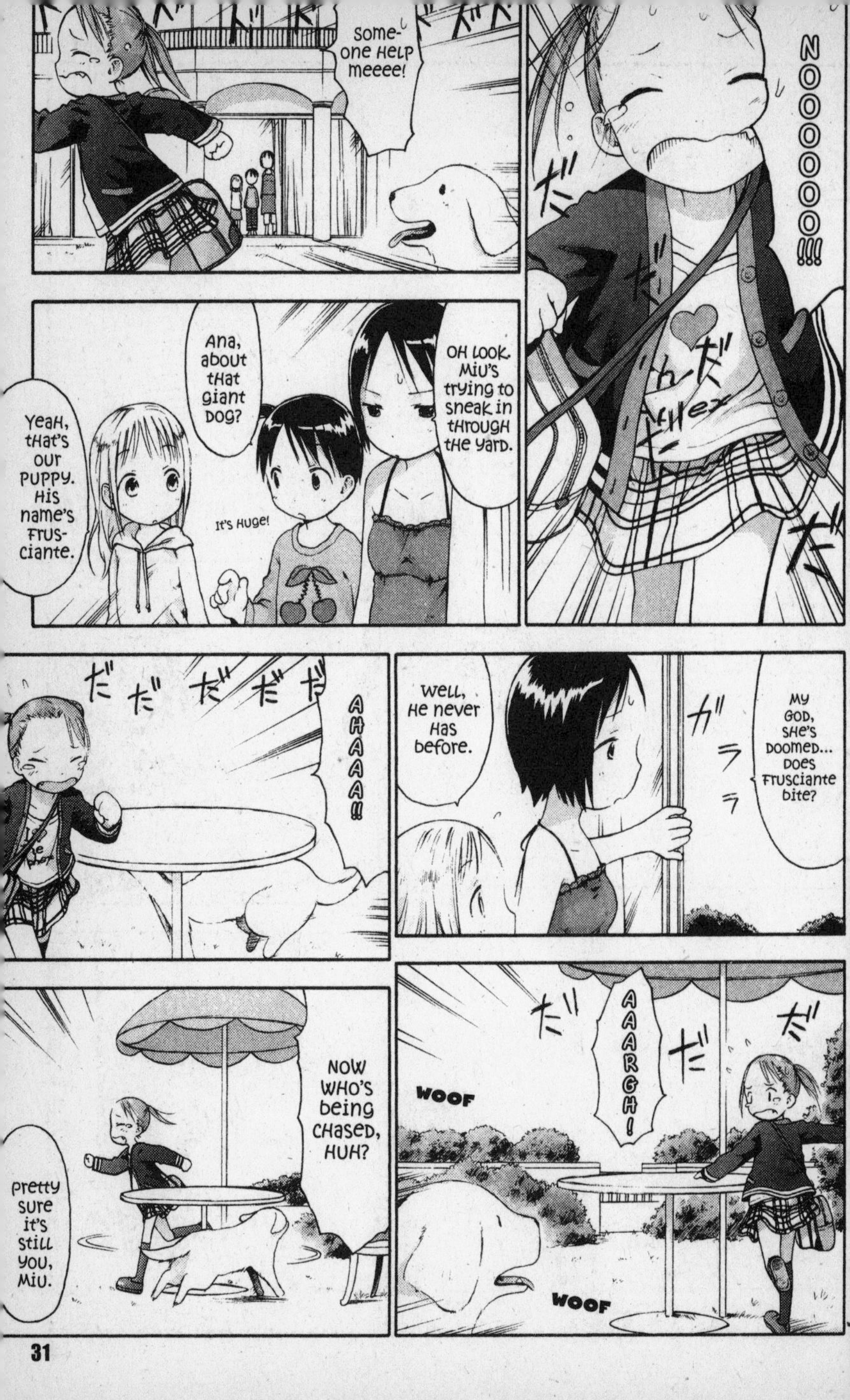
NOOOOOOO!!!
Someone help meeee!
Oh look. Miu's trying to sneak in through the yard.
Ana, about that giant dog?
It's huge!
Yeah, that's our puppy. His name's Frusciante.
My God, she's doomed... Does Frusciante bite?
Well, he never has before.
AHAAAA!!
AAAARGH!
WOOF
WOOF
Now who's being chased, huh?
Pretty sure it's still you, Miu.

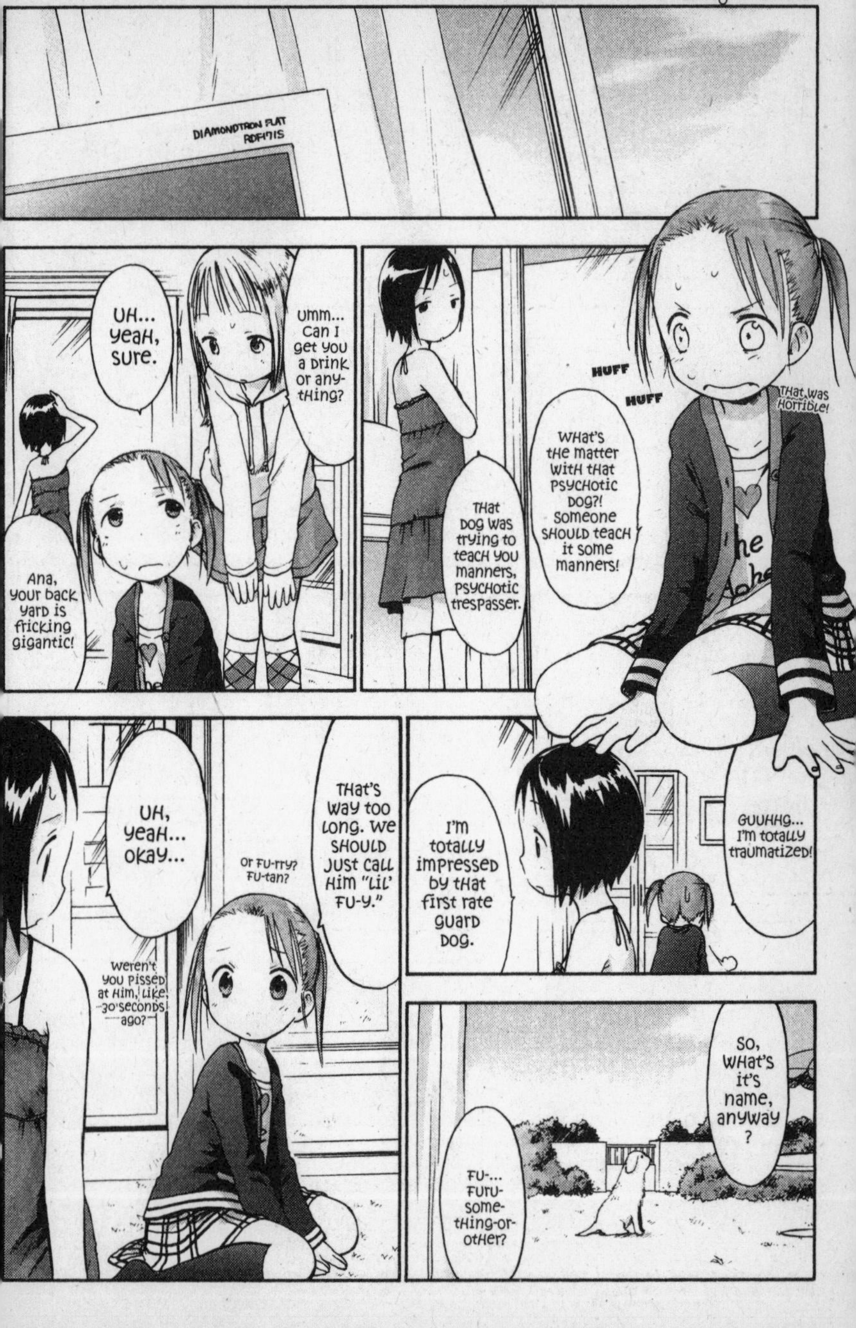
DIAMONDTRON FLAT RDF171S
That was Horrible!
HUFF
HUFF
What's the matter with that psychotic dog?! Someone should teach it some manners!
That dog was trying to teach you manners, psychotic trespasser.
Umm... can I get you a drink or any-thing?
Uh... yeah, sure.
Ana, your back yard is fricking gigantic!
Guuhhg... I'm totally traumatized!
I'm totally impressed by that first rate guard dog.
So, what's it's name, anyway?
Fu-... Furu-some-thing-or-other?
That's way too long. We should just call him "Lil' Fu-y."
Or Fu-rry? Fu-tan?
Uh, yeah... okay...
Weren't you pissed at him, like, 30 seconds ago?

He'd Be a "White" Man

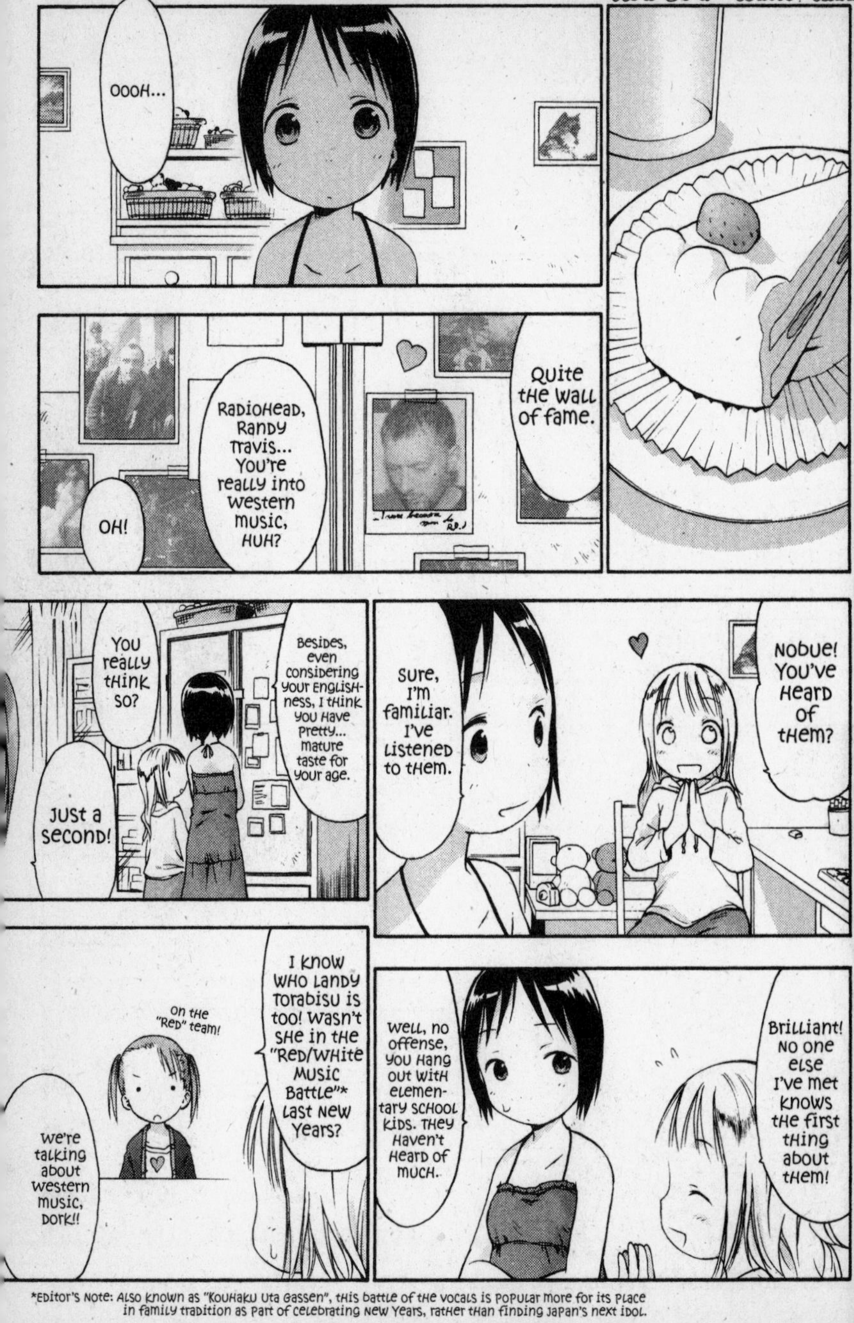
OOOH...
Quite the wall of fame.
RadioHead, Randy Travis... You're really into western music, HUH?
OH!
Nobue! You've Heard of them?
Sure, I'm familiar. I've listened to them.
Besides, even considering your English-ness, I think you have pretty... mature taste for your age.
You really think so?
Just a second!
Brilliant! No one else I've met knows the first thing about them!
Well, no offense, you hang out with elementary school kids. They haven't heard of much.
I know who Landy Torabisu is too! Wasn't she in the "Red/White Music Battle"* last New Years?
On the "Red" team!
We're talking about western music, Dork!!

*Editor's Note: Also known as "Kouhaku Uta Gassen", this battle of the vocals is popular more for its place in family tradition as part of celebrating New Years, rather than finding Japan's next idol.

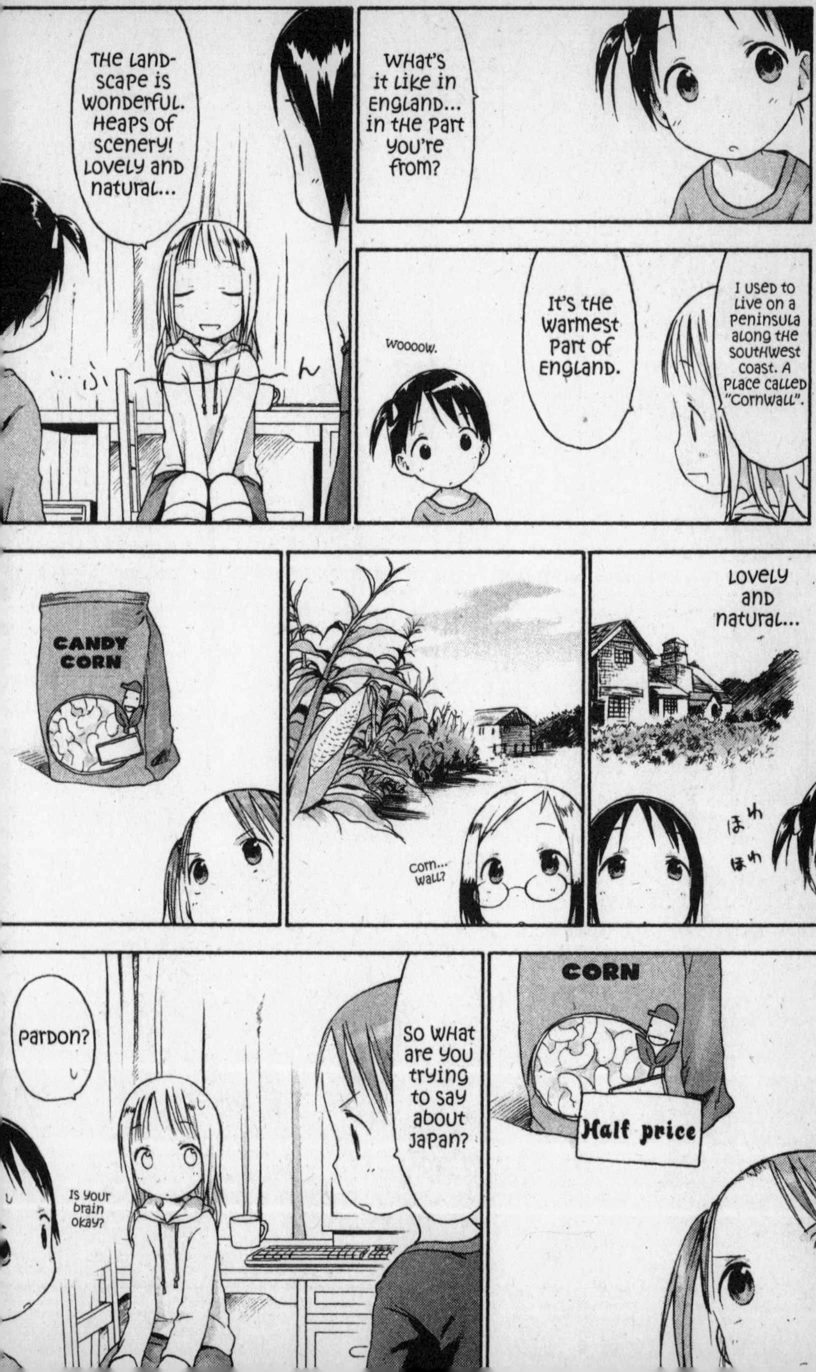
What's it like in England... in the part you're from?
I used to live on a peninsula along the southwest coast. A place called "Cornwall".
It's the warmest part of England.
Woooow.
The land-scape is wonderful. Heaps of scenery! Lovely and natural...
...ふ~ん
Lovely and natural...
ほわ ほわ
Corn... wall?
CANDY CORN
CORN
Half price
So what are you trying to say about Japan?
Pardon?
Is your brain okay?

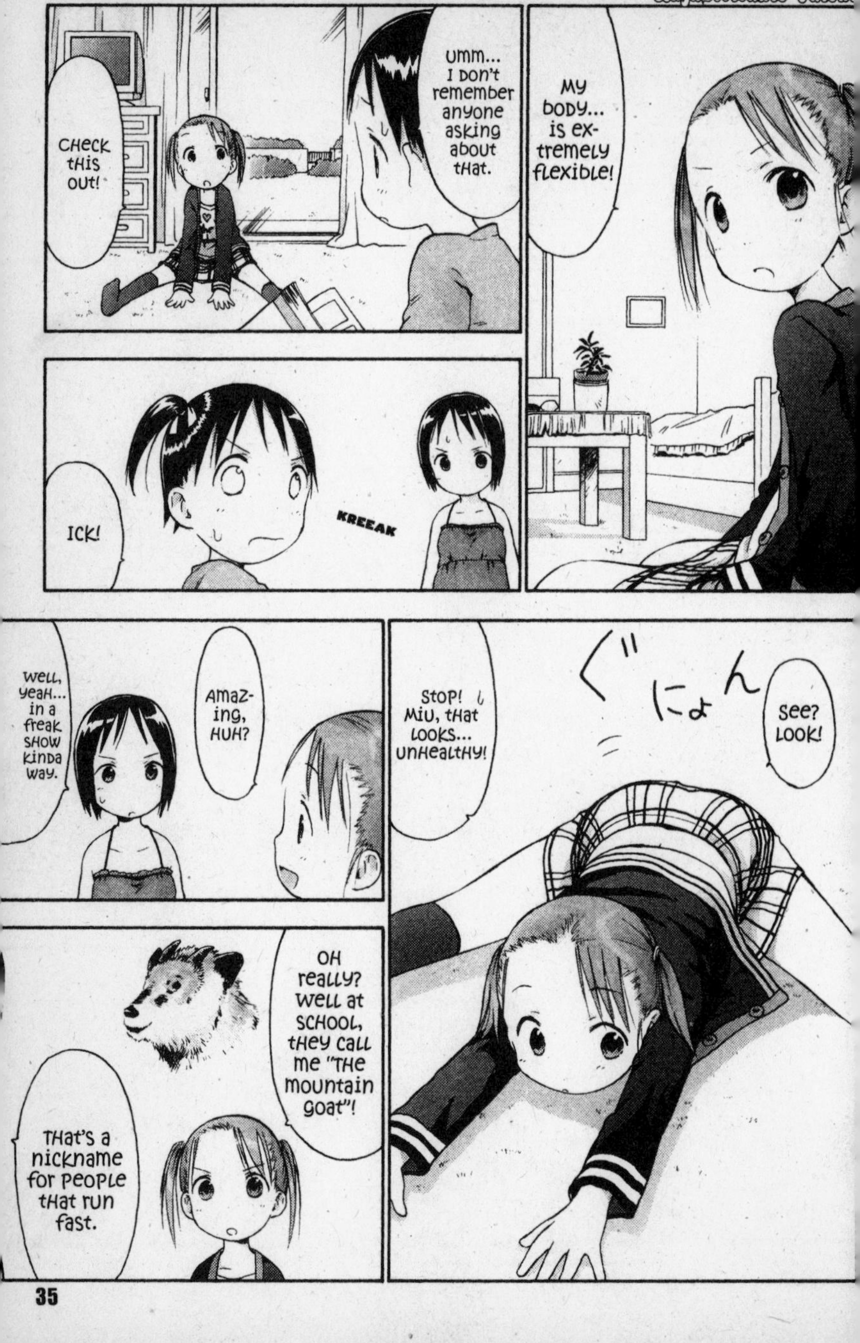
My body... is extremely flexible!
Umm... I don't remember anyone asking about that.
Check this out!
KREEAK
Ick!
See? Look!
ぐにょん
Stop! Miu, that looks... unhealthy!
Amazing, huh?
Well, yeah... in a freak show kinda way.
Oh really? Well at school, they call me "The mountain goat"!
That's a nickname for people that run fast.

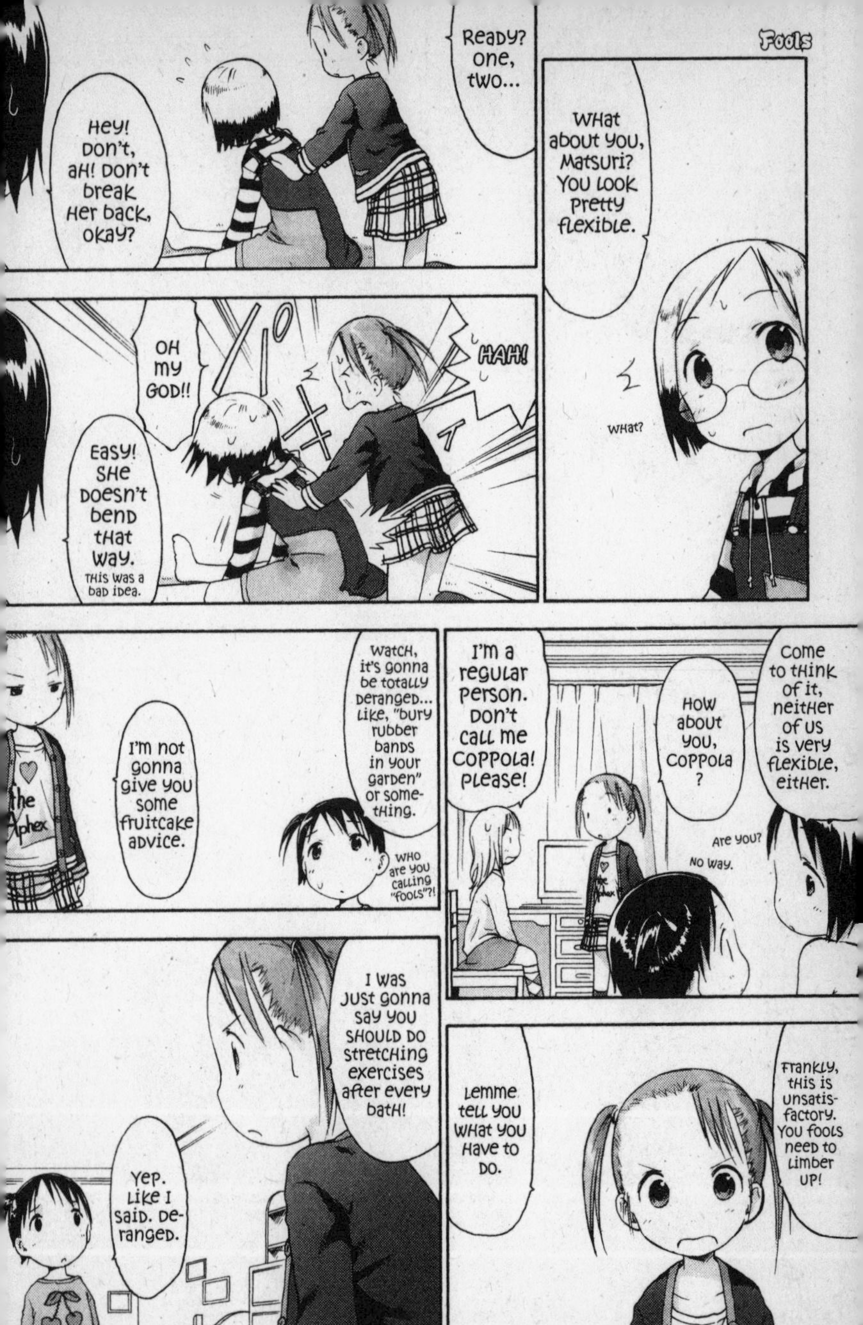
What about you, Matsuri? You look pretty flexible.
What?
Ready? one, two...
Hey! Don't, ah! Don't break her back, okay?
HAH!
OH my GOD!!
Easy! She doesn't bend that way.
This was a bad idea.
Come to think of it, neither of us is very flexible, either.
How about you, Coppola?
I'm a regular person. Don't call me Coppola! Please!
Are you?
No way.
Frankly, this is unsatis-factory. You fools need to limber up!
Lemme tell you what you have to do.
Watch, it's gonna be totally deranged... like, "bury rubber bands in your garden" or some-thing.
Who are you calling "fools"?!
I'm not gonna give you some fruitcake advice.
I was just gonna say you should do stretching exercises after every bath!
Yep. Like I said. De-ranged.

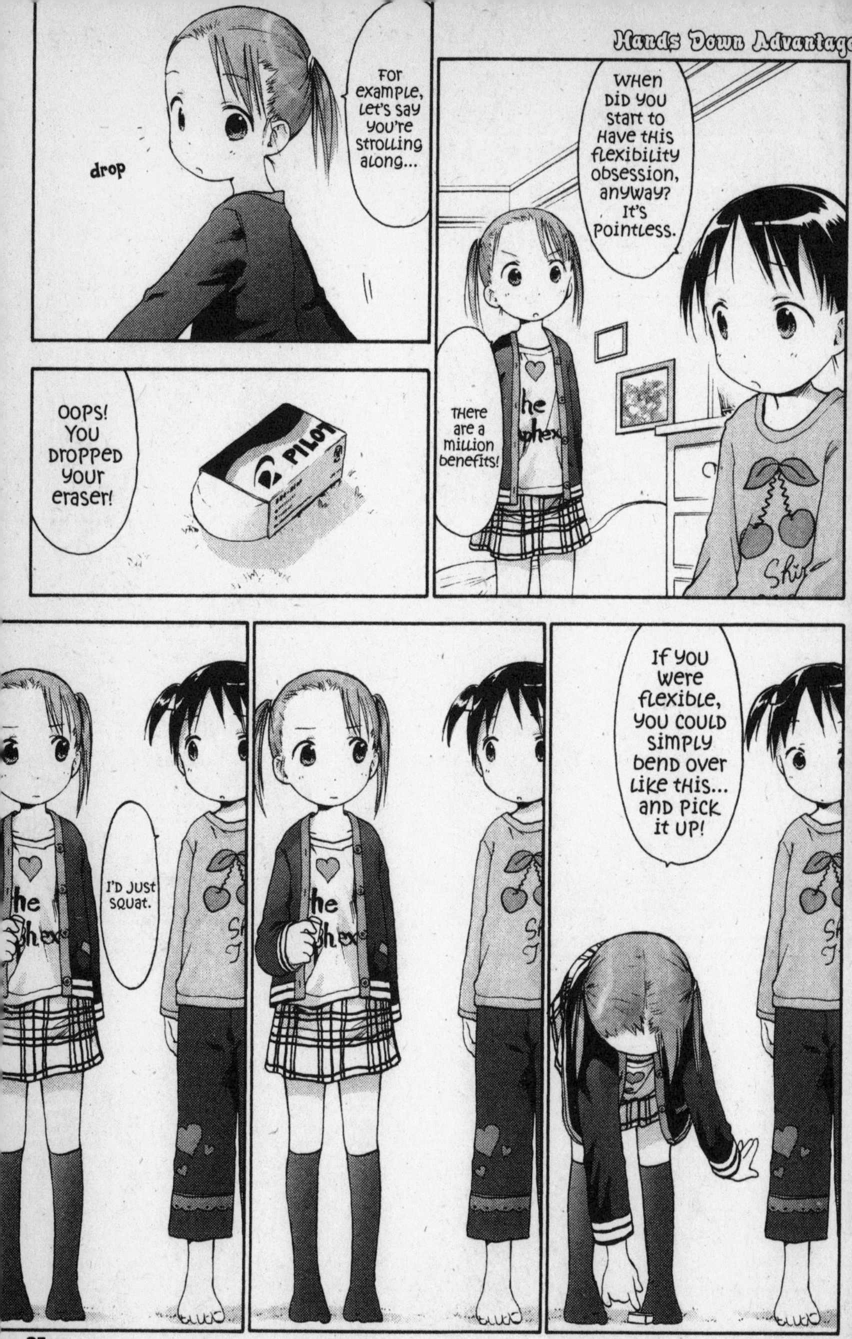
When did you start to have this flexibility obsession, anyway? It's pointless.
There are a million benefits!
For example, let's say you're strolling along...
drop
Oops! You dropped your eraser!
If you were flexible, you could simply bend over like this... and pick it up!
I'd just squat.

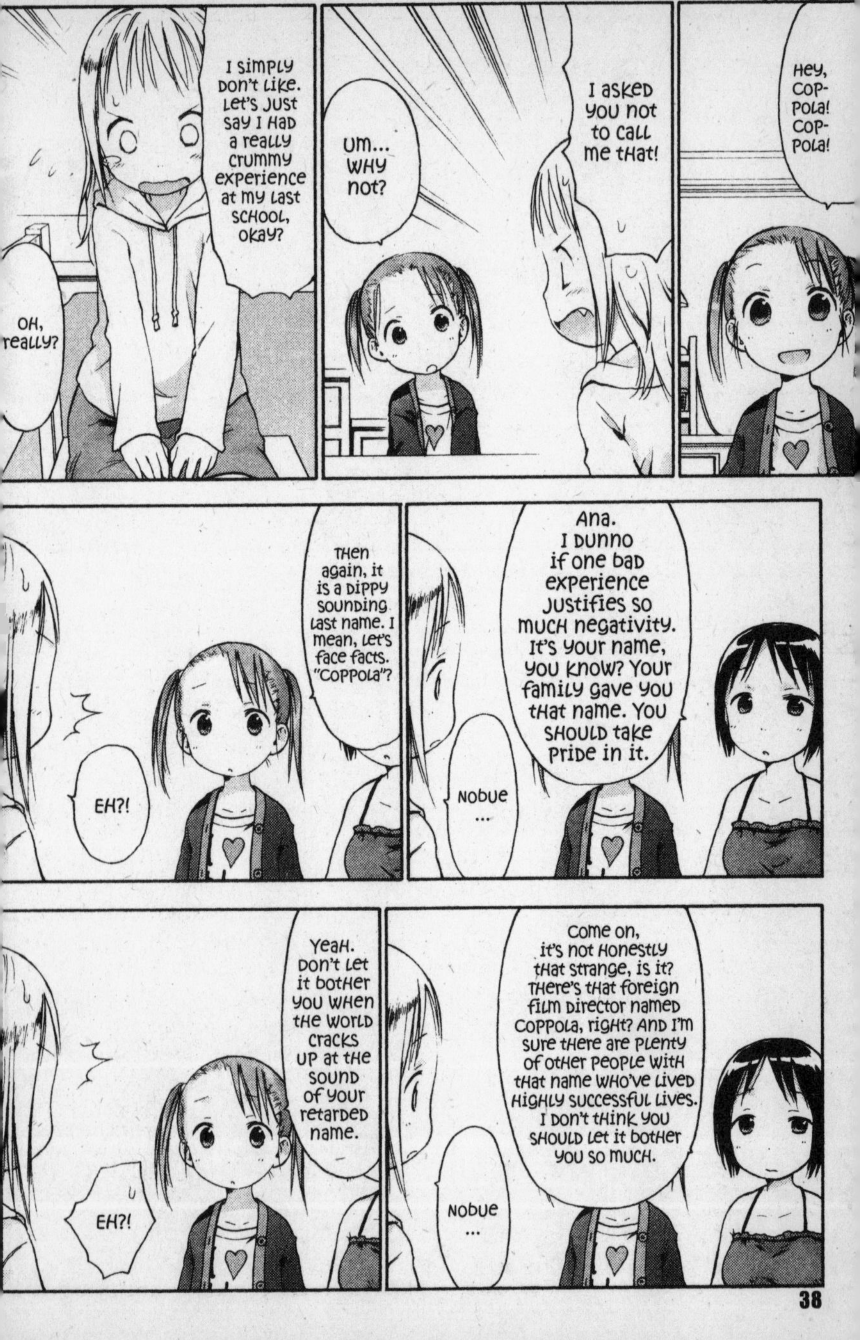
Hey, COP-POLA! COP-POLA!
I asked you not to call me that!
Um... WHY not?
I simply don't like. Let's just say I had a really crummy experience at my last school, okay?
Oh, really?
Ana. I dunno if one bad experience justifies so much negativity. It's your name, you know? Your family gave you that name. You should take pride in it.
Nobue ...
Then again, it is a dippy sounding last name. I mean, let's face facts. "Coppola"?
EH?!
Come on, it's not honestly that strange, is it? There's that foreign film director named Coppola, right? And I'm sure there are plenty of other people with that name who've lived highly successful lives. I don't think you should let it bother you so much.
Nobue ...
Yeah. Don't let it bother you when the world cracks up at the sound of your retarded name.
EH?!

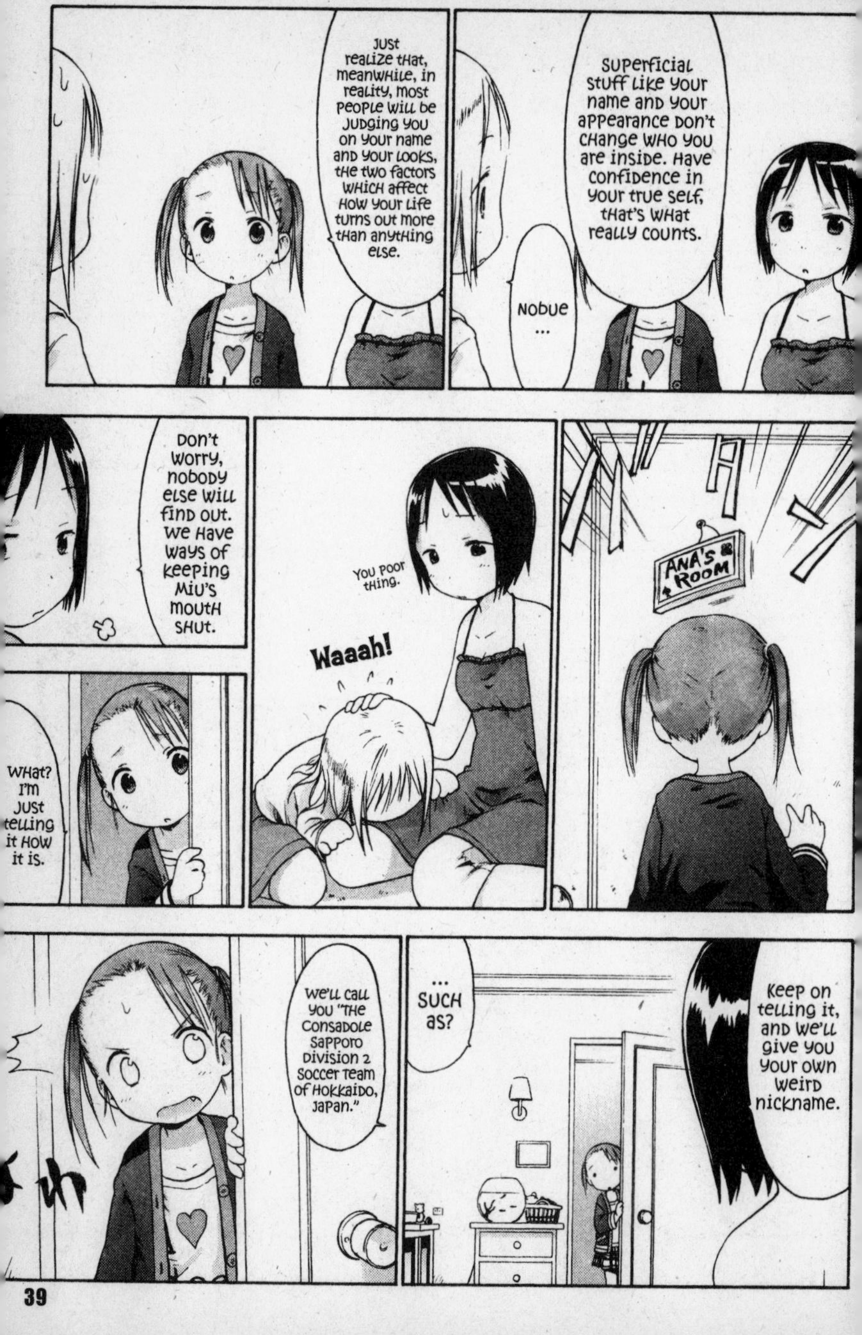
Superficial stuff like your name and your appearance don't change who you are inside. Have confidence in your true self, that's what really counts.
Nobue ...
Just realize that, meanwhile, in reality, most people will be judging you on your name and your looks, the two factors which affect how your life turns out more than anything else.
ANA's ROOM
You poor thing.
Waaah!
Don't worry, nobody else will find out. We have ways of keeping Miu's mouth shut.
What? I'm just telling it how it is.
Keep on telling it, and we'll give you your own weird nickname.
... Such as?
We'll call you "The Consadole Sapporo Division 2 Soccer Team of Hokkaido, Japan."

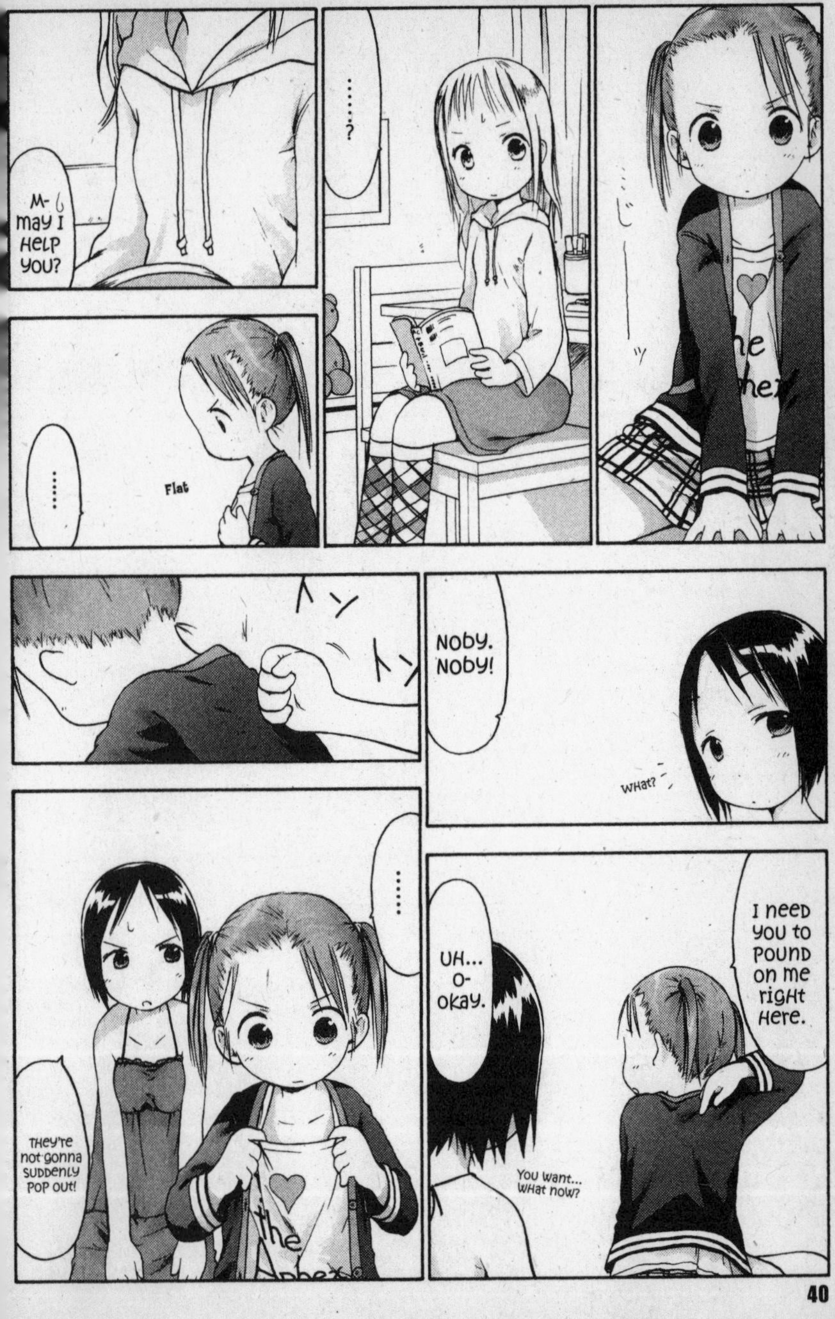
......?
M-may I help you?
......
Flat
Noby. Noby!
What?
トン
トン
I need you to pound on me right here.
Uh... O-okay.
You want... What now?
......
They're not gonna suddenly pop out!

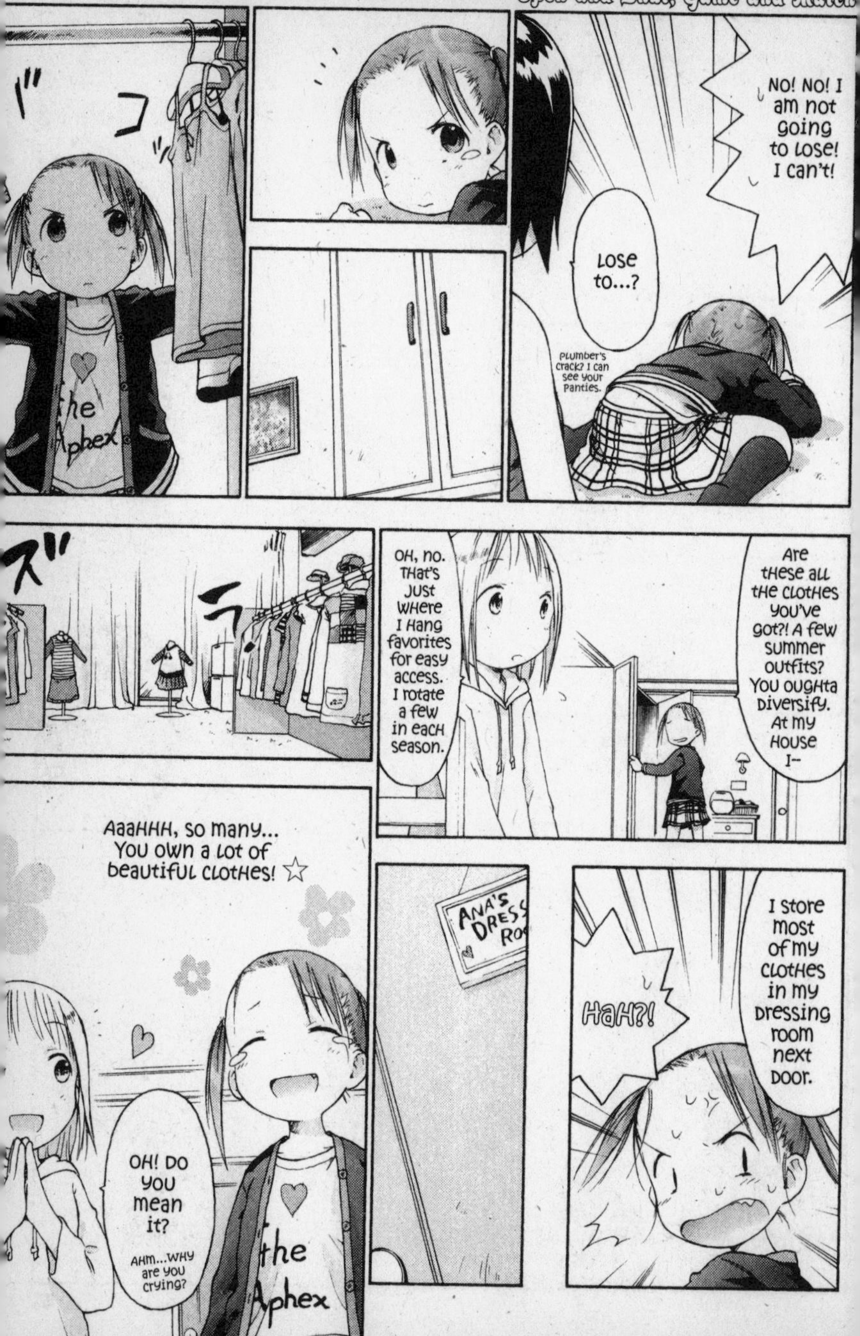
NO! NO! I am not going to lose! I can't!
Lose to...?
Plumber's crack? I can see your panties.
ドコ
Are these all the clothes you've got?! A few summer outfits? You oughta diversify. At my house I–
Oh, no. That's just where I hang favorites for easy access. I rotate a few in each season.
ズラ
I store most of my clothes in my dressing room next door.
HaH?!
ANA'S DRESS RO
AaaHHH, so many... You own a lot of beautiful clothes! ☆
OH! DO you mean it?
AHm...why are you crying?

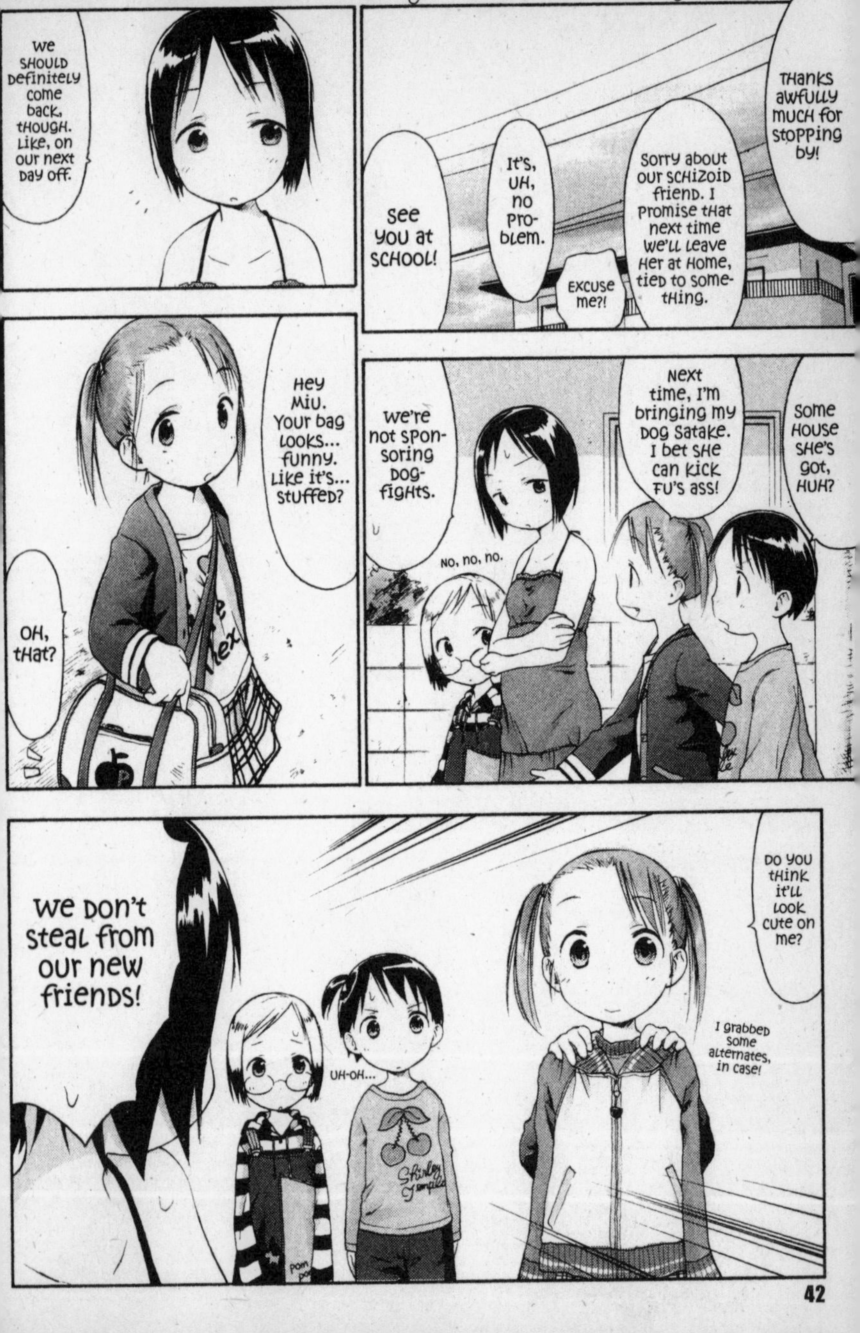
Thanks awfully much for stopping by!
Sorry about our schizoid friend. I promise that next time we'll leave her at home, tied to something.
Excuse me?!
It's, uh, no problem.
See you at school!
We should definitely come back, though. Like, on our next day off.
Some house she's got, huh?
Next time, I'm bringing my dog Satake. I bet she can kick Fu's ass!
We're not sponsoring dogfights.
No, no, no.
Hey Miu. Your bag looks... funny. Like it's... stuffed?
Oh, that?
Do you think it'll look cute on me?
I grabbed some alternates, in case!
Uh-oh...
We don't steal from our new friends!

HALLO WORK

matsuri

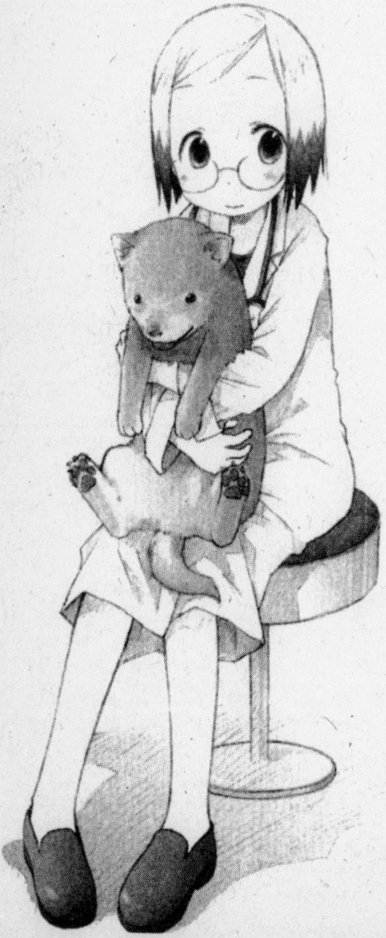

Veterinarian

HALLO WORK

miu

Stewardess

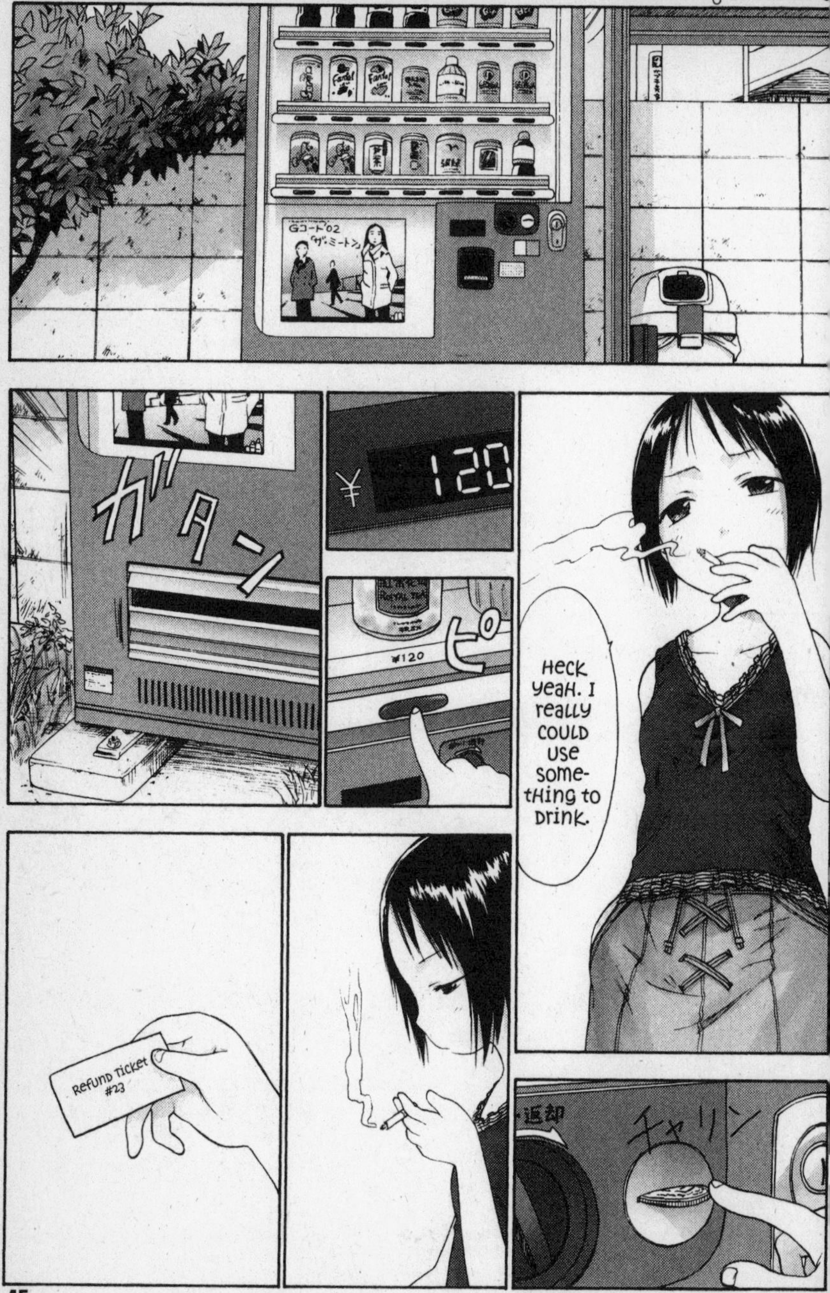
Gコード02
「ザ・ミートン」
Heck yeah. I really could use something to drink.
¥ 120
ROYAL TEA
¥120
ピ
ガターン
返却
チャリン
Refund Ticket #23

episode. 13

AN AMUSING STEW (USING MIU)

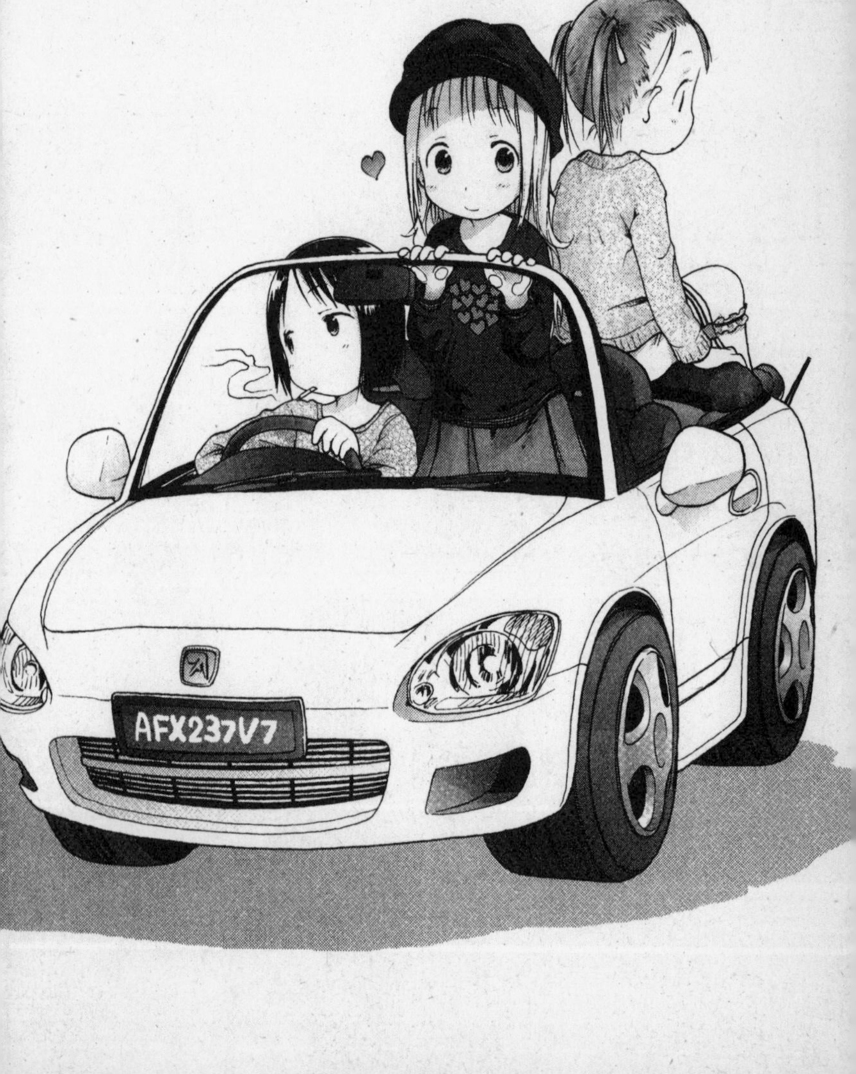
AFX237V7

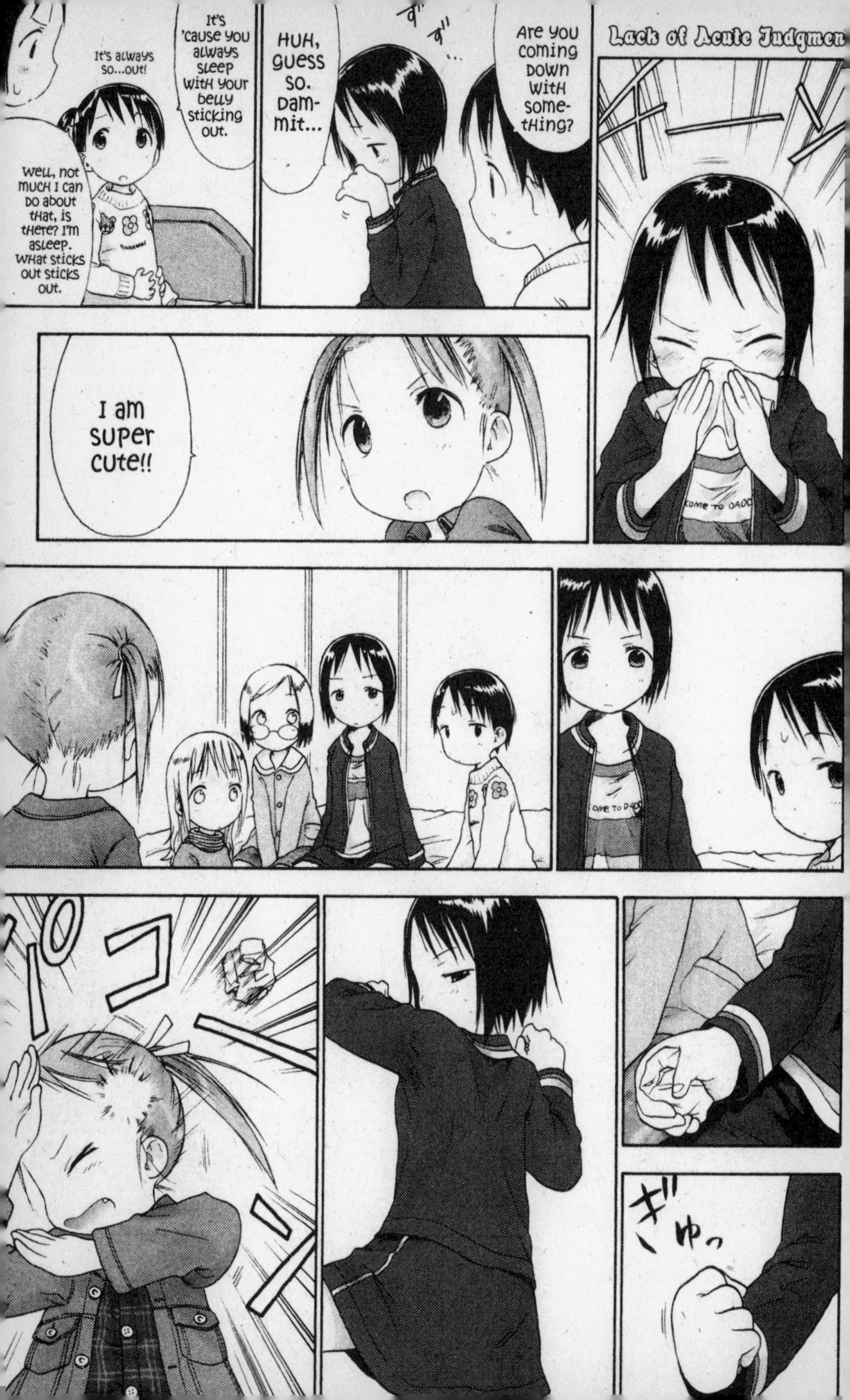
Lack of Acute Judgmen
Are you coming down with something?
ずず…
Huh, guess so. Dam-mit...
It's 'cause you always sleep with your belly sticking out.
It's always so...out!
Well, not much I can do about that, is there? I'm asleep. What sticks out sticks out.
I am super cute!!
ぎゅっ

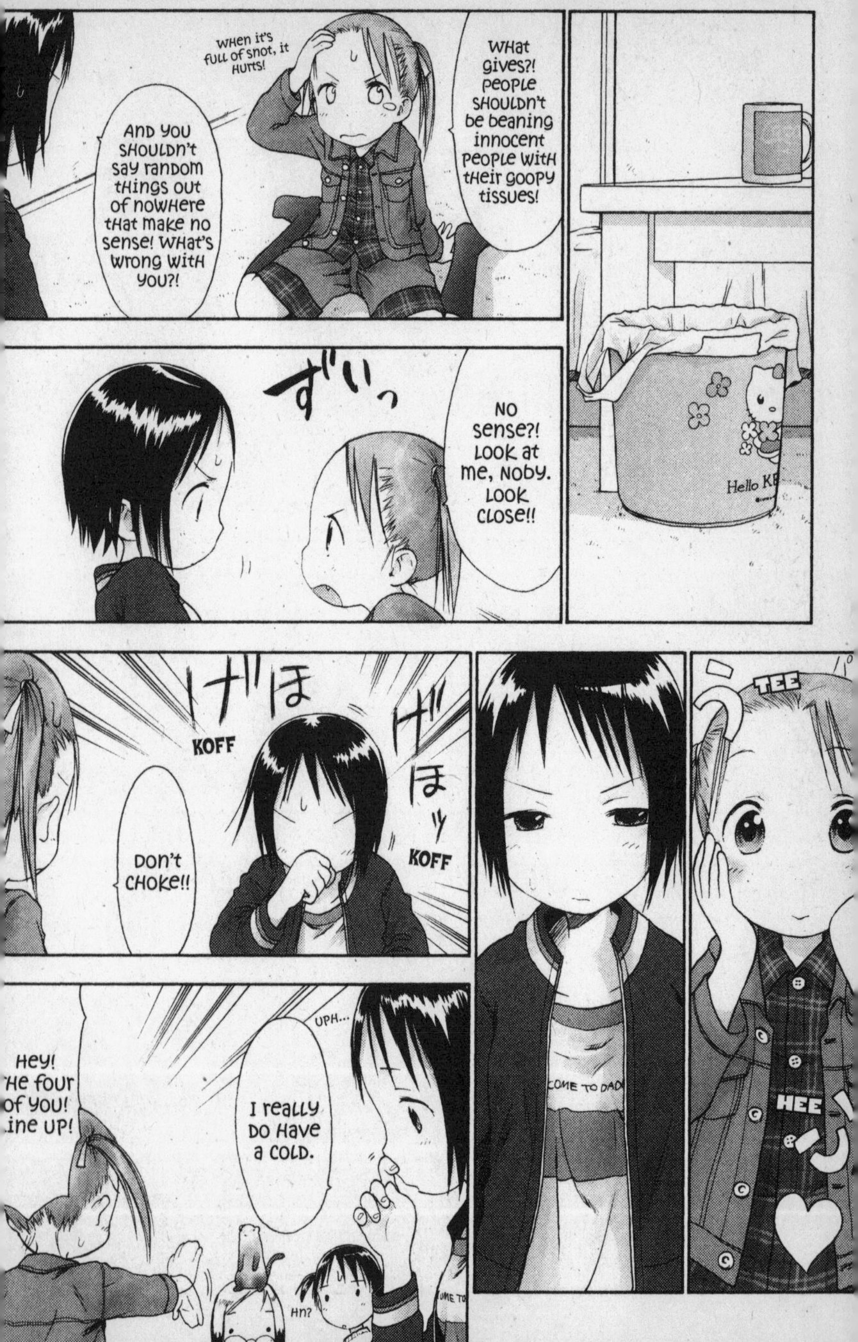
What gives?! People shouldn't be beaning innocent people with their goopy tissues!
When it's full of snot, it hurts!
And you shouldn't say random things out of nowhere that make no sense! What's wrong with you?!
No sense?! Look at me, Noby. Look close!!
ずいっ
TEE
HEE
げほ
KOFF
げほッ
KOFF
Don't choke!!
Uph...
I really do have a cold.
Hey! he four of you! ine up!
Hn?

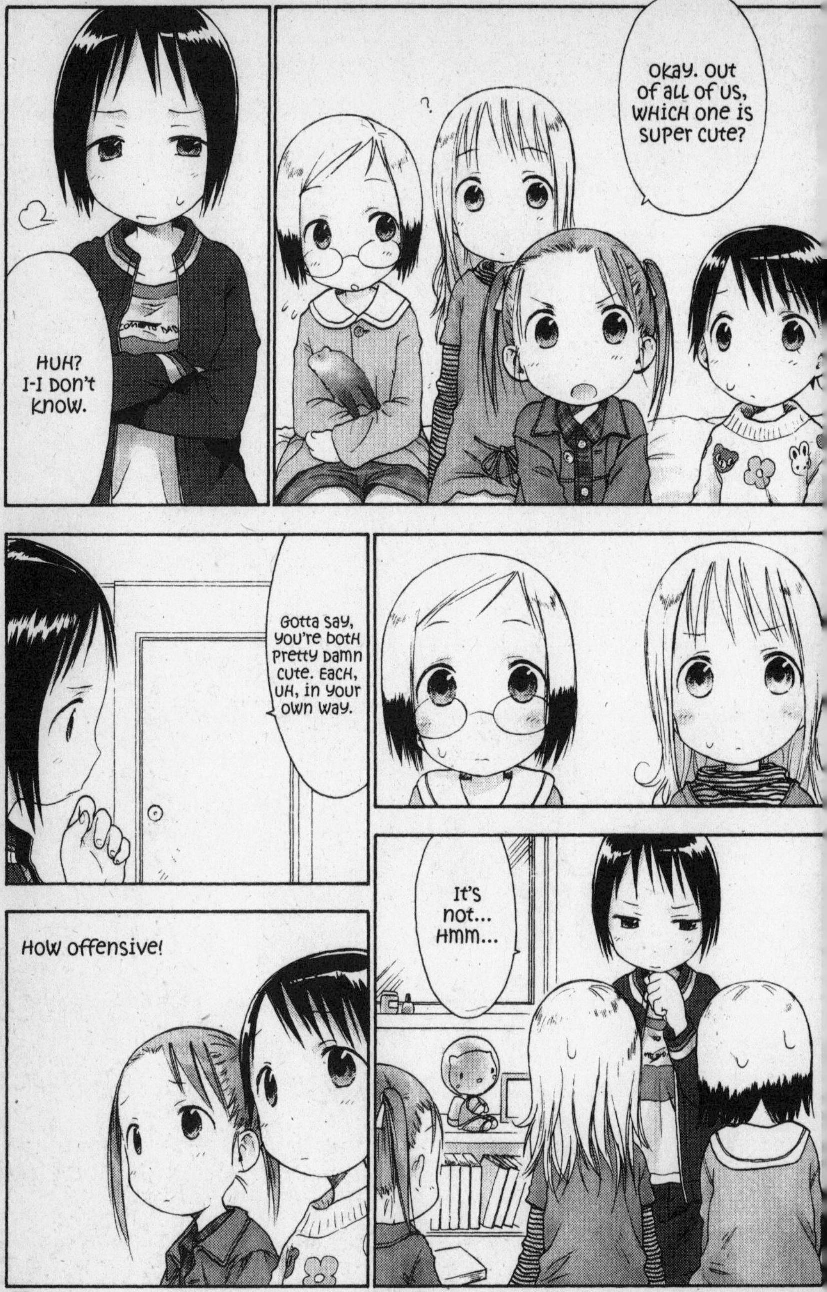
Okay. Out of all of us, WHICH one is super cute?
HUH? I-I Don't know.
Gotta say, you're both pretty damn cute. EacH, UH, in your own way.
It's not... Hmm...
How offensive!

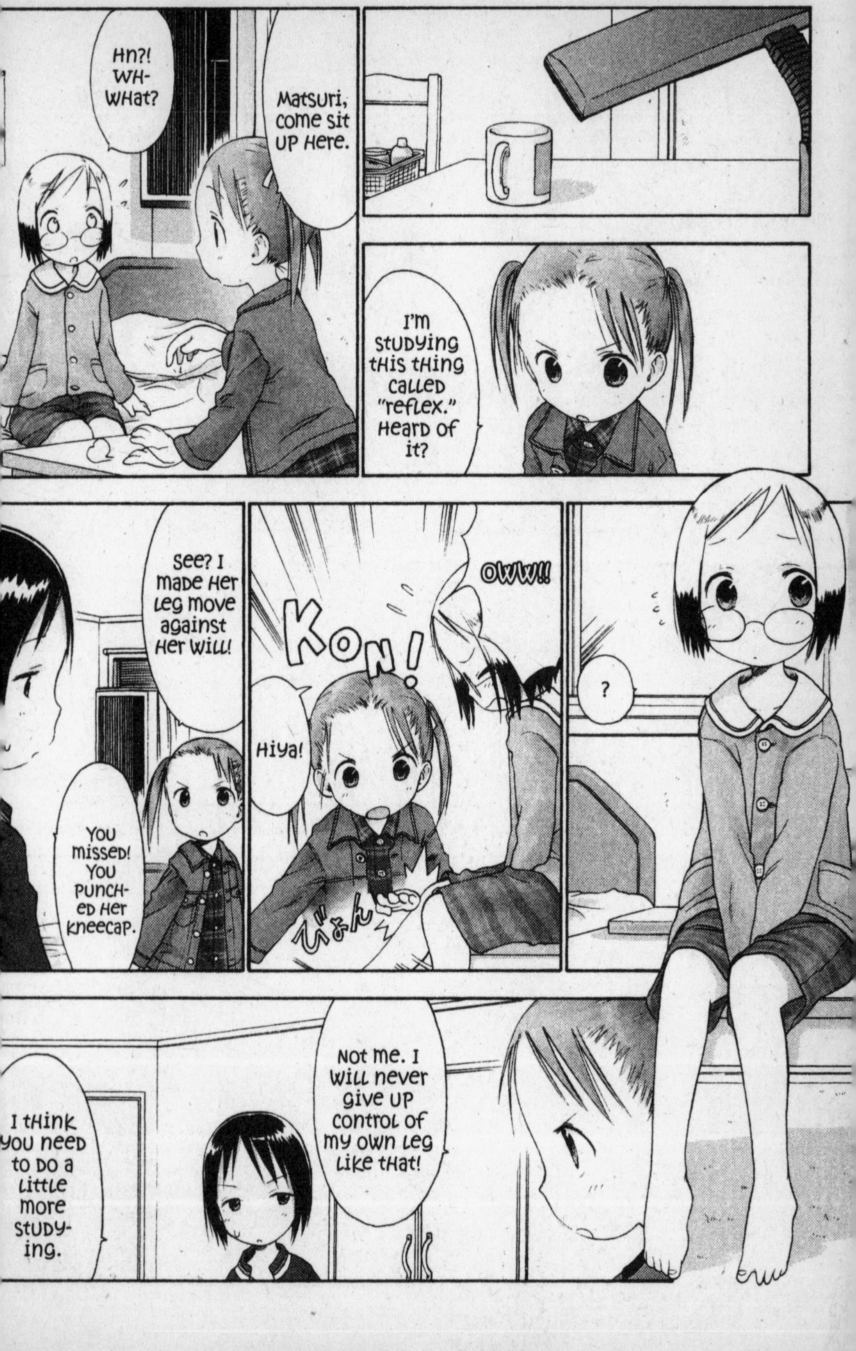
I'm studying this thing called "reflex." Heard of it?
Matsuri, come sit up here.
Hn?! WH-WHat?
?
OWW!!
KON!
Hiya!
びよん
See? I made her leg move against her will!
You missed! You punched her kneecap.
Not me. I will never give up control of my own leg like that!
I think you need to do a little more studying.

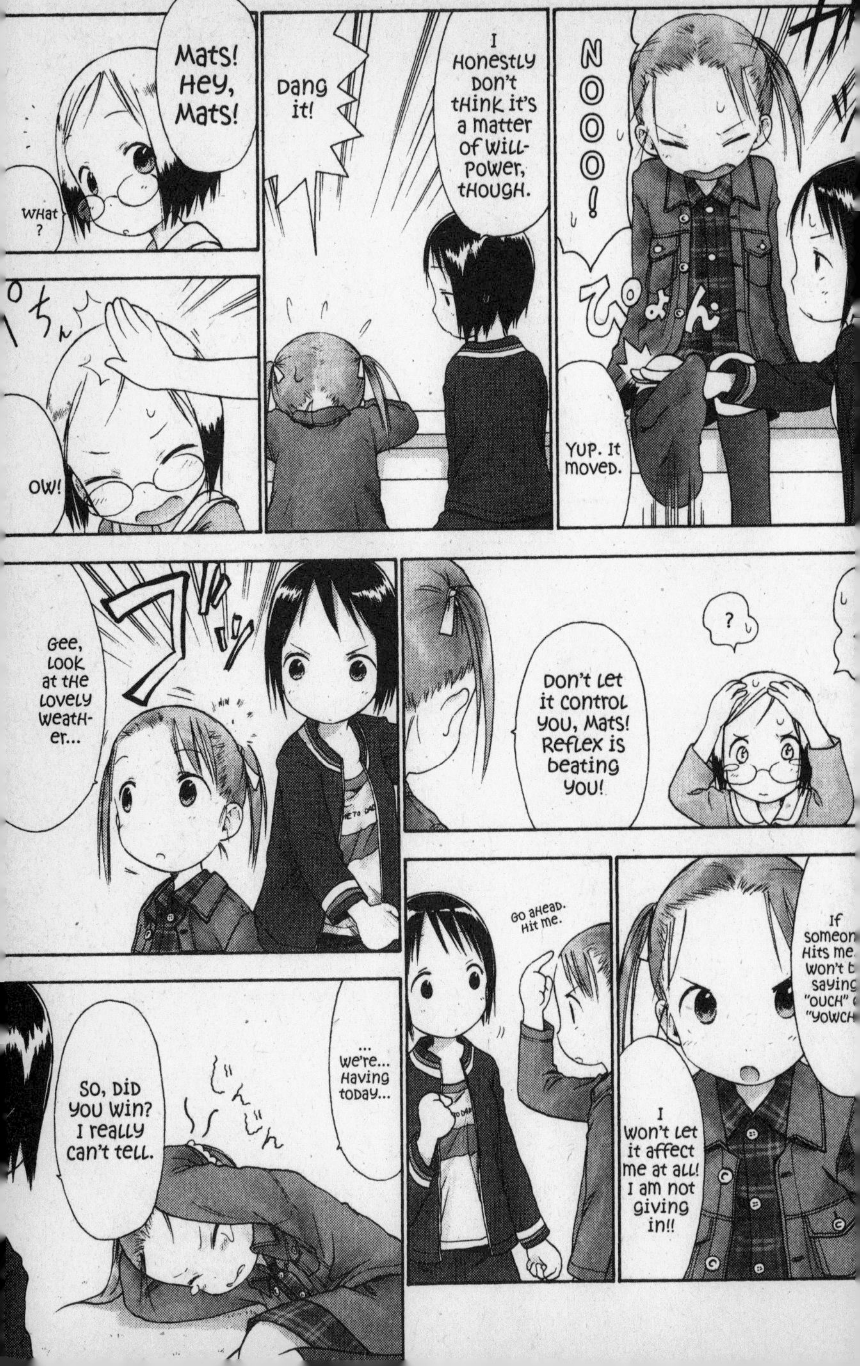
NOOOO!
ぴょん
Yup. It moved.
I honestly don't think it's a matter of will-power, though.
Dang it!
Mats! Hey, Mats!
What?
ぱちん
Ow!
?
Don't let it control you, Mats! Reflex is beating you!
Gee, look at the lovely weather...
If someon Hits me. won't b saying "OUCH" "YOWCH
I won't let it affect me at all! I am not giving in!!
Go ahead. Hit me.
...We're... having today...
じんじん
So, did you win? I really can't tell.

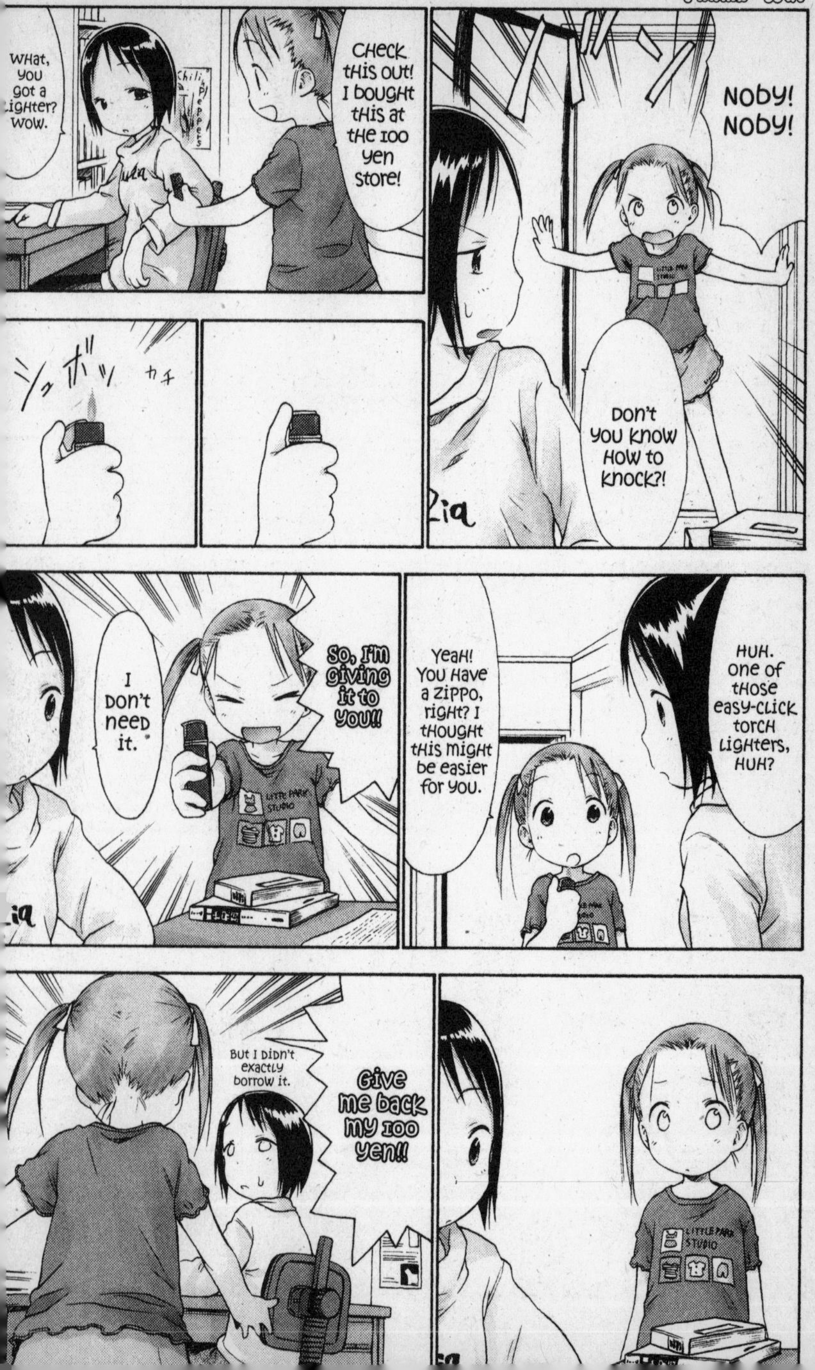
NOBY! NOBY!
DON'T YOU KNOW HOW TO KNOCK?!
CHECK THIS OUT! I BOUGHT THIS AT THE 100 YEN STORE!
WHAT, YOU GOT A LIGHTER? WOW.
シュボッ
カチ
HUH. ONE OF THOSE EASY-CLICK TORCH LIGHTERS, HUH?
YEAH! YOU HAVE A ZIPPO, RIGHT? I THOUGHT THIS MIGHT BE EASIER FOR YOU.
So, I'm giving it to you!!
I DON'T NEED IT.
Give me back my 100 yen!!
But I didn't exactly borrow it.

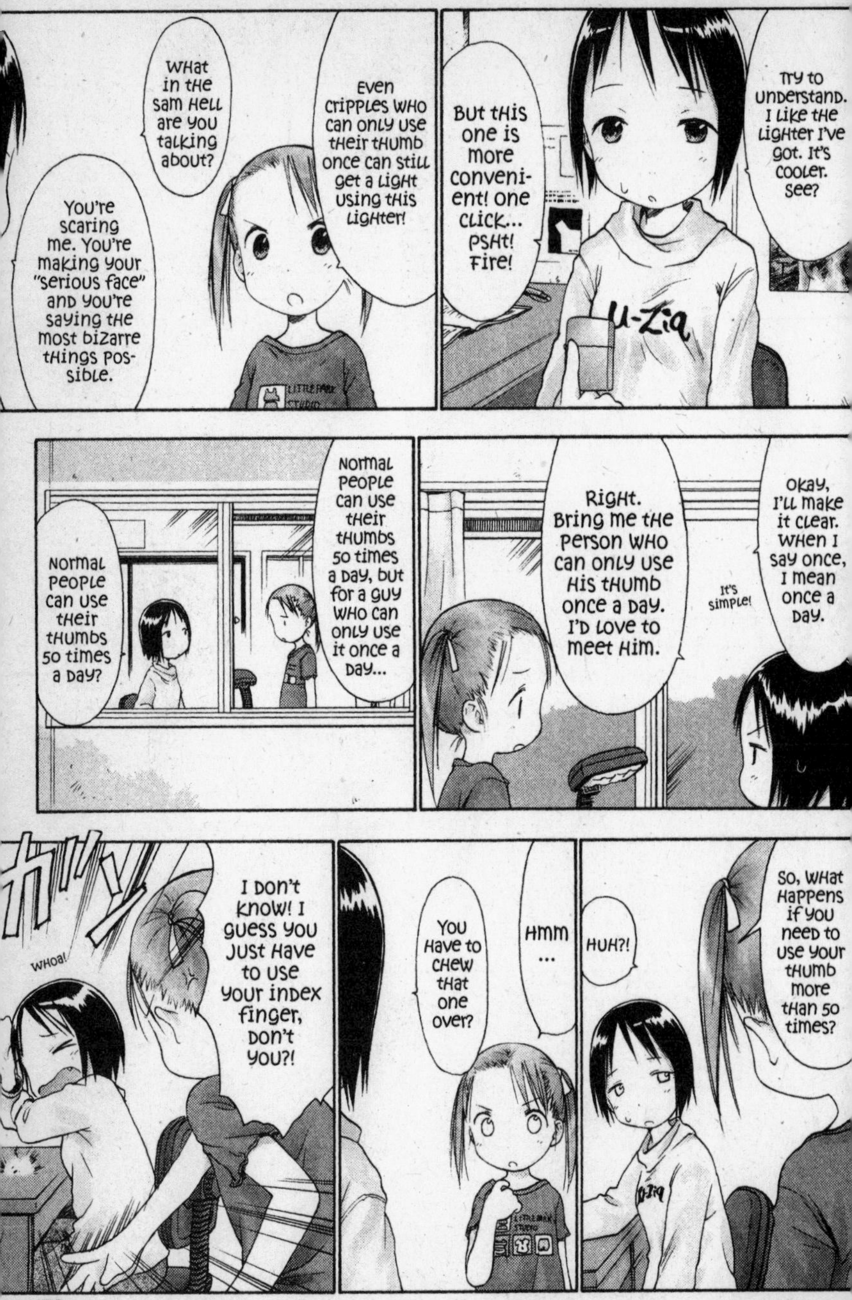
Try to understand. I like the lighter I've got. It's cooler. See?
But this one is more conveni-ent! One click... PSHT! Fire!
Even cripples who can only use their thumb once can still get a light using this lighter!
What in the sam hell are you talking about?
You're scaring me. You're making your "serious face" and you're saying the most bizarre things pos-sible.
Okay, I'll make it clear. When I say once, I mean once a day.
It's simple!
Right. Bring me the person who can only use his thumb once a day. I'd love to meet him.
Normal people can use their thumbs 50 times a day, but for a guy who can only use it once a day...
Normal people can use their thumbs 50 times a day?
So, what happens if you need to use your thumb more than 50 times?
HUH?!
Hmm ...
You have to chew that one over?
カッ
I don't know! I guess you just have to use your index finger, don't you?!
Whoa!

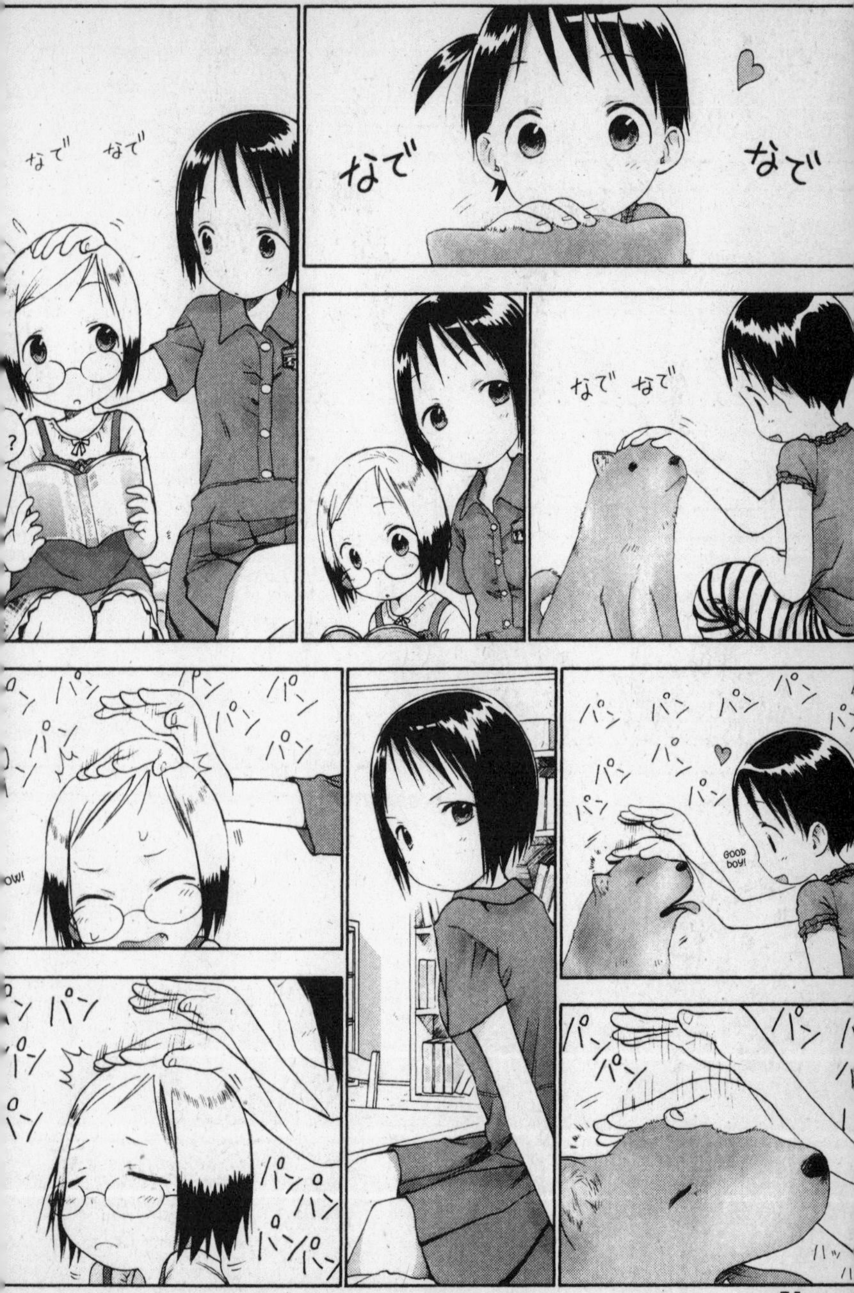
なで
なで
なで なで
なで なで
?
パン パン パン パン
パン パン パン
パン パン
GOOD BOY!
パン パン パン
ハッ ハ
パン パン パン パン パン
パン パン
OW!
パン パン パン パン
パンパン パンパン パンパーン

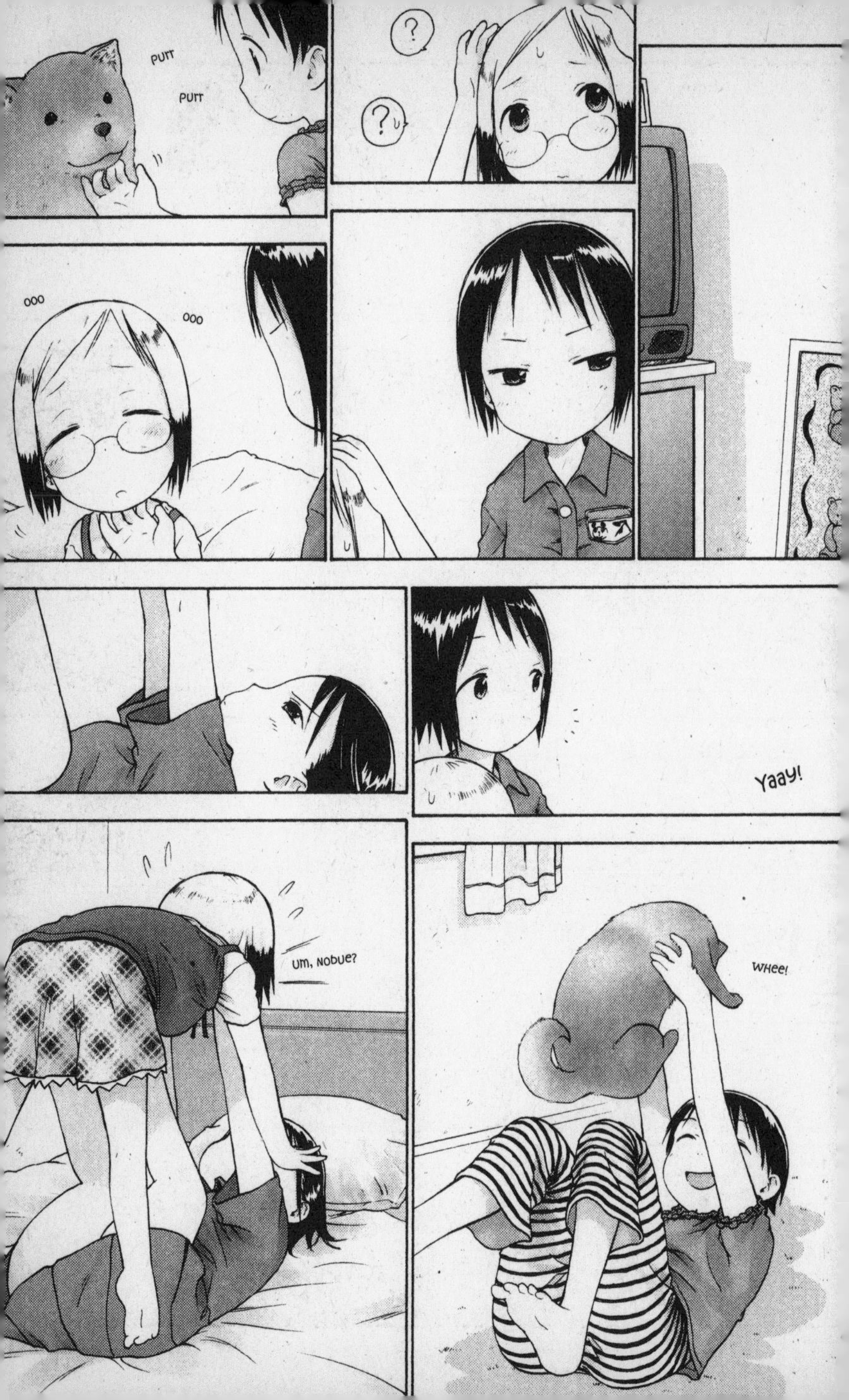
?
?
purr
purr
ooo
ooo
Yaay!
Whee!
Um, Nobue?

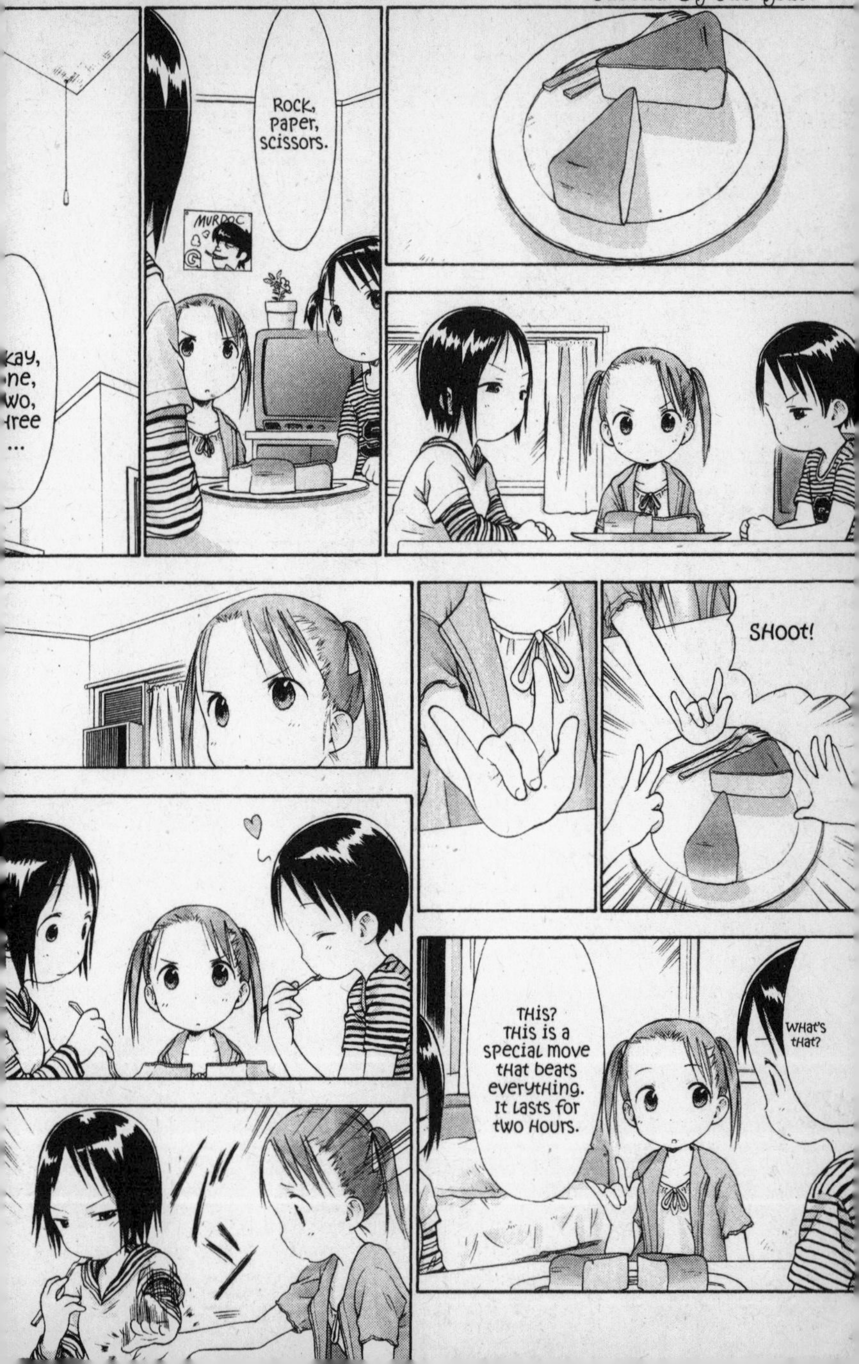
Rock, paper, scissors.
kay, ne, wo, hree …
SHOOT!
What's that?
THIS? THIS is a special move that beats everything. It lasts for two hours.

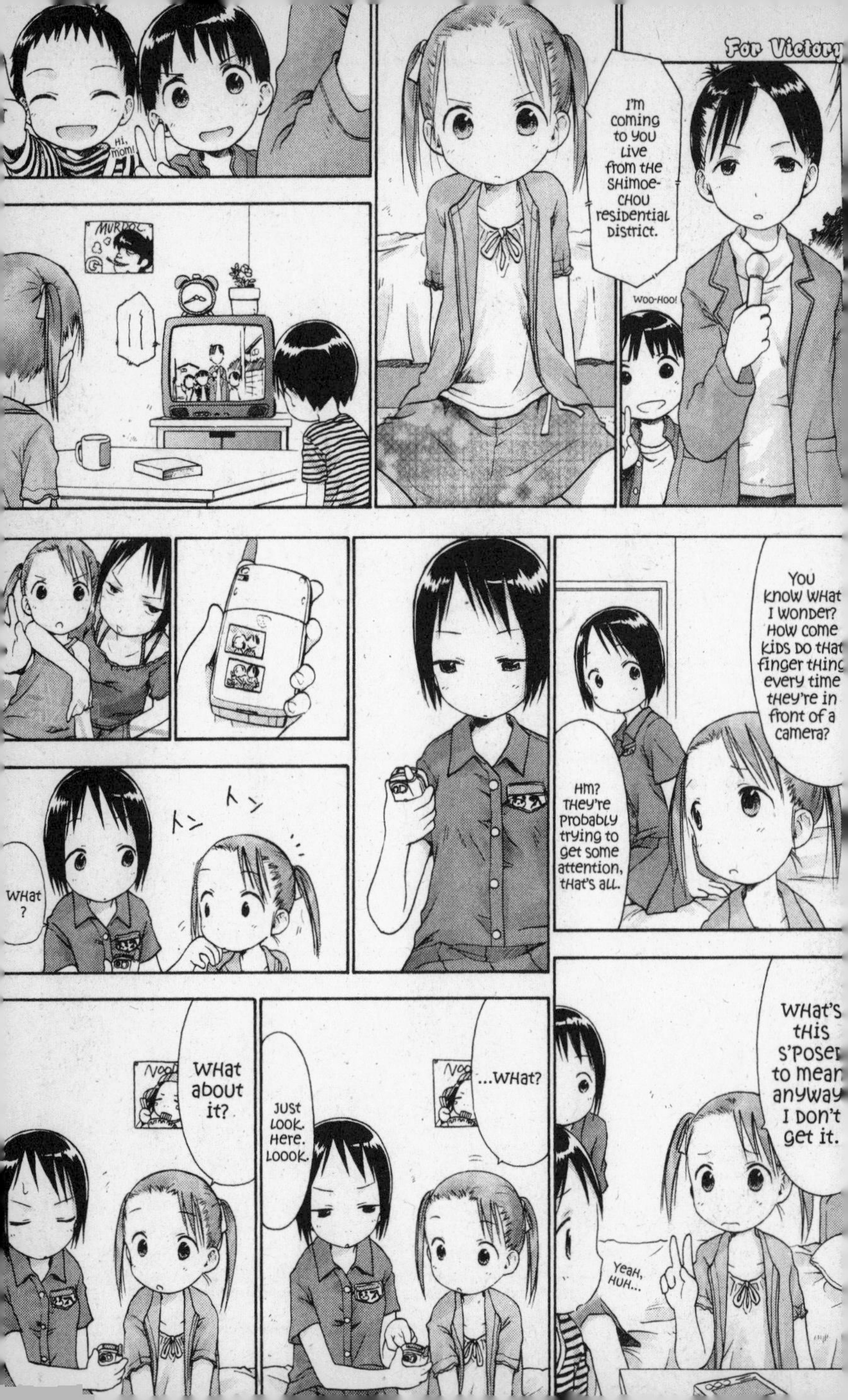
For Victory
I'm coming to you live from the Shimoe-chou residential district.
Woo-hoo!
Hi, mom!
You know what I wonder? How come kids do that finger thing every time they're in front of a camera?
Hm? They're probably trying to get some attention, that's all.
トン トン
What?
What's this s'posed to mean anyway. I don't get it.
Yeah, huh...
...What?
Just look. Here. Loook.
What about it?

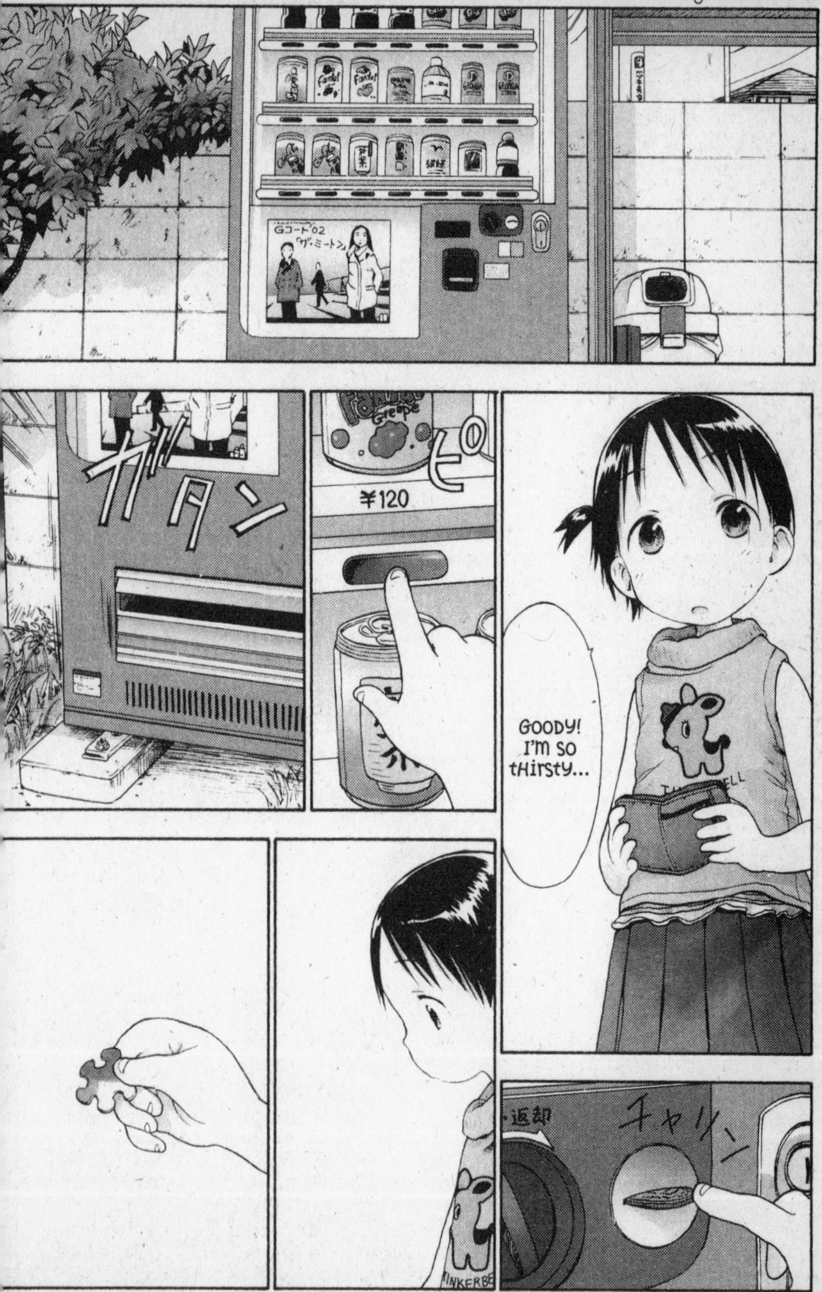
Gコード'02
「ザ・ミートン」
GOODY! I'm so thirsty...
ピ
Grape
¥120
ガタン
返却
チャリン

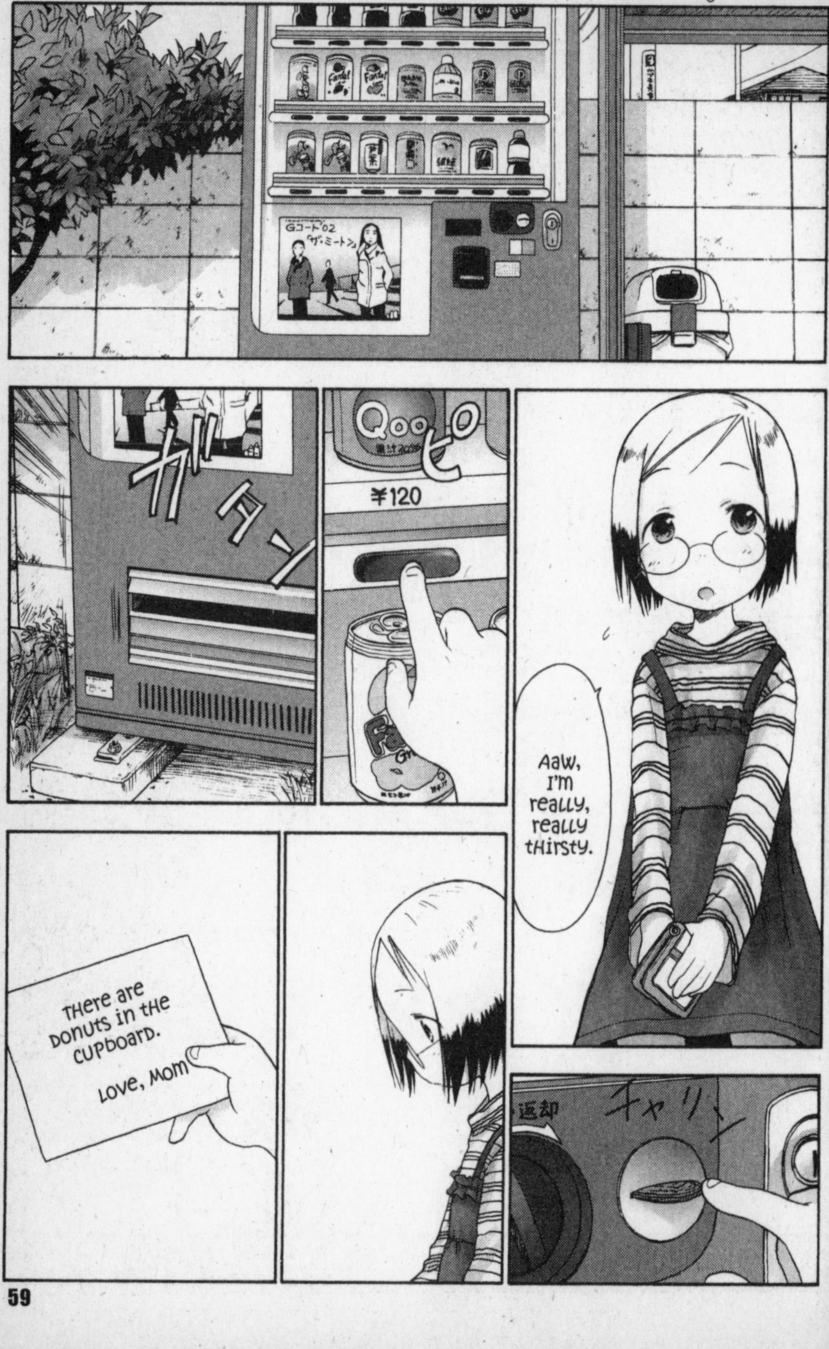
Gコード'02
「ザ・ミートン」
Aaw, I'm really, really thirsty.
Qoo
ピ
¥120
ガタン
返却
チャリン
There are donuts in the cupboard.
Love, Mom

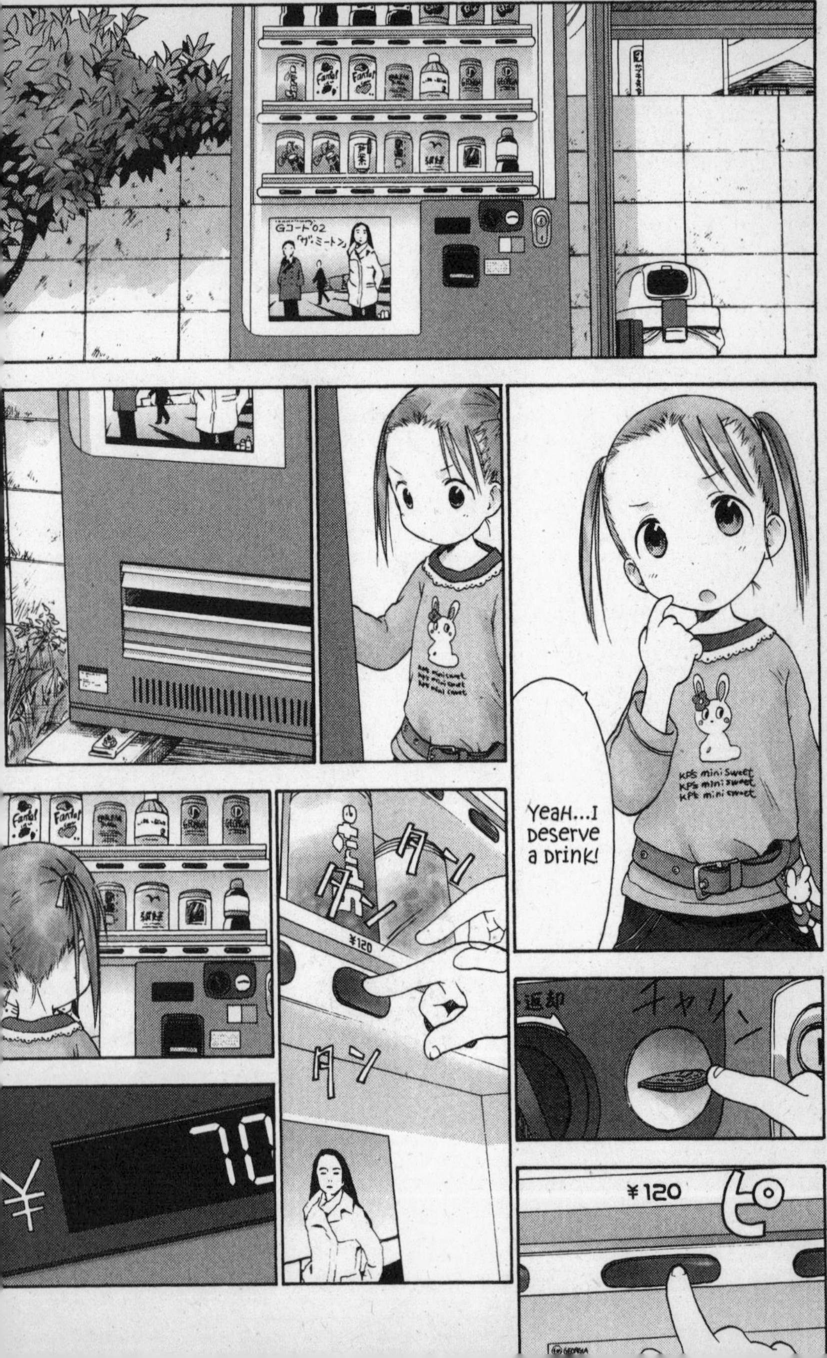
Gコード'02
「ザ・ミートン」
YeaH...I Deserve a Drink!
返却
チャリン
タン タン
¥120
タン
¥120
ピ
¥70

HALLO WORK

ana

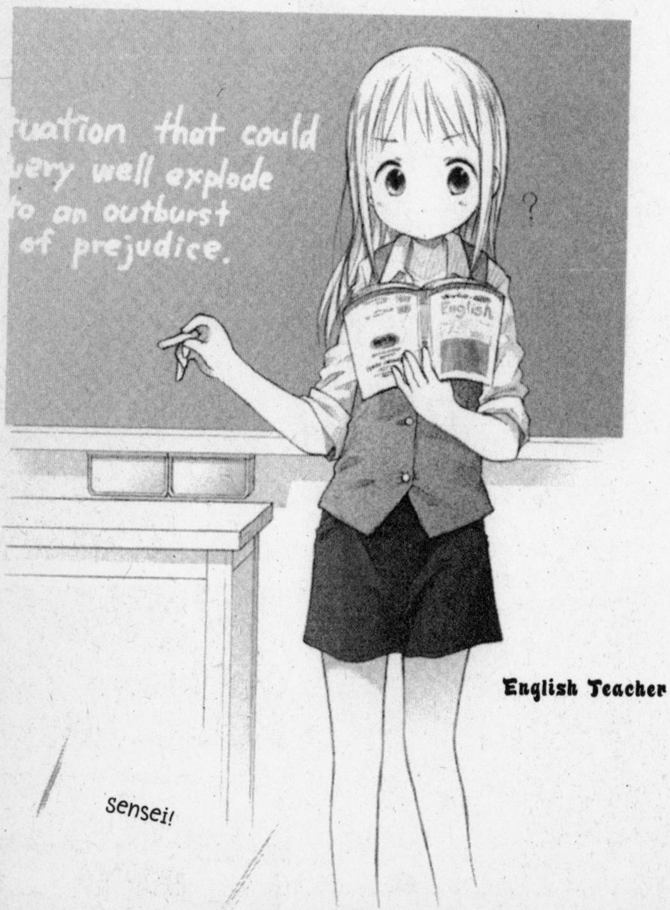

uation that could
very well explode
to an outburst
of prejudice.
?
English
English Teacher
sensei!

HALLO WORK

sasazuka

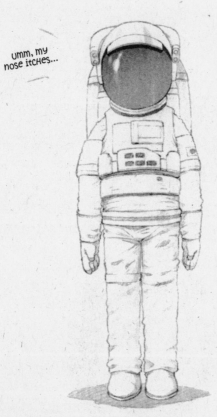

Astronaut

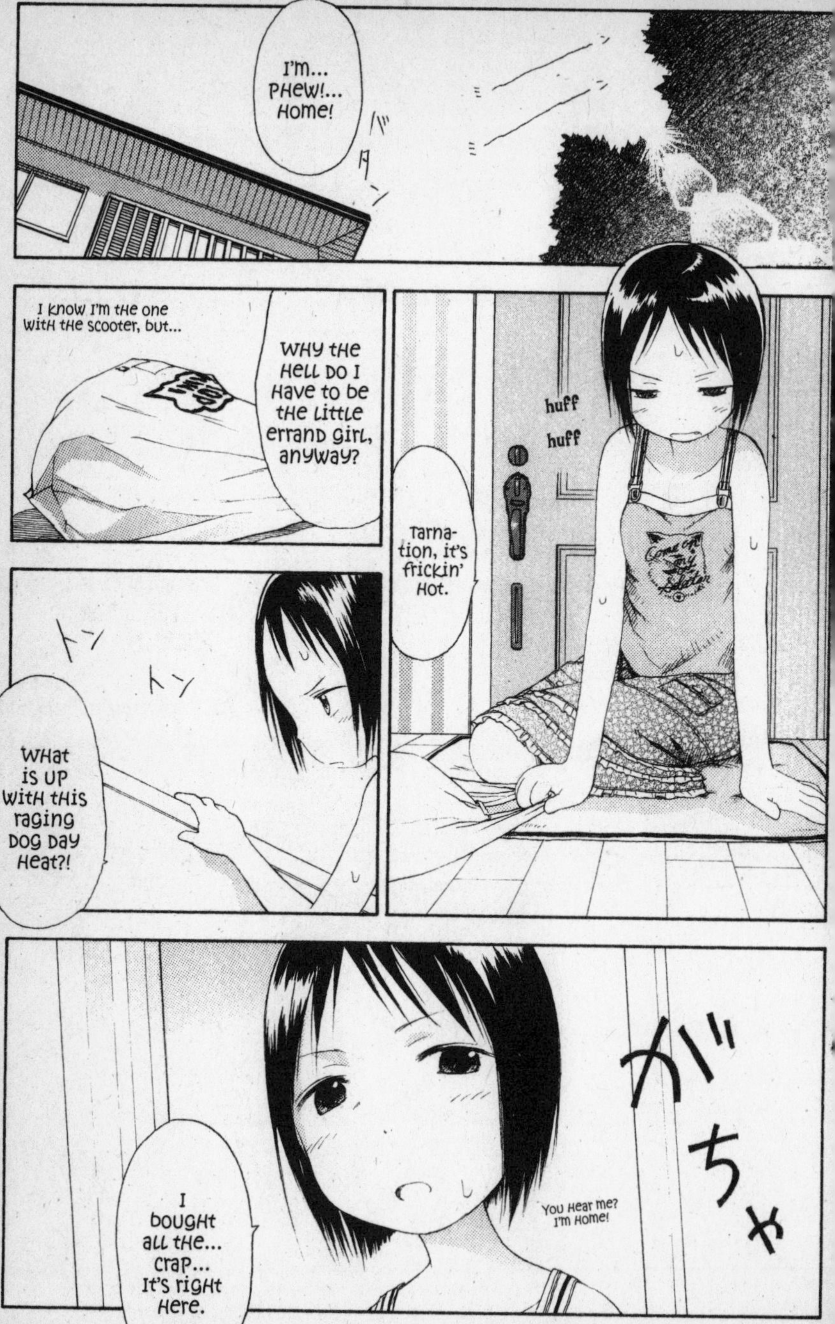
I'm... PHEW!... HOME!
バタン
huff
huff
Tarnation, it's frickin' hot.
I know I'm the one with the scooter, but...
WHY THE HELL DO I HAVE TO BE THE LITTLE ERRAND GIRL, ANYWAY?
トン
トン
WHAT IS UP WITH THIS RAGING DOG DAY HEAT?!
がちゃ
You hear me? I'm home!
I bought all the... crap... It's right here.

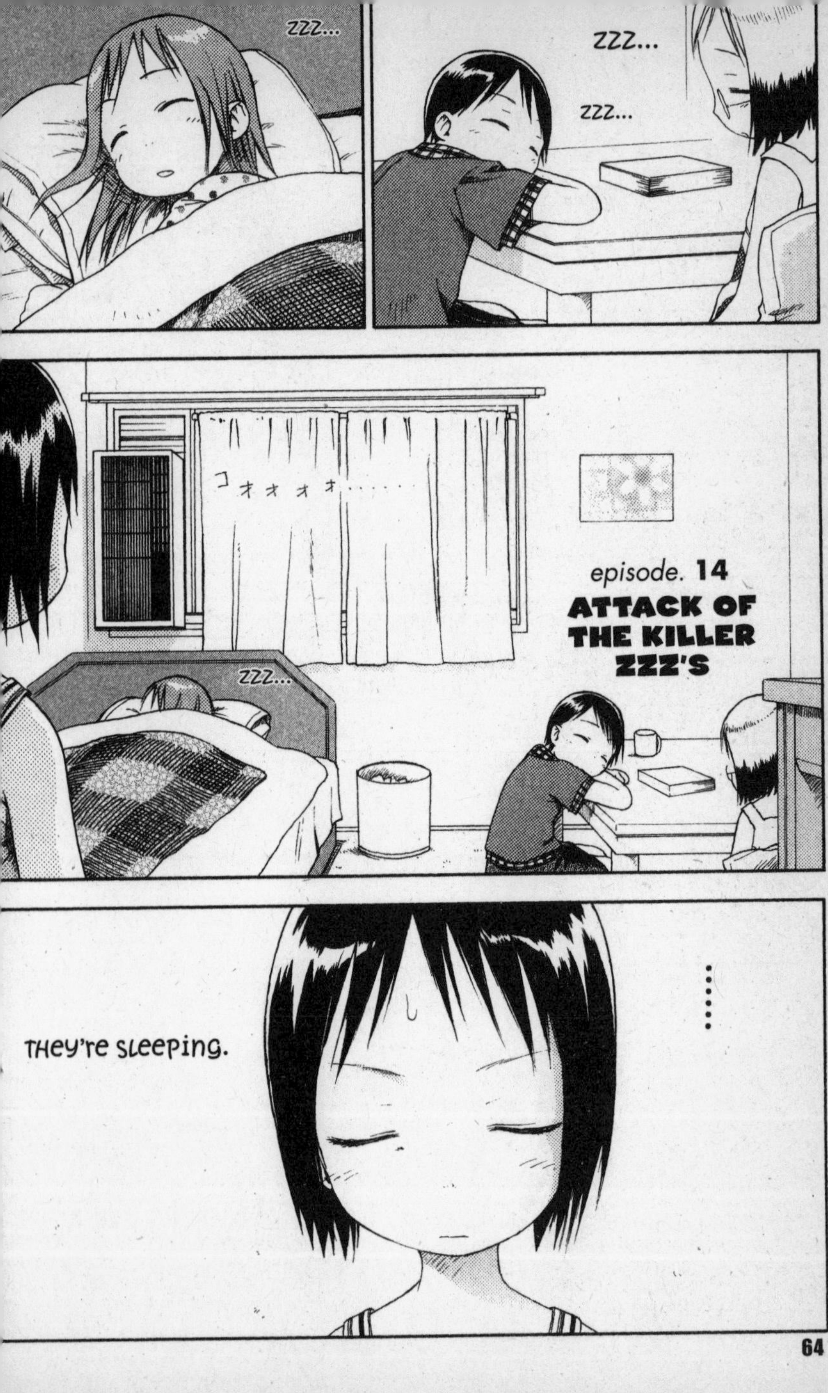
ZZZ...
ZZZ...
ZZZ...
コオオオオ……
episode. 14
ATTACK OF THE KILLER ZZZ'S
ZZZ...
……
They're sleeping.

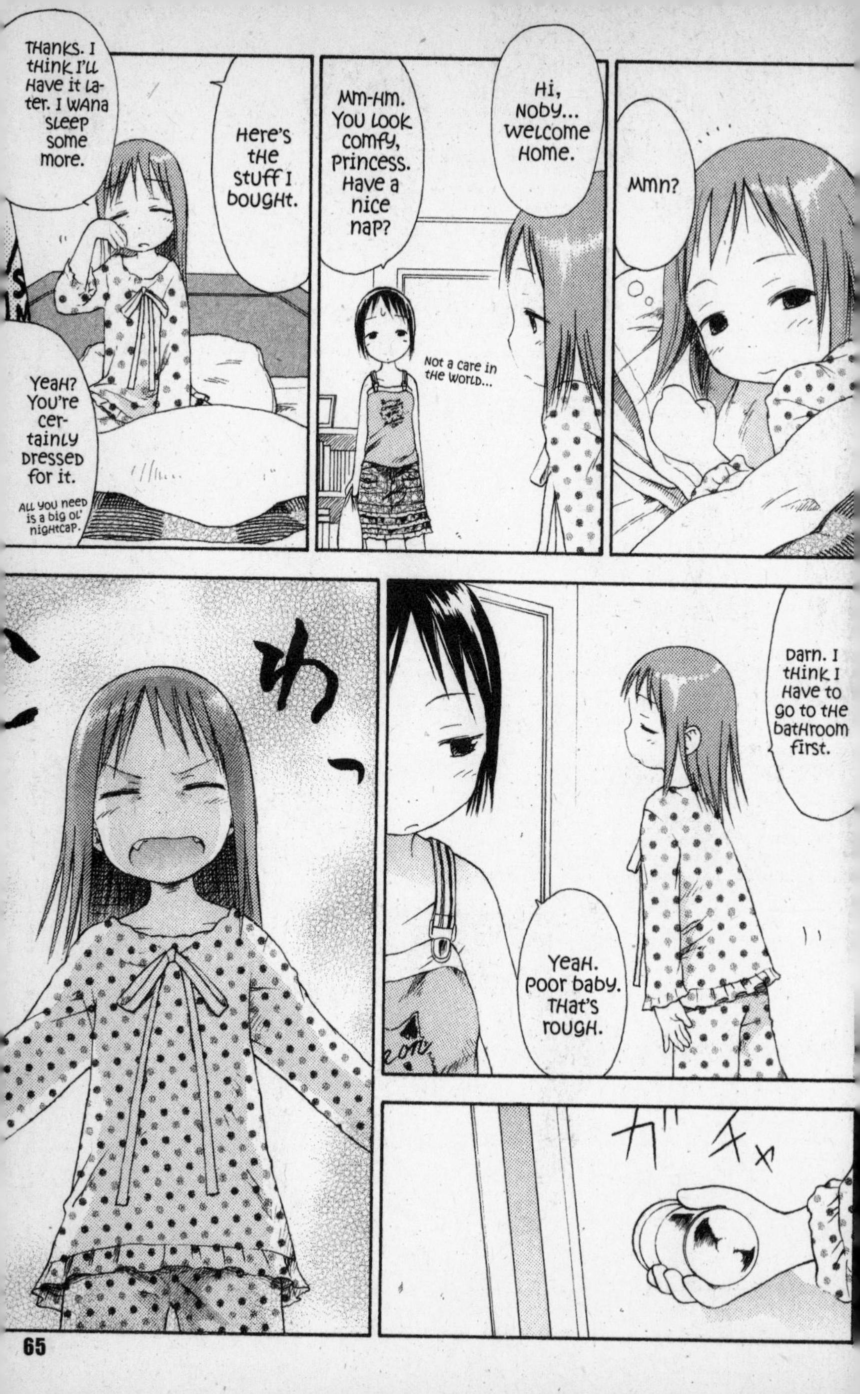
Mmn?
Hi, Noby... welcome home.
Mm-hm. You look comfy, princess. Have a nice nap?
Not a care in the world...
Here's the stuff I bought.
Thanks. I think I'll have it later. I wana sleep some more.
Yeah? You're certainly dressed for it.
All you need is a big ol' nightcap.
Darn. I think I have to go to the bathroom first.
Yeah. Poor baby. That's rough.
ガチャ
わっ

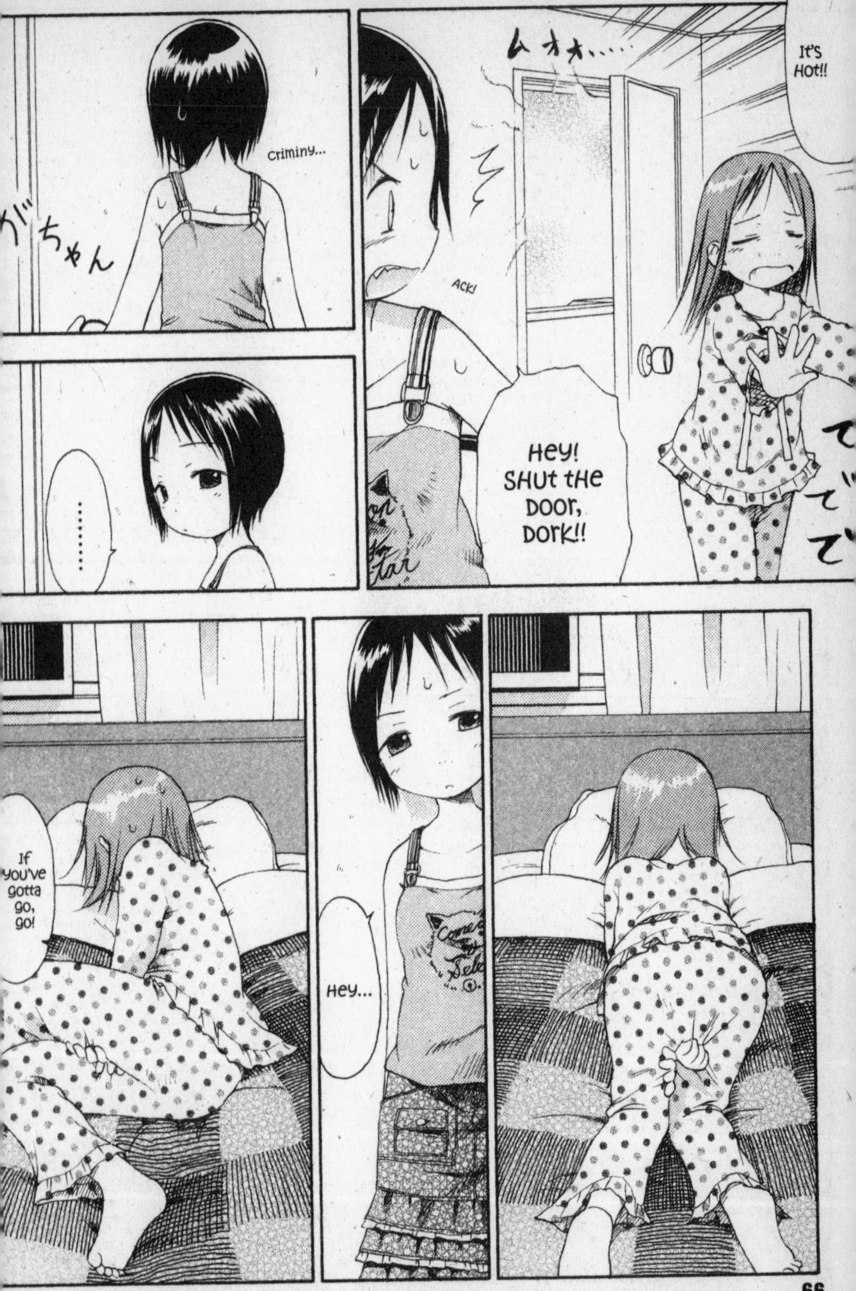
It's Hot!!
ムオォ……
ACK!
Hey! SHUT the Door, Dork!!
てでてで
Criminy...
ちゃん
....
Hey...
If you've gotta go, go!

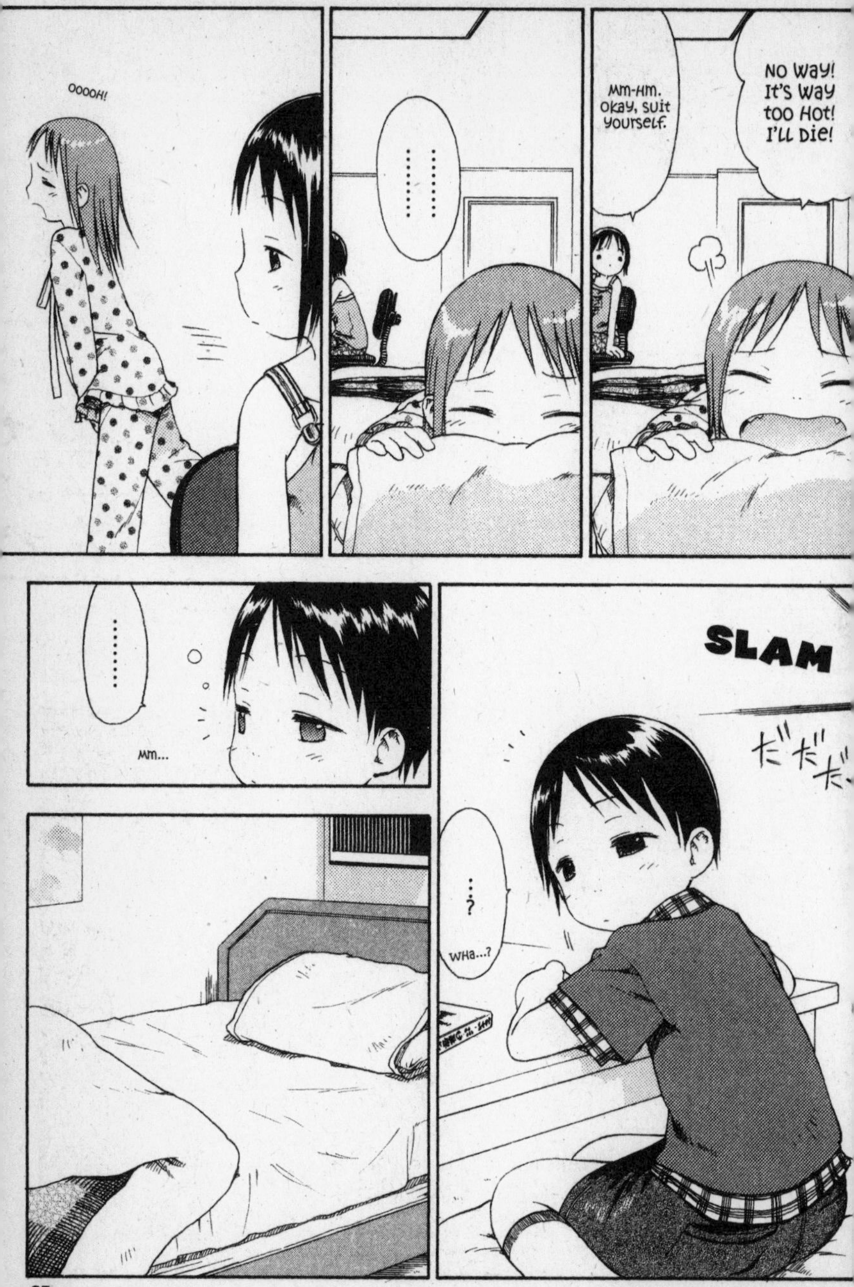
No Way! It's Way too Hot! I'll Die!
Mm-Hm. Okay, suit yourself.
......
OOOOH!
SLAM
だだだ
...?
Wha...?
......
Mm...

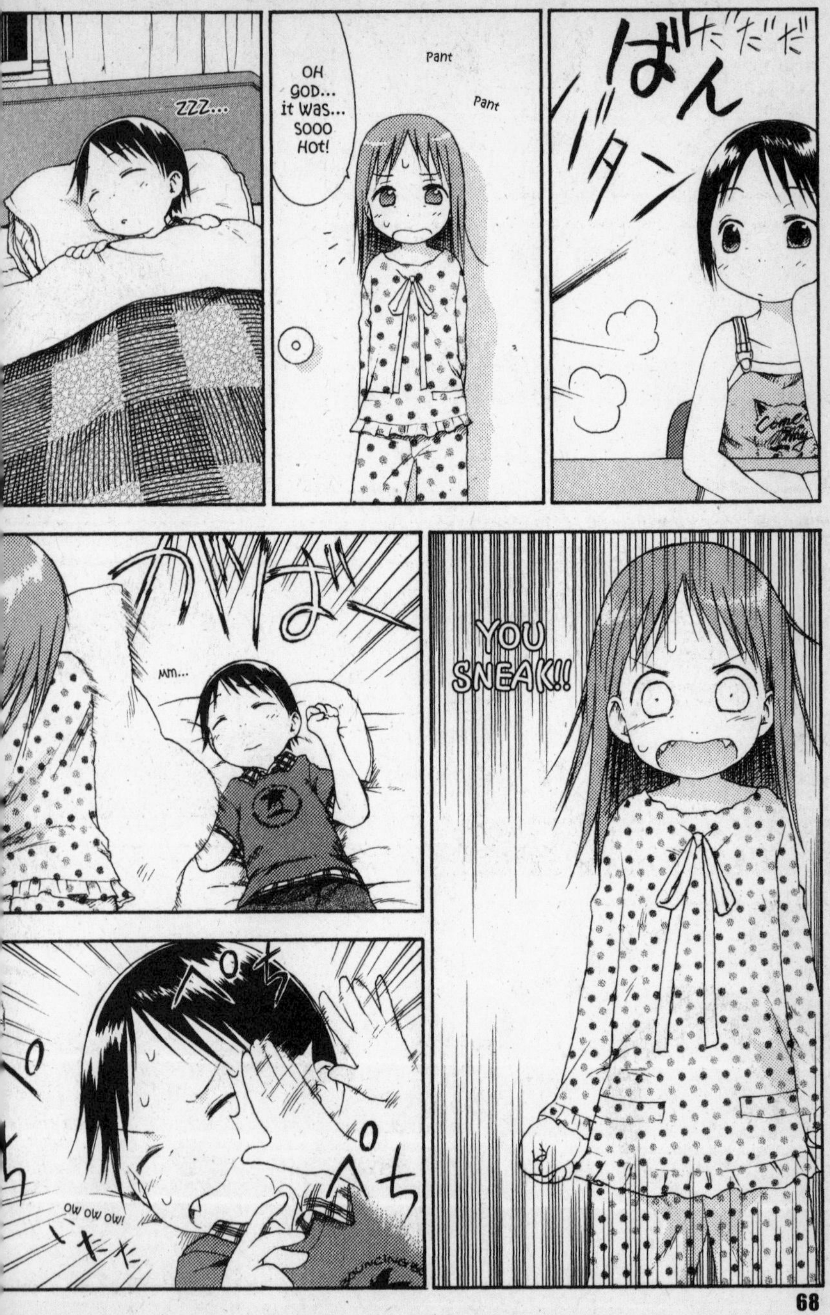
だだだ
ばん
バタン
Pant
Pant
OH GOD... it was... SOOO Hot!
ZZZ...
YOU SNEAK!!
MM...
ぺち
ぺち
OW OW OW!

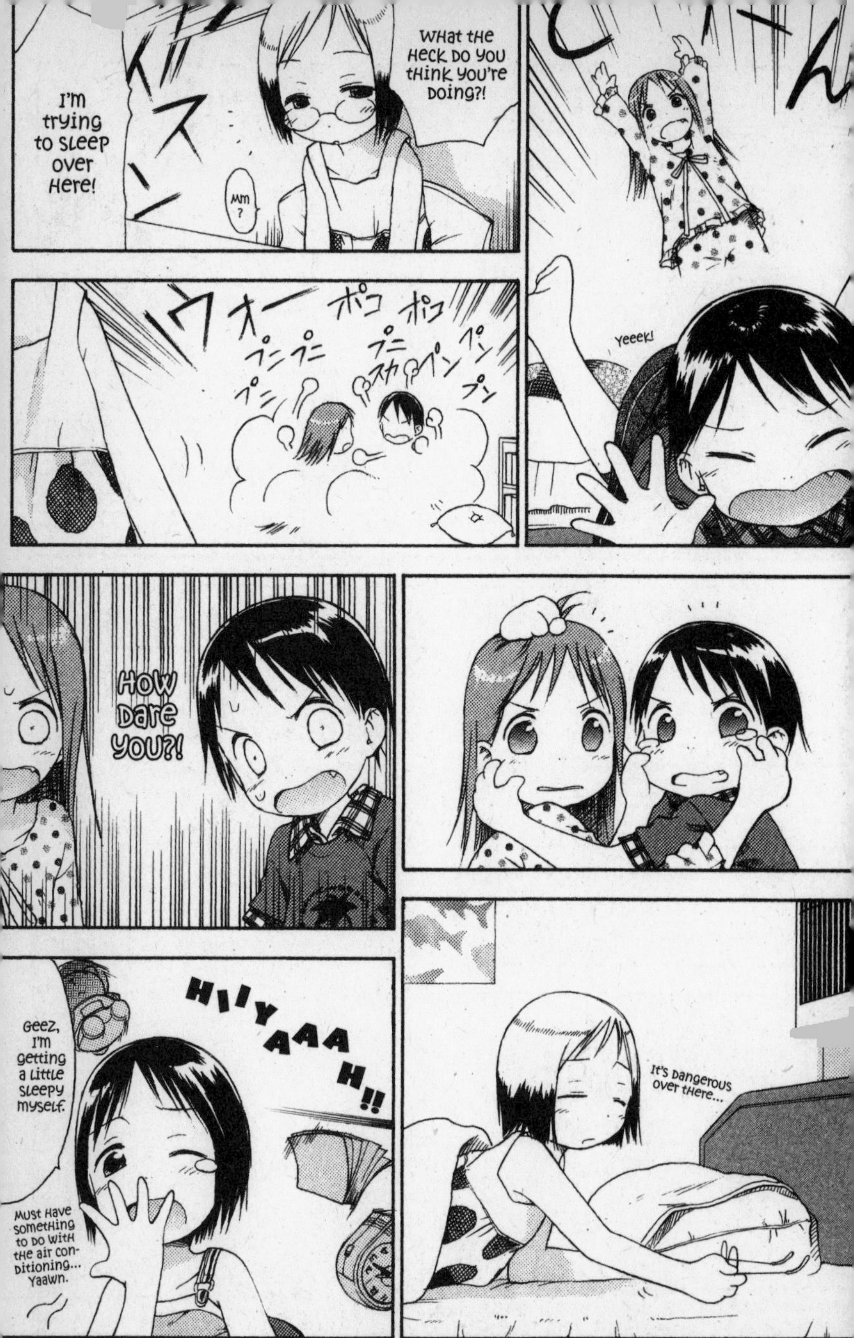

What the heck do you think you're doing?!
I'm trying to sleep over here!
Mm ?
Yeeek!
ウオー
ポコ ポコ
How dare you?!
It's dangerous over there...
HIIYAAAH!!
Geez, I'm getting a little sleepy myself.
Must have something to do with the air conditioning... Yaawn.

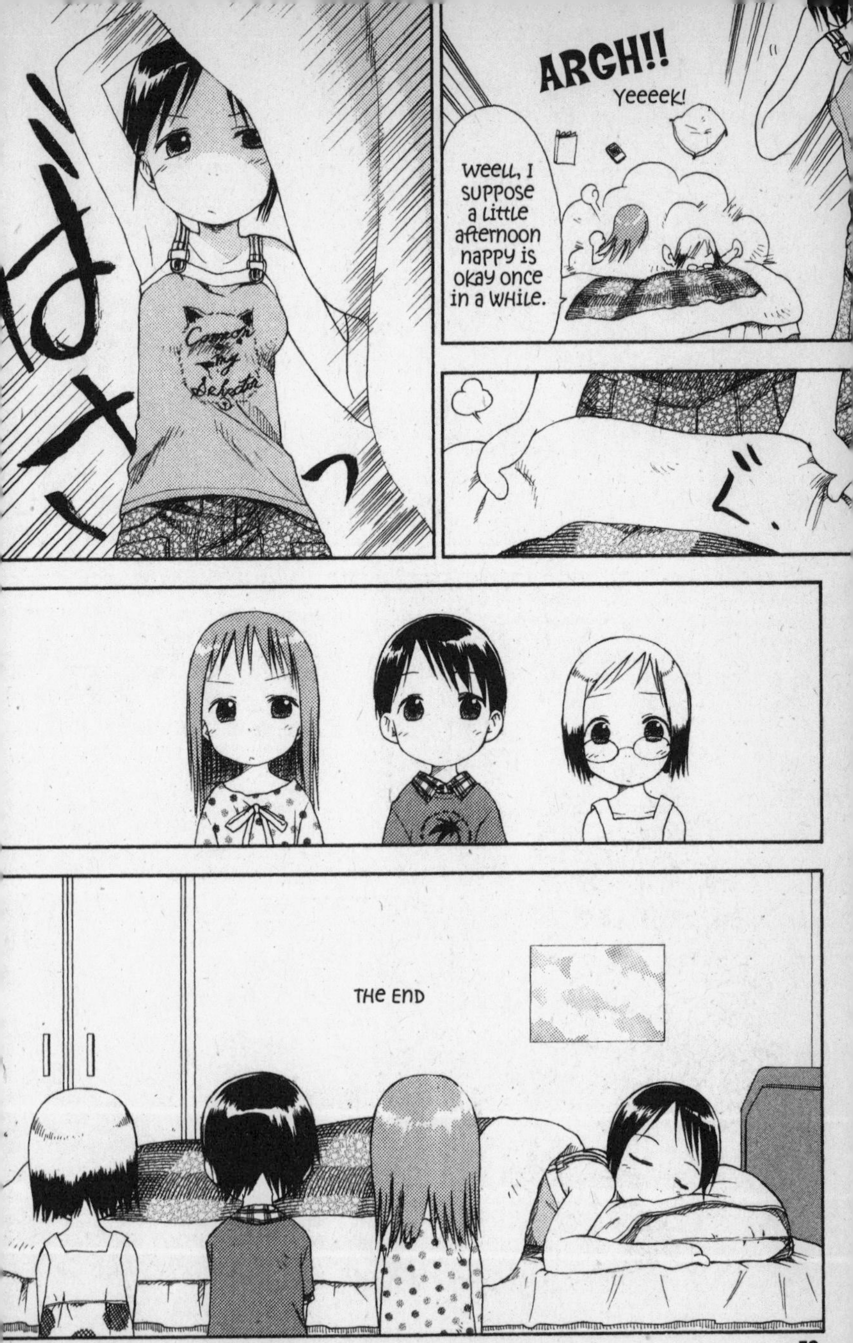
ARGH!!
Yeeeek!
Weeell, I suppose a little afternoon nappy is okay once in a while.
THE END

HALLO WORK

nobue

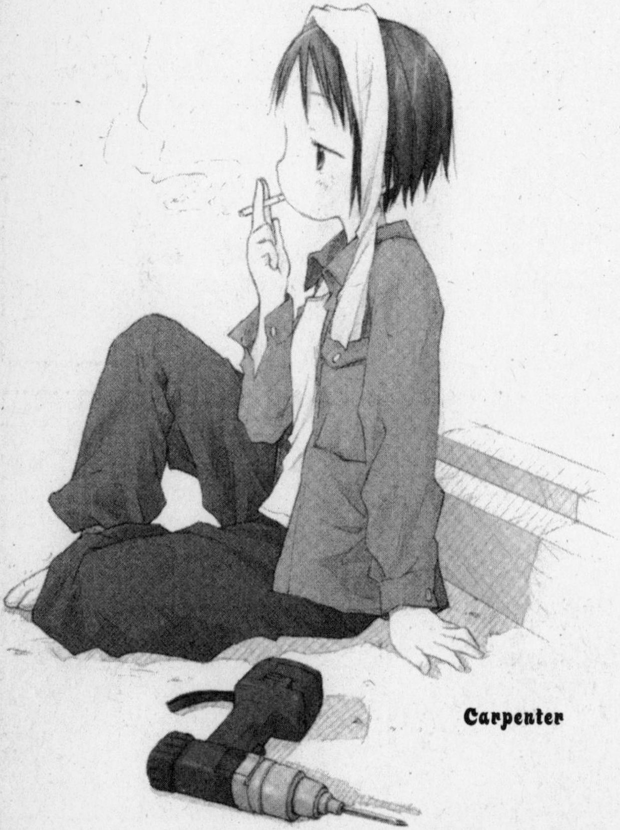
Carpenter

HALLO WORK
chika

Kindergarten
Teacher

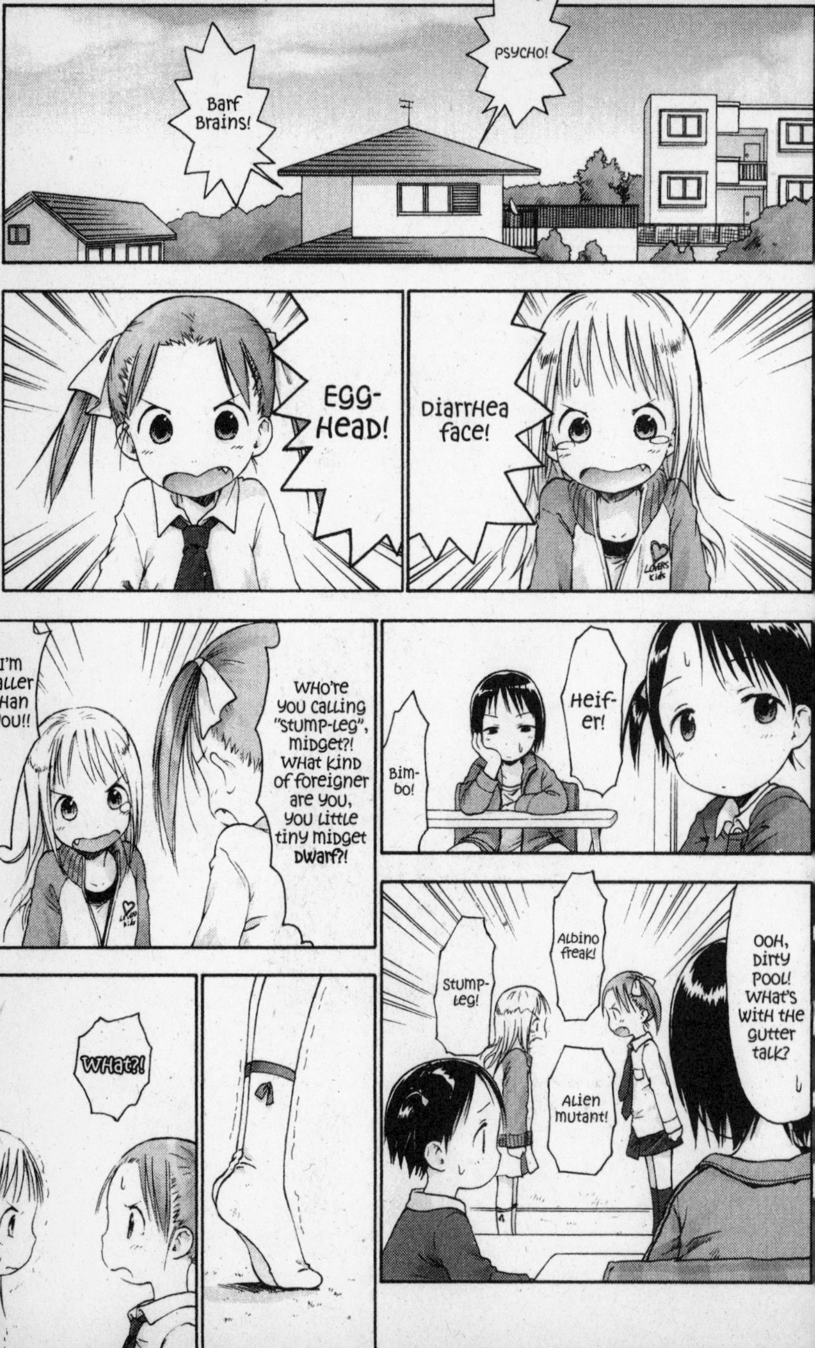
PSYCHO!
Barf Brains!
Diarrhea face!
EGG-HEAD!
Heif-er!
Bim-bo!
Who're you calling "stump-leg", midget?! What kind of foreigner are you, you little tiny midget DWARF?!
I'm taller than you!!
Ooh, dirty pool! What's with the gutter talk?
Albino freak!
Alien mutant!
Stump-leg!
WHAT?!

episode. **15**

ANA VS MIU

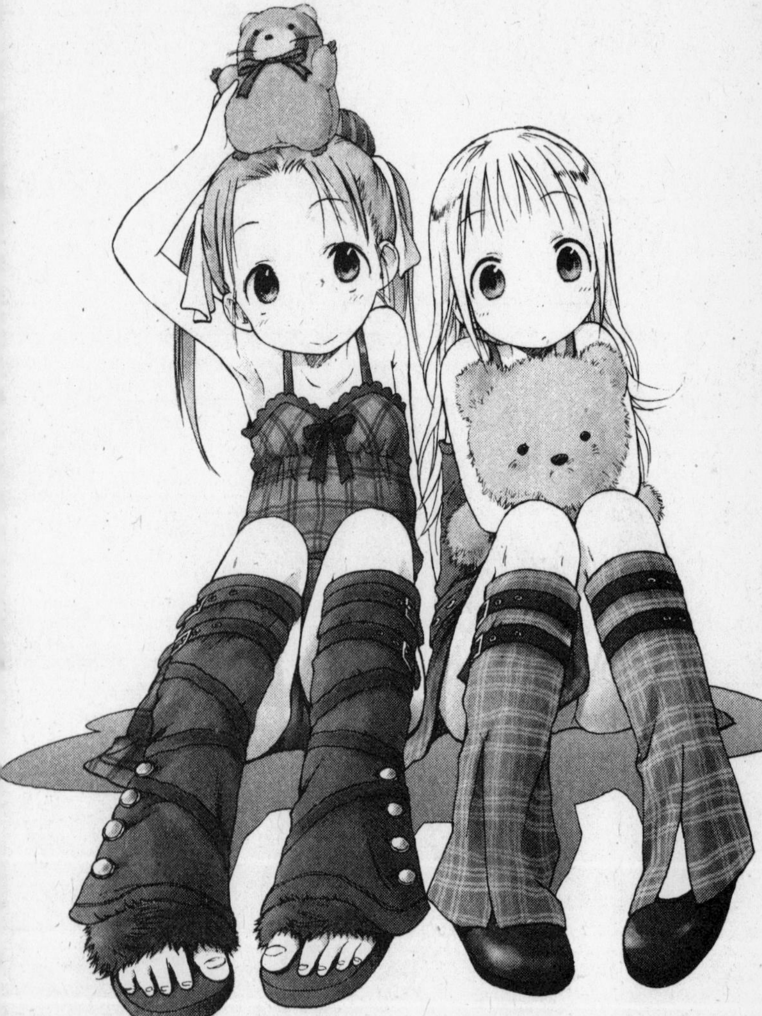

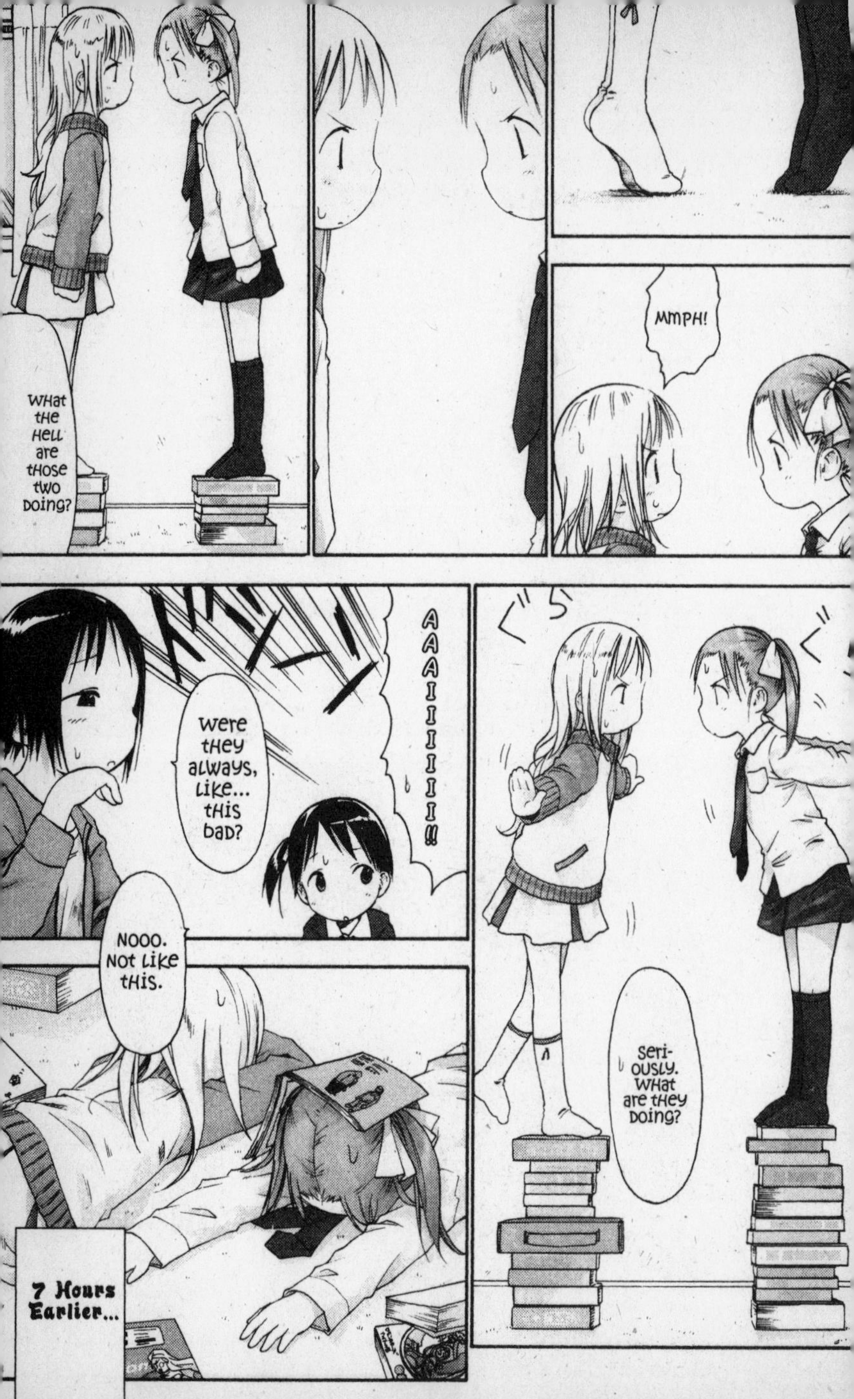

MMPH!
What the hell are those two doing?
ぐら
Seri-ously. What are they doing?
AAAIIIIIIIII!!
Were they always, like... this bad?
NOOO. Not like this.
7 Hours Earlier...

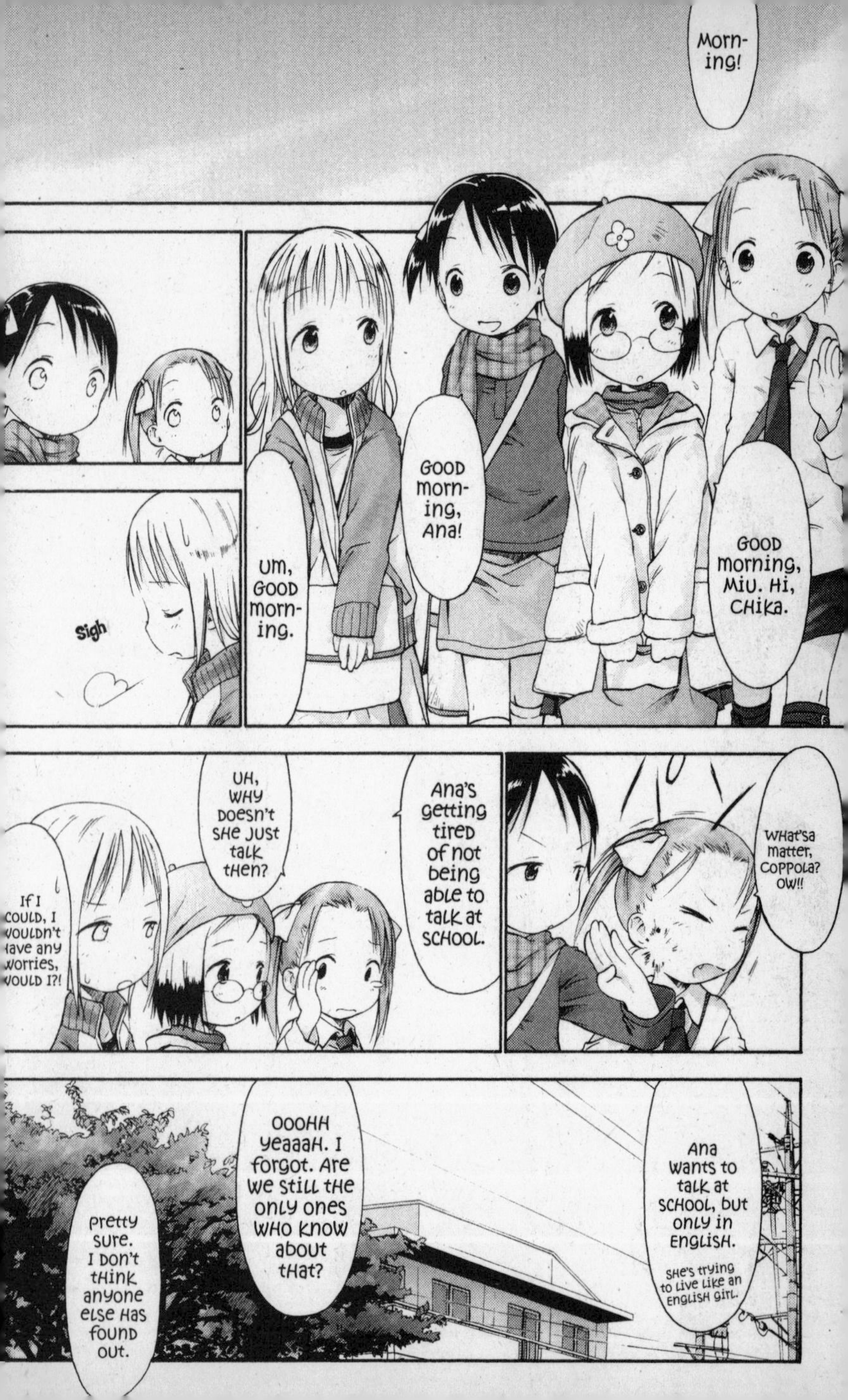
Morning!
Good morning, Miu. Hi, Chika.
Good morning, Ana!
Um, good morning.
Sigh
What'sa matter, Coppola? Ow!!
Ana's getting tired of not being able to talk at school.
Uh, why doesn't she just talk then?
If I could, I wouldn't have any worries, would I?!
Ana wants to talk at school, but only in English.
She's trying to live like an English girl.
Ooohh yeaaah. I forgot. Are we still the only ones who know about that?
Pretty sure. I don't think anyone else has found out.

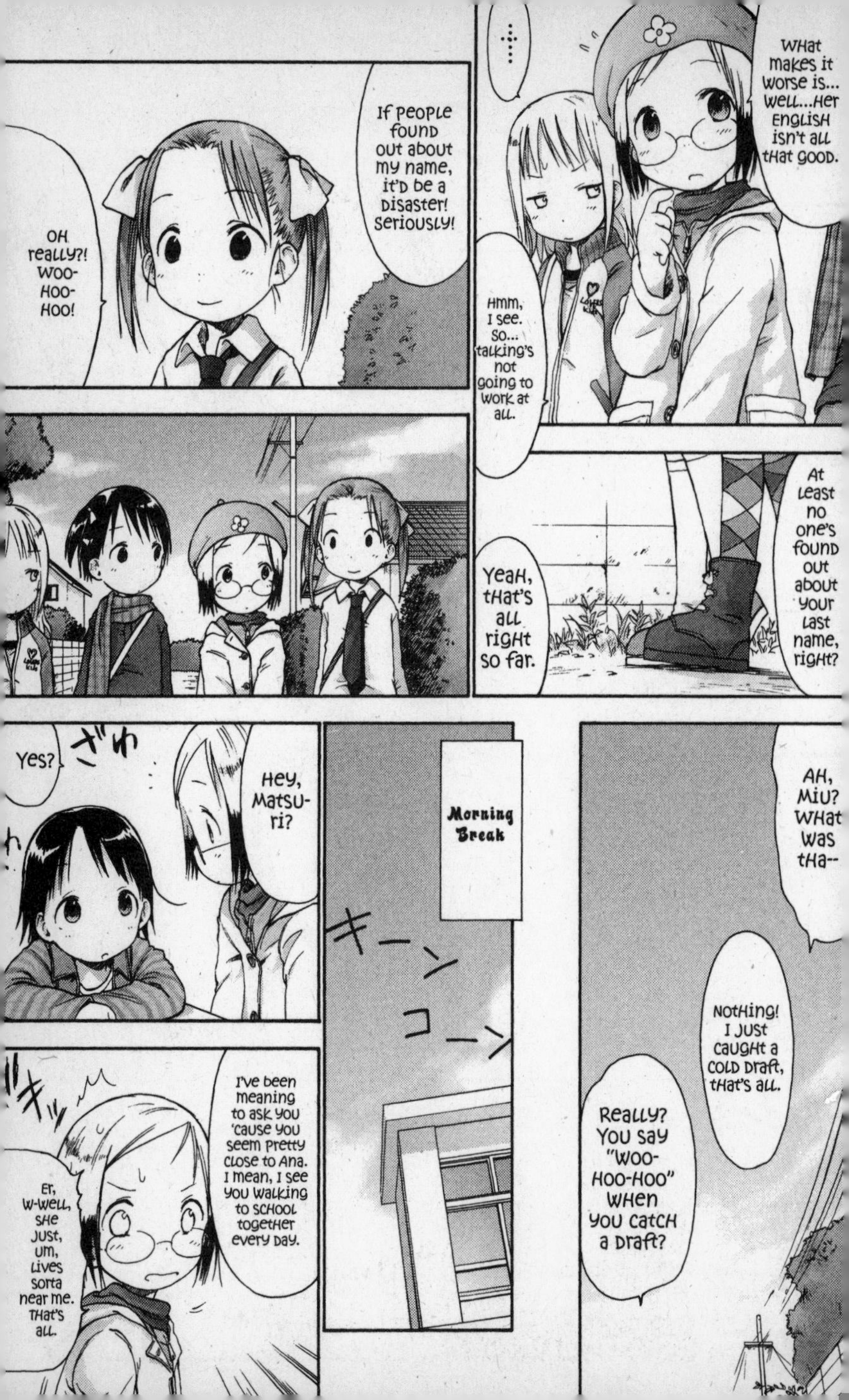
What makes it worse is... well...her English isn't all that good.
…
Hmm, I see. So... talking's not going to work at all.
If people found out about my name, it'd be a disaster! Seriously!
Oh really?! Woo-hoo-hoo!
At least no one's found out about your last name, right?
Yeah, that's all right so far.
Ah, Miu? What was tha--
Nothing! I just caught a cold draft, that's all.
Really? You say "Woo-hoo-hoo" when you catch a draft?
Morning Break
キーンコーン
Hey, Matsu-ri?
ざわ
Yes?
I've been meaning to ask you 'cause you seem pretty close to Ana. I mean, I see you walking to school together every day.
ギッ
Er, w-well, she just, um, lives sorta near me. That's all.

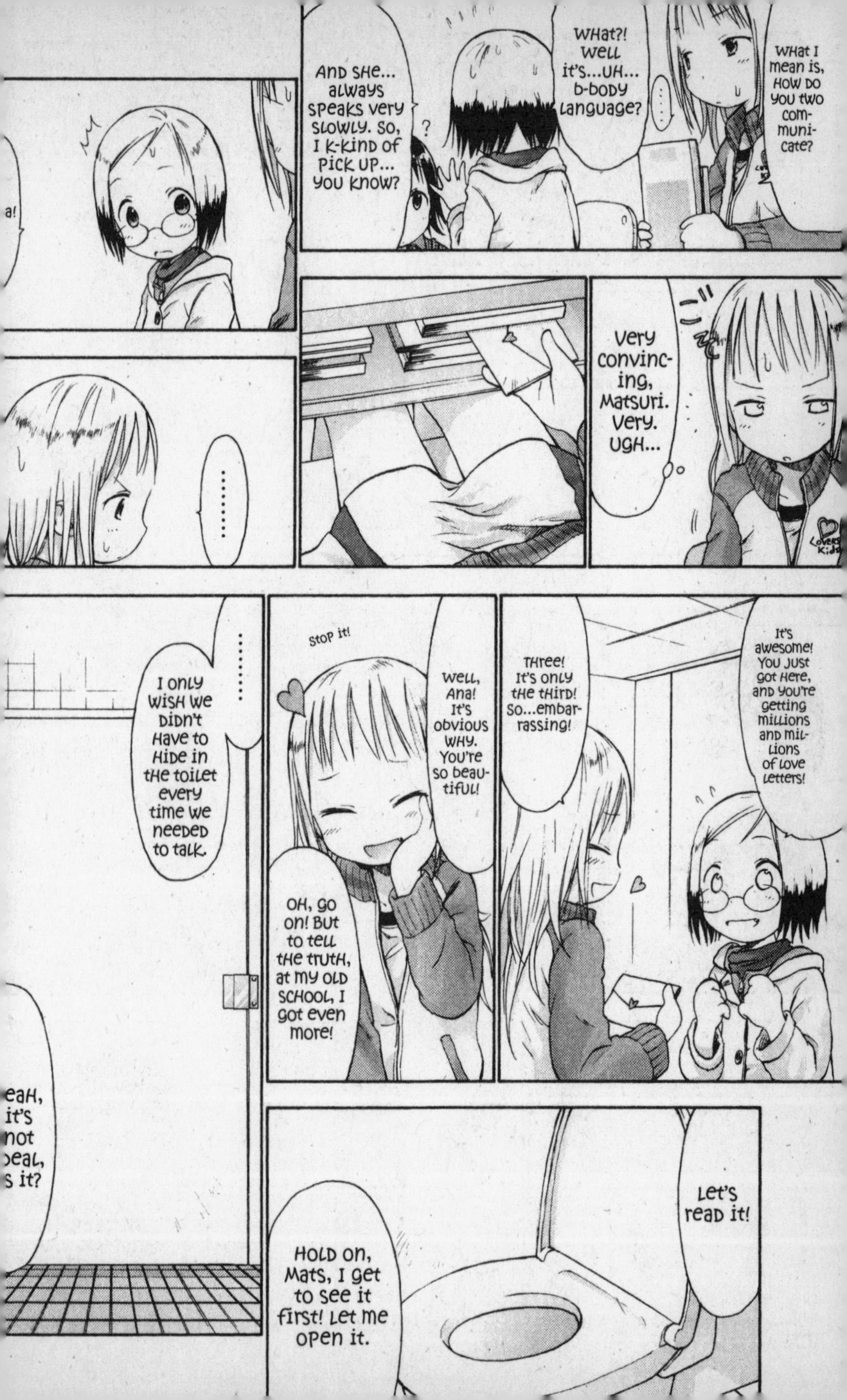

What I mean is, how do you two communicate?
What?! Well it's...uh... b-body language?
......
?
And she... always speaks very slowly. So, I k-kind of pick up... you know?
a!
Very convincing, Matsuri. Very. Ugh...
....
It's awesome! You just got here, and you're getting millions and millions of love letters!
Three! It's only the third! So...embarrassing!
Well, Ana! It's obvious why. You're so beautiful!
Stop it!
Oh, go on! But to tell the truth, at my old school, I got even more!
Let's read it!
Hold on, Mats, I get to see it first! Let me open it.
....
I only wish we didn't have to hide in the toilet every time we needed to talk.
eah, it's not deal, s it?

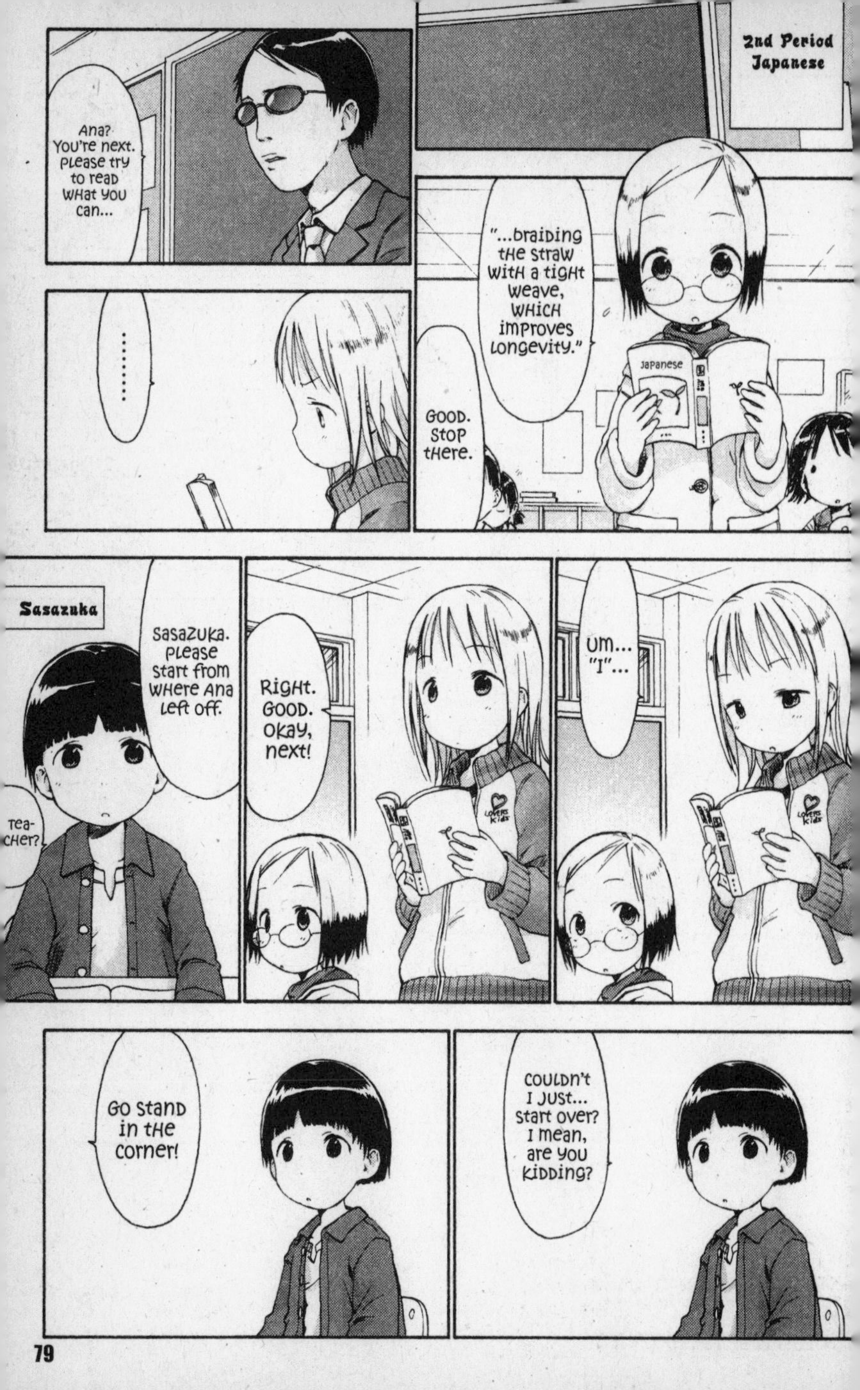
2nd Period Japanese
"...braiding the straw with a tight weave, which improves longevity."
Japanese
Good. Stop there.
Ana? You're next. Please try to read what you can...
......
Um... "I"...
Right. Good. Okay, next!
Sasazuka
Sasazuka. Please start from where Ana left off.
Tea-cher?
Couldn't I just... start over? I mean, are you kidding?
Go stand in the corner!

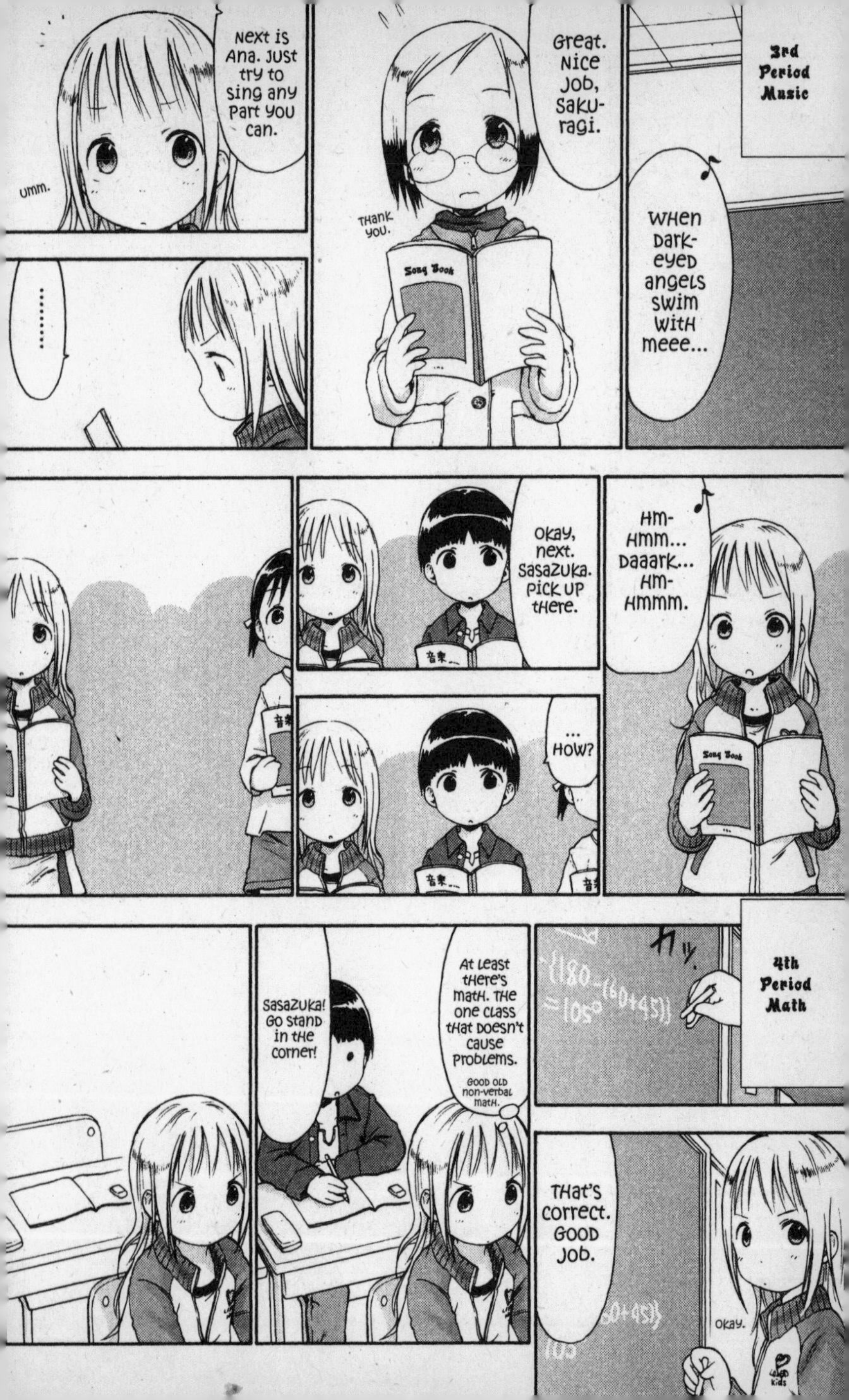
3rd Period Music
When dark-eyed angels swim with meee...
Great. Nice job, Saku-ragi.
Thank you.
Next is Ana. Just try to sing any part you can.
Umm.
....
Hm-hmm... Daaark... Hm-hmmm.
Song Book
Okay, next. Sasazuka. Pick up there.
...How?
4th Period Math
{180-(60+45)}
=105°
That's correct. Good job.
Okay.
At least there's math. The one class that doesn't cause problems.
Good old non-verbal math.
Sasazuka! Go stand in the corner!

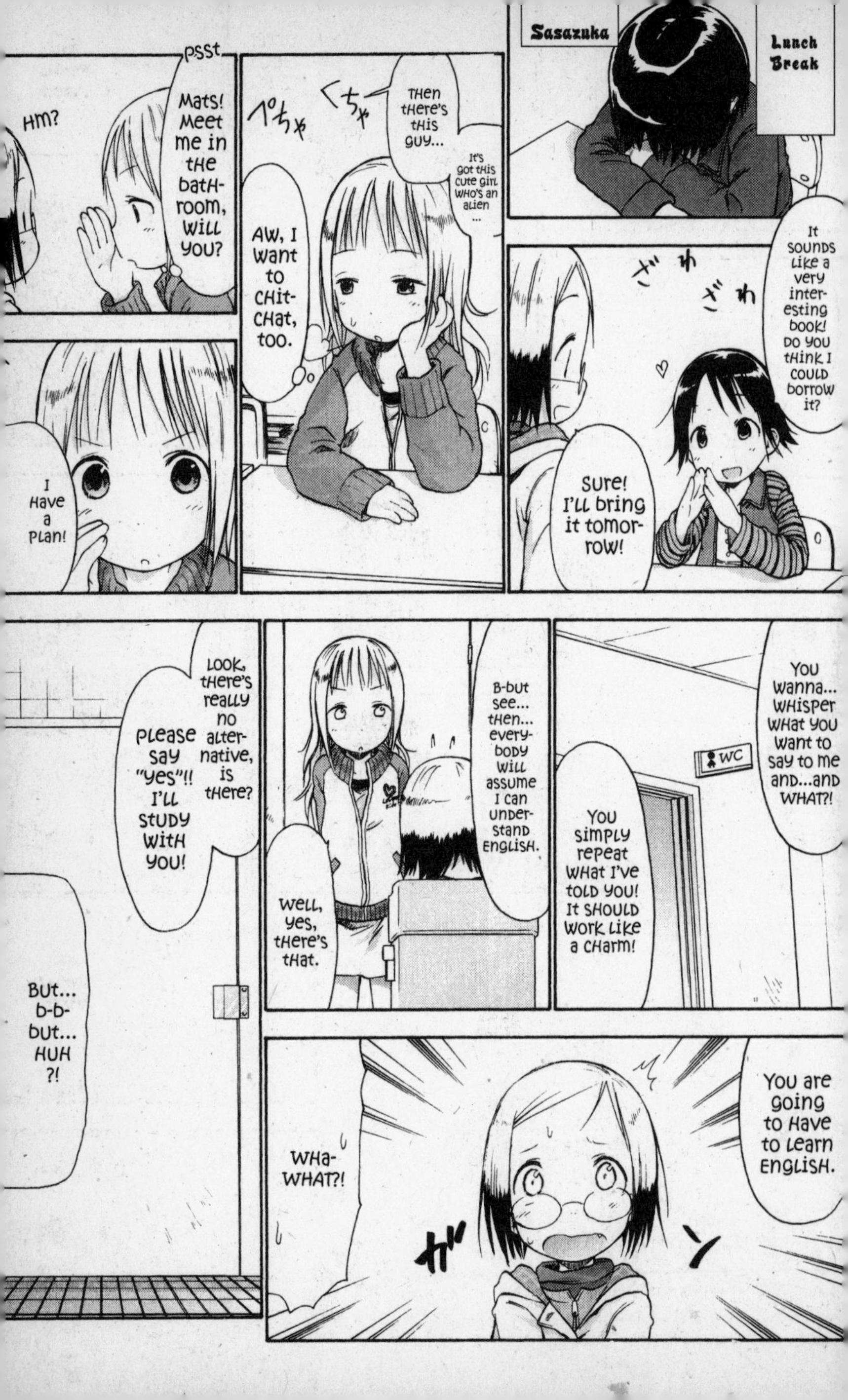

Lunch Break
Sasazuka
It sounds like a very interesting book! Do you think I could borrow it?
ざわ ざわ
Sure! I'll bring it tomorrow!
くちゃ
Then there's this guy...
It's got this cute girl who's an alien...
ぺちゃ
Aw, I want to chit-chat, too.
PSST
Mats! Meet me in the bathroom, will you?
Hm?
I have a plan!
You wanna... whisper what you want to say to me and...and WHAT?!
WC
You simply repeat what I've told you! It should work like a charm!
B-but see... then... everybody will assume I can understand English.
Well, yes, there's that.
You are going to have to learn English.
ガ ン
WHA-WHAT?!
Look, there's really no alternative, is there?
Please say "yes"!! I'll study with you!
But... b-b-but... HUH?!

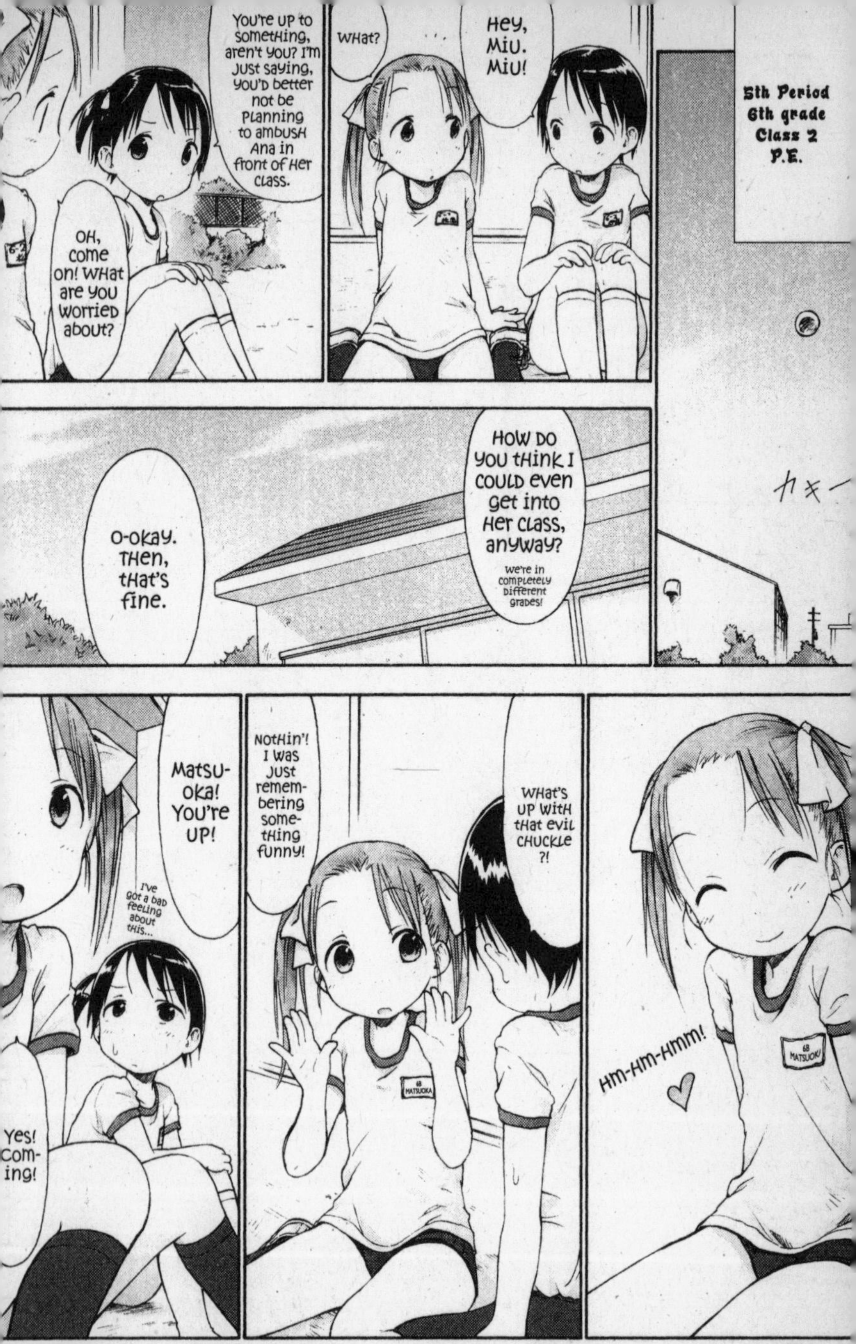
5th Period 6th grade Class 2 P.E.
Hey, Miu. Miu!
...
What?
You're up to something, aren't you? I'm just saying, you'd better not be planning to ambush Ana in front of her class.
Oh, come on! What are you worried about?
カキー
How do you think I could even get into her class, anyway?
We're in completely different grades!
O-okay. Then, that's fine.
Hm-hm-hmm!
What's up with that evil chuckle?!
Nothin'! I was just remembering something funny!
Matsuoka! You're up!
I've got a bad feeling about this...
Yes! Coming!

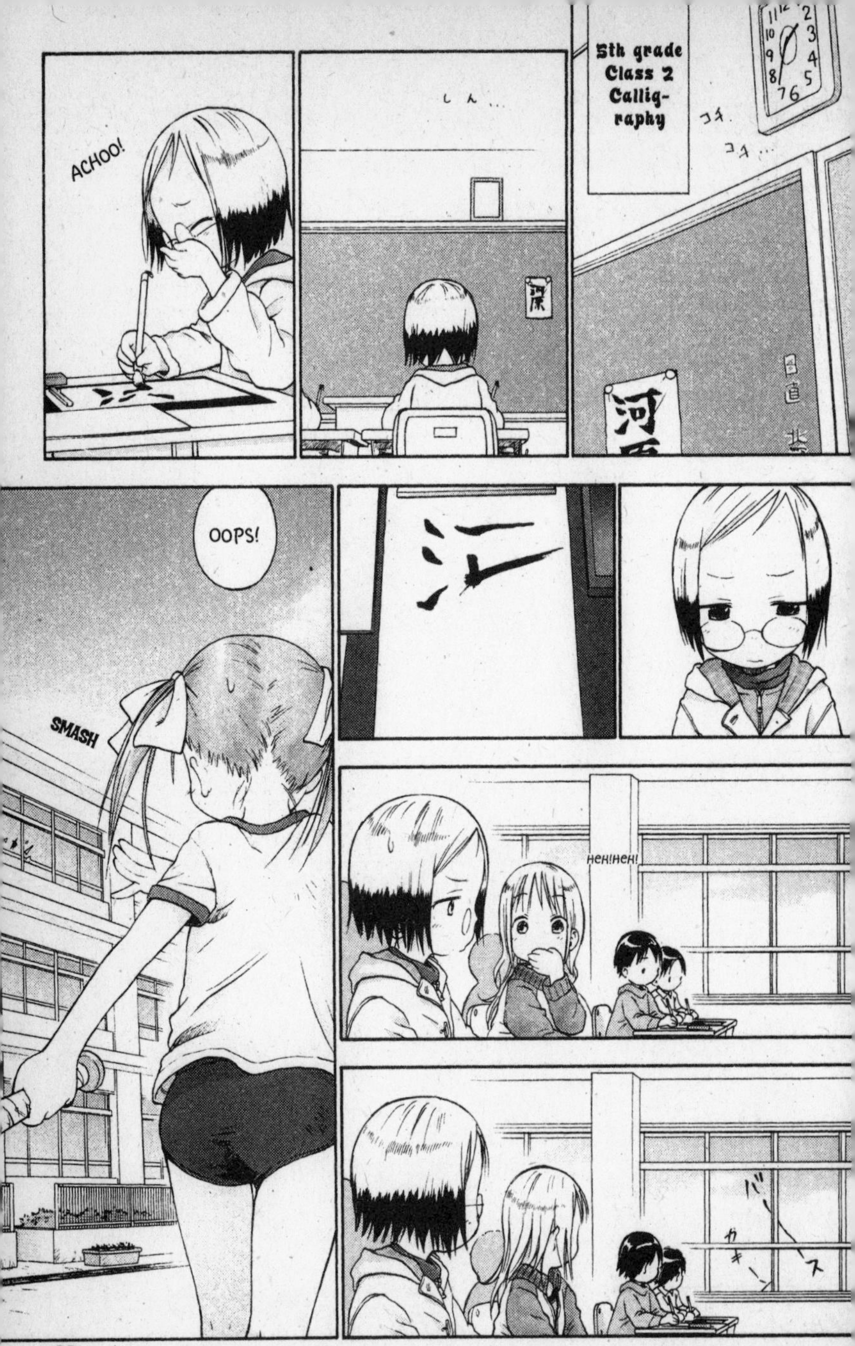
5th grade Class 2 Calligraphy
コチ.
コチ...
しん...
ACHOO!
HEH!HEH!
OOPS!
SMASH

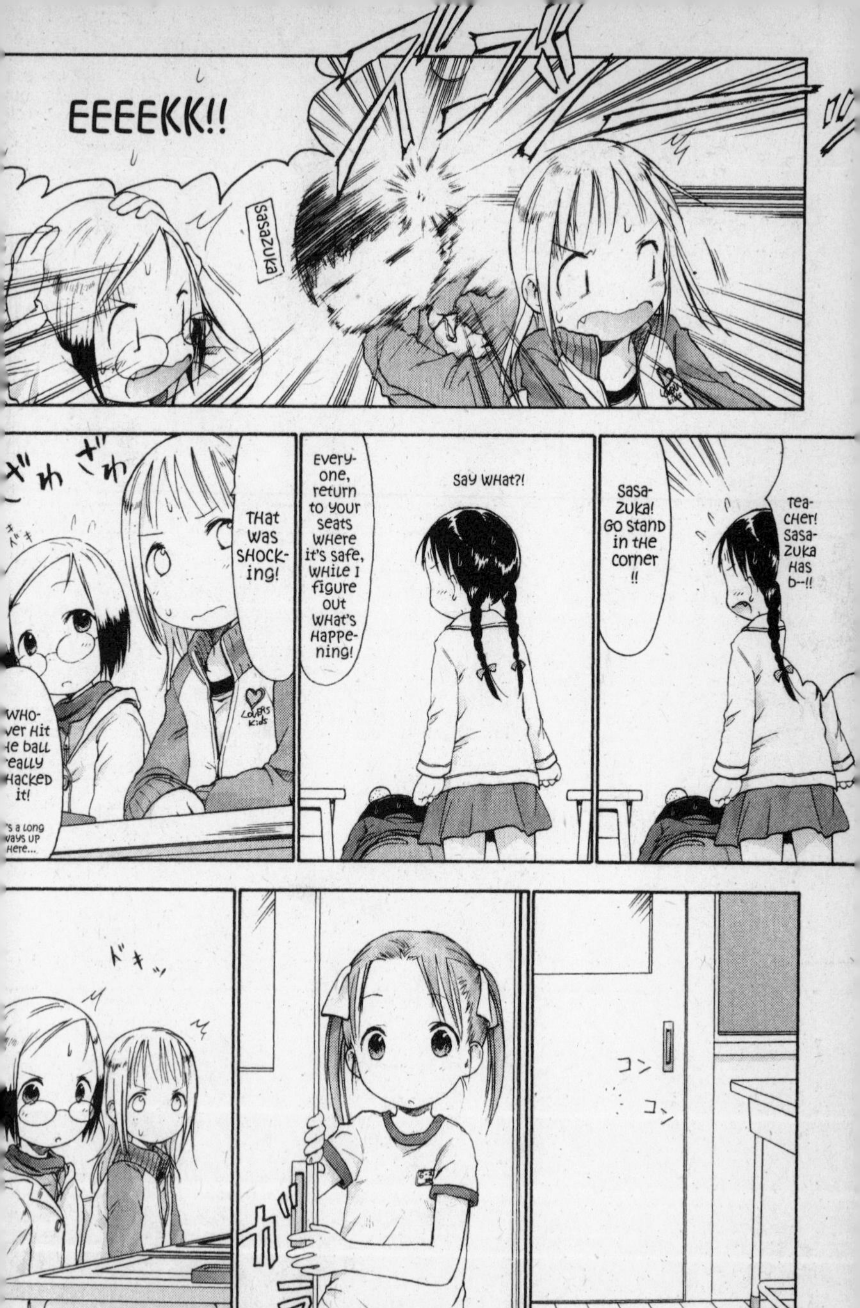
EEEEKK!!
Sasazuka
Teacher! Sasazuka has b--!!
Sasa-zuka! Go stand in the corner!!
Say what?!
Every-one, return to your seats where it's safe, while I figure out what's happe-ning!
ざわざわ
That was shock-ing!
Who-ver hit he ball eally hacked it!
's a long ways up here...
コン
コン
ガラ
ドキッ

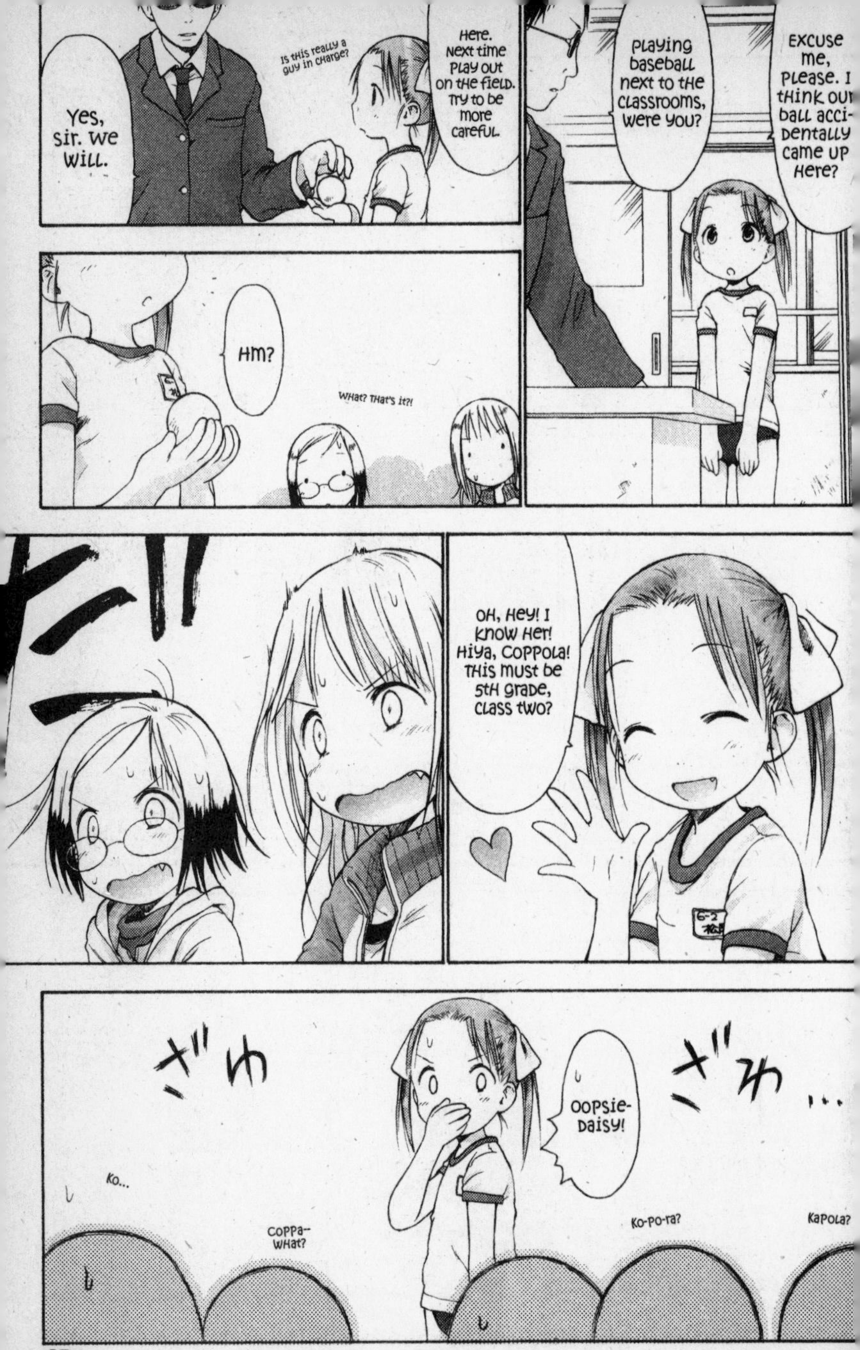
Excuse me, please. I think our ball accidentally came up here?
Playing baseball next to the classrooms, were you?
Here. Next time play out on the field. Try to be more careful.
Is this really a guy in charge?
Yes, sir. We will.
Hm?
What? That's it?!
Oh, hey! I know her! Hiya, Coppola! This must be 5th grade, class two?
6-2
ざわ…
Oopsie-daisy!
ざわ
Kapola?
Ko-po-ra?
Coppa-what?
Ko...

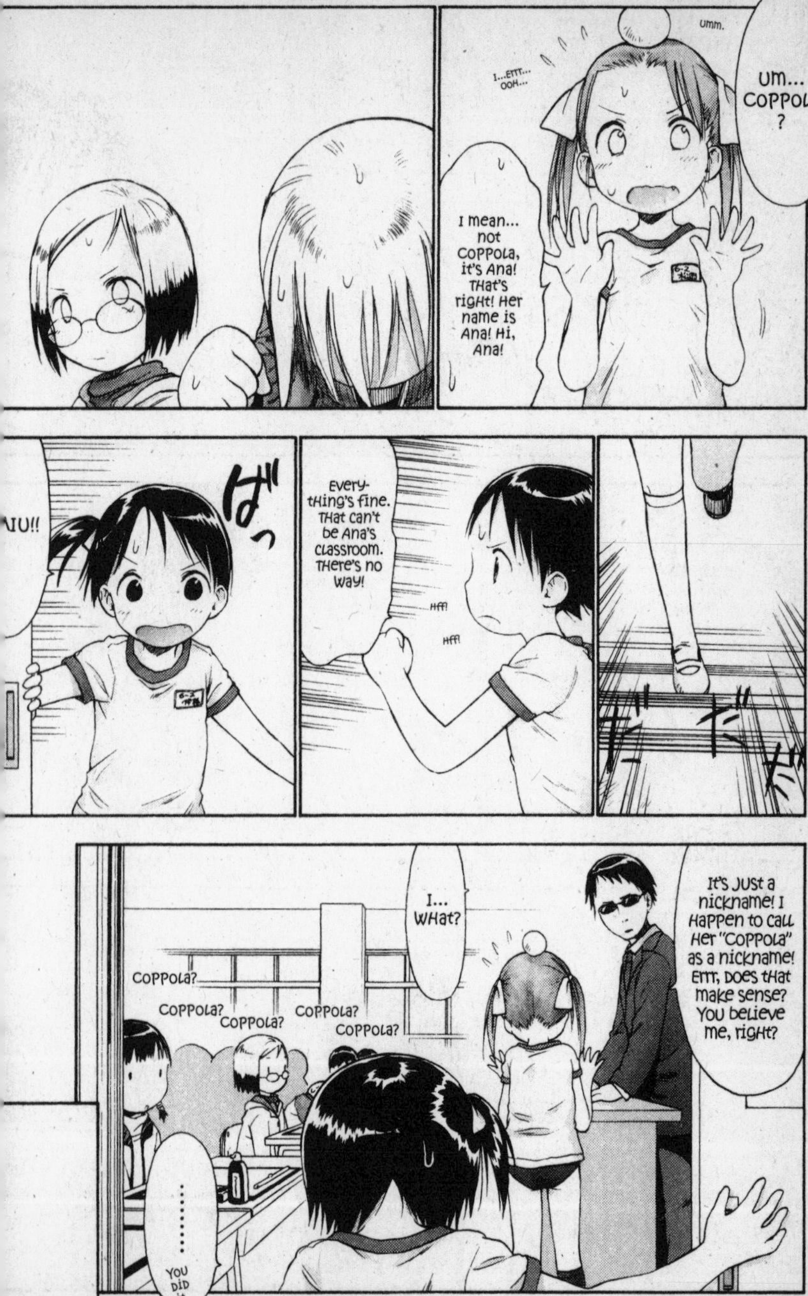

umm.
Um... Coppola?
I...Errr... Ooh...
I mean... not Coppola, it's Ana! That's right! Her name is Ana! Hi, Ana!
ダ ダ ダ
Every-thing's fine. That can't be Ana's classroom. There's no way!
Hff! Hff!
ばっ
IU!!
It's just a nickname! I happen to call her "Coppola" as a nickname! Errr, does that make sense? You believe me, right?
I... What?
Coppola? Coppola? Coppola? Coppola? Coppola?
......
You did it.

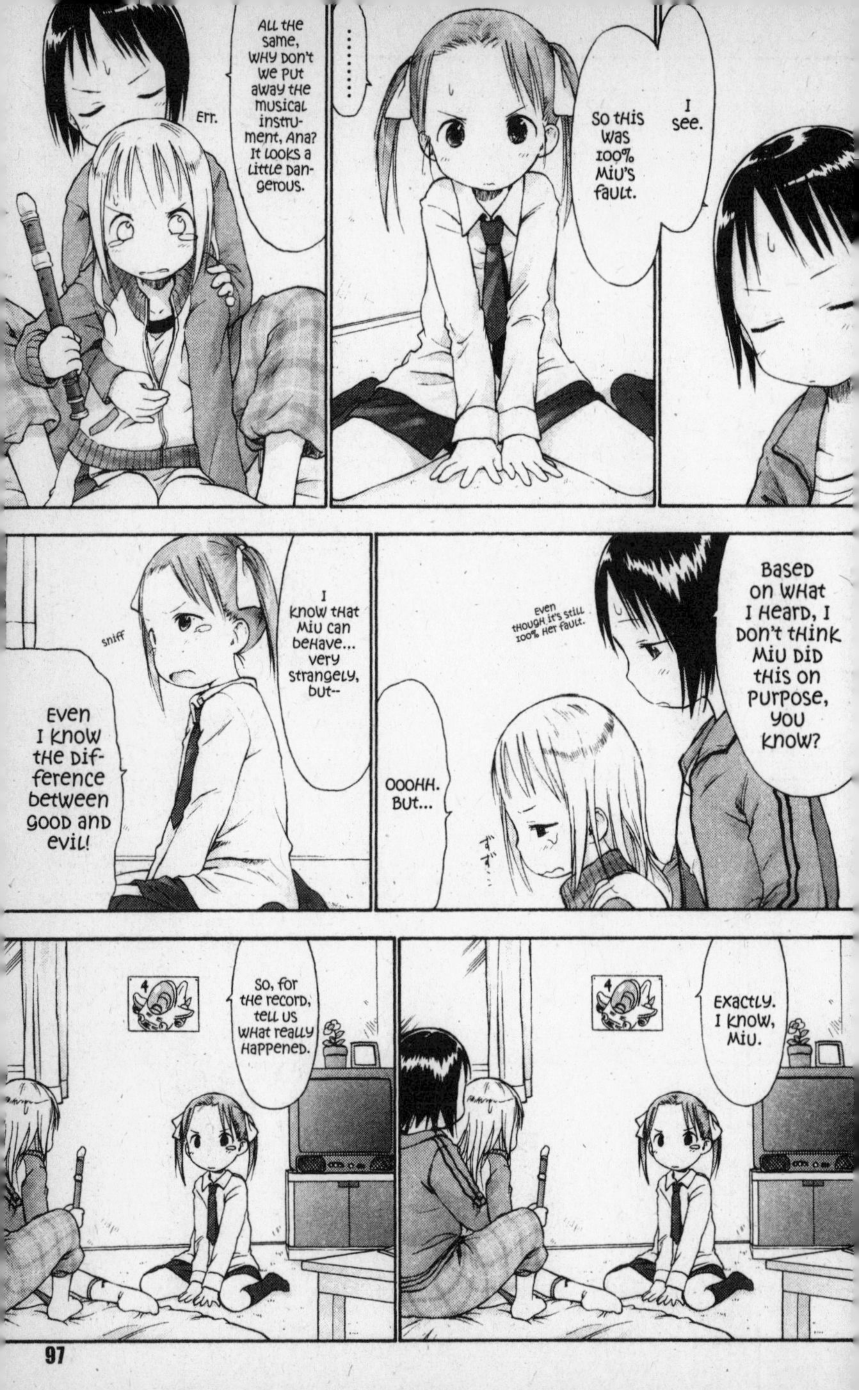
I see.
So this was 100% Miu's fault.
......
All the same, why don't we put away the musical instrument, Ana? It looks a little dangerous.
Err.
Based on what I heard, I don't think Miu did this on purpose, you know?
Even though it's still 100% her fault.
Ooohh. But...
ずず…
I know that Miu can behave... very strangely, but--
sniff
Even I know the difference between good and evil!
Exactly. I know, Miu.
So, for the record, tell us what really happened.

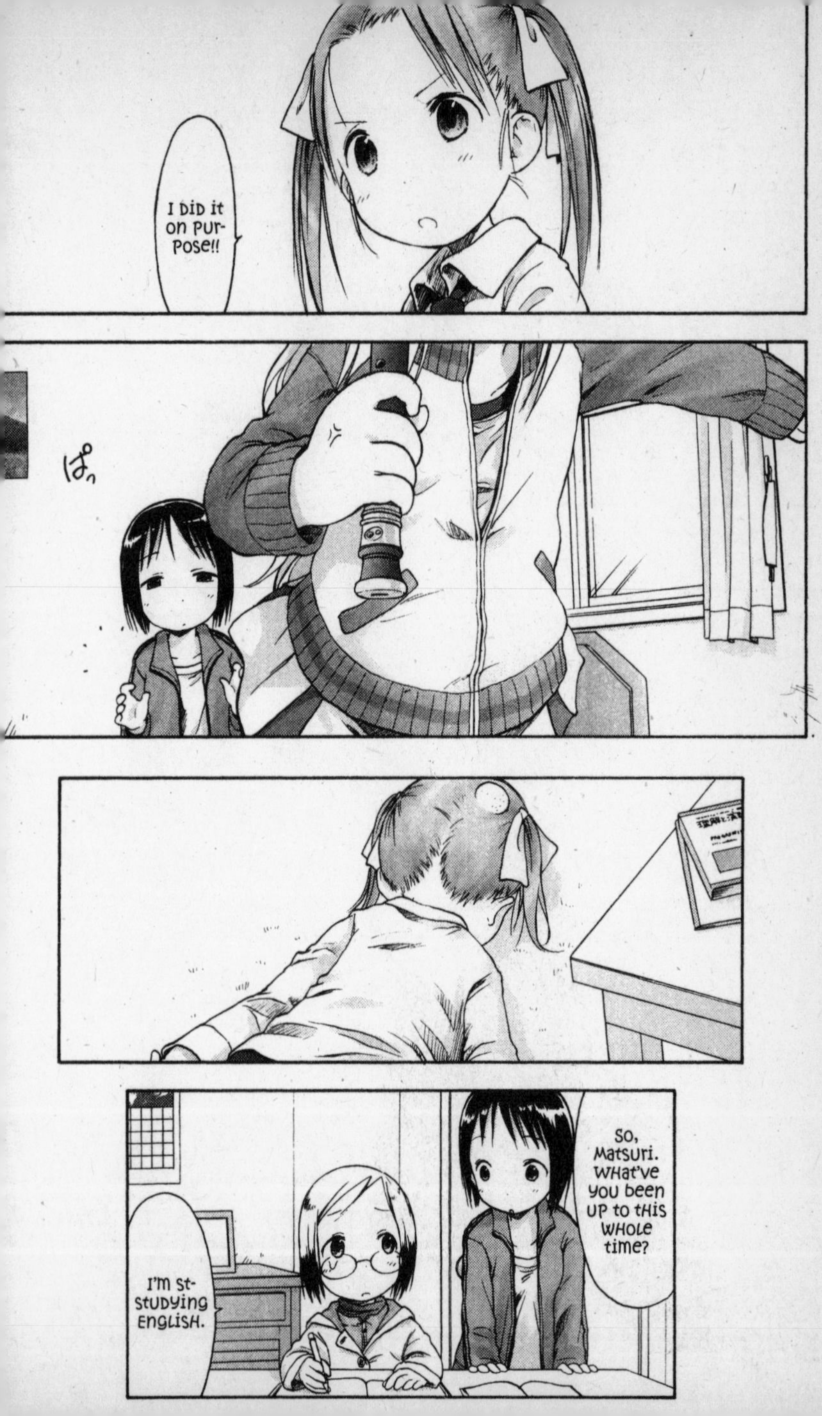
I DID it on pur-pose!!
ぱっ
So, Matsuri. WHat've you been up to tHIS WHOLE time?
I'm st-studying ENGLISH.

HALLO WORK

matsuri

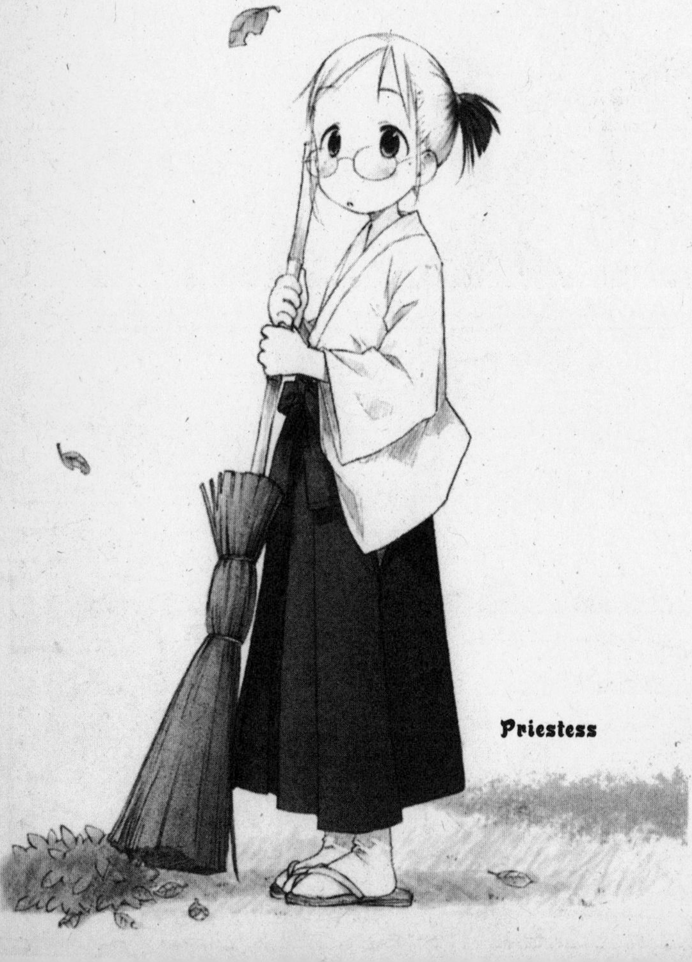

Priestess

HALLO WORK

miu

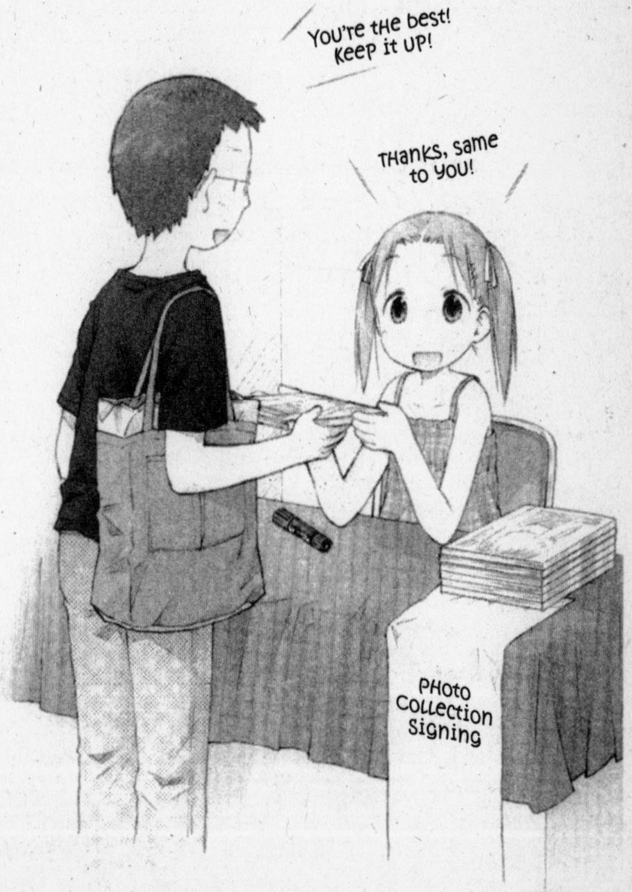
You're the best! Keep it up!
Thanks, same to you!
Photo Collection Signing

Idol

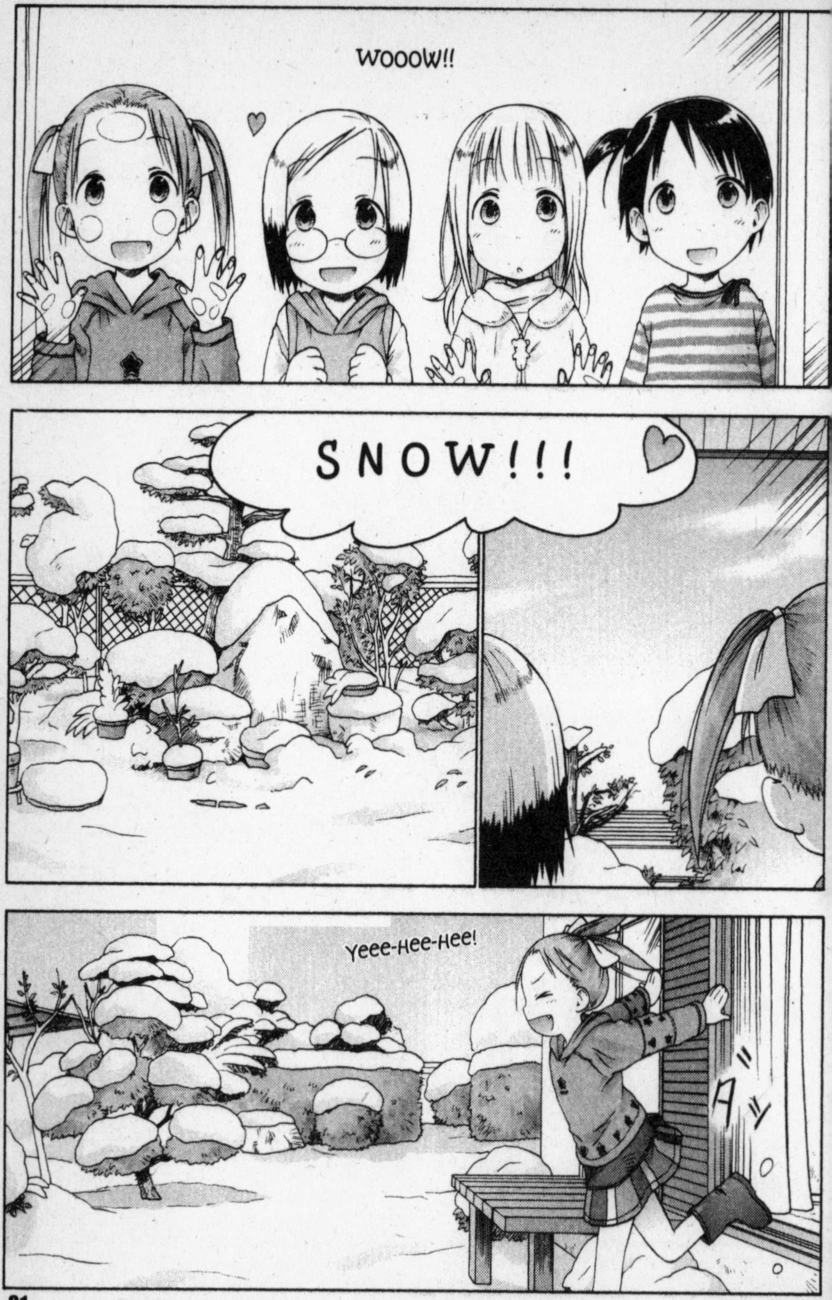
WOOOW!!
SNOW!!!
Yeee-Hee-Hee!
ダッ

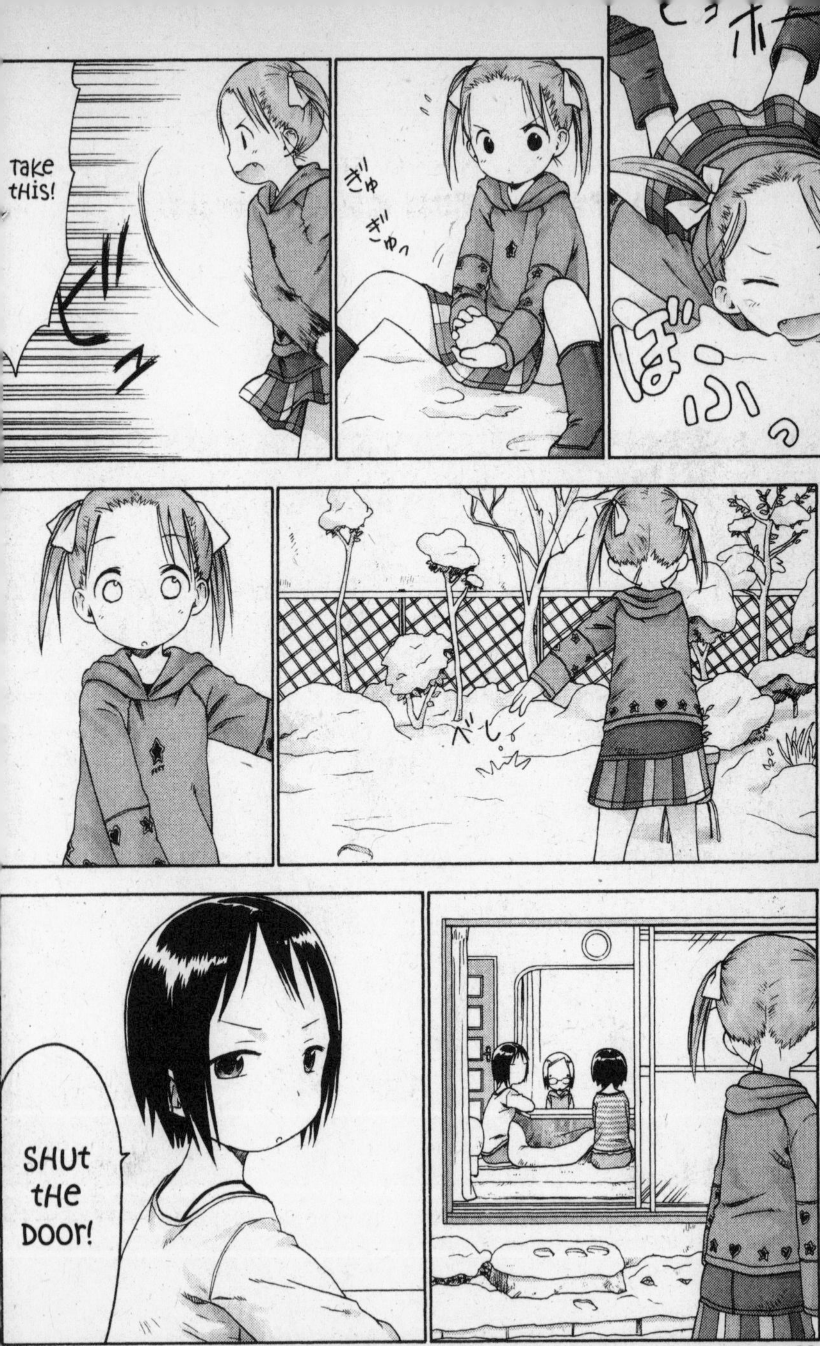
ぼふっ
ぎゅ
ぎゅっ
Take this!
べしっ
SHUT the DOOR!

episode. 16

A JAPANESE CHRISTMAS

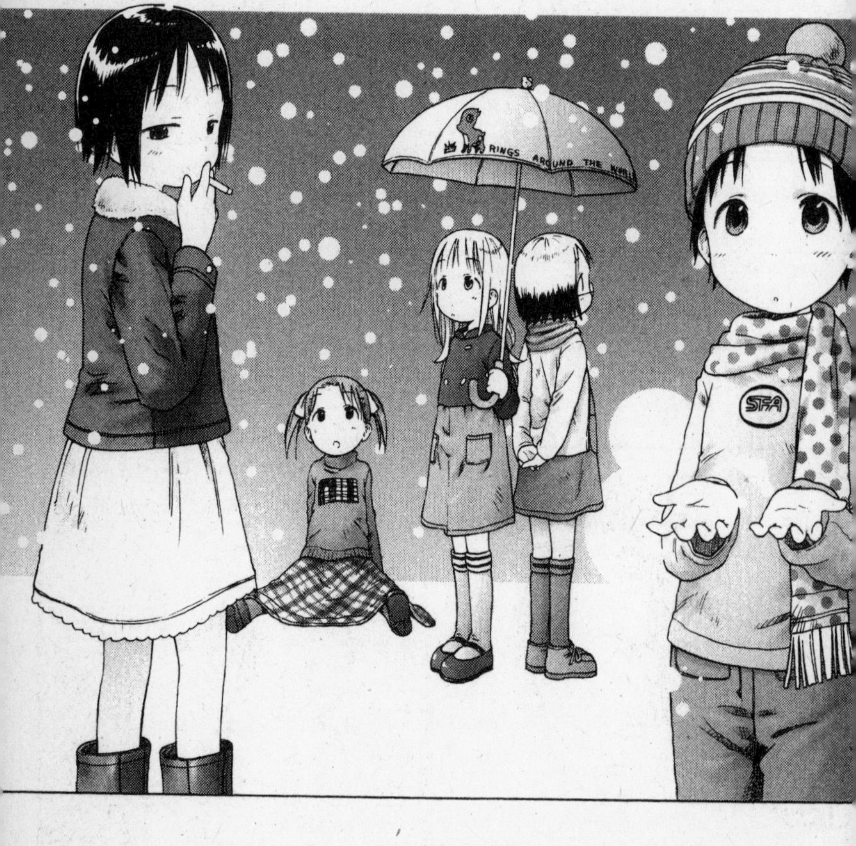
RINGS AROUND THE
SFA

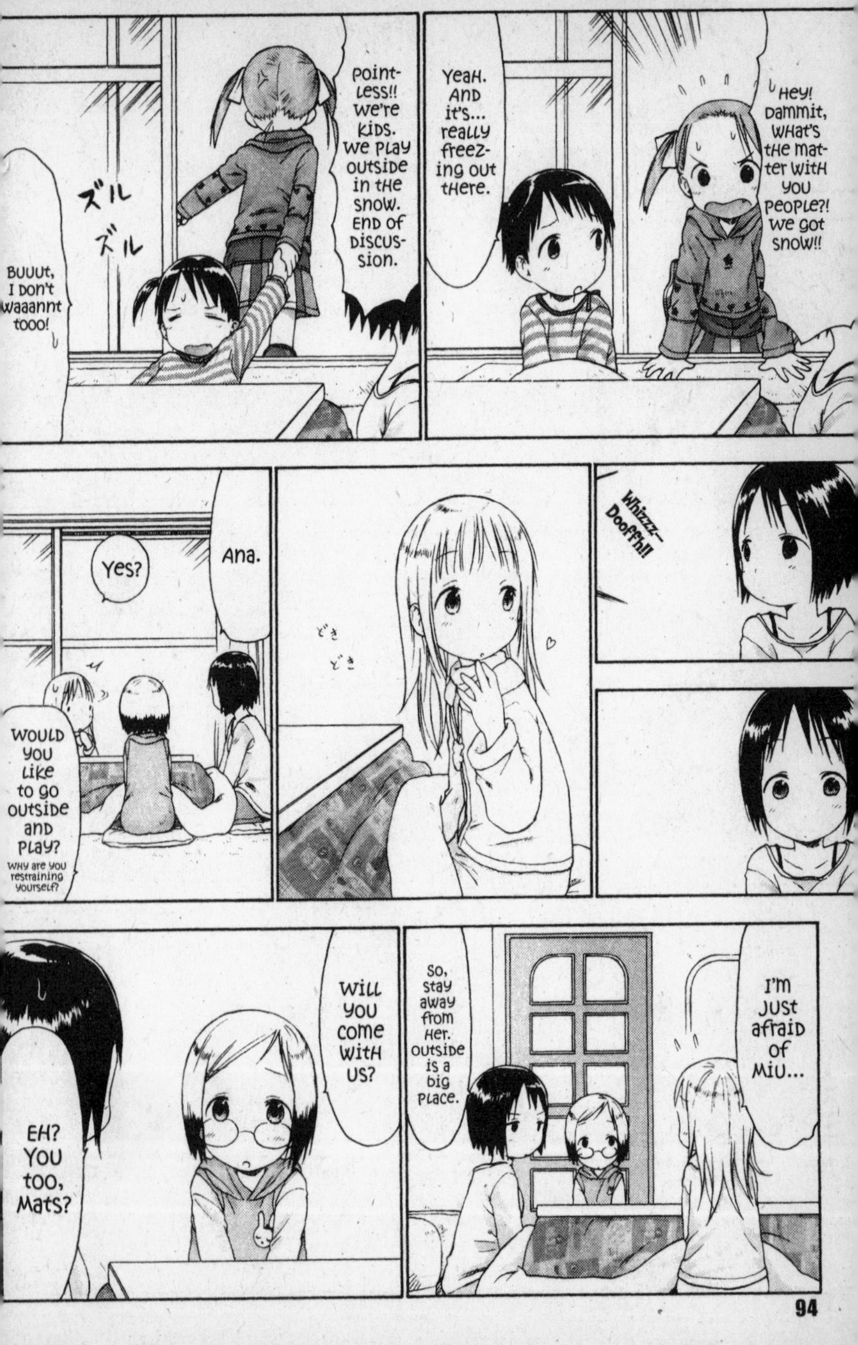

Hey! Dammit, what's the matter with you people?! We got snow!!
Yeah. And it's... really freezing out there.
Pointless!! We're kids. We play outside in the snow. End of discussion.
ズル ズル
Buuut, I don't waaannt tooo!
Whizzz-Dooff'n!!
どき どき
Ana.
Yes?
Would you like to go outside and play?
Why are you restraining yourself?
I'm just afraid of Miu...
So, stay away from her. Outside is a big place.
Will you come with us?
Eh? You too, Mats?

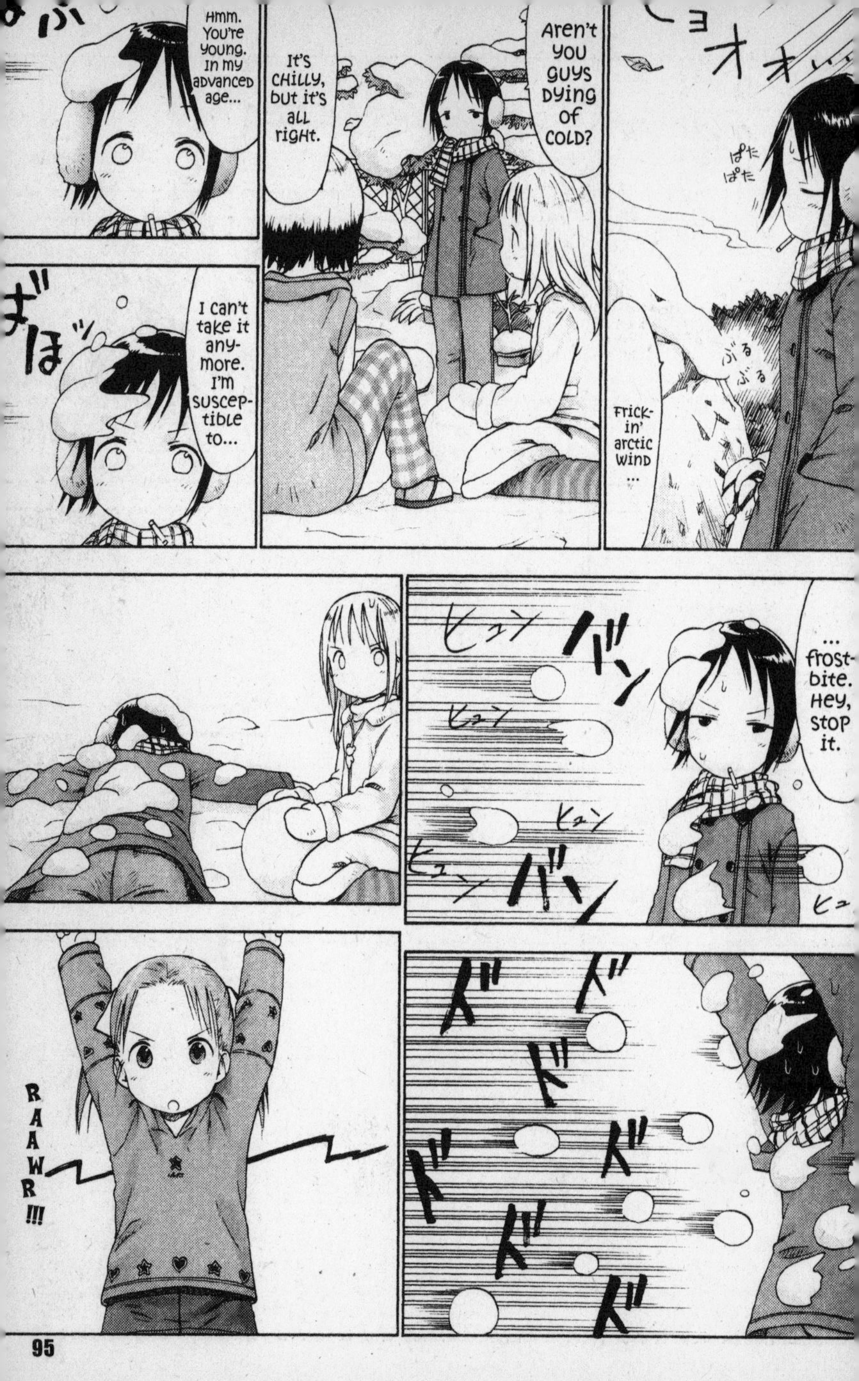
ぱたぱた
ぶるぶる
Frick-in' arctic wind ...
Aren't you guys dying of cold?
It's chilly, but it's all right.
Hmm. You're young. In my advanced age...
ずぼッ
I can't take it any-more. I'm suscep-tible to...
... frost-bite. Hey, stop it.
RAAAWR!!!

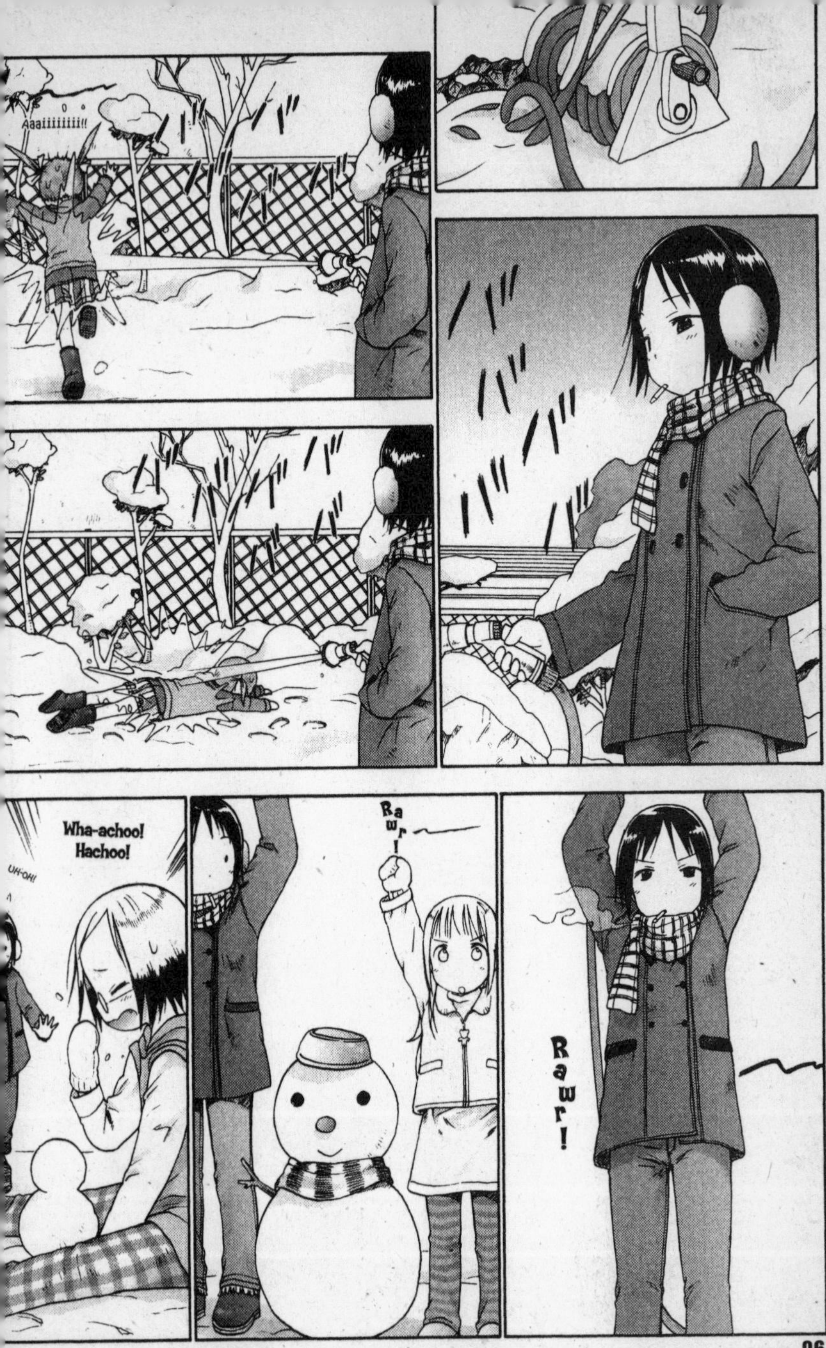
Aaaiiiiiiiii!!
Rawr!
Rawr!~
Wha-achoo!
Hachoo!
UH-OH!

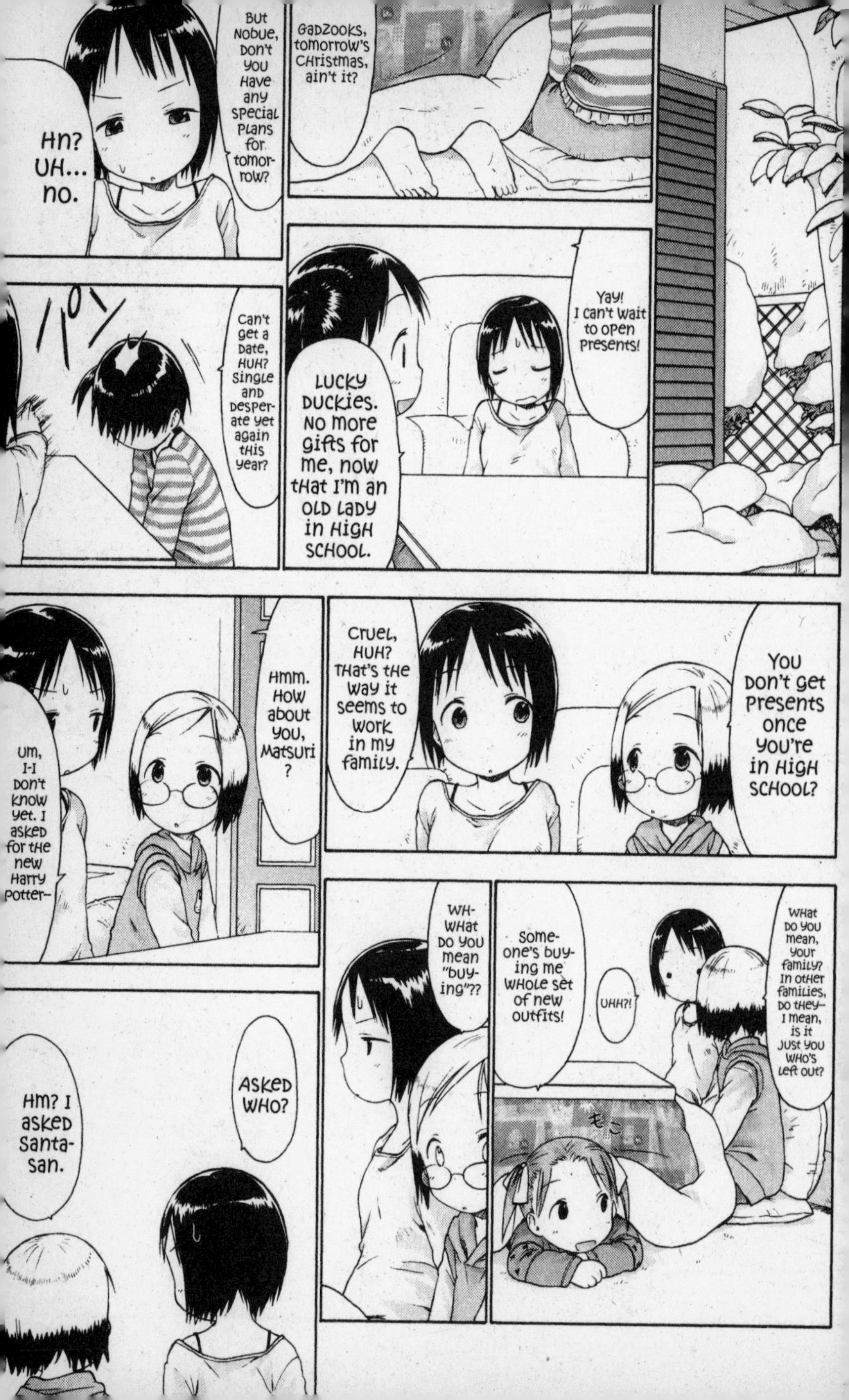

Gadzooks, tomorrow's Christmas, ain't it?
But Nobue, don't you have any special plans for tomorrow?
Hn? Uh... no.
Yay! I can't wait to open presents!
Lucky duckies. No more gifts for me, now that I'm an old lady in high school.
Can't get a date, huh? Single and desperate yet again this year?
You don't get presents once you're in high school?
Cruel, huh? That's the way it seems to work in my family.
Hmm. How about you, Matsuri?
Um, I-I don't know yet. I asked for the new Harry Potter–
What do you mean, your family? In other families, do they– I mean, is it just you who's left out?
UHH?!
Someone's buying me whole set of new outfits!
もこ
Wh-what do you mean "buying"??
Asked who?
Hm? I asked Santa-san.

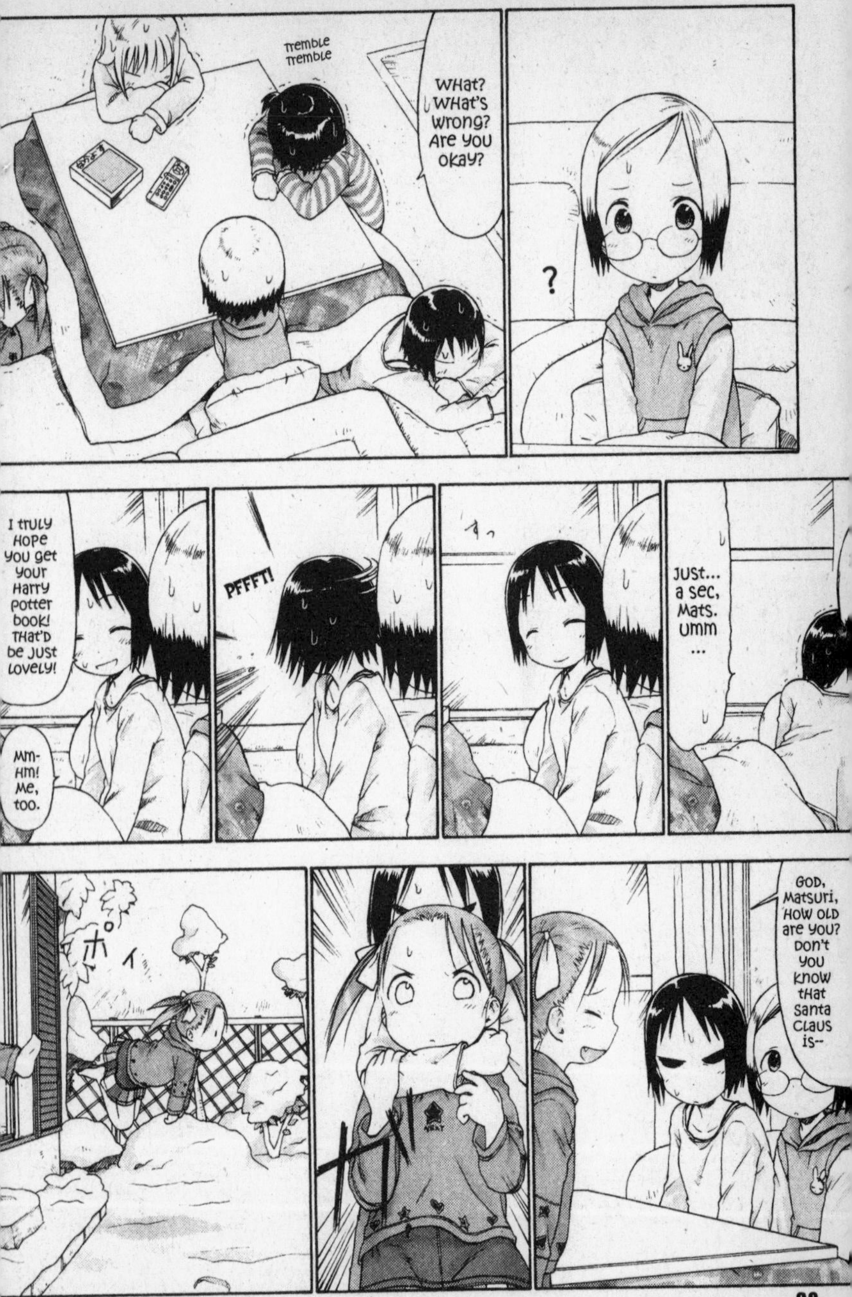
?
WHAT? WHAT'S WRONG? ARE YOU OKAY?
TREMBLE TREMBLE
JUST... A SEC, MATS. UMM ...
すっ
PFFFT!
I TRULY HOPE YOU GET YOUR HARRY POTTER BOOK! THAT'D BE JUST LOVELY!
MM-HM! ME, TOO.
GOD, MATSURI, HOW OLD ARE YOU? DON'T YOU KNOW THAT SANTA CLAUS IS--
ポイ

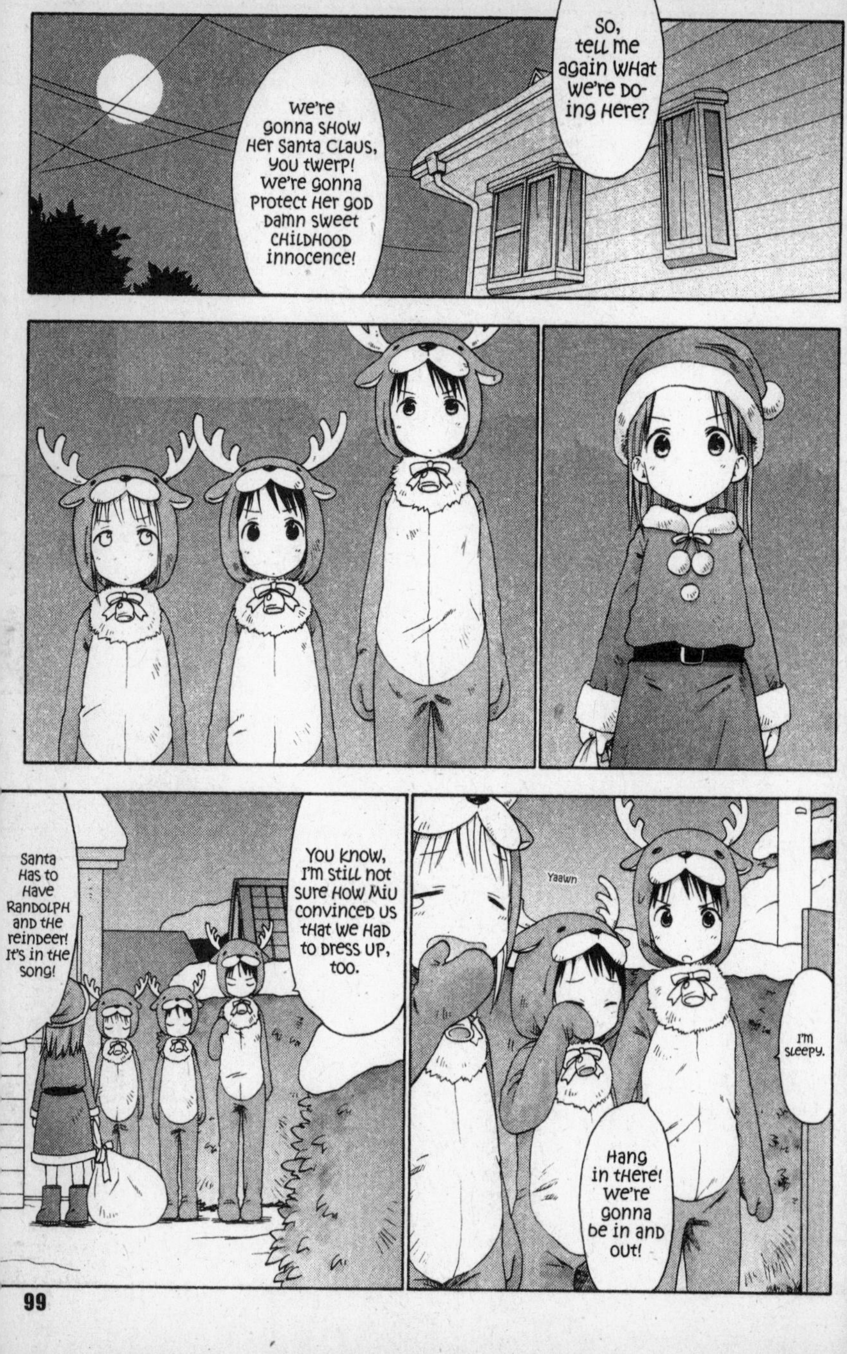
So, tell me again what we're doing here?
We're gonna show her Santa Claus, you twerp! We're gonna protect her god damn sweet childhood innocence!
Yaawn
I'm sleepy.
Hang in there! We're gonna be in and out!
You know, I'm still not sure how Miu convinced us that we had to dress up, too.
Santa has to have Randolph and the reindeer! It's in the song!

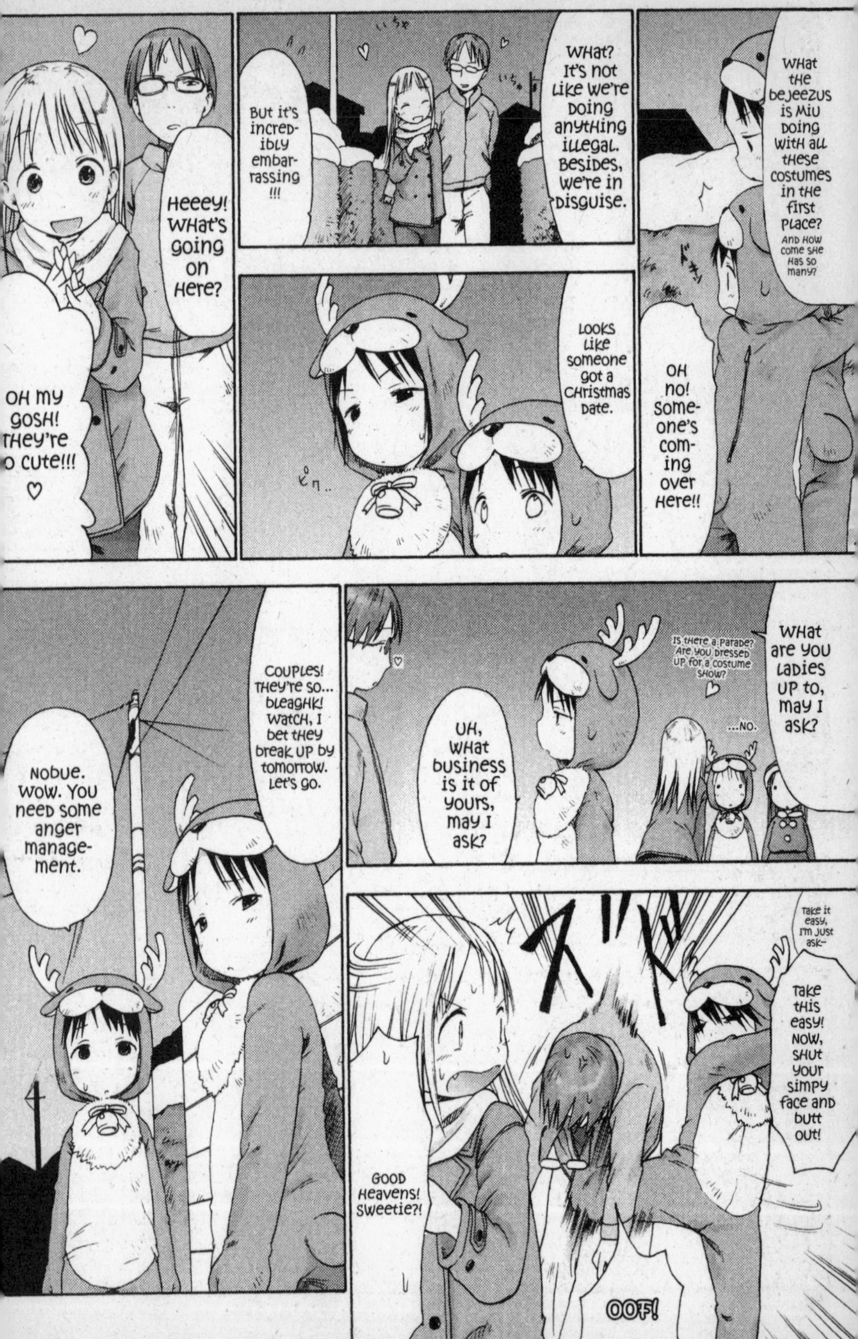
What the bejeezus is Miu doing with all these costumes in the first place?
And how come she has so many?
Oh no! Someone's coming over here!!
What? It's not like we're doing anything illegal. Besides, we're in disguise.
But it's incredibly embarrassing!!!
Looks like someone got a Christmas date.
Heeey! What's going on here?
Oh my gosh! They're o cute!!! ♡
What are you ladies up to, may I ask?
Is there a parade? Are you dressed up for a costume show? ♡
...No.
Uh, what business is it of yours, may I ask?
Take it easy, I'm just ask–
Take this easy! Now, shut your simpy face and butt out!
Good heavens! Sweetie?!
OOF!
Couples! They're so... bleaghk! Watch, I bet they break up by tomorrow. Let's go.
Nobue. Wow. You need some anger management.

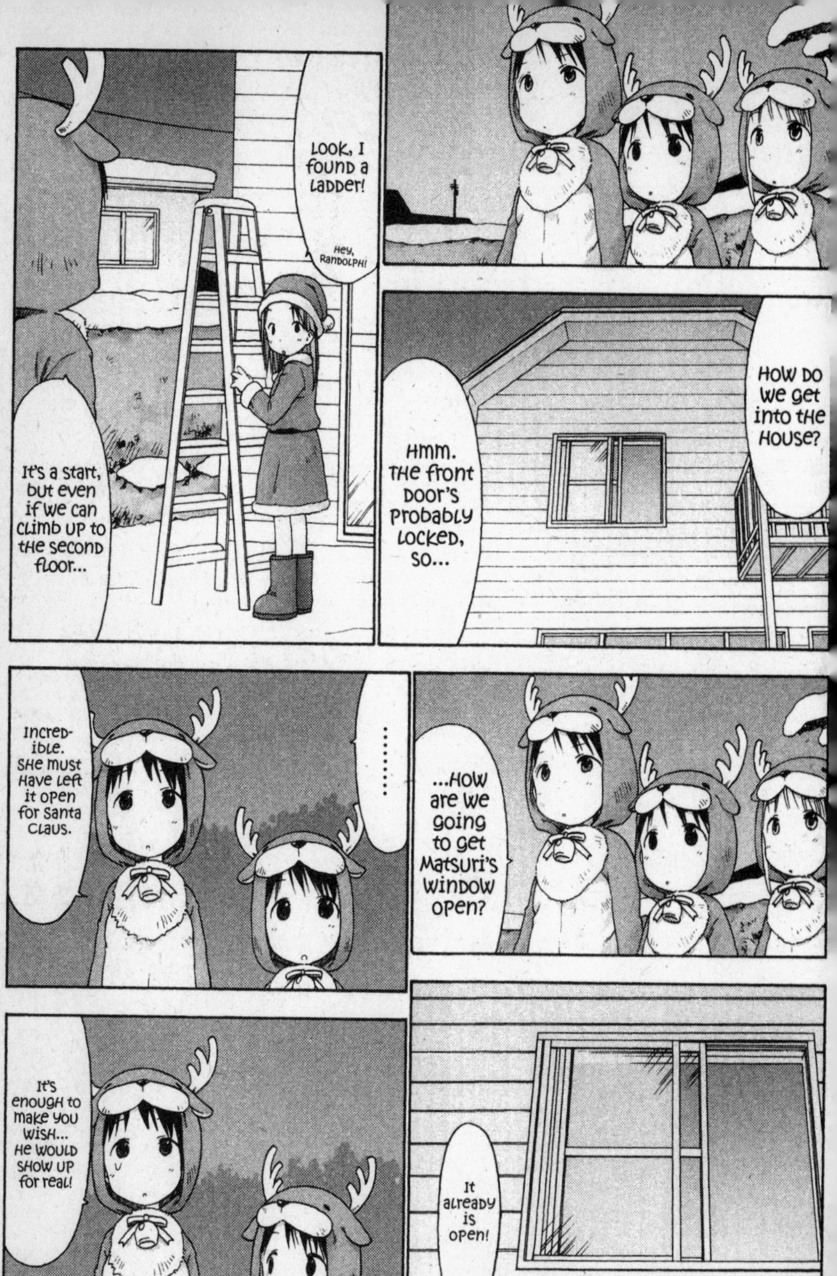
How do we get into the house?
Hmm. The front door's probably locked, so...
Look, I found a ladder!
Hey, Randolph!
It's a start, but even if we can climb up to the second floor...
...How are we going to get Matsuri's window open?
It already is open!
....
Incred-ible. She must have left it open for Santa Claus.
It's enough to make you wish... he would show up for real!

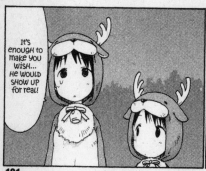

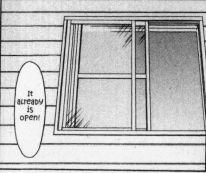

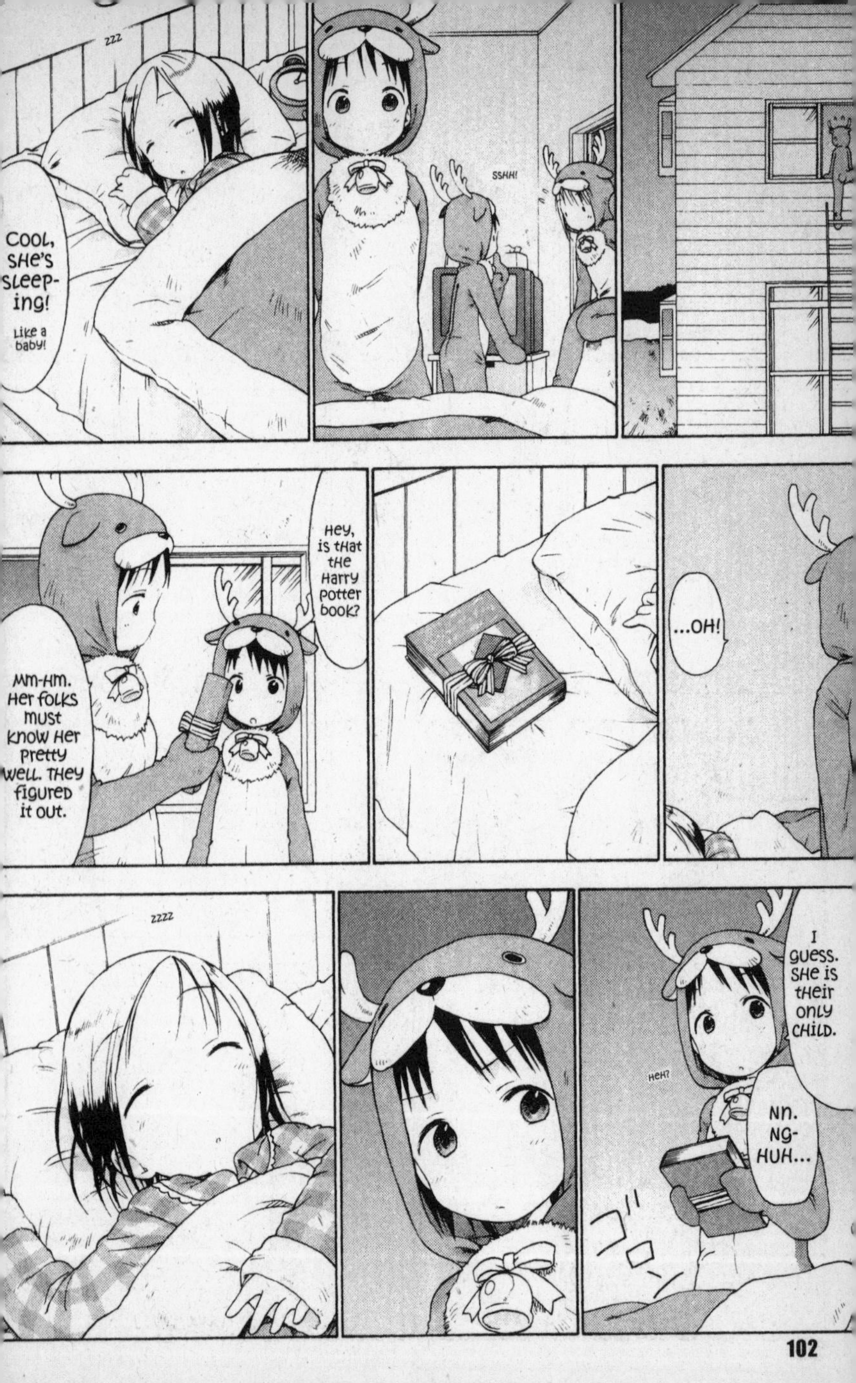
SSHH!
ZZZ
COOL, SHE'S SLEEP-ING!
Like a baby!
...OH!
Hey, is that the Harry Potter book?
Mm-hm. Her folks must know her pretty well. They figured it out.
I guess. She is their only child.
HEH?
Nn. Ng-huh...
ZZZZ

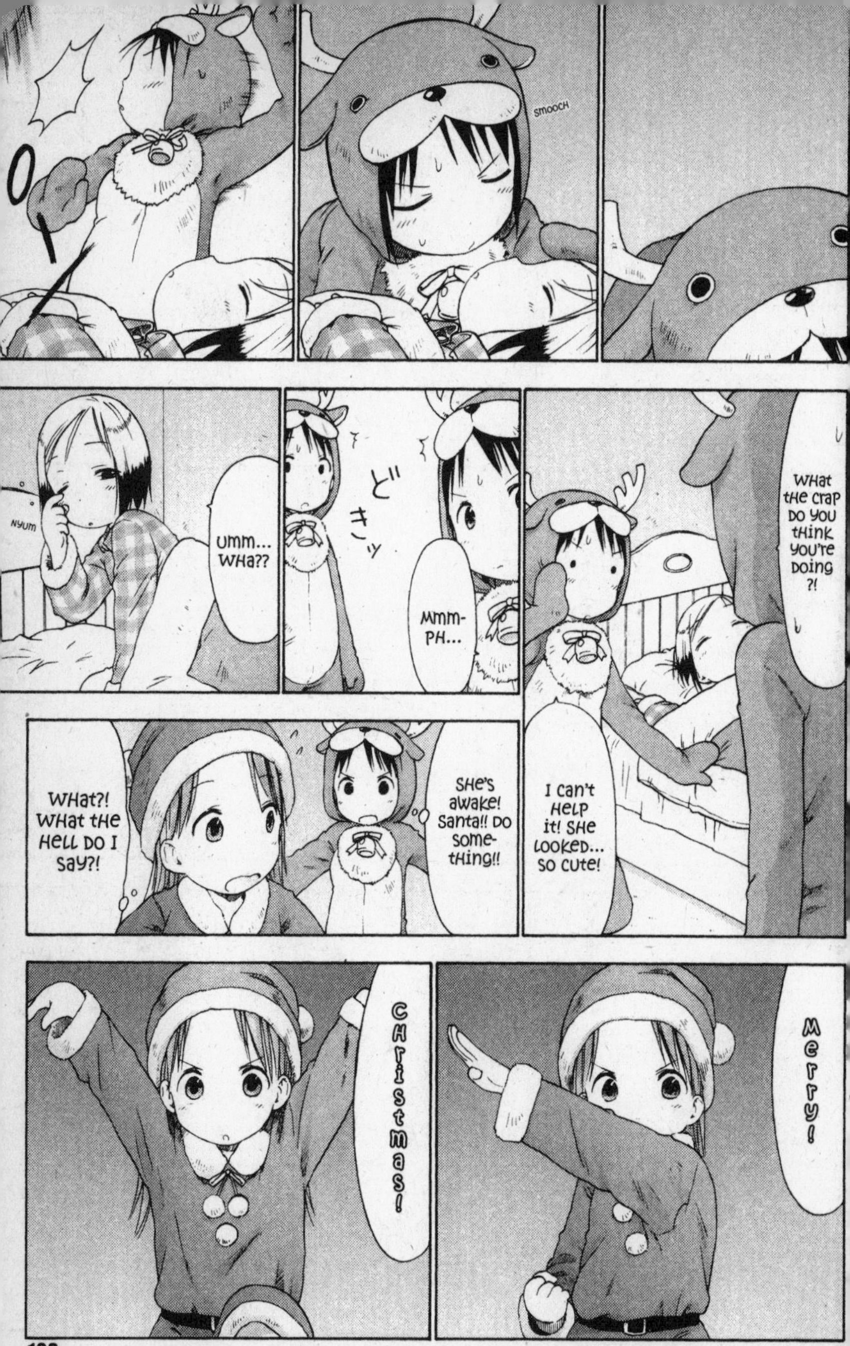
SMOOCH
WHAT THE CRAP DO YOU THINK YOU'RE DOING?!
どきッ
MMM-PH...
NYUM
UMM... WHA??
I CAN'T HELP IT! SHE LOOKED... SO CUTE!
SHE'S AWAKE! SANTA!! DO SOME-THING!!
WHAT?! WHAT THE HELL DO I SAY?!
MERRY!
CHRISTMAS!

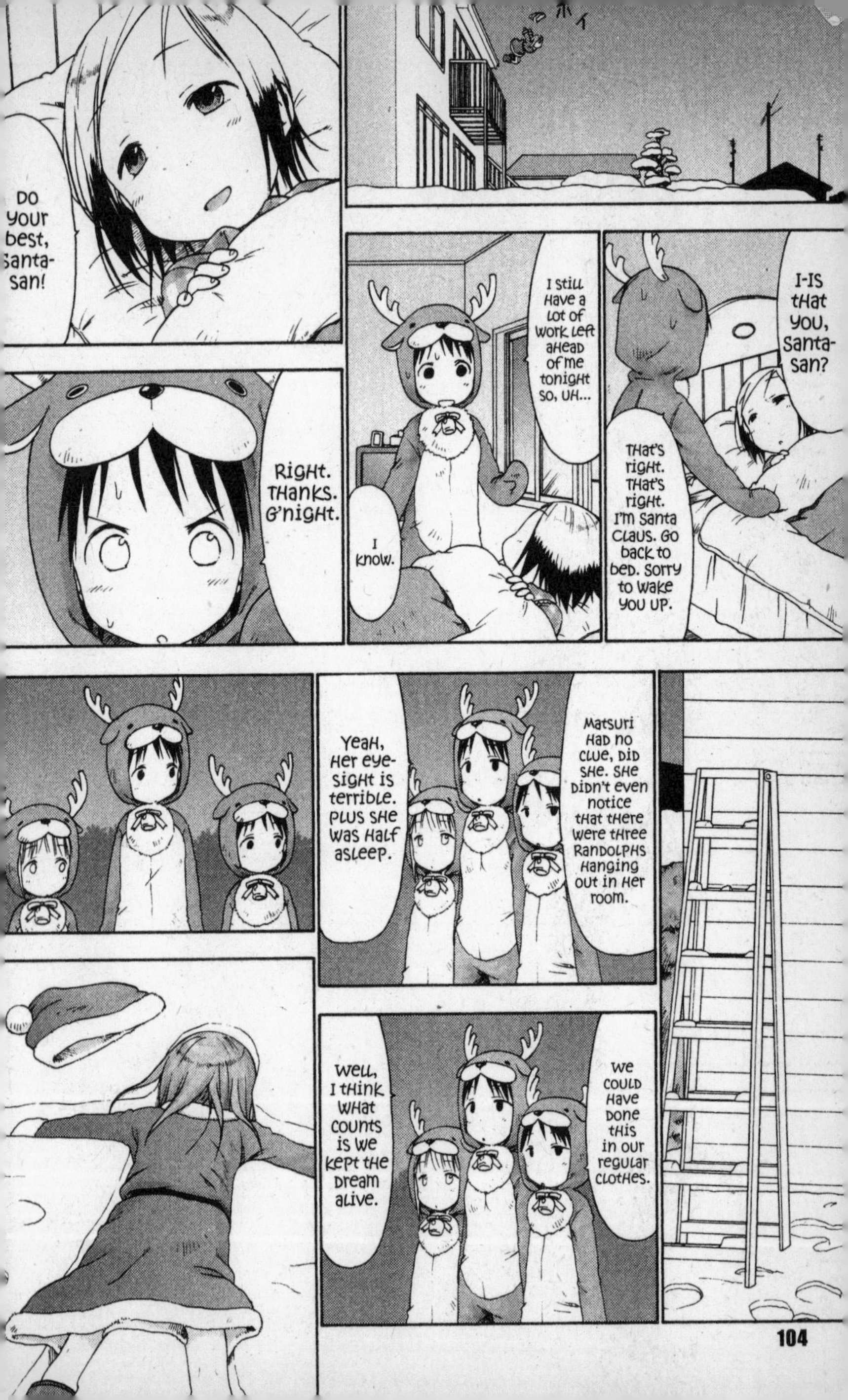
Do your best, Santa-san!
I-Is that you, Santa-san?
That's right. That's right. I'm Santa Claus. Go back to bed. Sorry to wake you up.
I still have a lot of work left ahead of me tonight so, uh...
I know.
Right. Thanks. G'night.
Matsuri had no clue, did she. She didn't even notice that there were three Randolphs hanging out in her room.
Yeah, her eye-sight is terrible. Plus she was half asleep.
We could have done this in our regular clothes.
Well, I think what counts is we kept the dream alive.

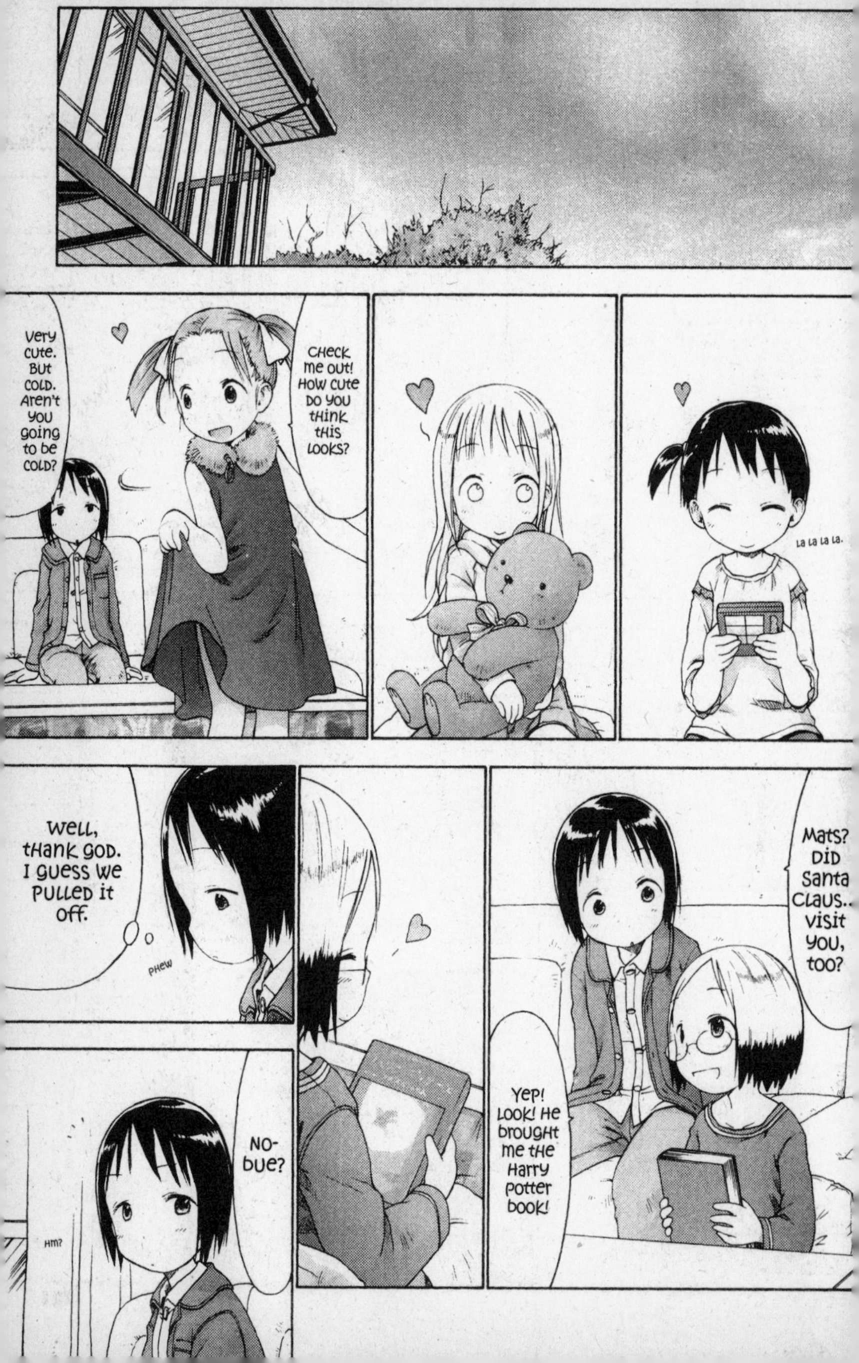
La la la la.
Check me out! How cute do you think this looks?
Very cute. But cold. Aren't you going to be cold?
Mats? Did Santa Claus... visit you, too?
Yep! Look! He brought me the Harry Potter book!
Well, thank God. I guess we pulled it off.
PHEW
No-bue?
Hm?

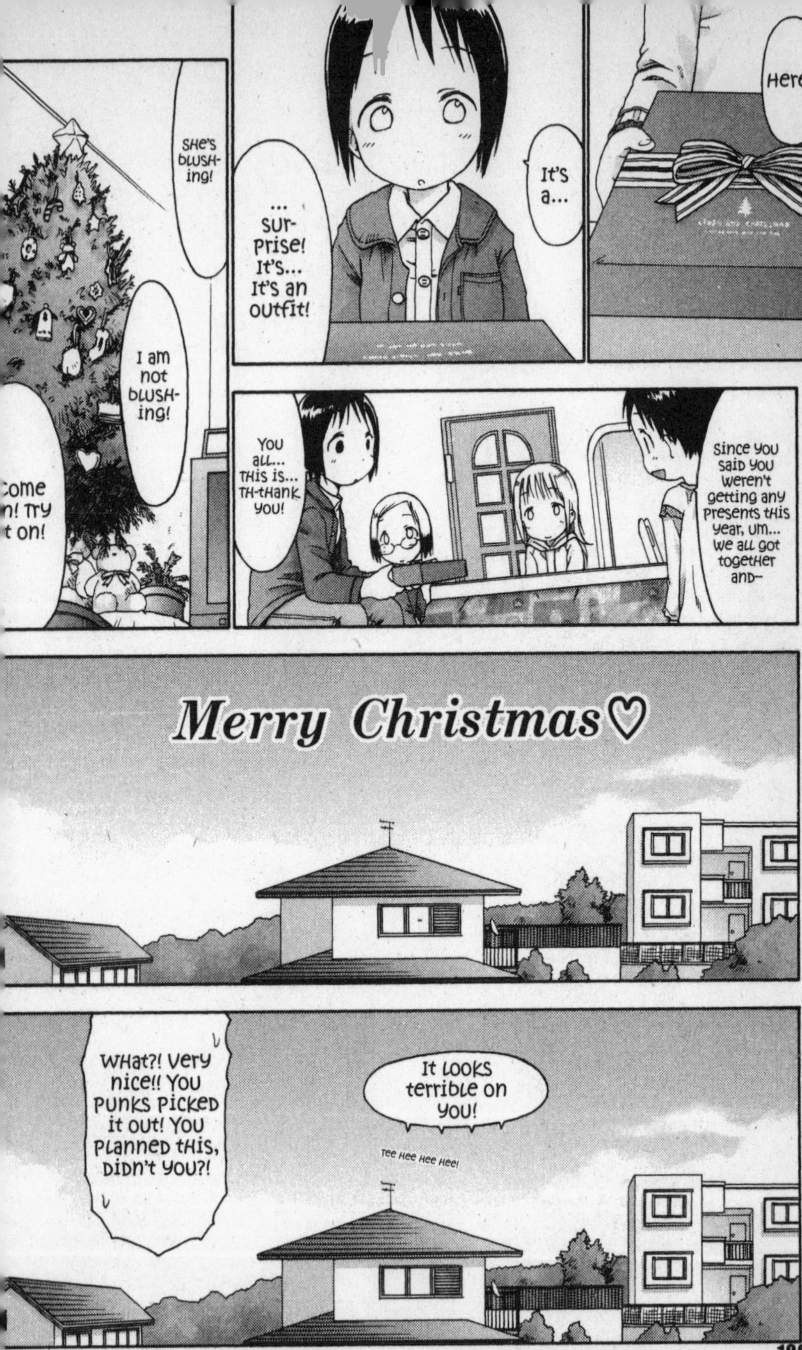
Here!
It's a...
... surprise! It's... It's an outfit!
Since you said you weren't getting any presents this year, um... we all got together and—
You all... This is... Th-thank you!
She's blushing!
I am not blushing!
come n! Try t on!
Merry Christmas♡
It looks terrible on you!
Tee hee hee hee!
What?! Very nice!! You punks picked it out! You planned this, didn't you?!

HALLO WORK

ana

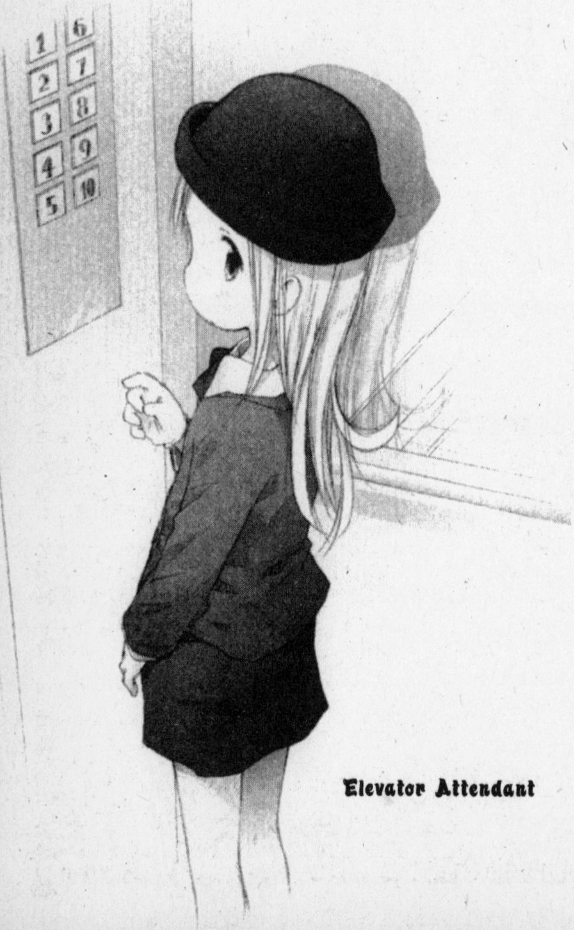

Elevator Attendant

HALLO WORK

sasazuka

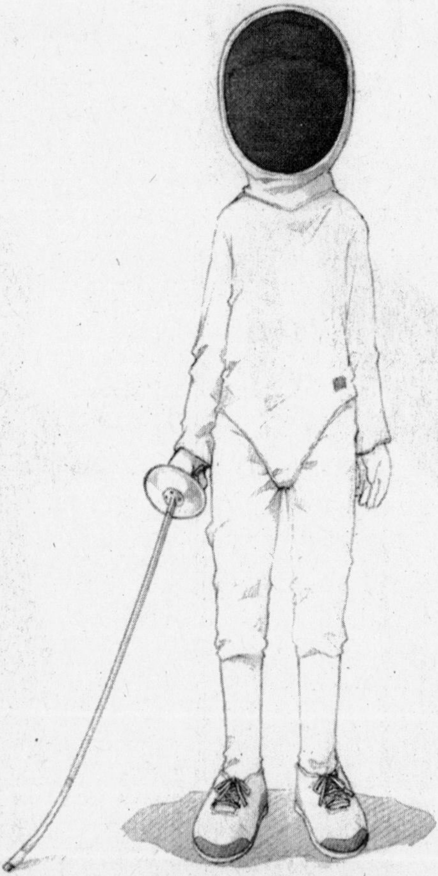
Fencer

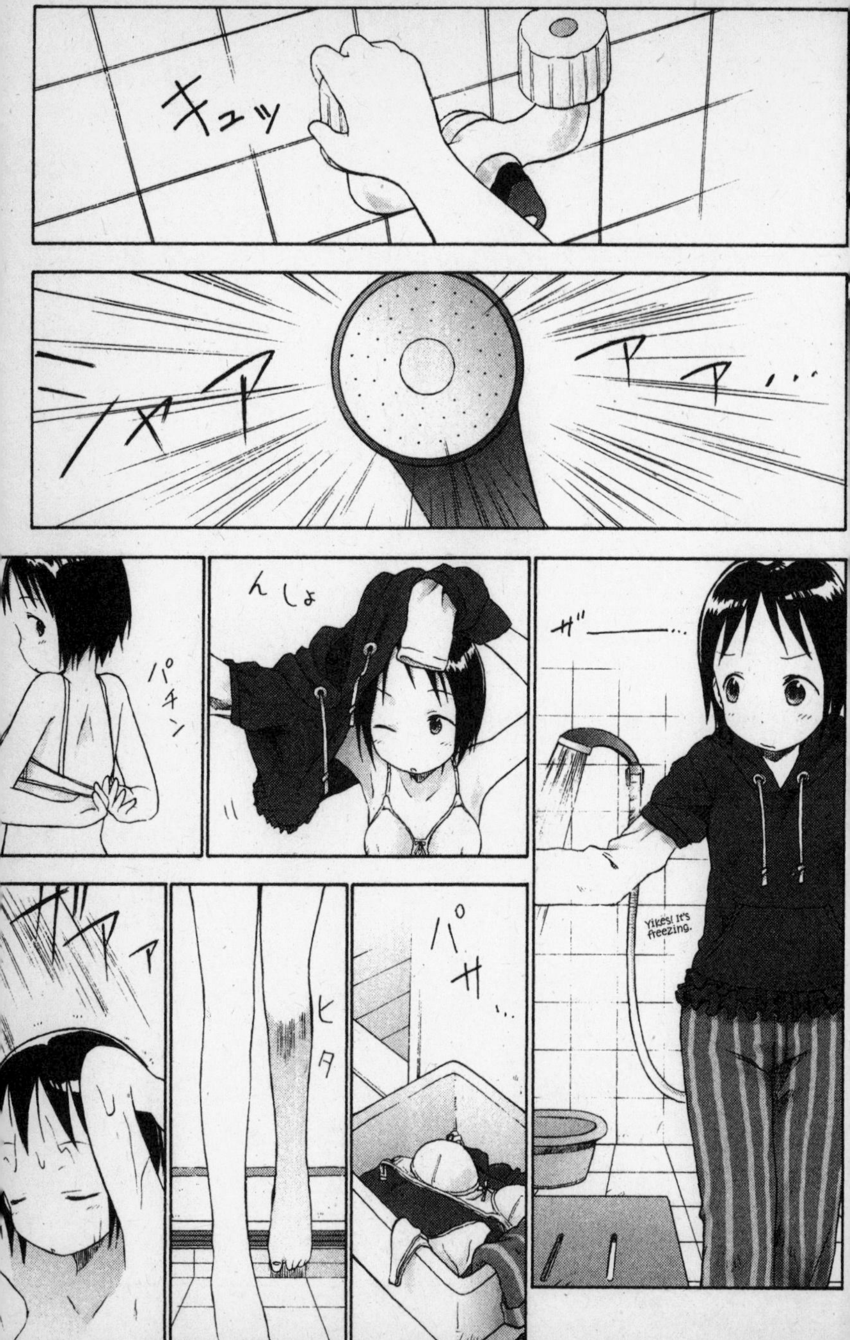
キュッ
シャアア
アア…
ザー…
Yikes! It's freezing.
んしょ
パチン
パサ…
ヒタ
ザァア

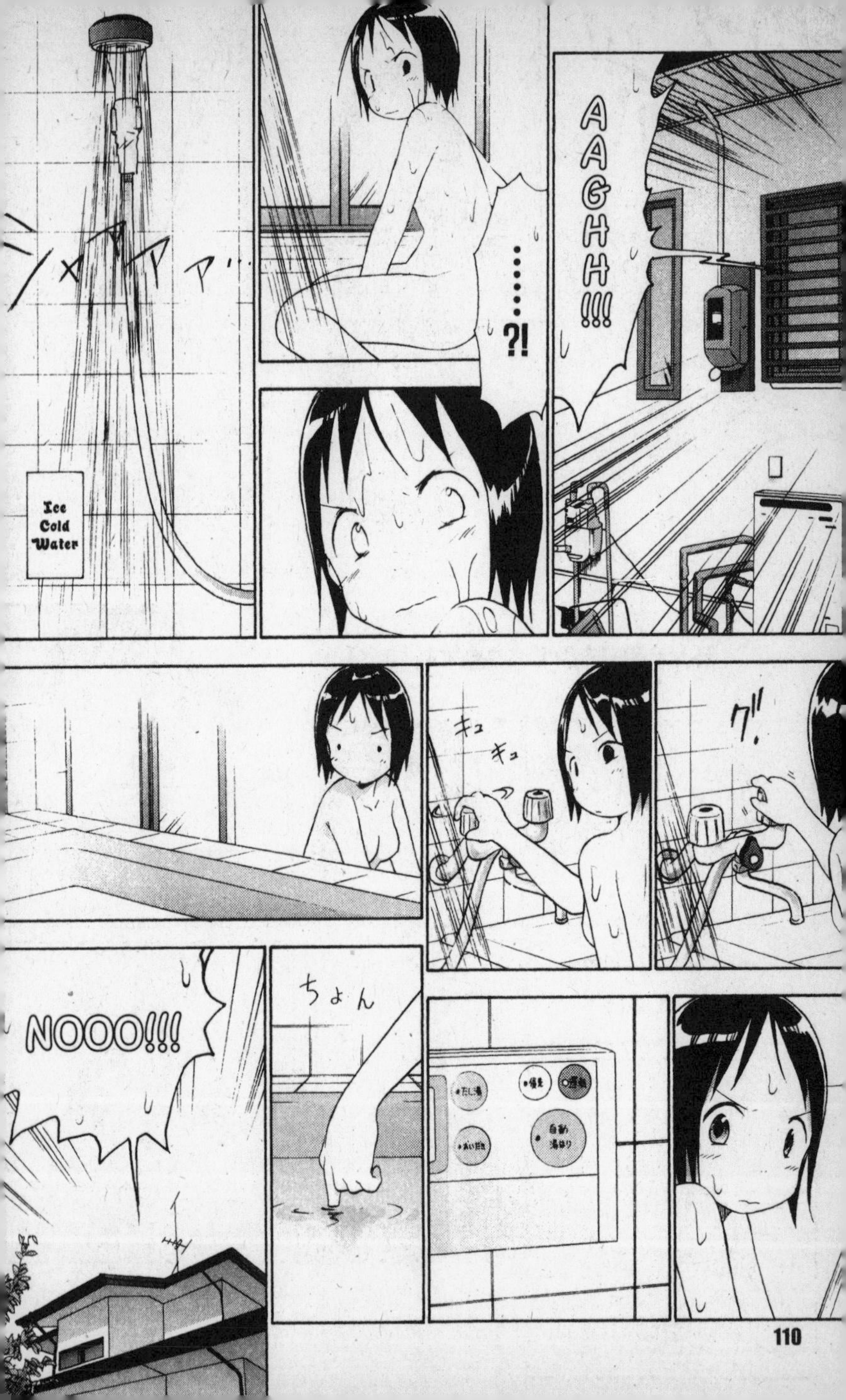
AAGHH!!!
……?!
シャアア…
Ice Cold Water
グ!
キュ
キュ
ちょん
NOOO!!!

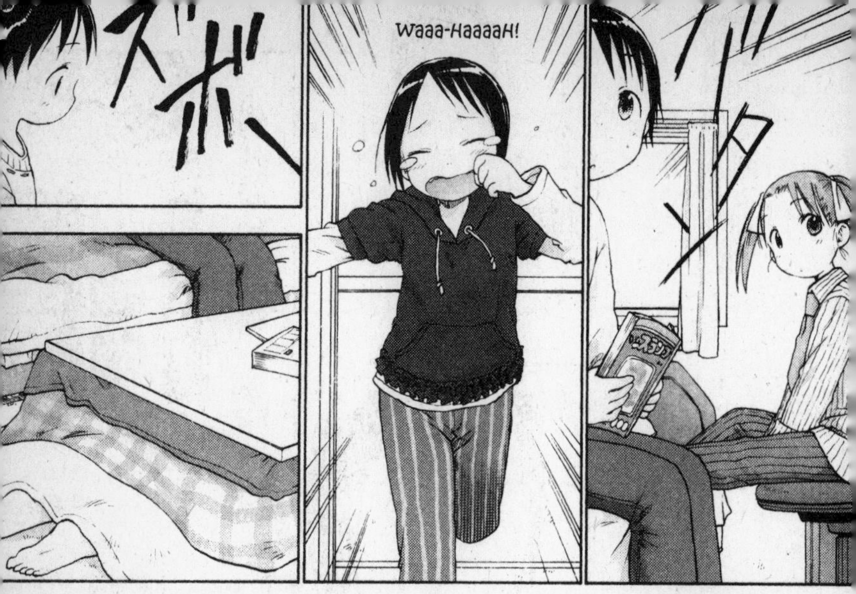
バタ
Waaa-HaaaaH!
ズボ

episode. 17
INTO HOT WATER

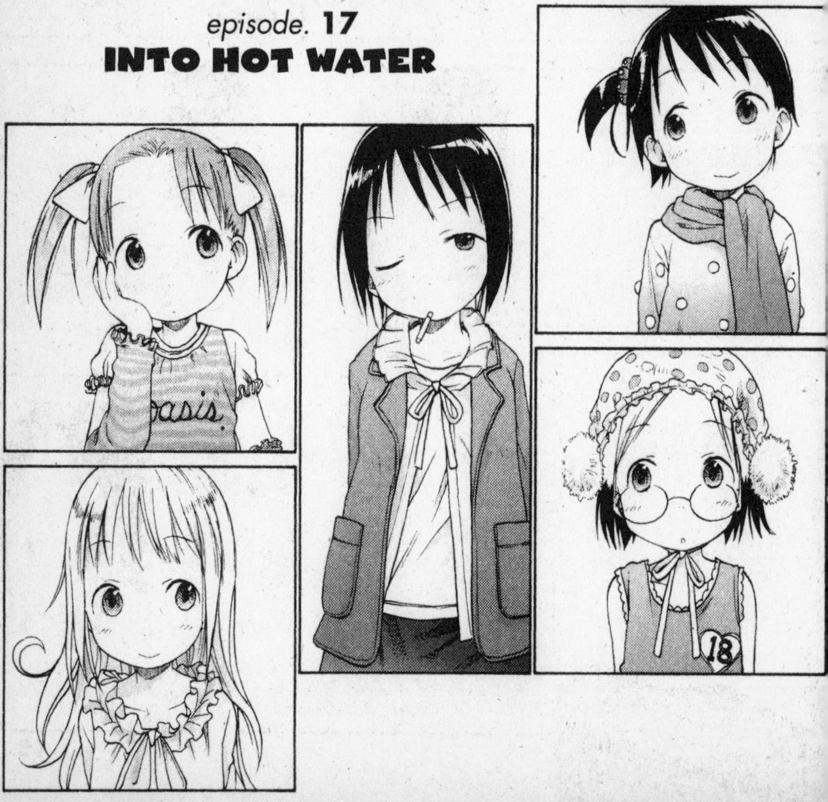
oasis
18

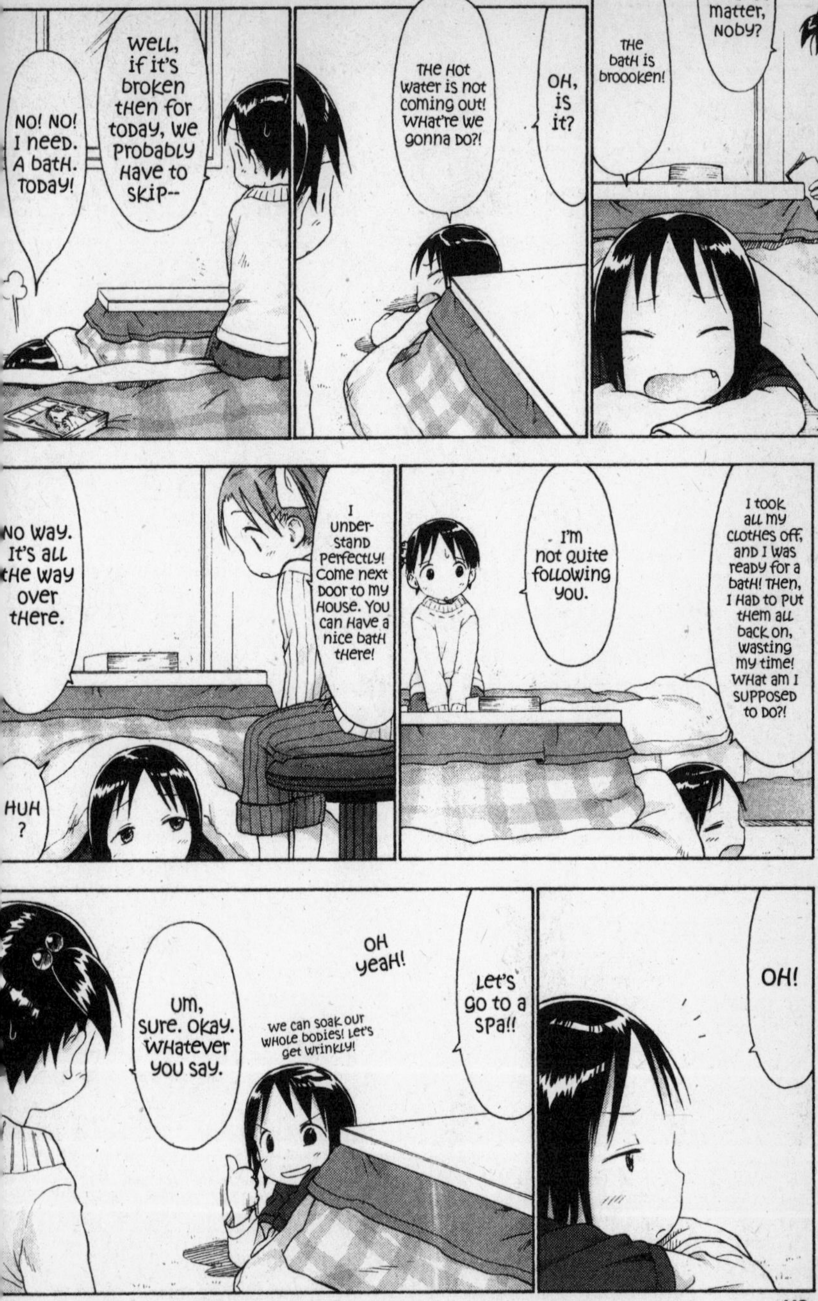
What'sa matter, Noby?
The bath is broooken!
Oh, is it?
The hot water is not coming out! What're we gonna do?!
Well, if it's broken then for today, we probably have to skip--
No! No! I need. A bath. Today!
I took all my clothes off, and I was ready for a bath! Then, I had to put them all back on, wasting my time! What am I supposed to do?!
I'm not quite following you.
I understand perfectly! Come next door to my house. You can have a nice bath there!
No way. It's all the way over there.
Huh?
Oh!
Let's go to a spa!!
Oh yeah!
We can soak our whole bodies! Let's get wrinkly!
Um, sure. Okay. Whatever you say.

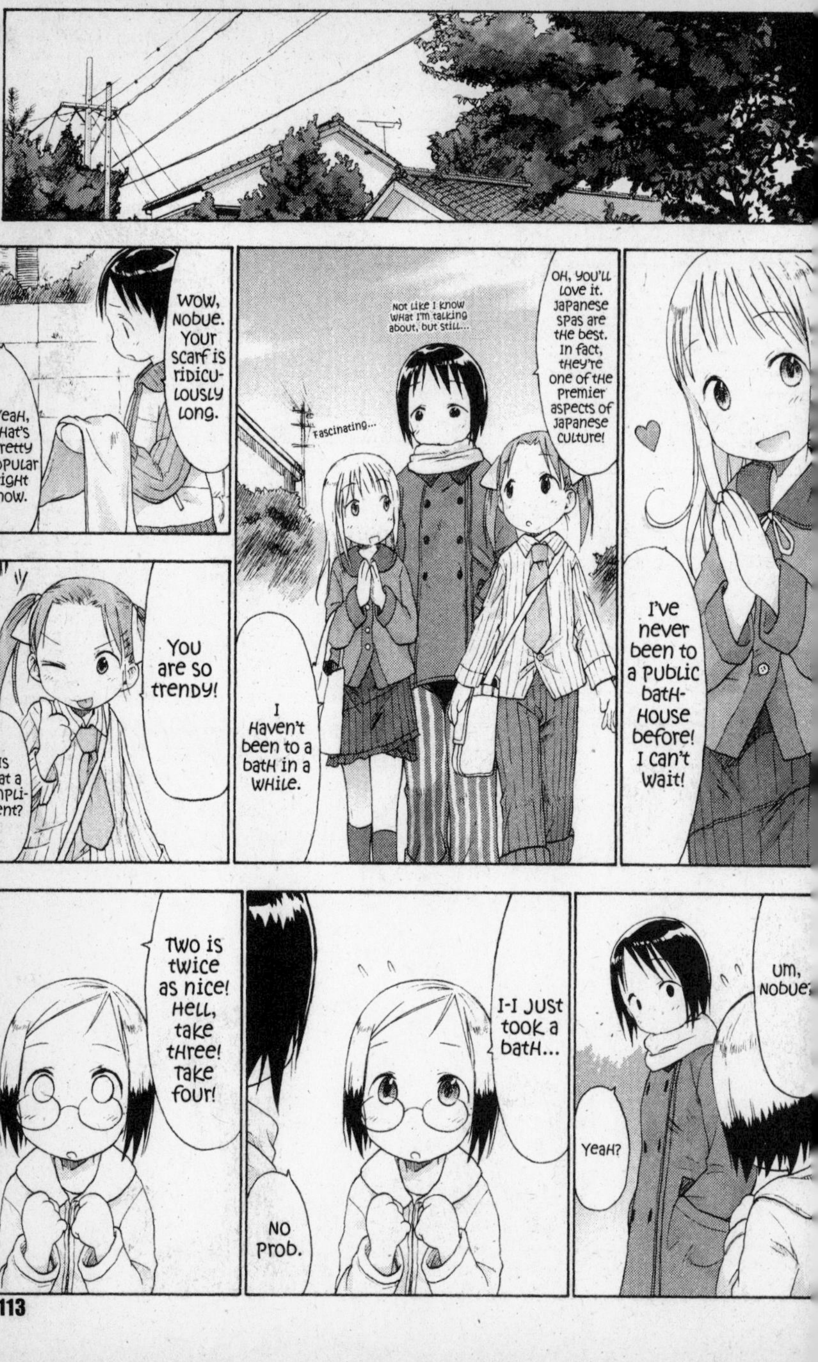
I've never been to a public bath-house before! I can't wait!
Oh, you'll love it. Japanese spas are the best. In fact, they're one of the premier aspects of Japanese culture!
Not like I know what I'm talking about, but still...
Fascinating...
I haven't been to a bath in a while.
Wow, Nobue. Your scarf is ridicu-lously long.
Yeah, that's pretty popular right now.
ビッ
You are so trendy!
Is that a compli-ment?
Um, Nobue?
Yeah?
I-I just took a bath...
No prob.
Two is twice as nice! Hell, take three! Take four!

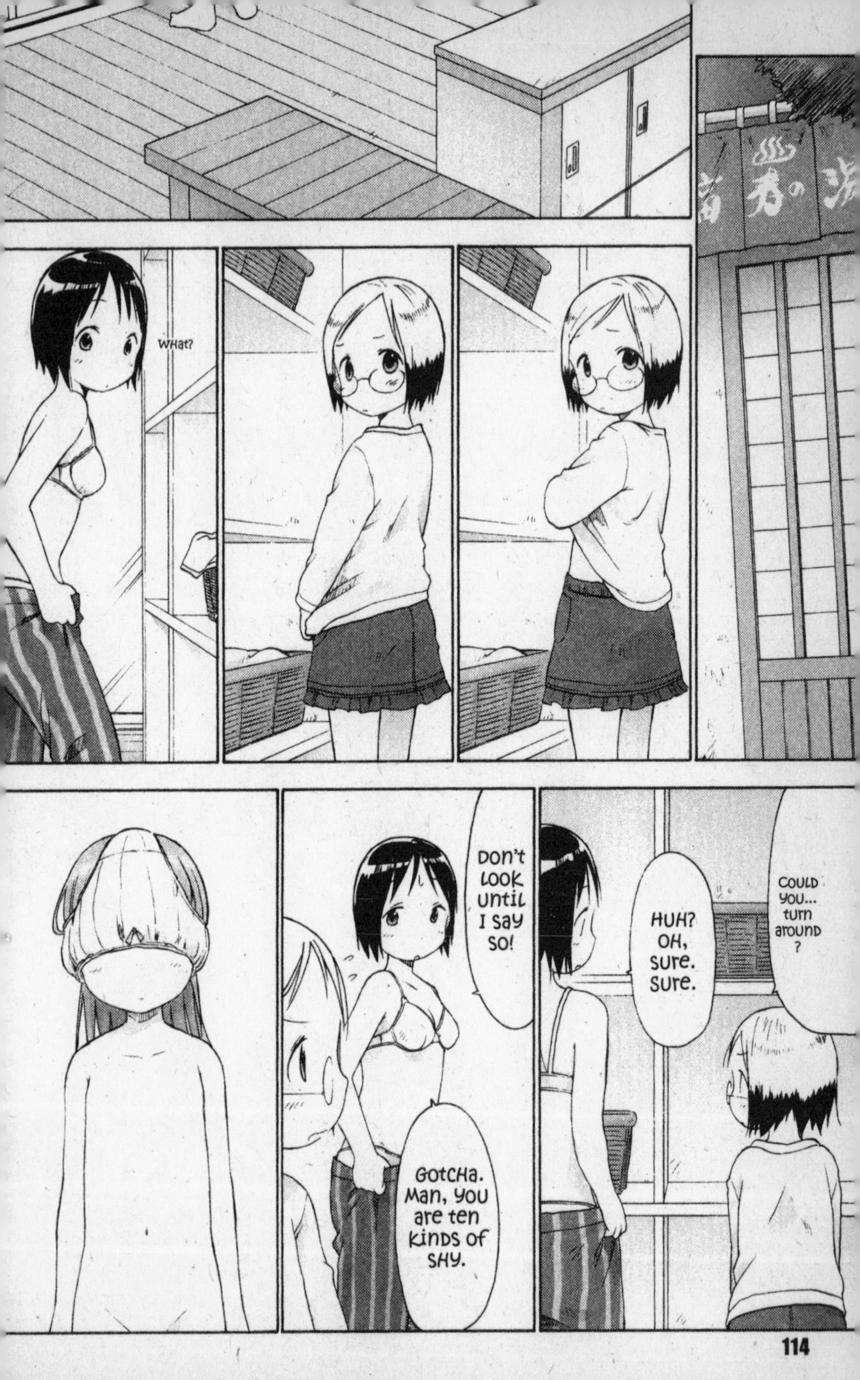
What?
Could you... turn around?
Huh? Oh, sure. Sure.
Don't look until I say so!
Gotcha. Man, you are ten kinds of shy.

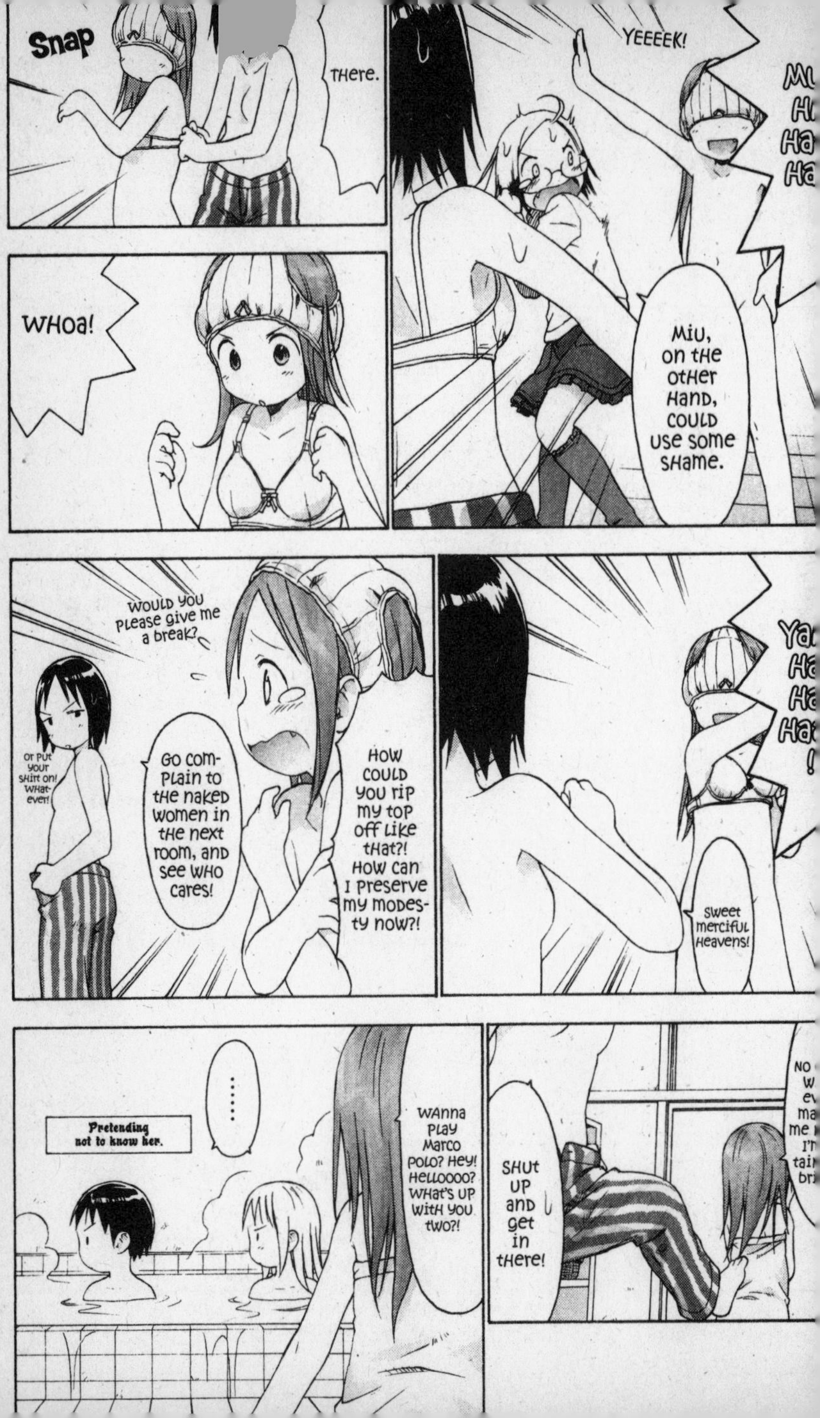
YEEEEK!
Miu, on the other hand, could use some shame.
Snap
There.
WHOA!
Sweet merciful Heavens!
How could you rip my top off like that?! How can I preserve my modesty now?!
Would you please give me a break?
Go complain to the naked women in the next room, and see who cares!
Or put your shirt on! Whatever!
Shut up and get in there!
Wanna play Marco Polo? Hey! Hellooooo? What's up with you two?!
......
Pretending not to know her.

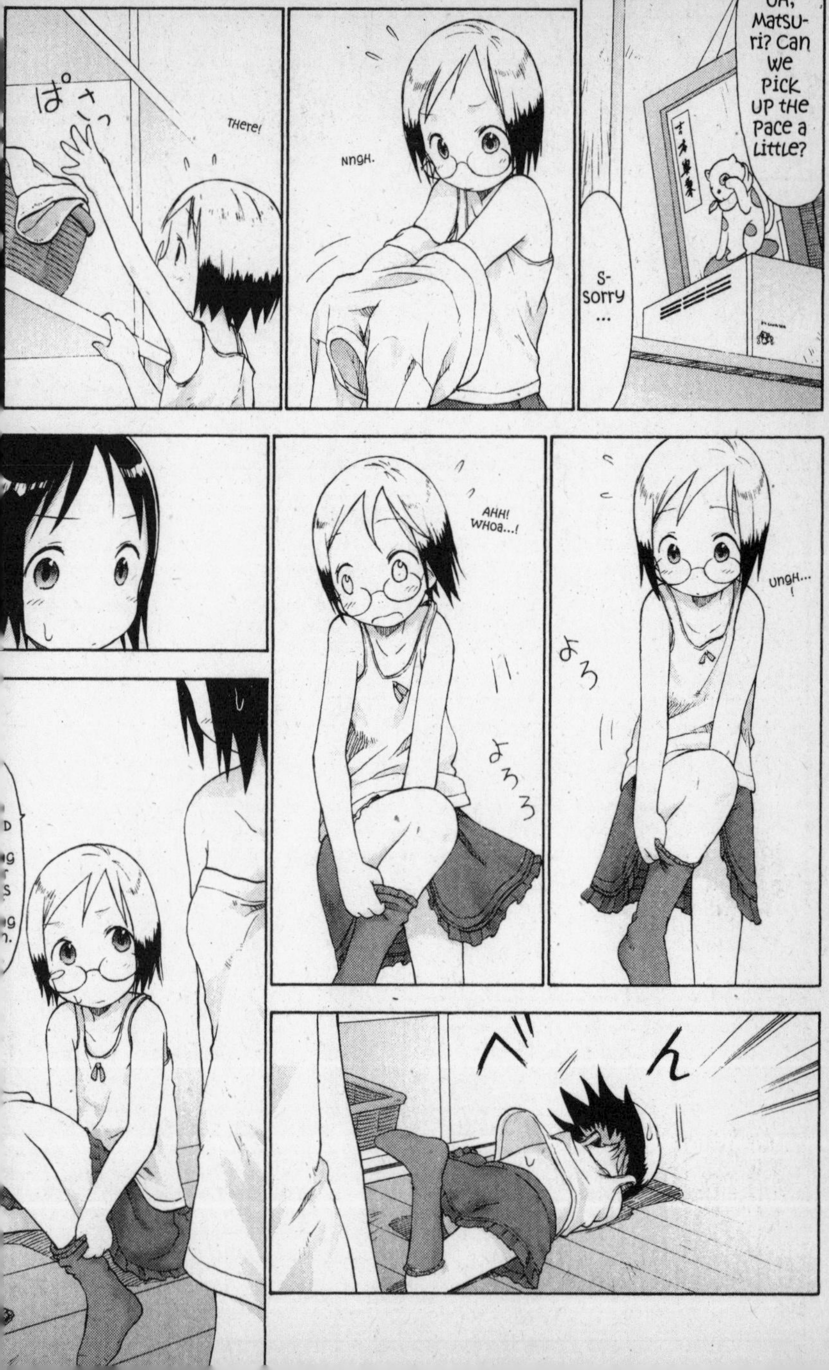
UH, MATSURI? CAN WE PICK UP THE PACE A LITTLE?
S-SORRY...
NNGH.
ぱさっ
THERE!
UNGH...!
よろ
AHH! WHOA...!
よろろ
べん

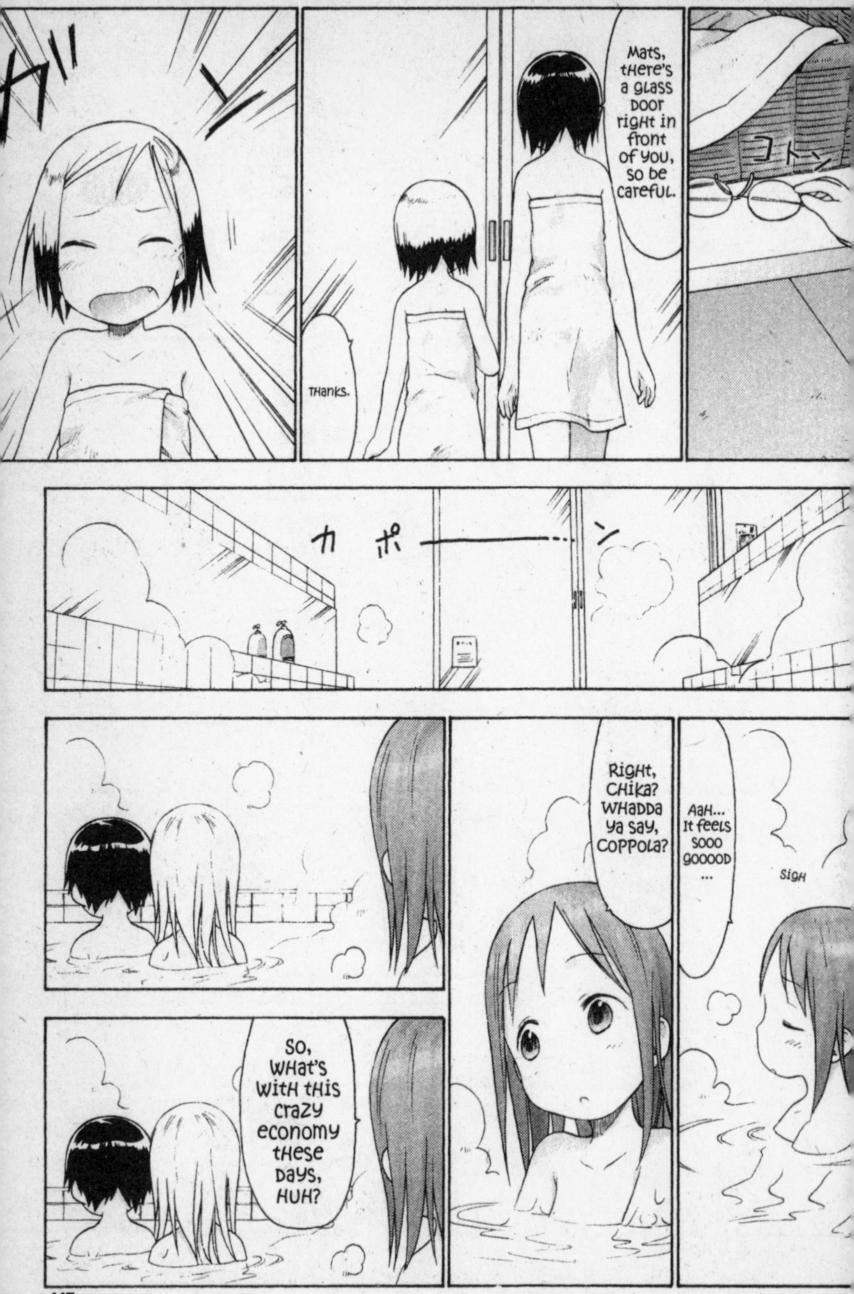
コトン
Mats, there's a glass door right in front of you, so be careful.
Thanks.
ガン
カポーーン
Sigh
Aah... It feels sooo goooood ...
Right, Chika? Whadda ya say, Coppola?
So, what's with this crazy economy these days, huh?

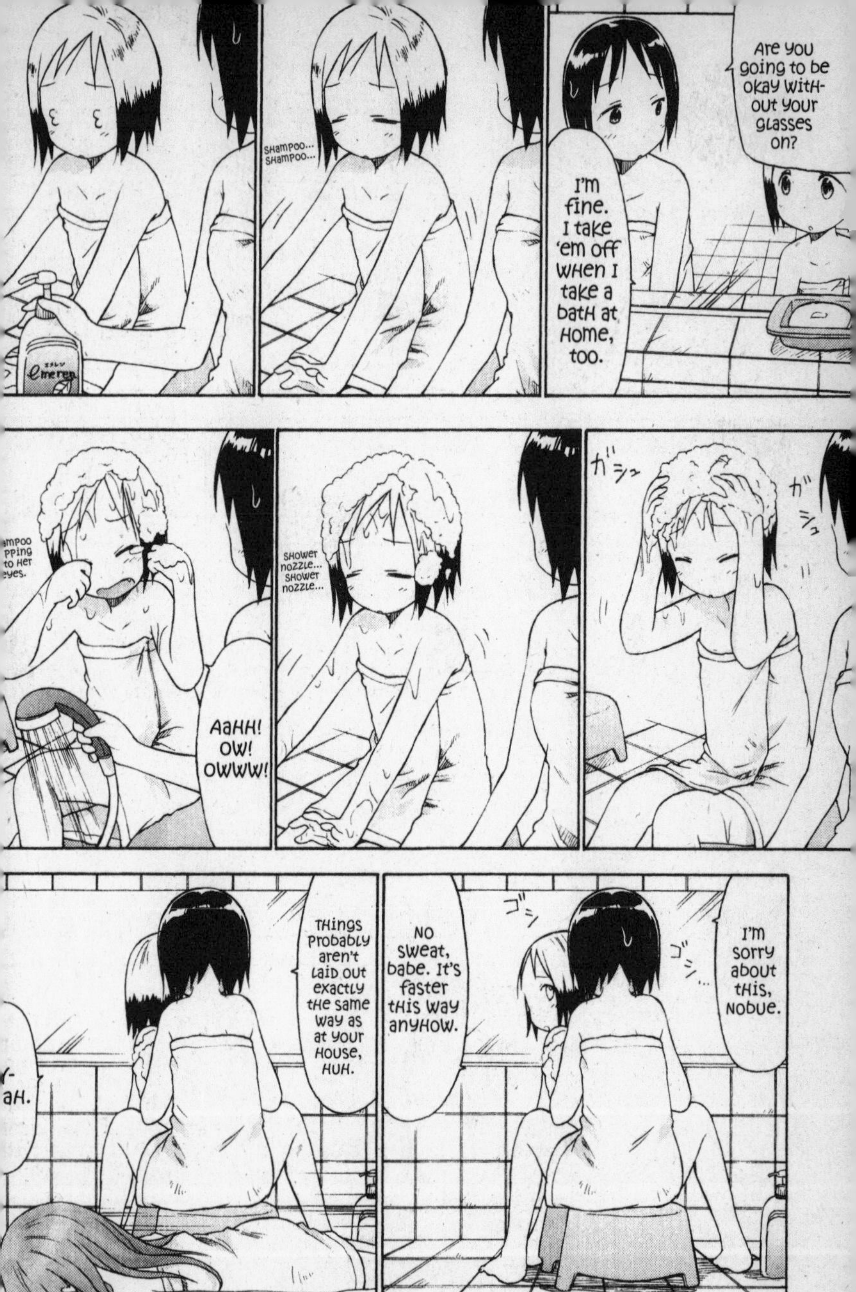
Are you going to be okay with-out your glasses on?
I'm fine. I take 'em off when I take a bath at home, too.
Shampoo... Shampoo...
ガシュ
ガシュ
Shower nozzle... Shower nozzle...
AaHH! OW! OWWW!
I'm sorry about this, Nobue.
ゴシ
ゴシ...
No sweat, babe. It's faster this way anyhow.
Things probably aren't laid out exactly the same way as at your house, huh.

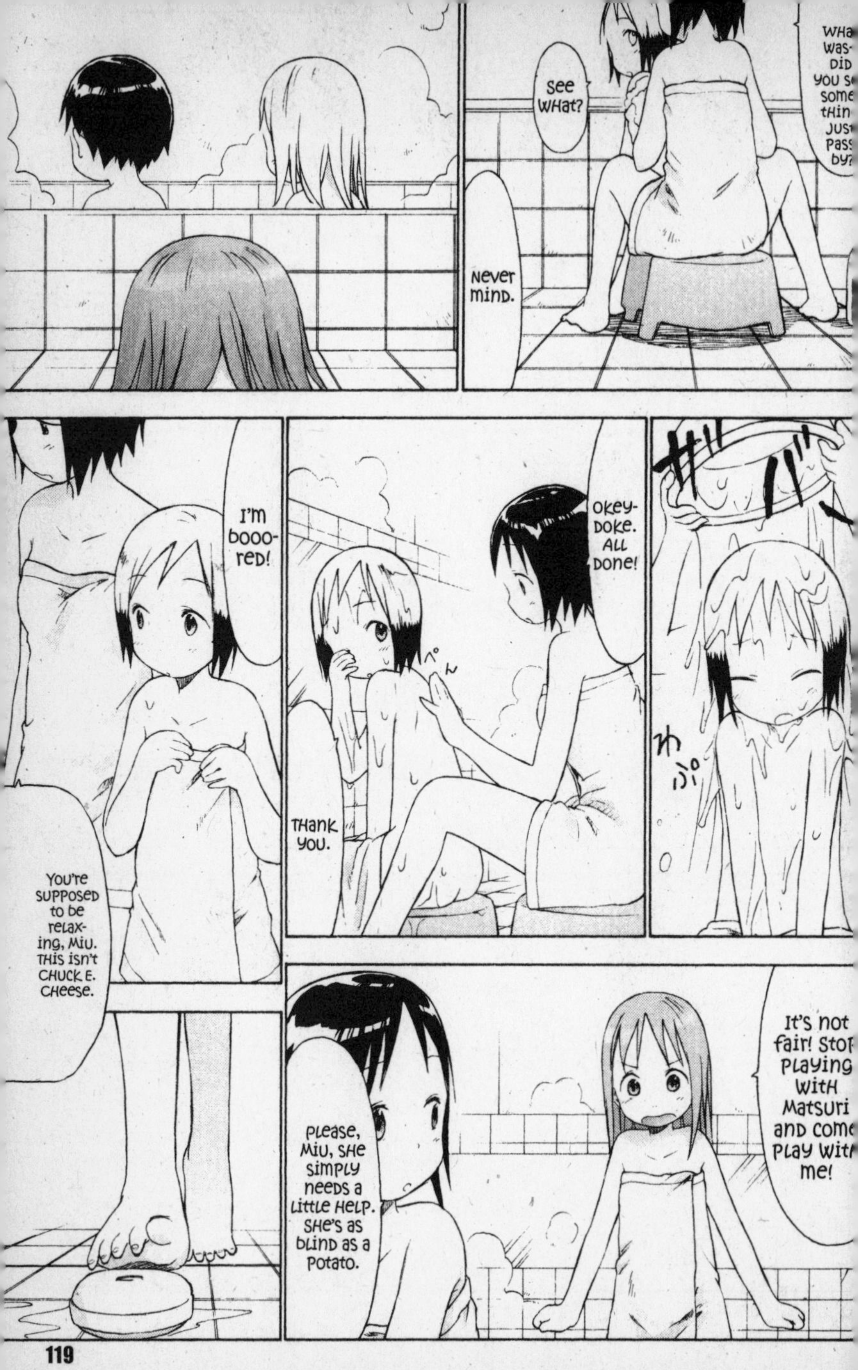
What was- did you s some thin just pass by?
See what?
Never mind.
ザ バ
わぷ
Okey-doke. All done!
ぺん
Thank you.
I'm booored!
You're supposed to be relaxing, Miu. This isn't Chuck E. Cheese.
It's not fair! Sto playing with Matsuri and come play wit me!
Please, Miu, she simply needs a little help. She's as blind as a potato.

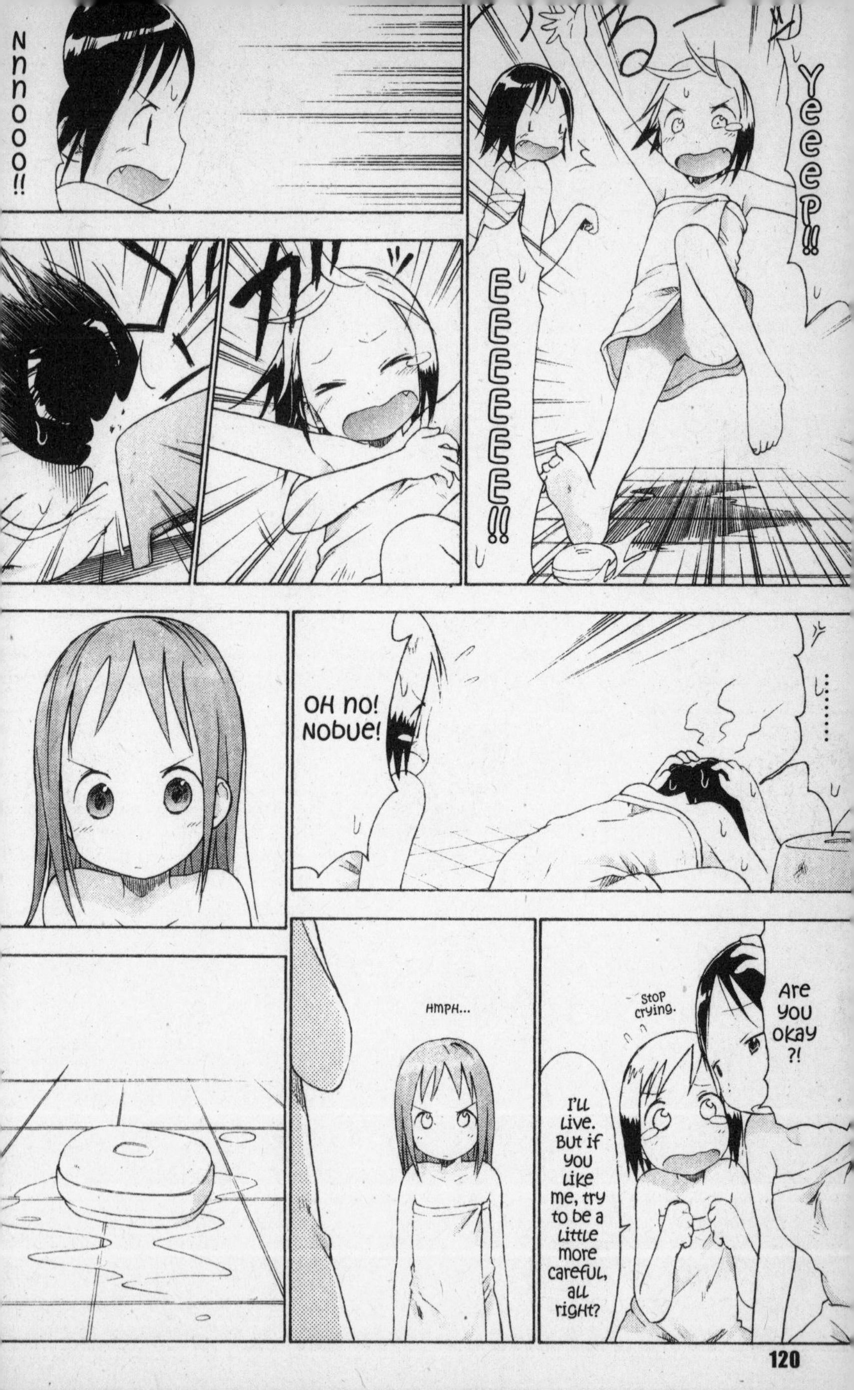
Yeeep!!
EEEEEEE!!
Nnnooo!!
......
OH no! Nobue!
Are you okay?!
Stop crying.
I'll live. But if you like me, try to be a little more careful, all right?
Hmph...

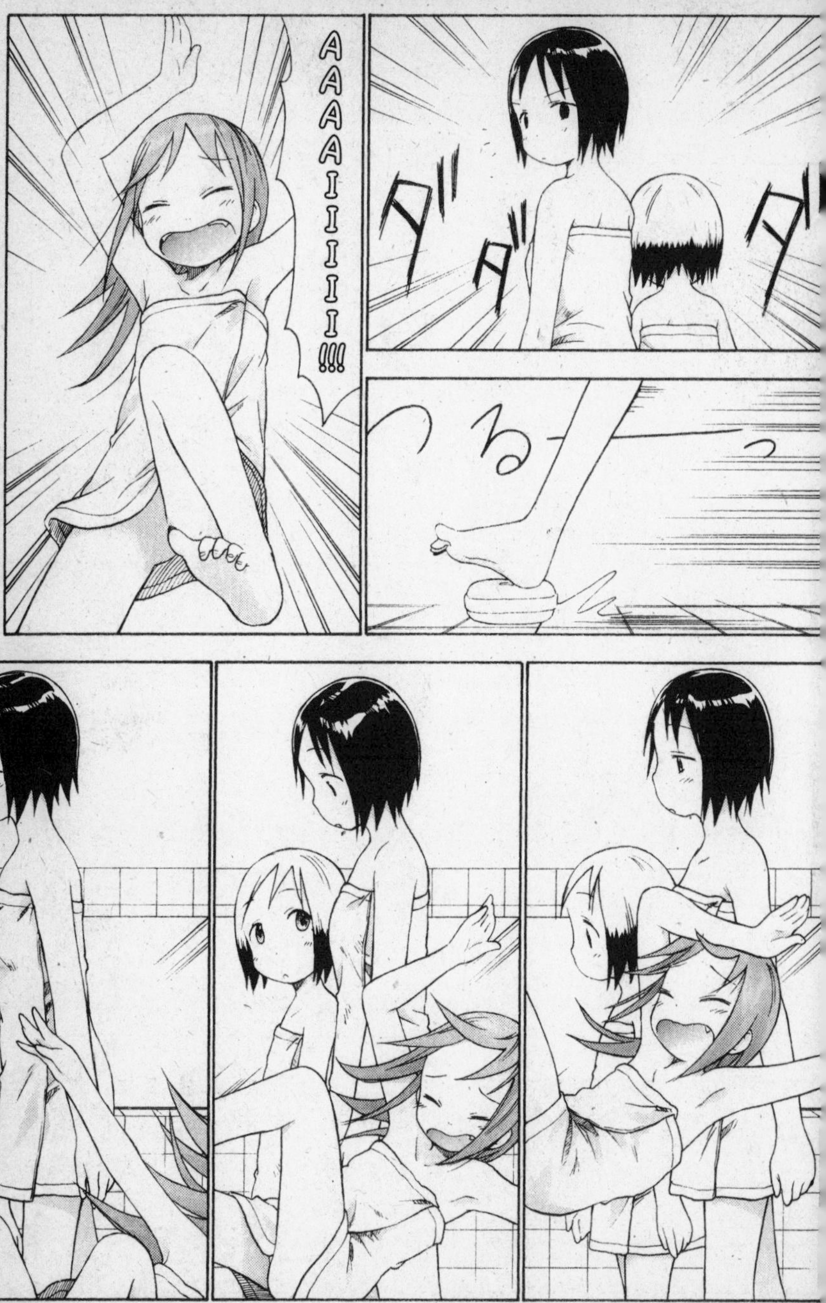
ダ
ダ
ダ
つるーっ
AAAAIIIII!!!

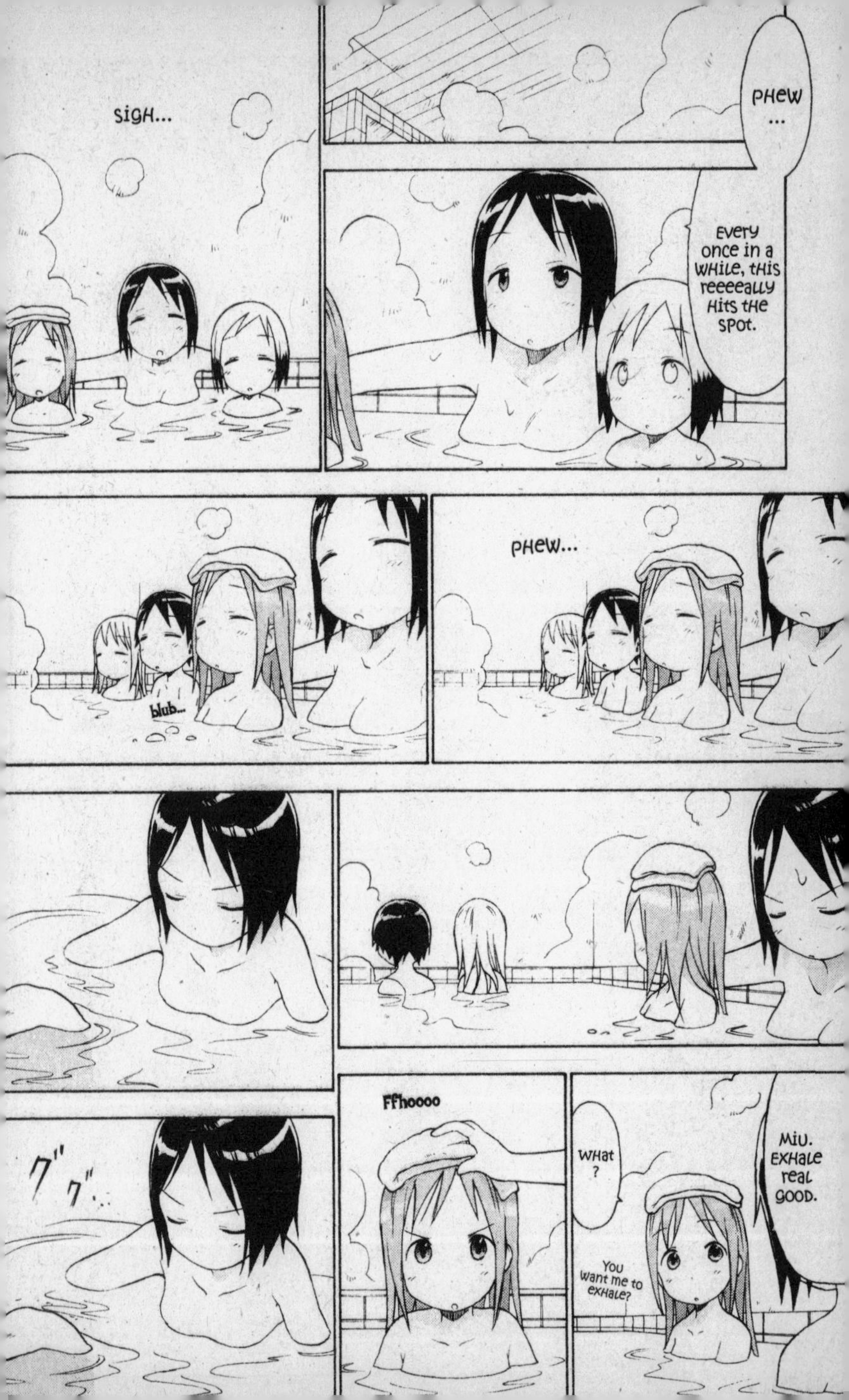
PHEW ...
Every once in a WHILE, this reeeeally Hits the spot.
SIGH...
PHEW...
blub...
MIU. EXHALE real GOOD.
WHAT ?
You want me to exhale?
Ffhoooo
グ グ...

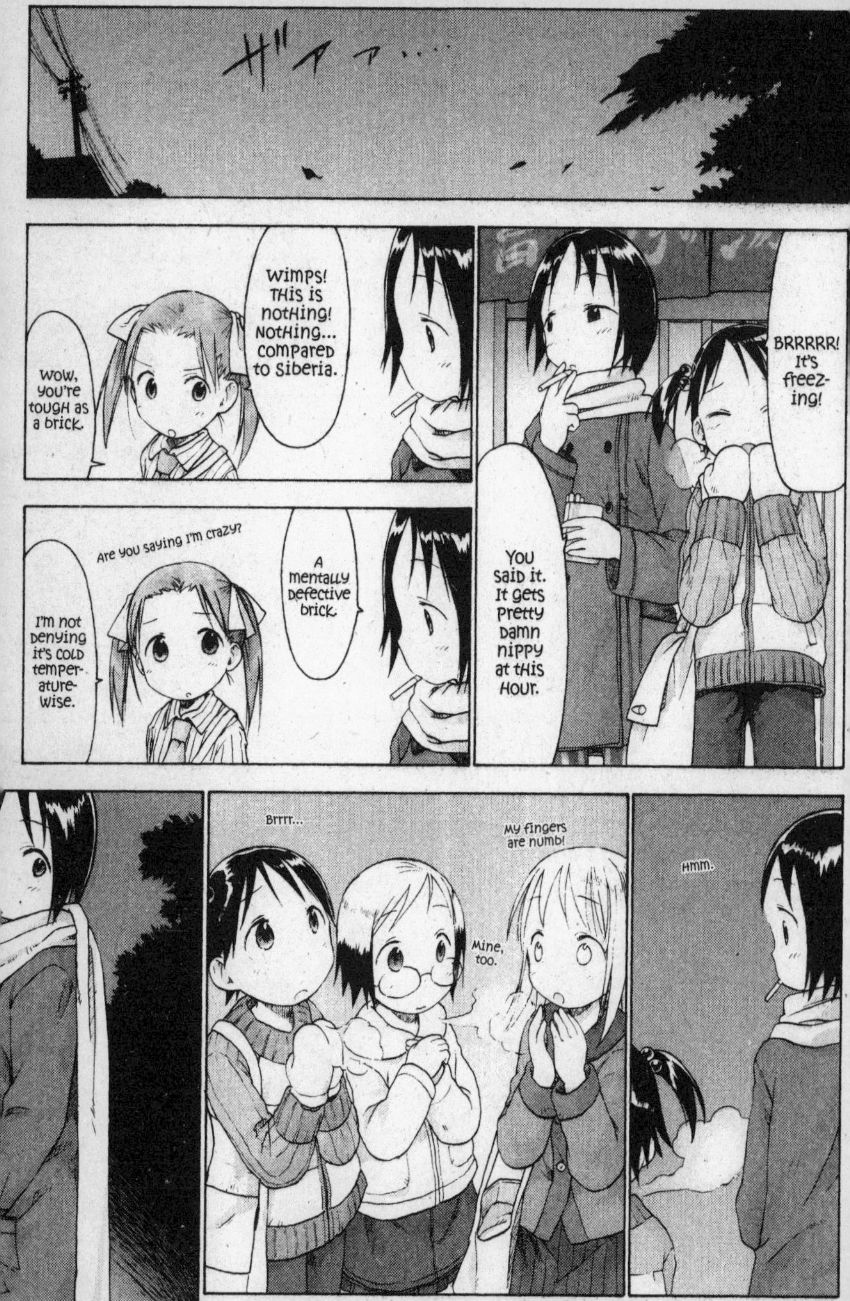
ザァ…
BRRRRR! It's freez-ing!
You said it. It gets pretty damn nippy at this hour.
Wimps! This is nothing! Nothing... compared to Siberia.
Wow, you're tough as a brick.
A mentally defective brick.
Are you saying I'm crazy?
I'm not denying it's cold temper-ature-wise.
Hmm.
My fingers are numb!
Brrrr...
Mine, too.

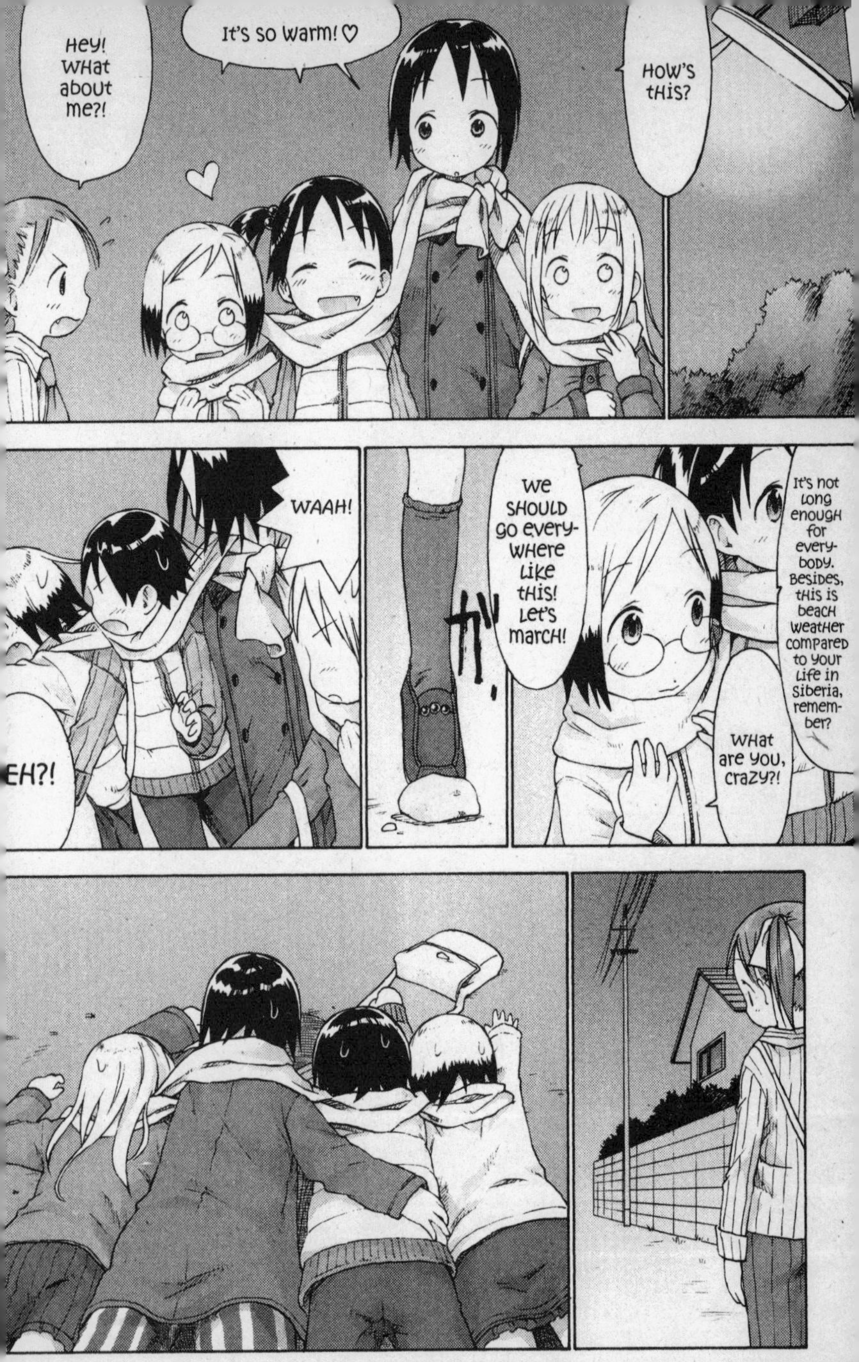
How's this?
It's so warm! ♡
Hey! What about me?!
We should go every-where like this! Let's march!
What are you, crazy?!
It's not long enough for every-body. Besides, this is beach weather compared to your life in Siberia, remember?
ガッ
WAAH!
EH?!

HALLO WORK

nobue

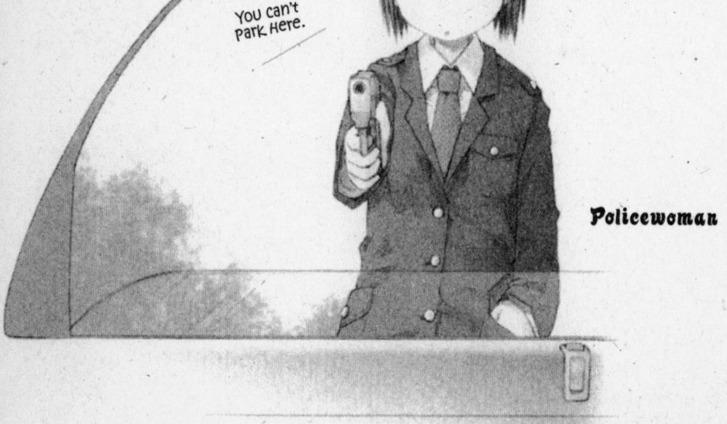
You can't Park Here.
Policewoman

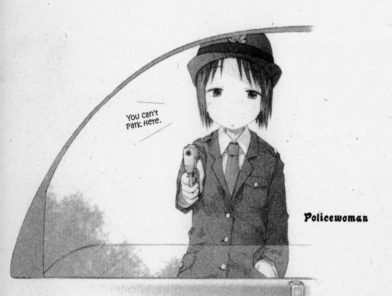

HALLO WORK

chika

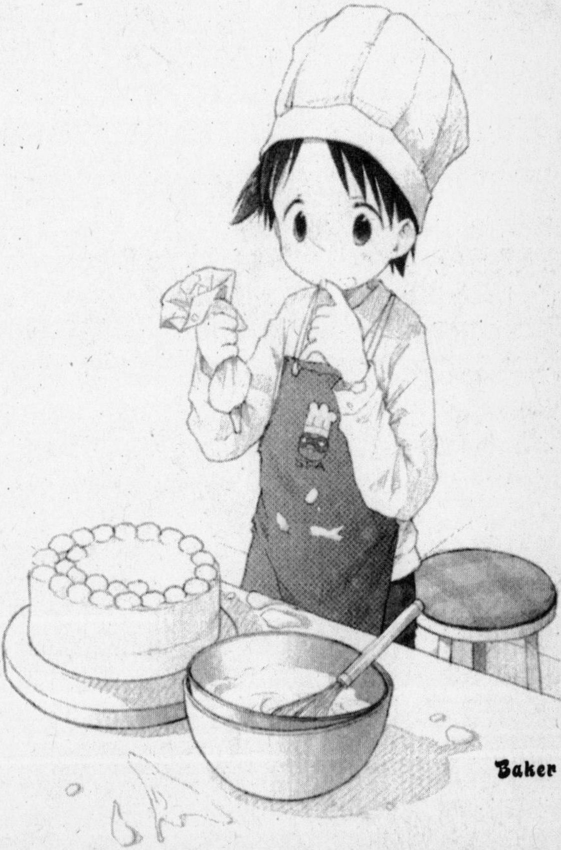

Baker

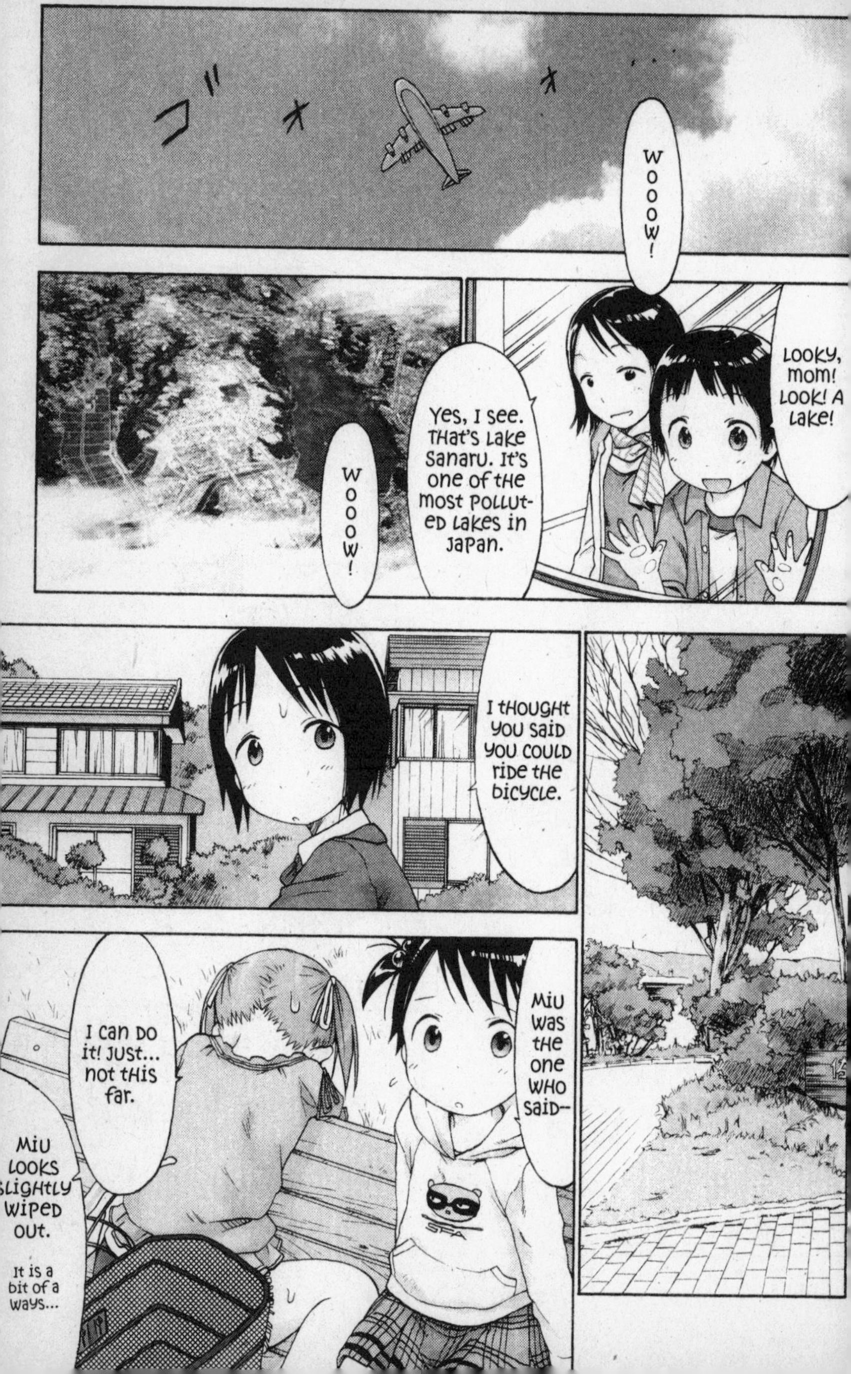
Woooow!
ゴオオ
Looky, mom! Look! A lake!
Yes, I see. That's Lake Sanaru. It's one of the most pollut-ed lakes in Japan.
Woooow!
I thought you said you could ride the bicycle.
Miu was the one who said--
I can do it! Just... not this far.
Miu looks slightly wiped out.
It is a bit of a ways...

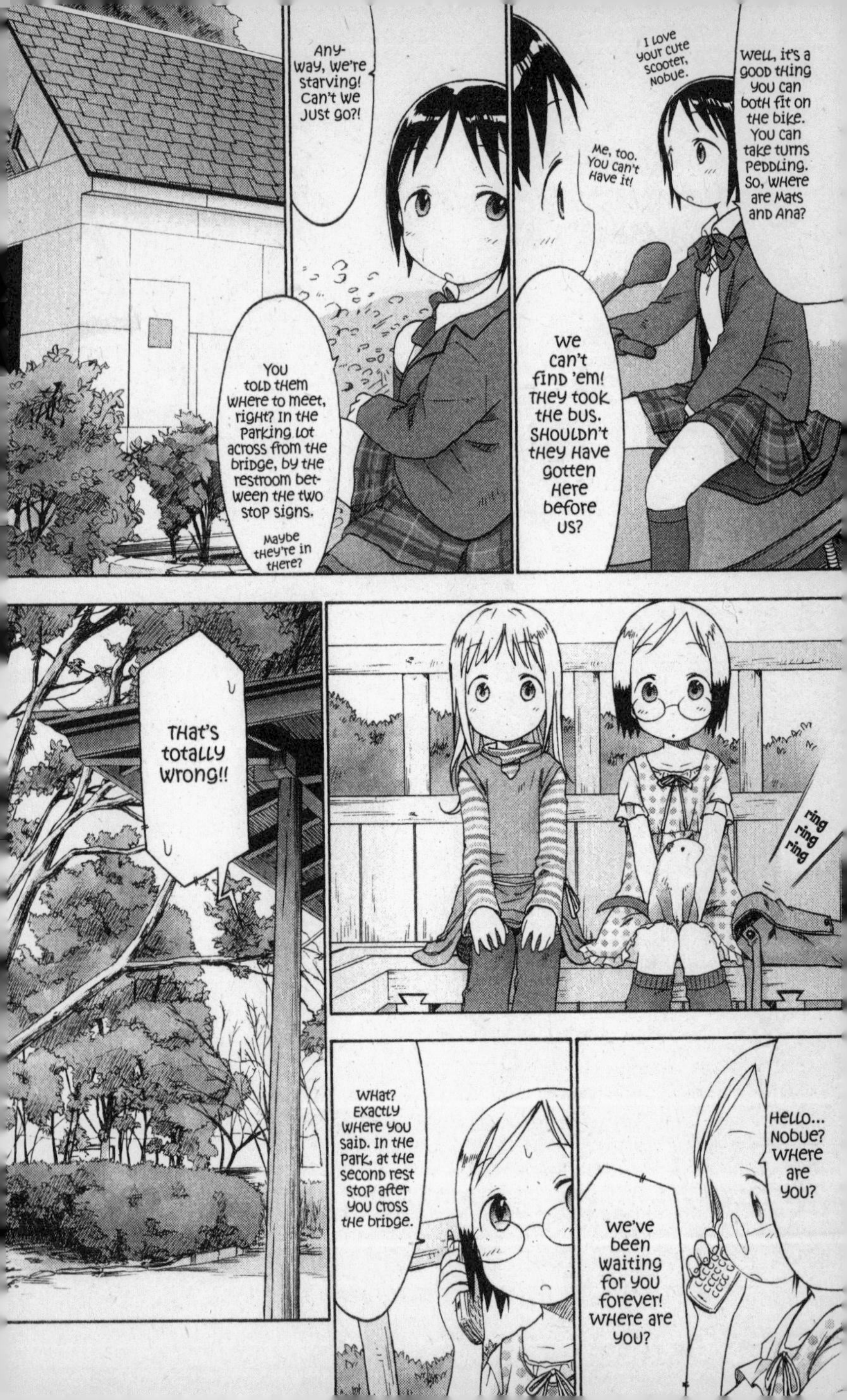

Well, it's a good thing you can both fit on the bike. You can take turns peddling. So, where are Mats and Ana?
I love your cute scooter, Nobue.
Me, too. You can't have it!
We can't find 'em! They took the bus. Shouldn't they have gotten here before us?
Any-way, we're starving! Can't we just go?!
You told them where to meet, right? In the parking lot across from the bridge, by the restroom bet-ween the two stop signs.
Maybe they're in there?
ring ring ring
Hello... Nobue? Where are you?
We've been waiting for you forever! Where are you?
What? Exactly where you said. In the park, at the second rest stop after you cross the bridge.
That's totally wrong!!

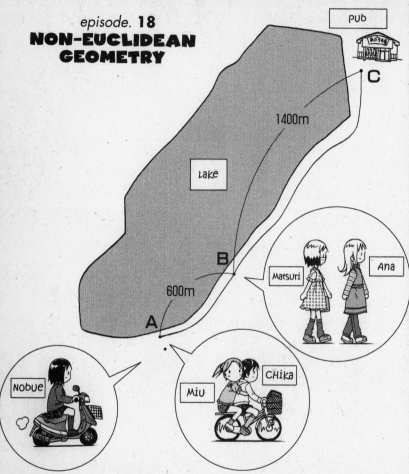

episode. **18**
NON-EUCLIDEAN GEOMETRY

pub

C

1400m

Lake

B

Matsuri

Ana

600m

A

Nobue

Miu

Chika

First read the previous two pages and the following four pages, then solve this math problem:

Miu, Chika and Nobue are at point (A), 2km away from the pub (C). Matsuri and Ana are at point (B), 1.4km away from the pub(C).

At 1:10pm, Nobue sets off for the pub on her scooter at 600m/minute. At the same time, Miu and Chika depart on their bicycle, traveling at 150m/minute. Meanwhile, Matsuri and Ana are walking to the pub at 70m/minute. When Nobue catches up to Matsuri and Ana, she picks them up and takes them with her on the scooter.

At what time do each of the girls arrive at the pub?

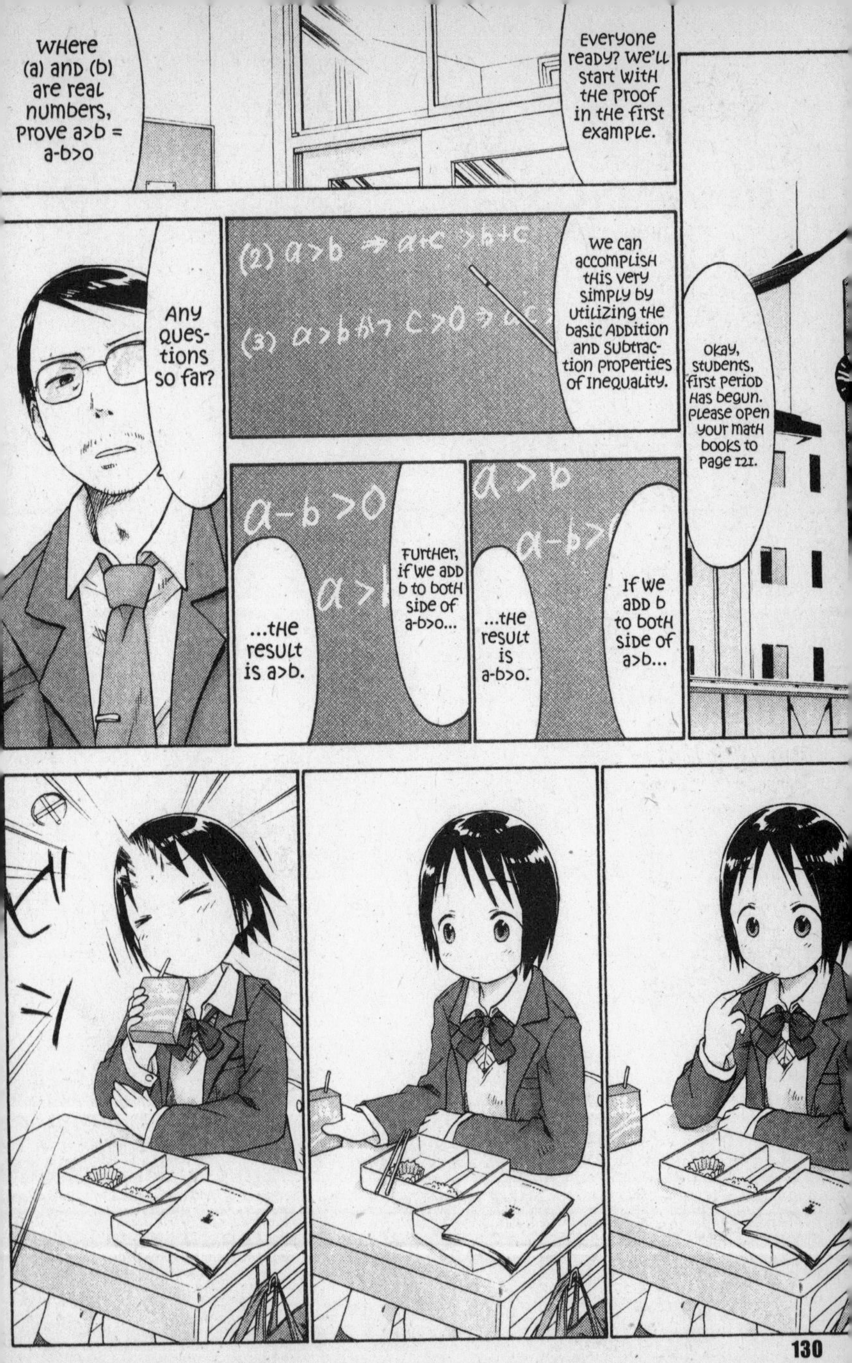
Okay, students, first period has begun. Please open your math books to page 121.
Everyone ready? We'll start with the proof in the first example.
Where (a) and (b) are real numbers, prove a>b = a-b>o
We can accomplish this very simply by utilizing the basic addition and subtraction properties of inequality.
If we add b to both side of a>b...
...the result is a-b>o.
Further, if we add b to both side of a-b>o...
...the result is a>b.
Any ques-tions so far?

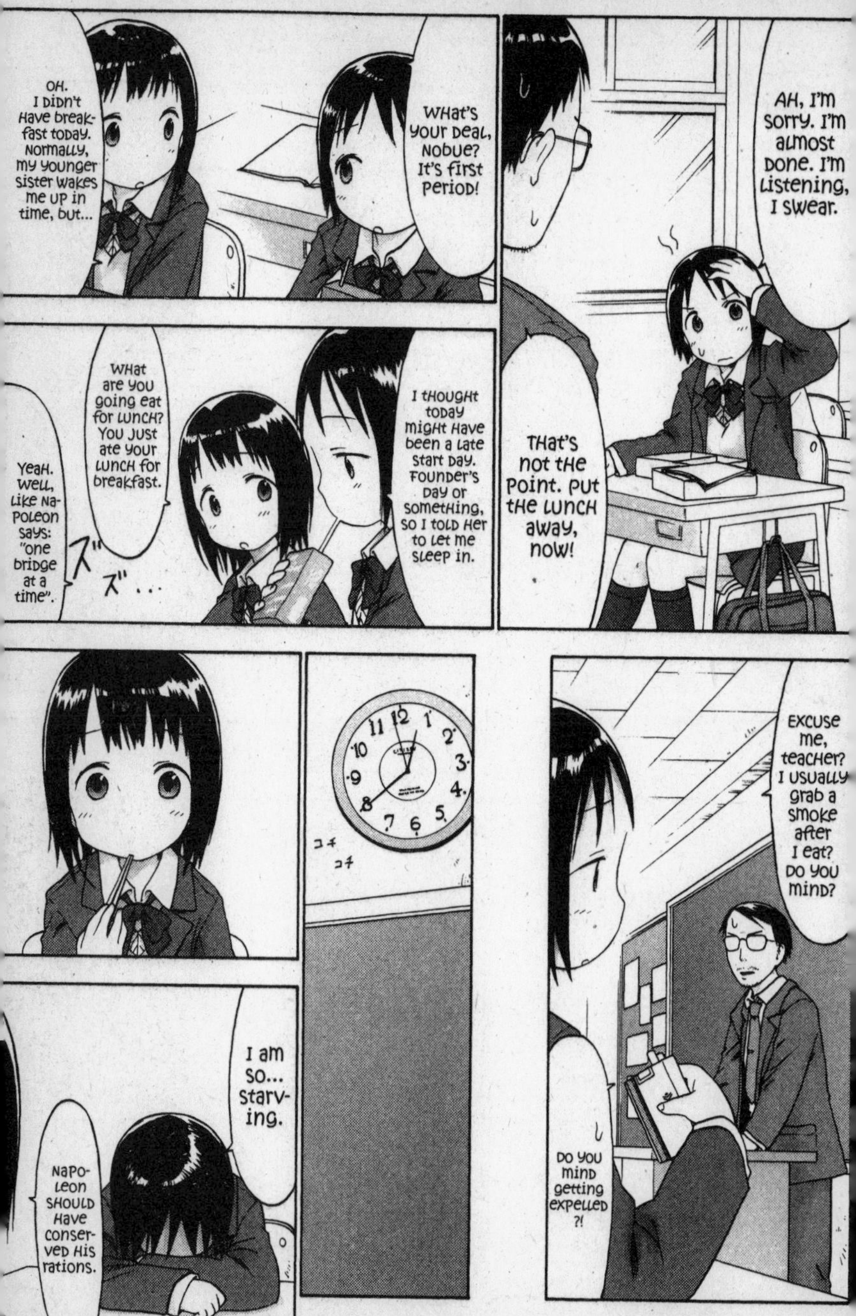

AH, I'M SORRY. I'M ALMOST DONE. I'M LISTENING, I SWEAR.
THAT'S NOT THE POINT. PUT THE LUNCH AWAY, NOW!
WHAT'S YOUR DEAL, NOBUE? IT'S FIRST PERIOD!
OH. I DIDN'T HAVE BREAKFAST TODAY. NORMALLY, MY YOUNGER SISTER WAKES ME UP IN TIME, BUT...
I THOUGHT TODAY MIGHT HAVE BEEN A LATE START DAY. FOUNDER'S DAY OR SOMETHING, SO I TOLD HER TO LET ME SLEEP IN.
WHAT ARE YOU GOING EAT FOR LUNCH? YOU JUST ATE YOUR LUNCH FOR BREAKFAST.
ズズ...
YEAH. WELL, LIKE NAPOLEON SAYS: "ONE BRIDGE AT A TIME".
EXCUSE ME, TEACHER? I USUALLY GRAB A SMOKE AFTER I EAT? DO YOU MIND?
DO YOU MIND GETTING EXPELLED ?!
コチ
コチ
I AM SO... STARVING.
NAPOLEON SHOULD HAVE CONSERVED HIS RATIONS.

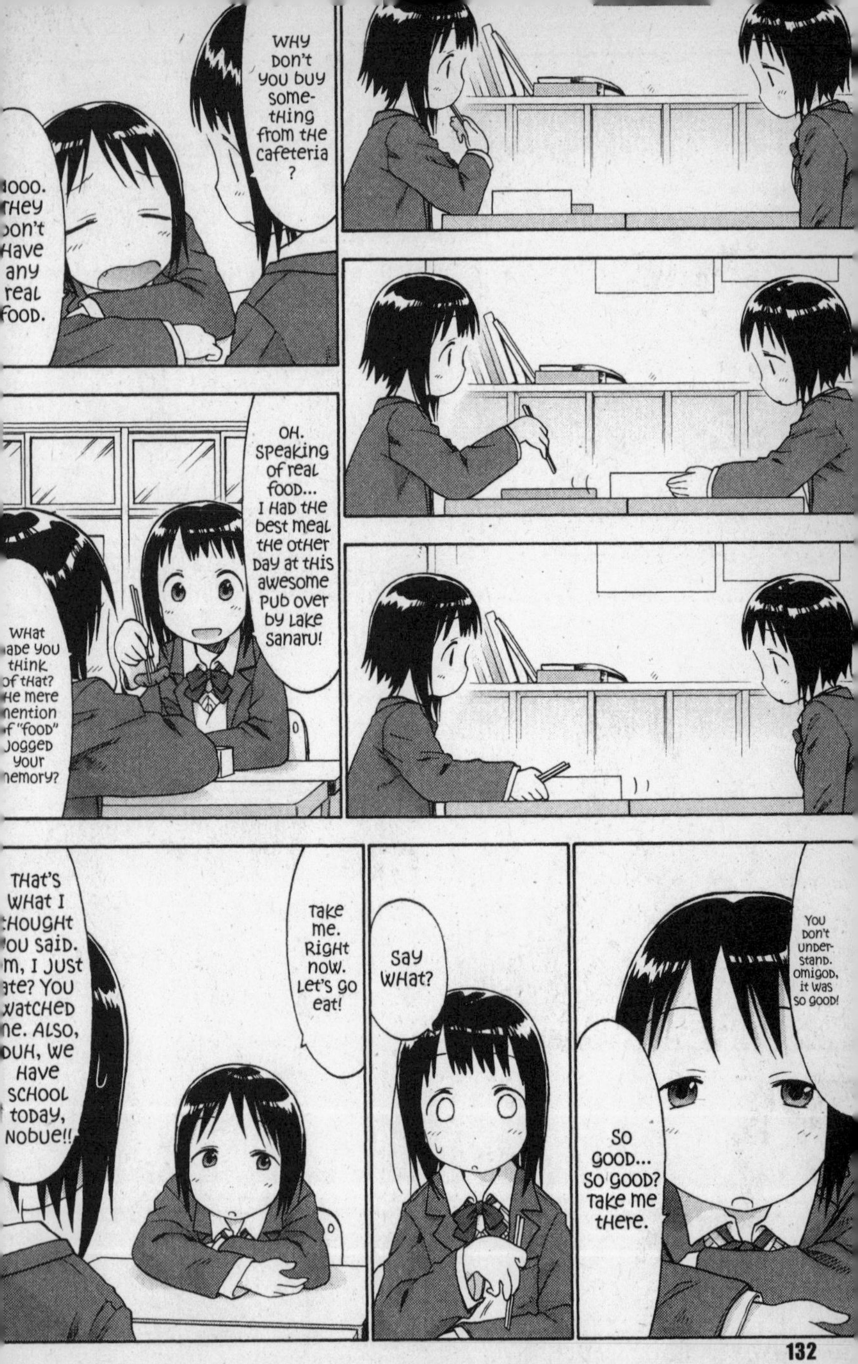
WHY DON'T YOU BUY SOMETHING FROM THE CAFETERIA?
NOOO. THEY DON'T HAVE ANY REAL FOOD.
OH. SPEAKING OF REAL FOOD... I HAD THE BEST MEAL THE OTHER DAY AT THIS AWESOME PUB OVER BY LAKE SANARU!
WHAT MADE YOU THINK OF THAT? THE MERE MENTION OF "FOOD" JOGGED YOUR MEMORY?
YOU DON'T UNDERSTAND. OMIGOD, IT WAS SO GOOD!
SO GOOD... SO GOOD? TAKE ME THERE.
SAY WHAT?
TAKE ME. RIGHT NOW. LET'S GO EAT!
THAT'S WHAT I THOUGHT YOU SAID. UM, I JUST ATE? YOU WATCHED ME. ALSO, DUH, WE HAVE SCHOOL TODAY, NOBUE!!

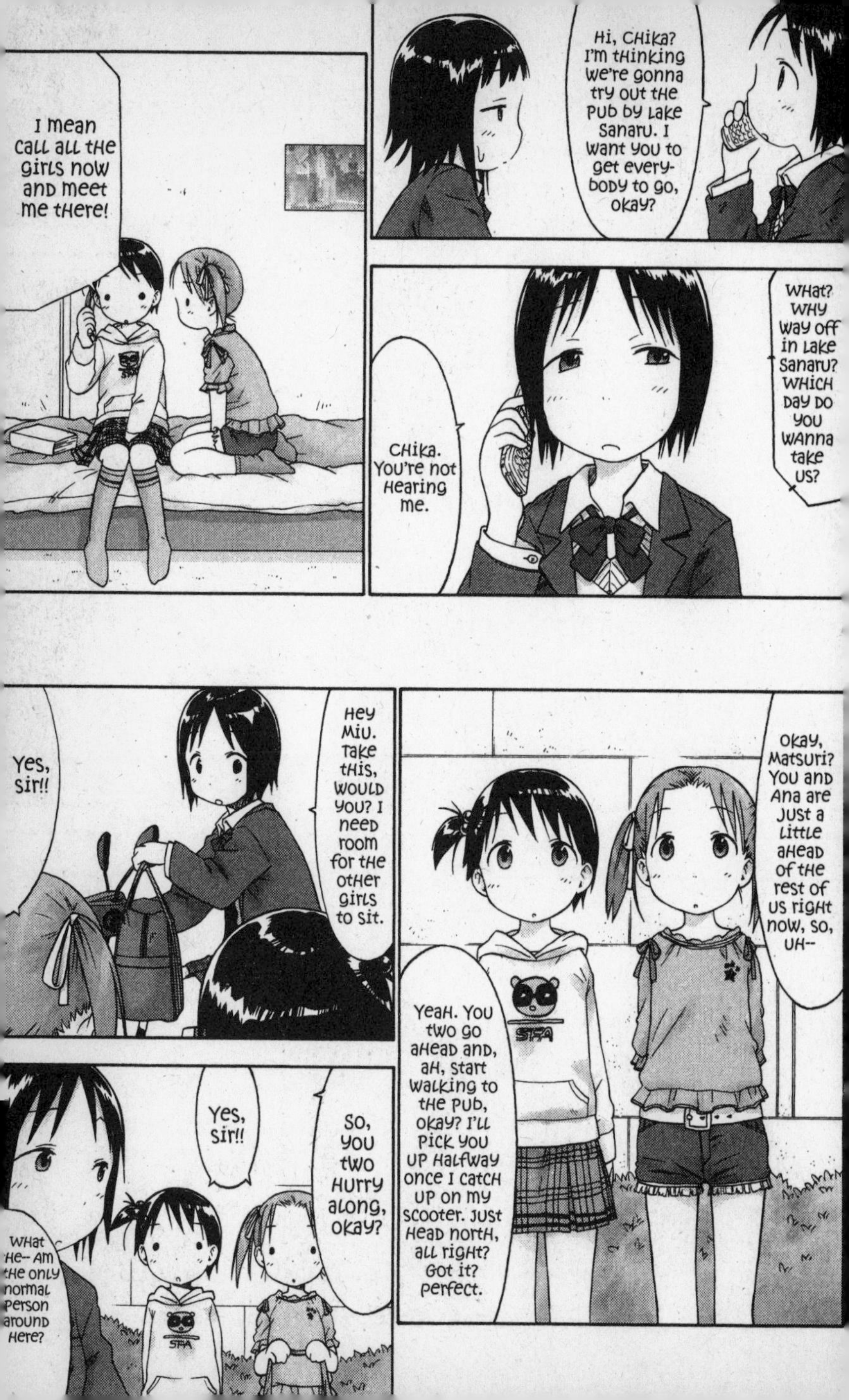
Hi, Chika? I'm thinking we're gonna try out the pub by Lake Sanaru. I want you to get every-body to go, okay?
What? Why way off in Lake Sanaru? Which day do you wanna take us?
Chika. You're not hearing me.
I mean call all the girls now and meet me there!
Okay, Matsuri? You and Ana are just a little ahead of the rest of us right now, so, uh--
Yeah. You two go ahead and, ah, start walking to the pub, okay? I'll pick you up halfway once I catch up on my scooter. Just head north, all right? Got it? perfect.
Hey Miu. Take this, would you? I need room for the other girls to sit.
Yes, sir!!
So, you two hurry along, okay?
Yes, sir!!
What he-- am the only normal person around here?

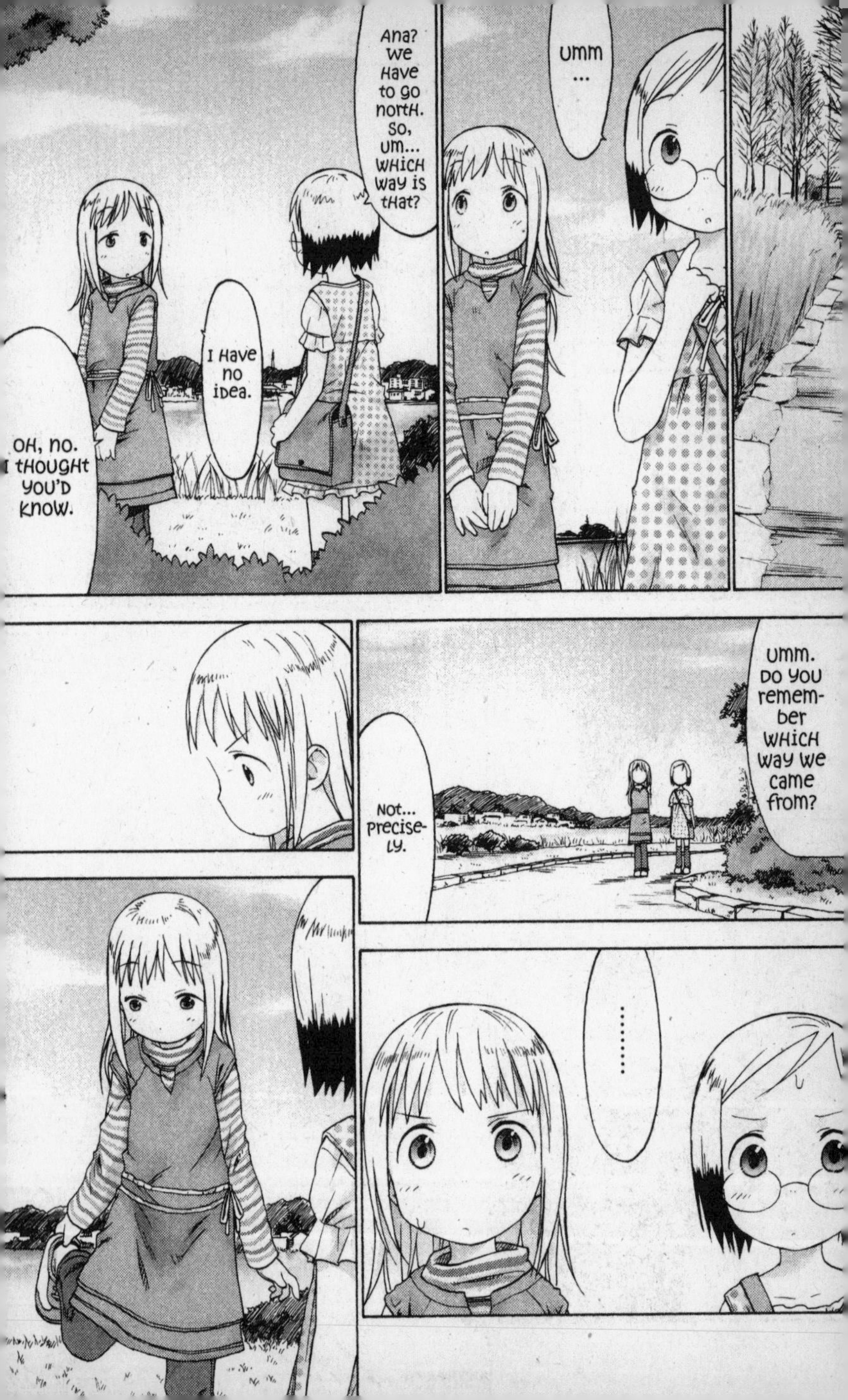
Umm ...
Ana? We have to go north. So, um... which way is that?
I have no idea.
Oh, no. I thought you'd know.
Umm. Do you remem-ber which way we came from?
Not... precise-ly.
....

ぽさっ

I'm getting tired. Can we swap now?

Hmn? It's just a little further. You can do it!

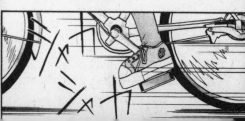

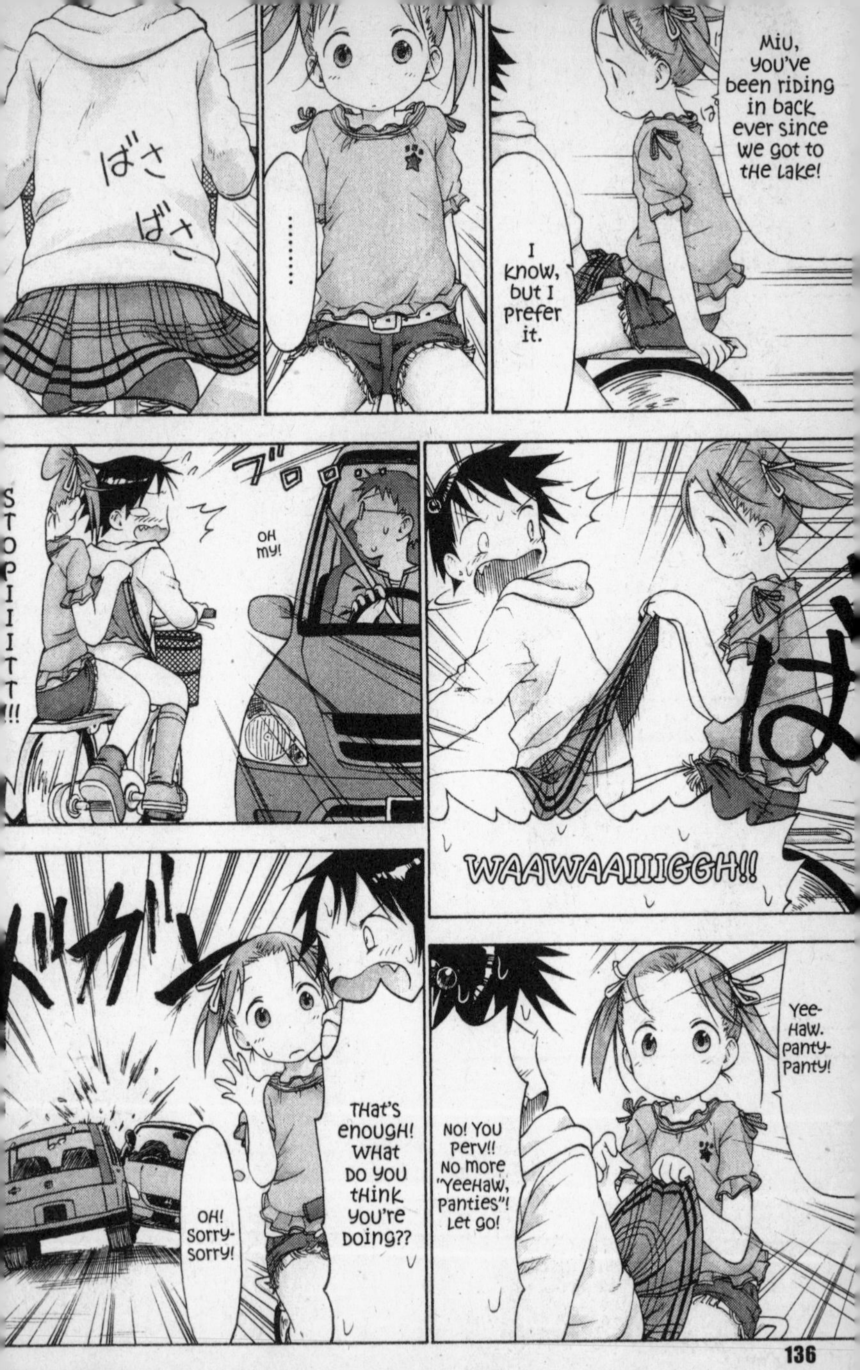
Miu, you've been riding in back ever since we got to the lake!
I know, but I prefer it.
......
ばさ ばさ
ば
WAAWAAIIIGGH!!
ブロロ
OH my!
STOPIIIITTT!!!
Yee-Haw. Panty-Panty!
No! You Perv!! No more "YeeHaw, Panties"! Let go!
ドガン
That's enough! What do you think you're doing??
OH! Sorry-sorry!

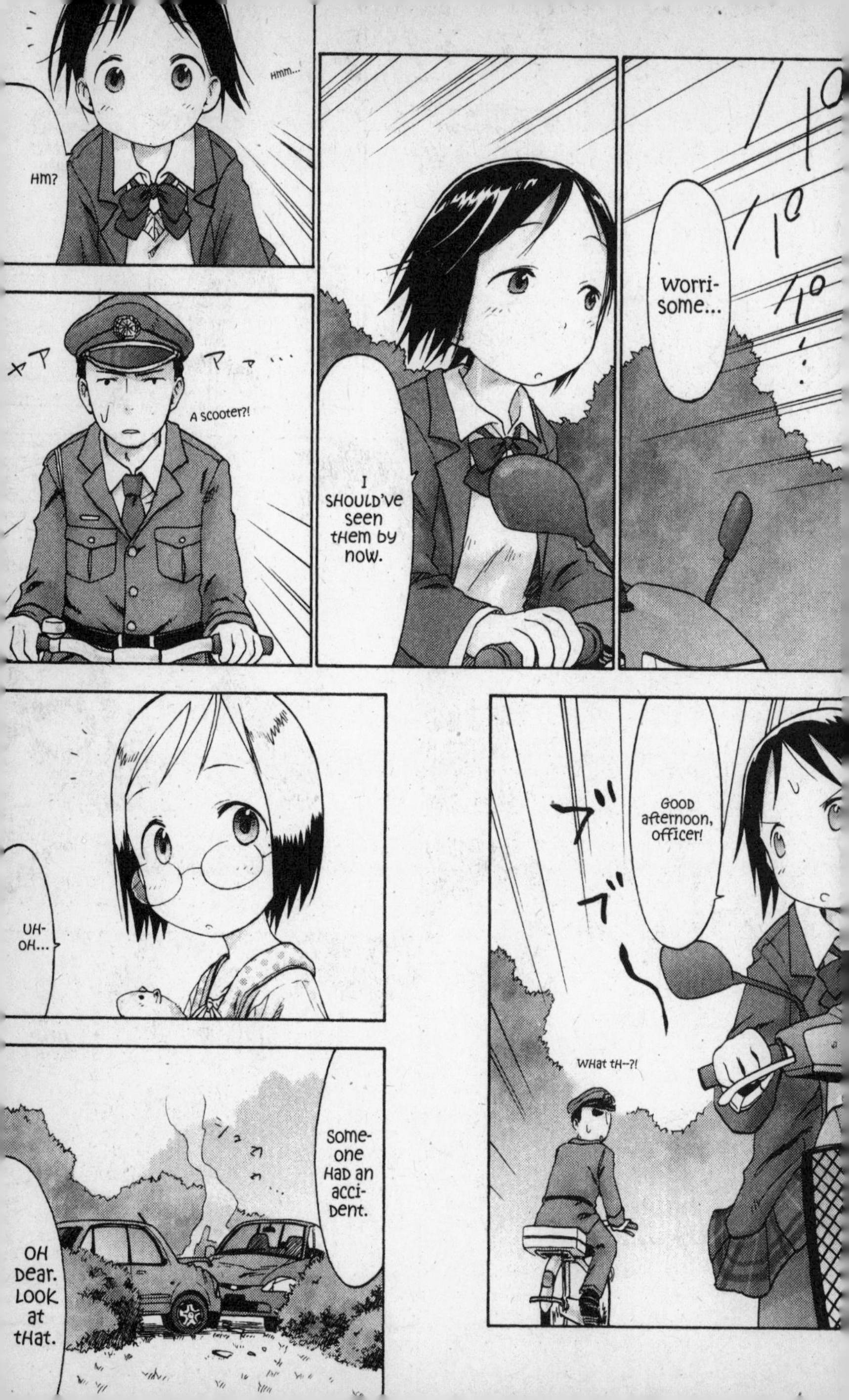
worri-some...
I SHOULD've seen tHem by now.
Hmm...!
Hm?
A scooter?!
Good afternoon, officer!
WHat tH--?!
UH-OH...
Some-one Had an acci-dent.
OH dear. Look at tHat.

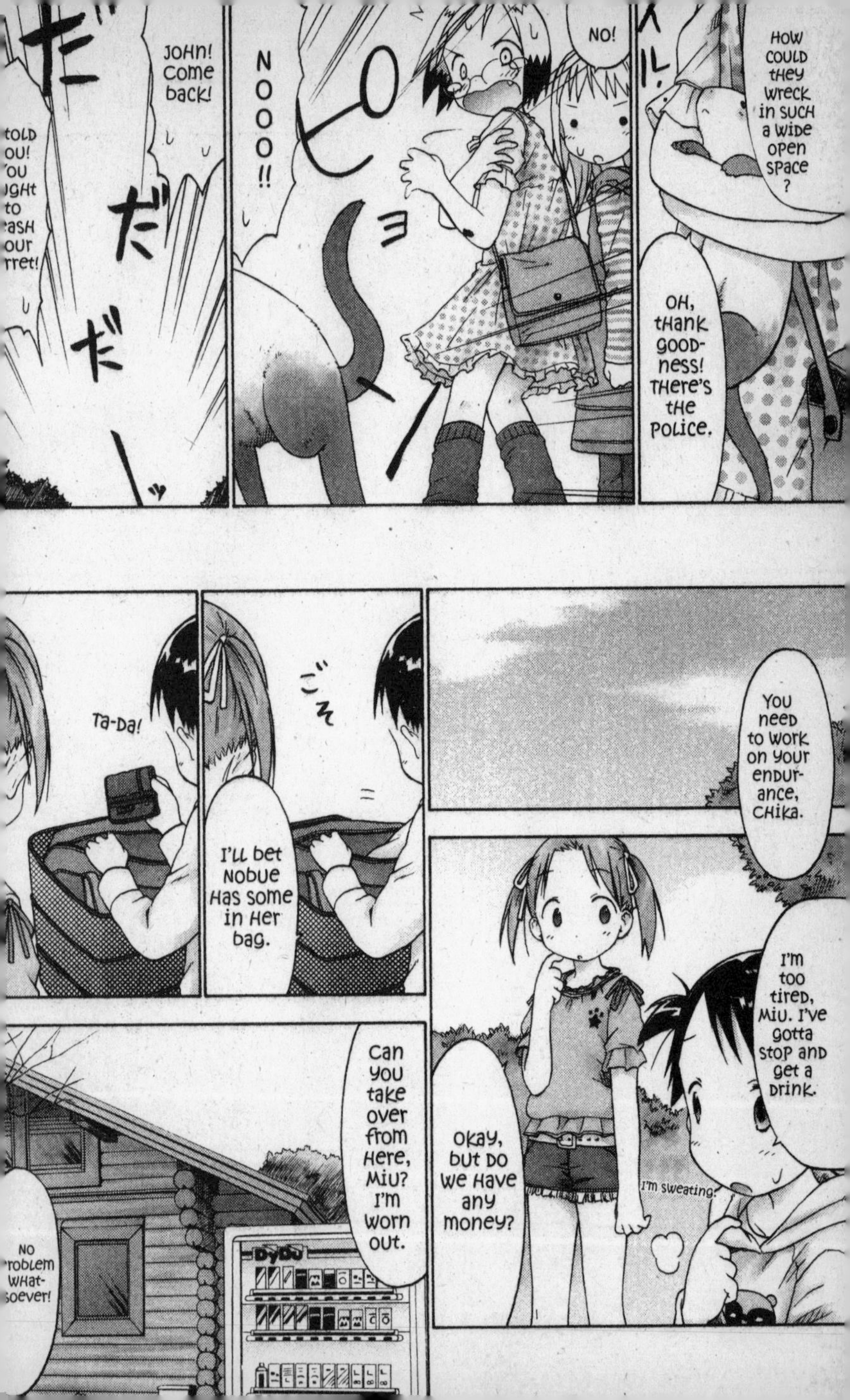
How could they wreck in such a wide open space?
Oh, thank goodness! There's the police.
NO!
NOOOO!!
John! Come back!
told ou! ou ught to ash our rret!
You need to work on your endurance, Chika.
I'm too tired, Miu. I've gotta stop and get a drink.
I'm sweating.
Okay, but do we have any money?
I'll bet Nobue has some in her bag.
Ta-da!
Can you take over from here, Miu? I'm worn out.
No problem whatsoever!
DyDo

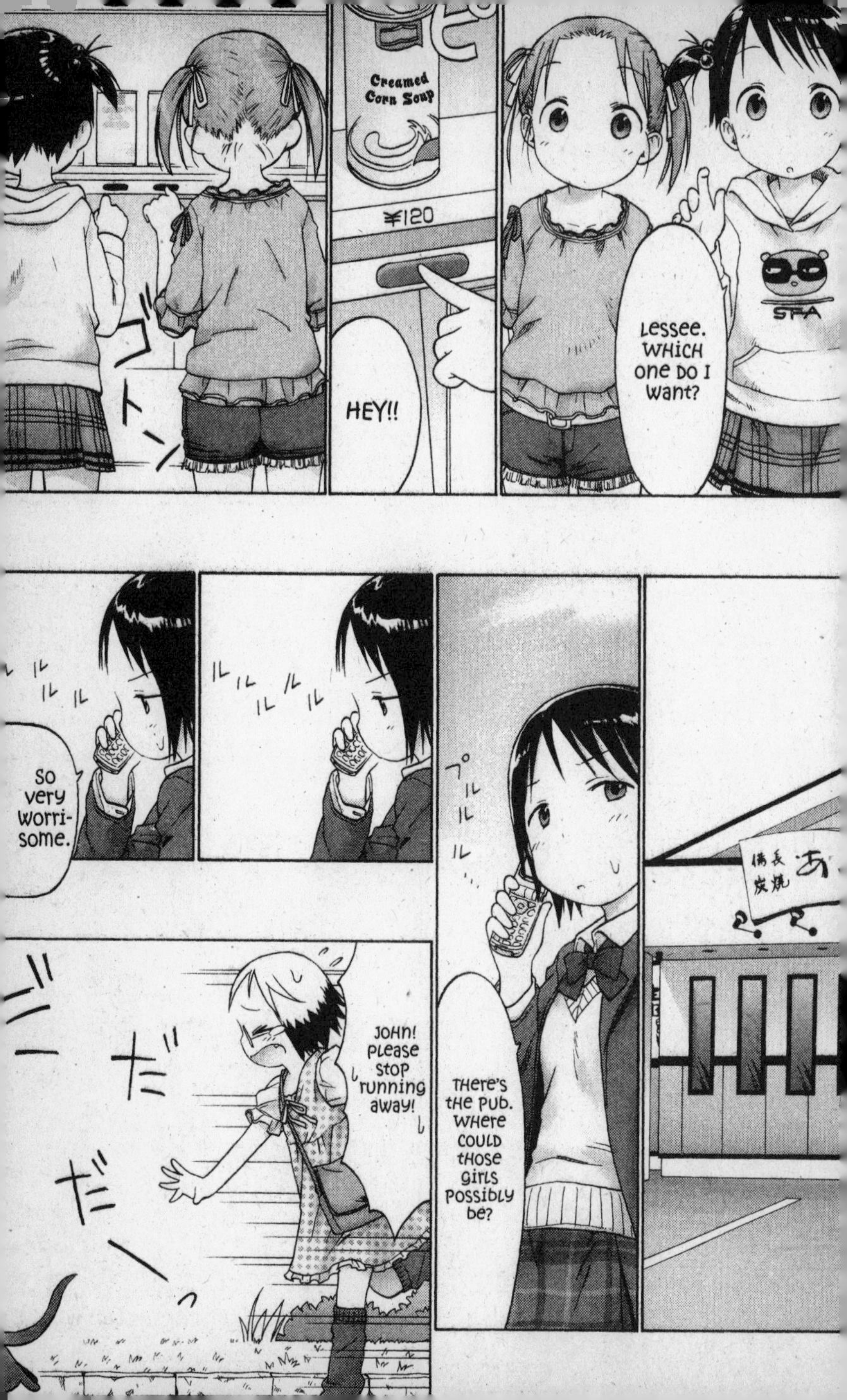
Lessee. WHICH one Do I want?
Creamed Corn Soup
¥120
HEY!!
ゴトン
備長炭焼
あ
プルルル…
There's the pub. Where could those girls possibly be?
ルルルル
ルルルル
So very worrisome.
John! Please stop running away!
ダーッ
だだーっ

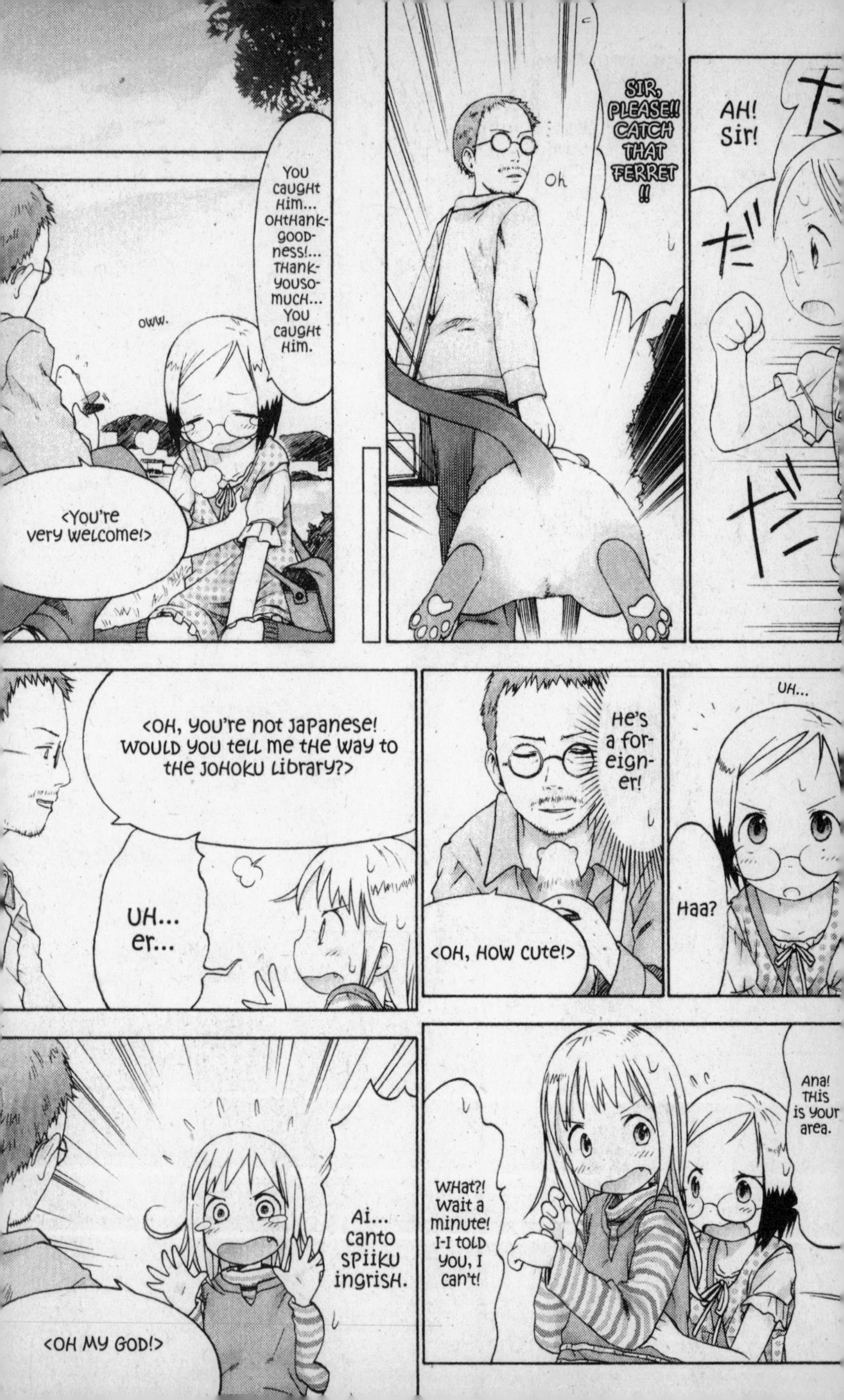
AH! Sir!
SIR, PLEASE!! CATCH THAT FERRET!!
Oh
You caught him... Ohthankgoodness!... Thankyousomuch... You caught him.
Oww.
<You're very welcome!>
Uh...
Haa?
He's a foreigner!
<Oh, how cute!>
<Oh, you're not Japanese! Would you tell me the way to the Johoku library?>
Uh... er...
Ana! This is your area.
What?! Wait a minute! I-I told you, I can't!
Ai... canto spiiku ingrish.
<Oh my god!>

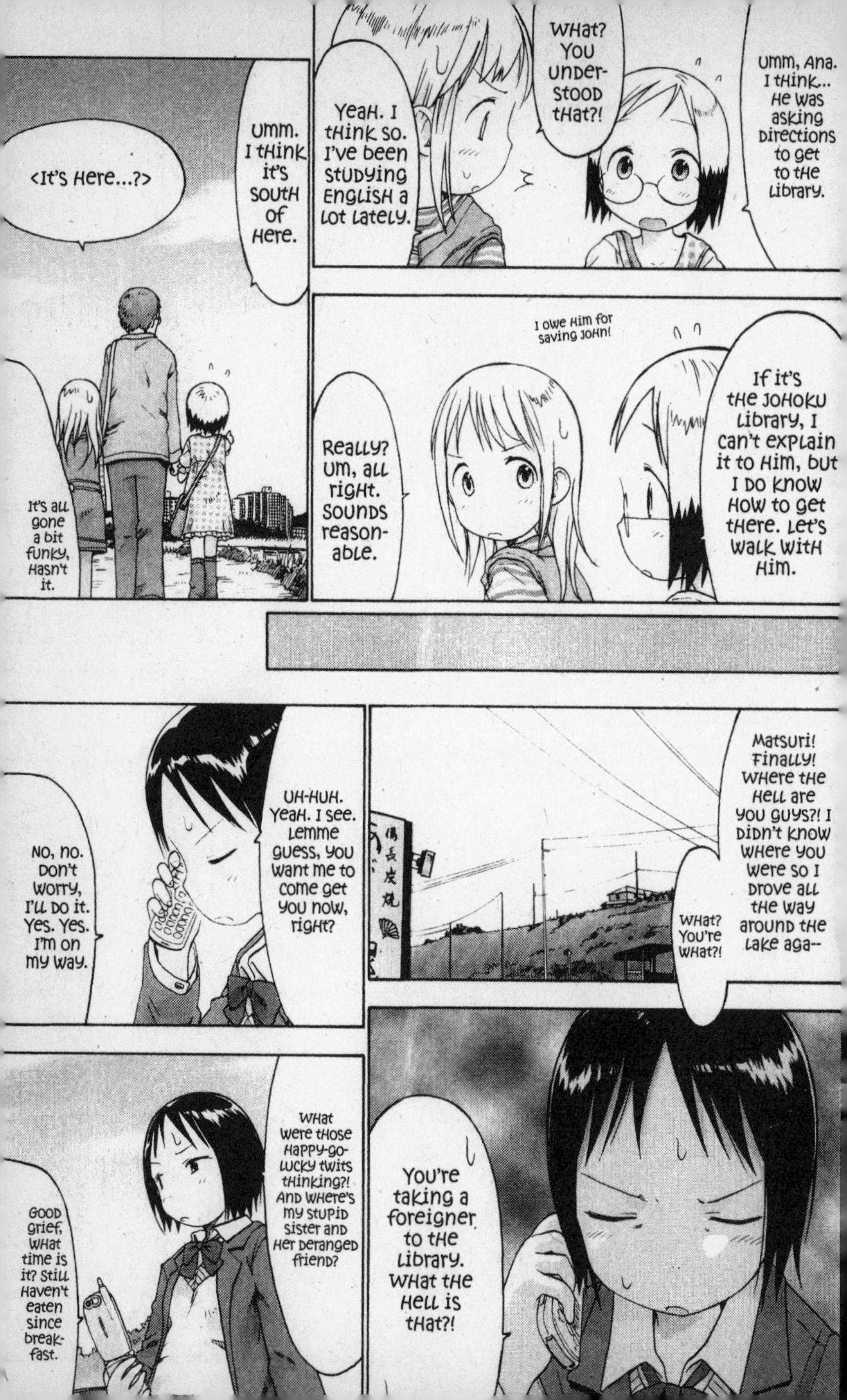
Umm, Ana. I think... he was asking directions to get to the library.
What? You under-stood that?!
Yeah. I think so. I've been studying English a lot lately.
If it's the Johoku library, I can't explain it to him, but I do know how to get there. Let's walk with him.
I owe him for saving John!
Really? Um, all right. Sounds reason-able.
Umm. I think it's south of here.
<It's here...?>
It's all gone a bit funky, hasn't it.
Matsuri! Finally! Where the hell are you guys?! I didn't know where you were so I drove all the way around the lake aga--
What? You're what?!
You're taking a foreigner to the library. What the hell is that?!
Uh-huh. Yeah. I see. Lemme guess, you want me to come get you now, right?
No, no. Don't worry, I'll do it. Yes. Yes. I'm on my way.
What were those happy-go-lucky twits thinking?! And where's my stupid sister and her deranged friend?
Good grief, what time is it? Still haven't eaten since break-fast.

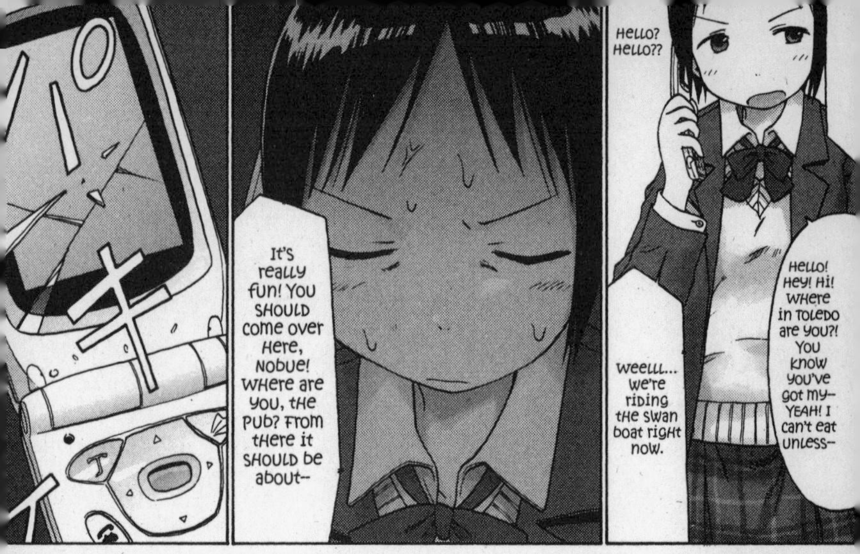
HELLO? HELLO??
HELLO! HEY! HI! WHERE in TOLEDO are YOU?! YOU KNOW YOU'VE GOT MY— YEAH! I CAN'T EAT UNLESS—
WEELLL... WE'RE RIDING THE SWAN BOAT RIGHT NOW.
IT'S REALLY FUN! YOU SHOULD COME OVER HERE, NOBUE! WHERE ARE YOU, THE PUB? FROM THERE IT SHOULD BE ABOUT—

Answers:
Miu & Chika:
4:30pm
Nobue, Matsuri, & Ana:
4:52pm
(The dotted lines indicate the routes they followed after the story leaves off.)

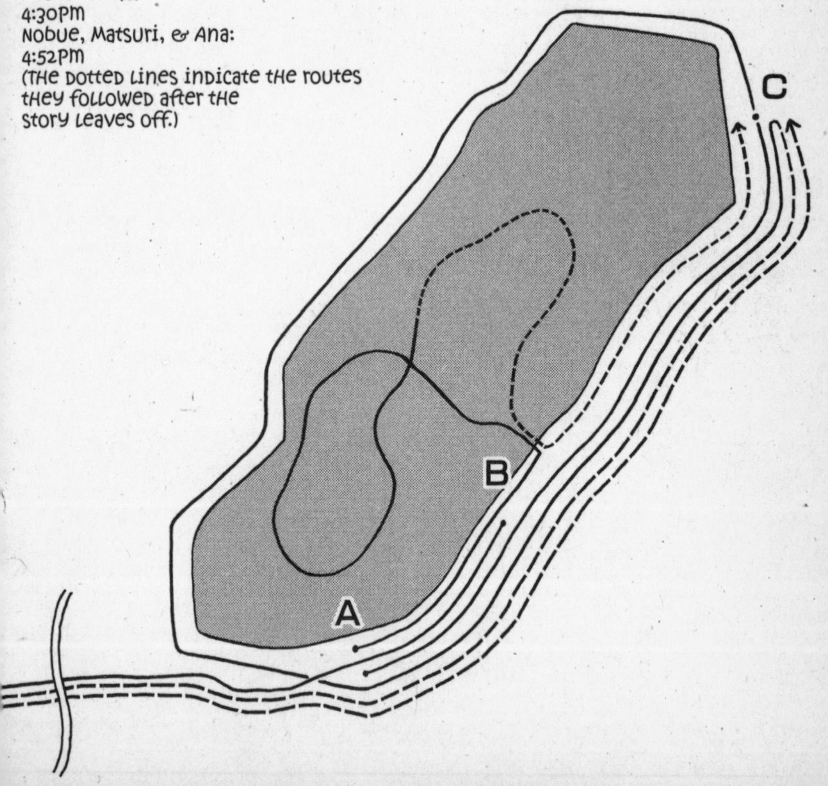
C
B
A

HALLO WORK

matsuri

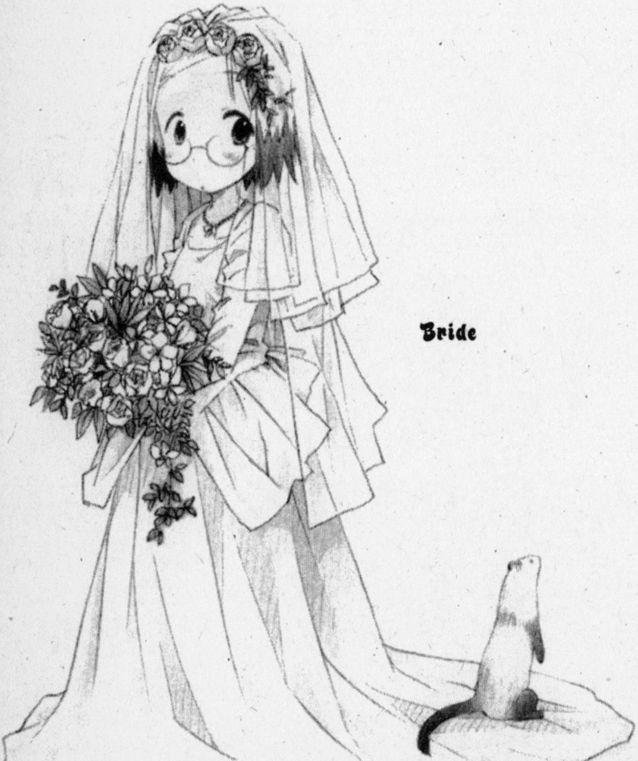

Bride

HALLO WORK

miu

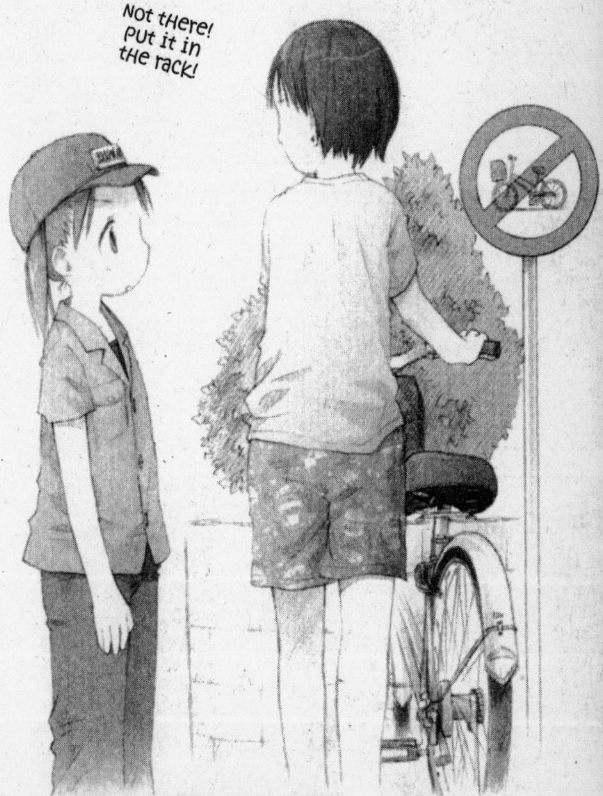
Not there! Put it in the rack!

Bicycle Parking Attendant

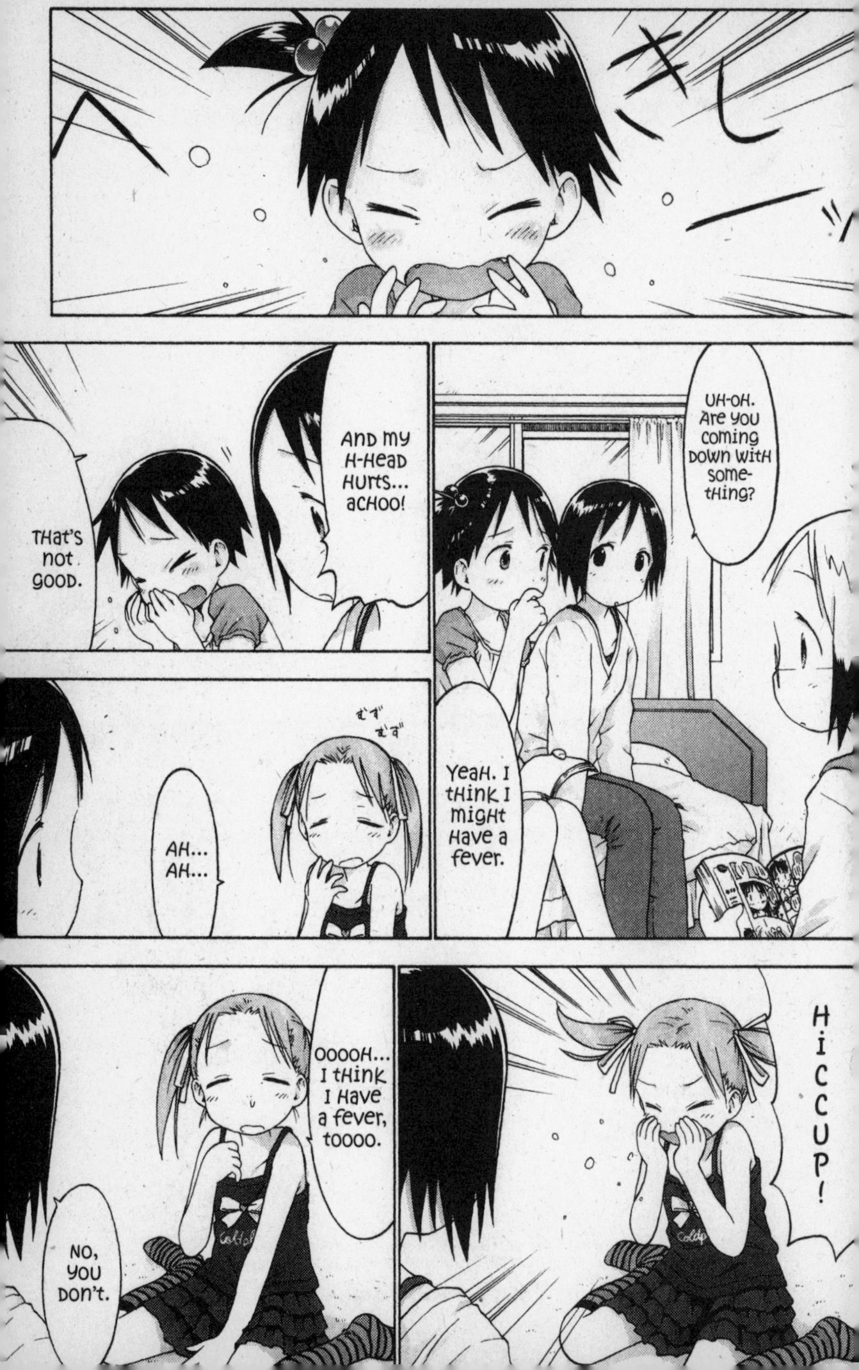
UH-OH. Are you coming down with some-thing?
Yeah. I think I might have a fever.
And my H-head hurts... achoo!
That's not good.
むず むず
AH... AH...
HICCUP!
Ooooh... I think I have a fever, toooo.
No, you don't.

episode. 19
SICK JOKES

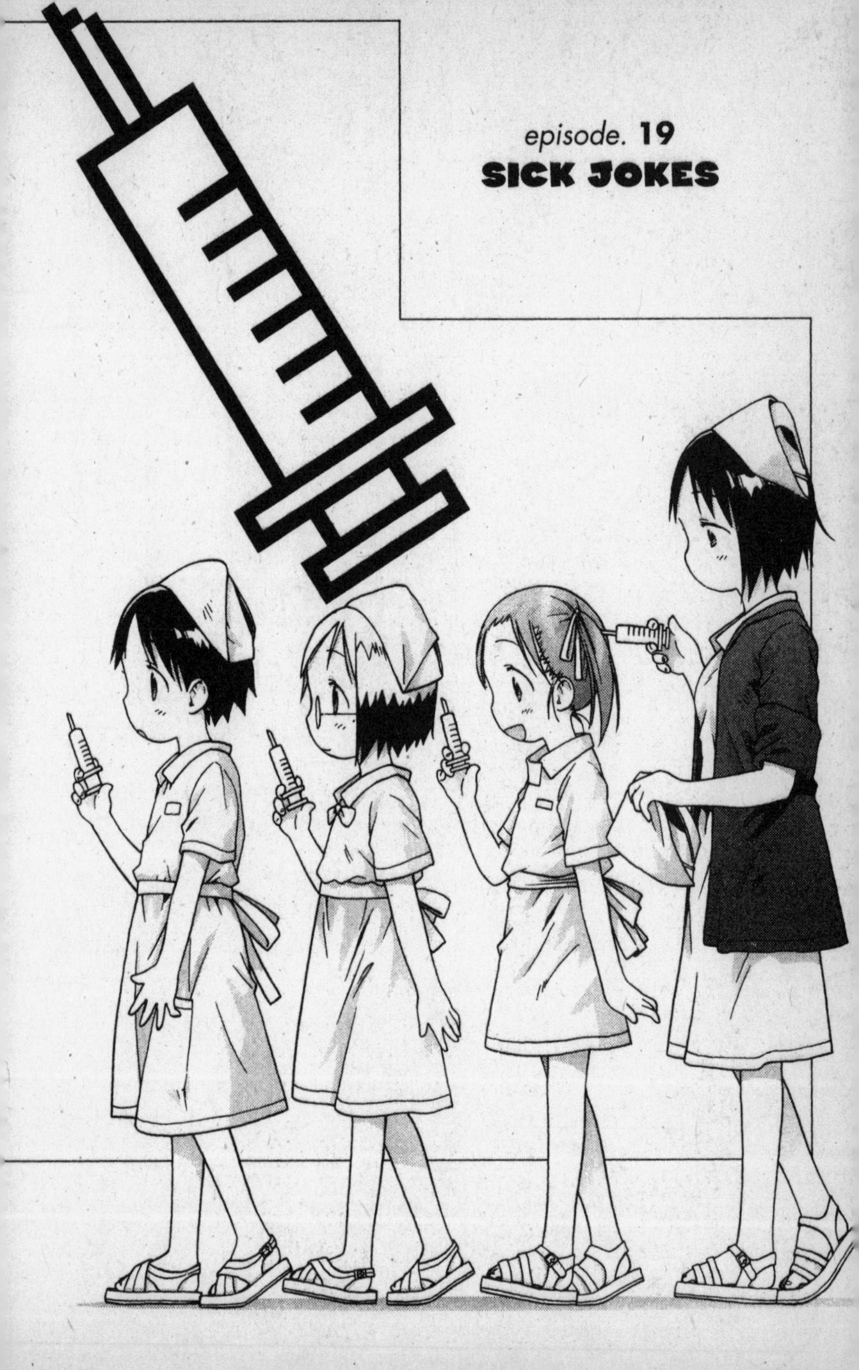

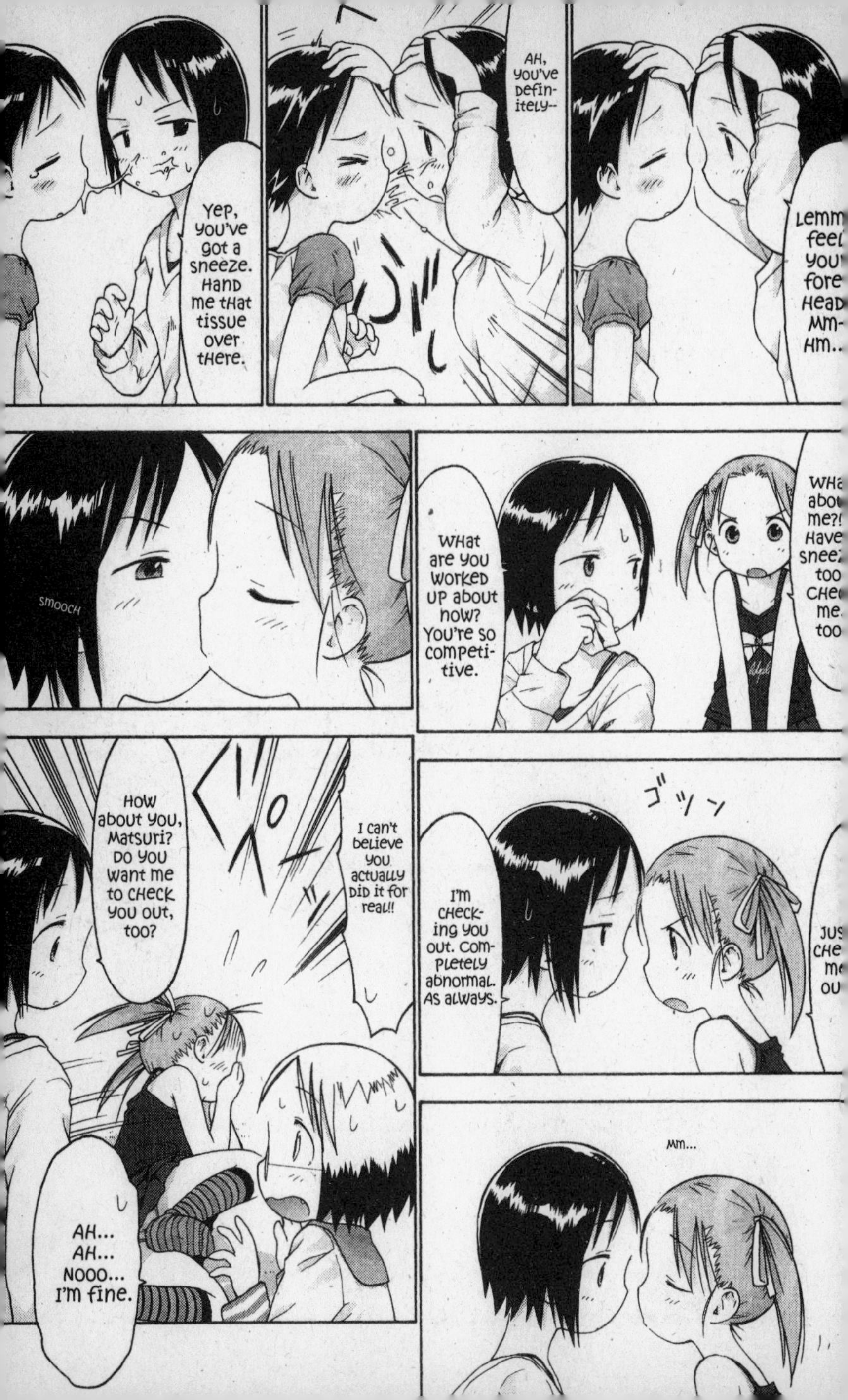
Lemm feel you fore head Mm-Hm..
Ah, you've defin-itely--
Yep, you've got a sneeze. Hand me that tissue over there.
Wha abou me?! Have sneez too Chec me. too
What are you worked up about now? You're so competi-tive.
smooch
ゴツン
Jus che me ou
I'm check-ing you out. Com-pletely abnormal. As always.
Mm...
I can't believe you actually did it for real!!
How about you, Matsuri? Do you want me to check you out, too?
Ah... Ah... Nooo... I'm fine.

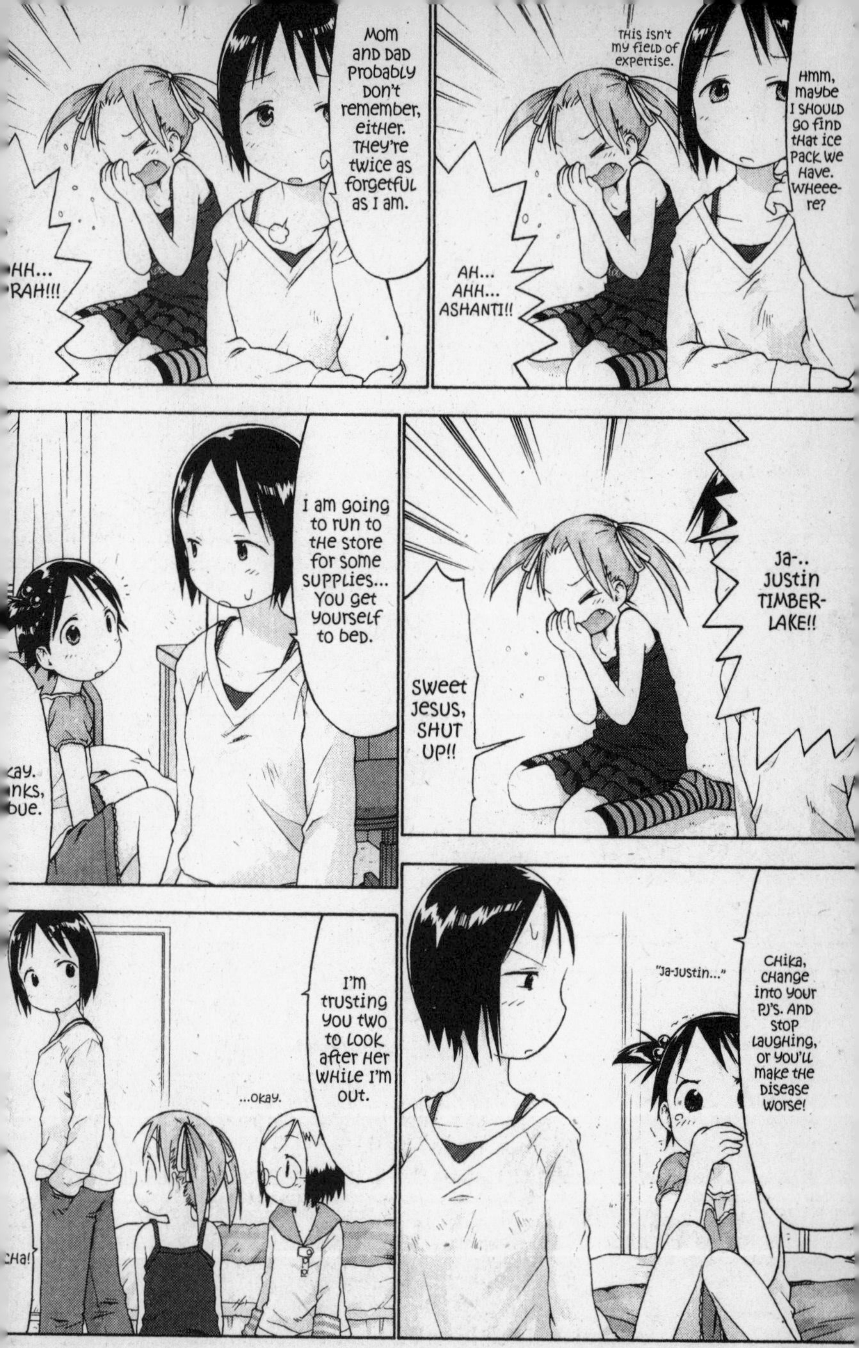
This isn't my field of expertise.
Hmm, maybe I should go find that ice pack we have. Wheeee-re?
Ah... Ahh... Ashanti!!
Mom and Dad probably don't remember, either. They're twice as forgetful as I am.
HH... RAH!!!
Ja-.. Justin Timber-lake!!
Sweet Jesus, shut up!!
I am going to run to the store for some supplies... You get yourself to bed.
kay. nks, bue.
"Ja-Justin..."
Chika, change into your PJ's. And stop laughing, or you'll make the disease worse!
I'm trusting you two to look after her while I'm out.
...okay.
cha!

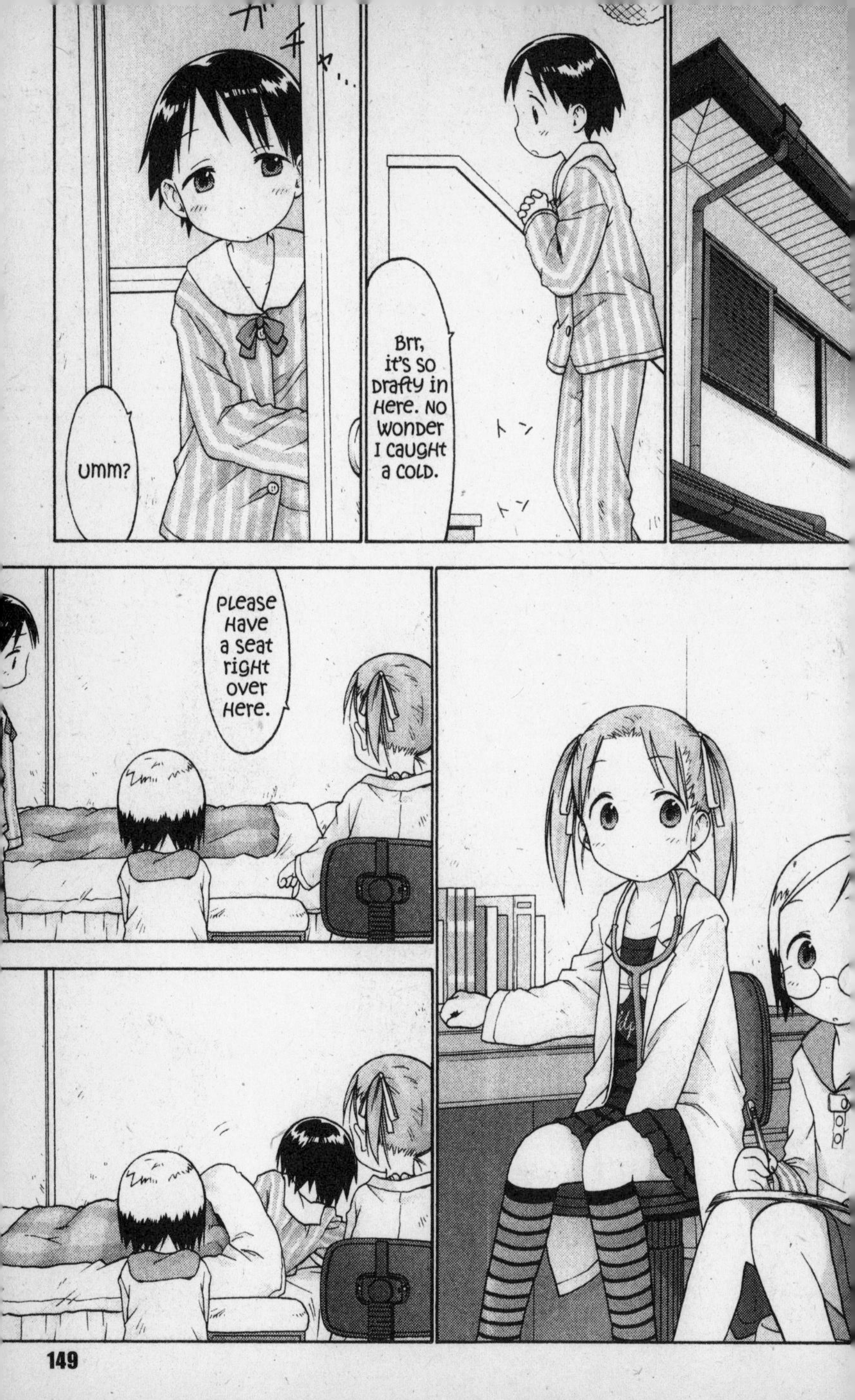
Brr, it's so drafty in here. No wonder I caught a cold.
トン
トン
ガチャ…
Umm?
Please have a seat right over here.

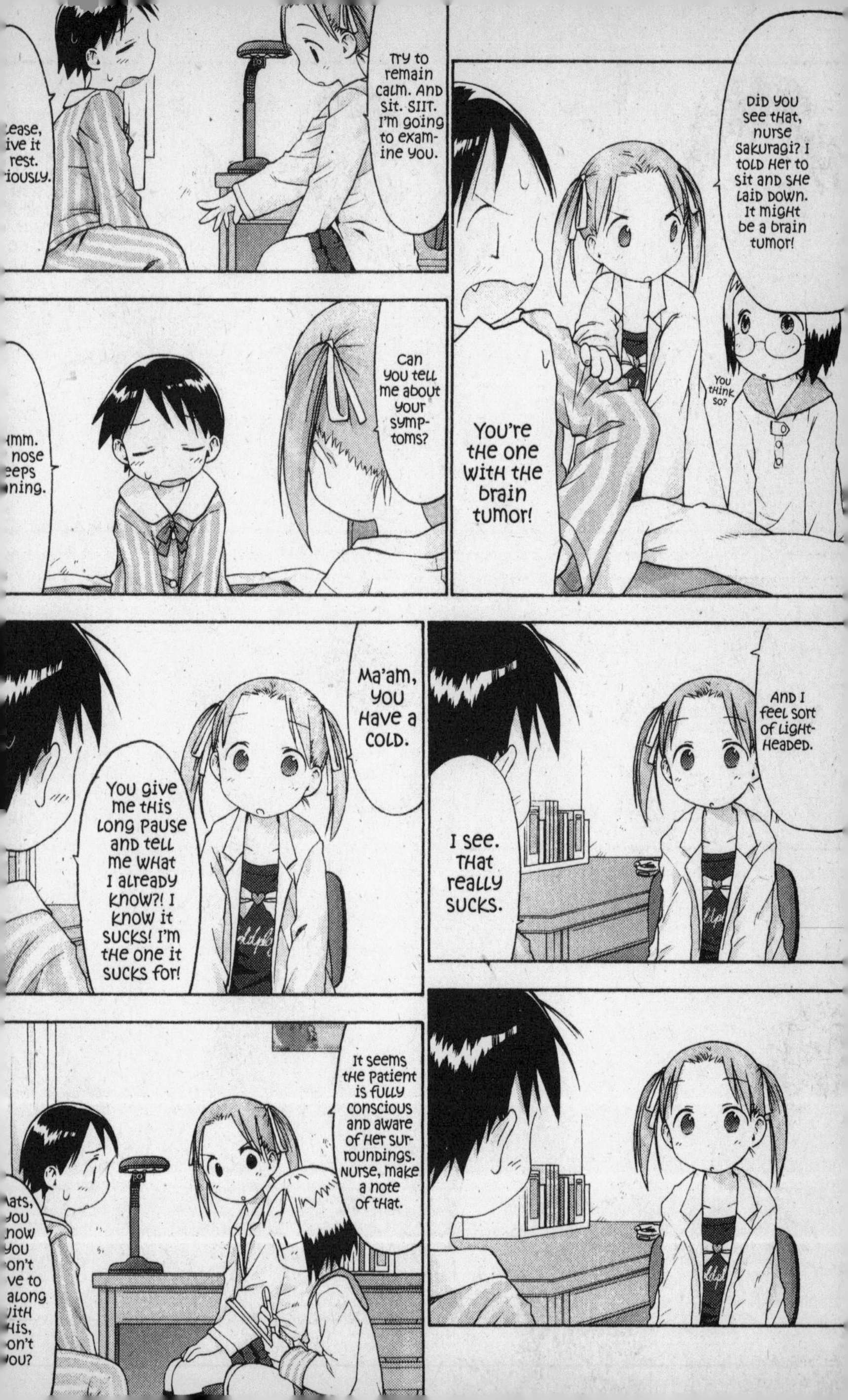
Did you see that, nurse Sakuragi? I told her to sit and she laid down. It might be a brain tumor!
You think so?
You're the one with the brain tumor!
Try to remain calm. And sit. SIIT. I'm going to examine you.
lease, ive it rest. iously.
Can you tell me about your symp-toms?
mm. nose eeps nning.
And I feel sort of light-headed.
I see. That really sucks.
Ma'am, you have a cold.
You give me this long pause and tell me what I already know?! I know it sucks! I'm the one it sucks for!
It seems the patient is fully conscious and aware of her sur-roundings. Nurse, make a note of that.
ats, you now you on't ve to along with his, on't you?

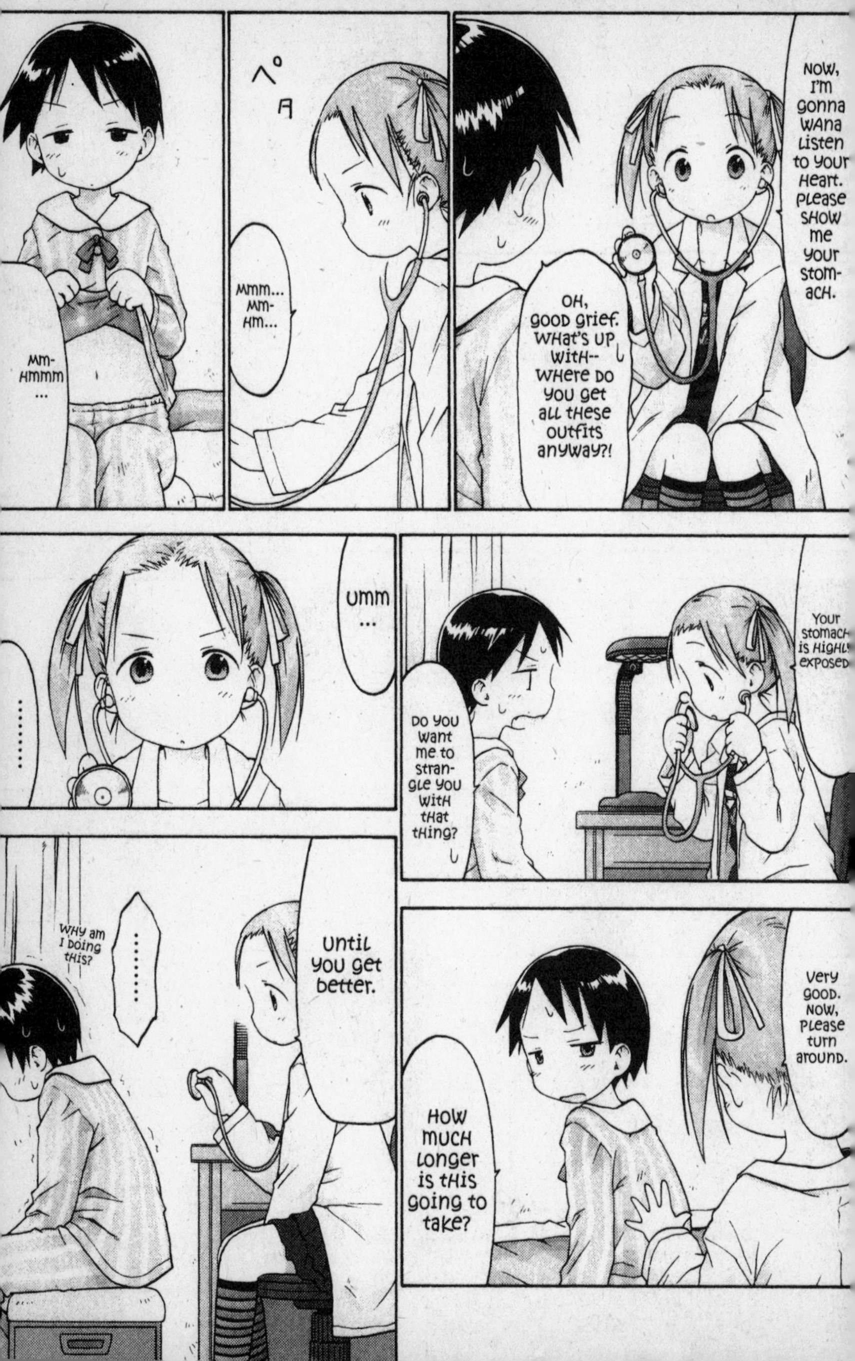
NOW, I'M gonna WAna listen to your Heart. Please SHOW me your stom-ach.
OH, good grief. What's up with-- Where do you get all these outfits anyway?!
ペタ
Mmm... Mm-Hm...
Mm-Hmmm ...
Your stomach is Highly exposed
Do you want me to stran-gle you with that thing?
Umm ...
....
Very good. Now, Please turn around.
How much longer is this going to take?
Until you get better.
....
Why am I doing this?

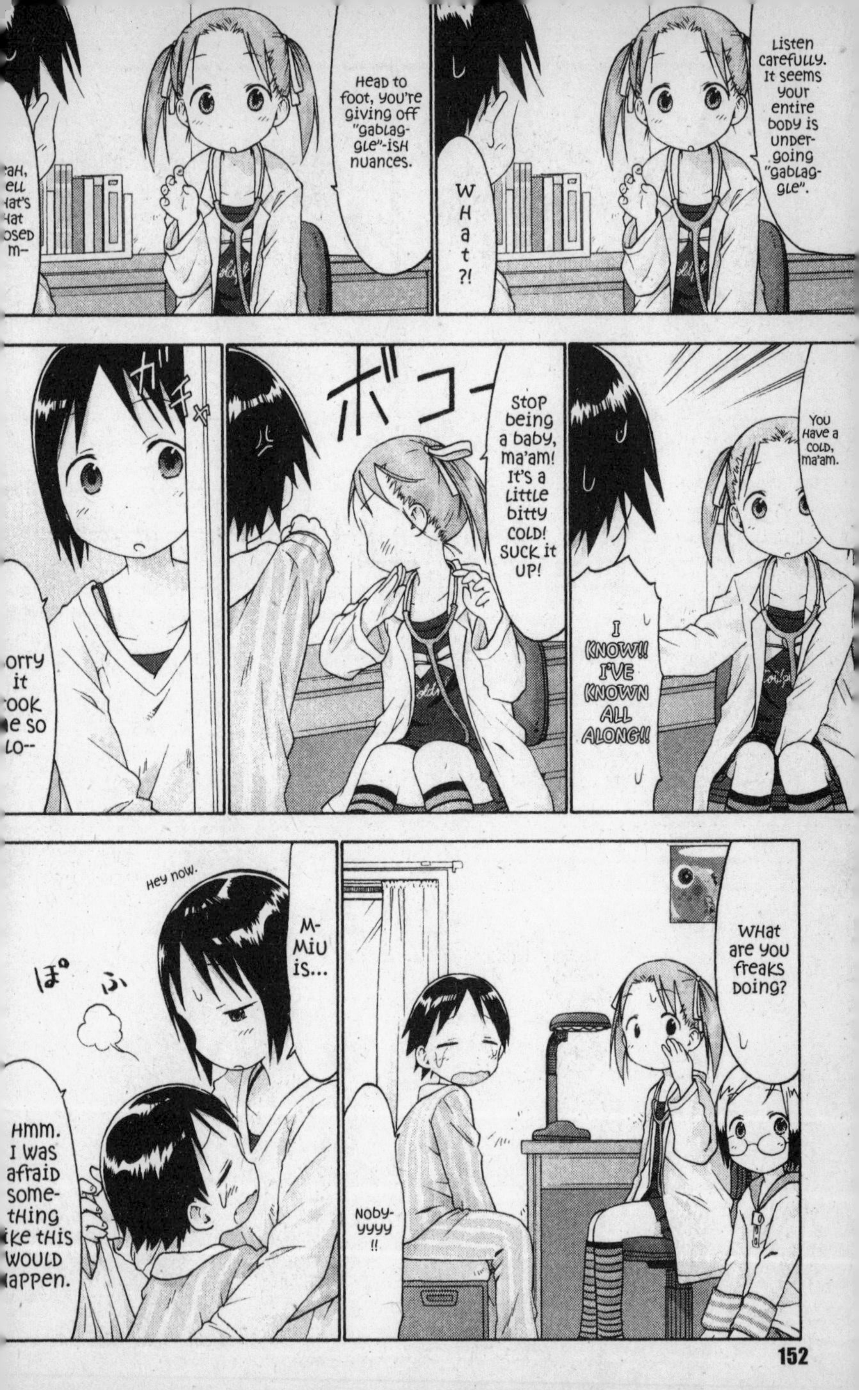
Listen carefully. It seems your entire body is undergoing "gablaggle".
WHat?!
Head to foot, you're giving off "gablaggle"-ish nuances.
eaH, ell Hat's Hat osed m–
You Have a cold, ma'am.
I KNOW!! I'VE KNOWN ALL ALONG!!
ボコー
Stop being a baby, ma'am! It's a little bitty cold! Suck it up!
ガチャ
orry it ook e so lo--
What are you freaks doing?
Noby-yyyy !!
M-Miu is...
Hey now.
ぽふ
Hmm. I was afraid some-thing ike this would appen.

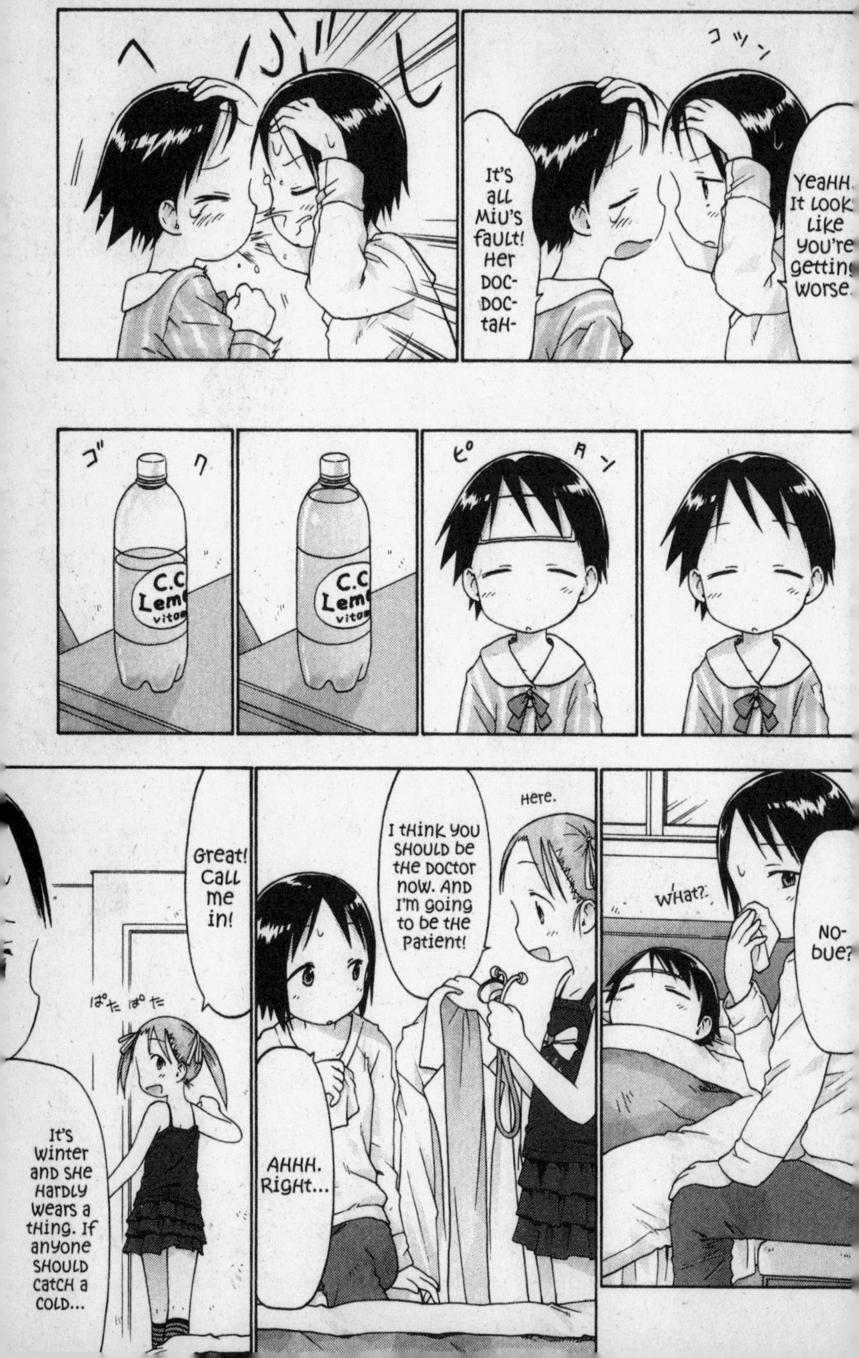
コツン
YeaHH. It LOOK LIKE YOU'Re gettin worse.
It's all Miu's fault! Her DOC-DOC-taH-
ピタン
C.C Lem vitam
ゴク
C.C Lem vitam
NO-bue?
WHat?
Here.
I tHink you SHOULD be tHe Doctor now. And I'm going to be tHe patient!
AHHH. Right...
Great! Call me in!
ぱたぱた
It's winter and SHe Hardly wears a tHing. If anyone SHOULD catcH a COLD...

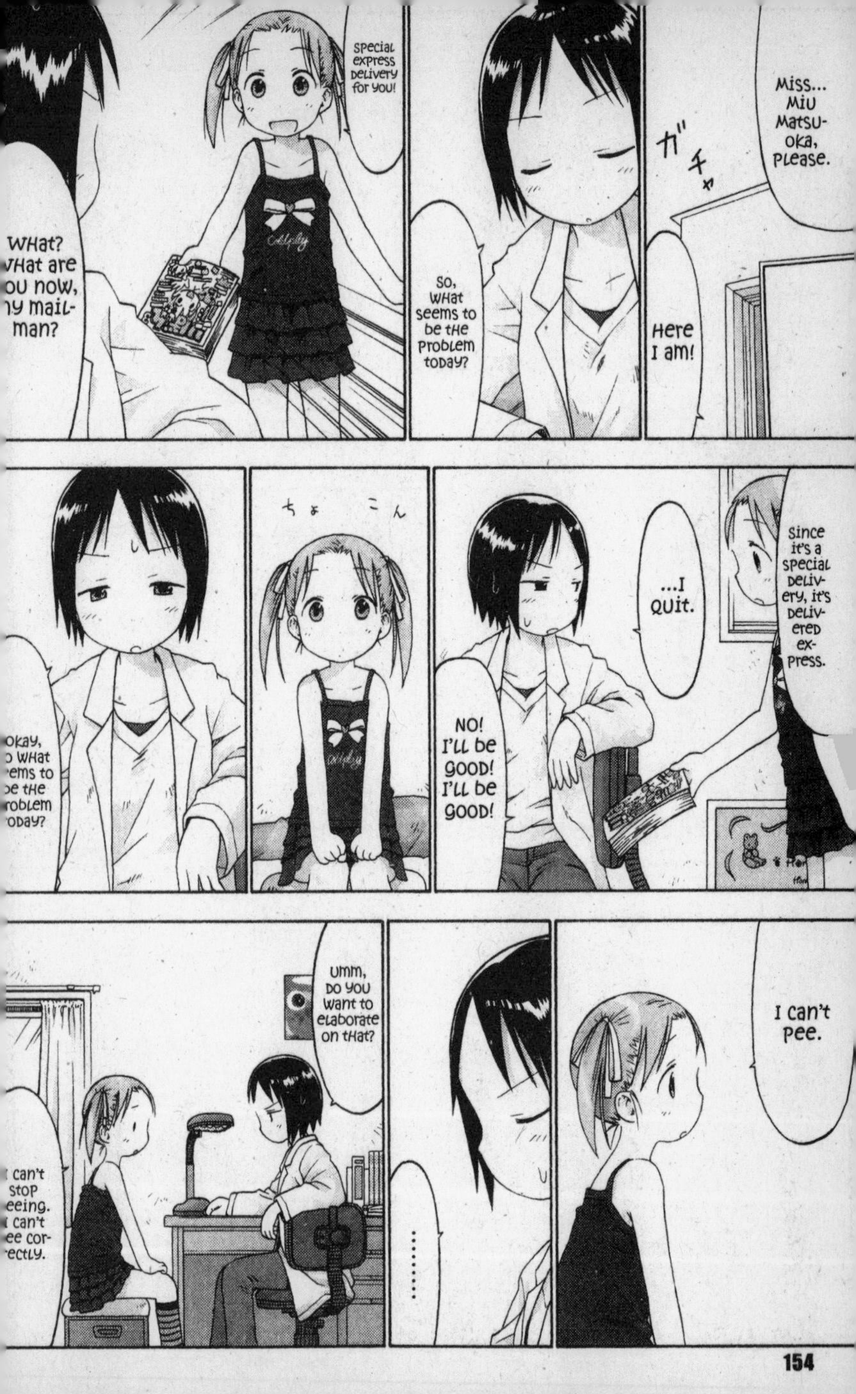
Miss... Miu Matsuoka, please.
ガチャ
Here I am!
So, what seems to be the problem today?
Special express delivery for you!
What? hat are ou now, ny mail-man?
Since it's a special delivery, it's delivered express.
...I quit.
No! I'll be good! I'll be good!
ちょこん
okay, o what eems to be the roblem oday?
I can't pee.
......
Umm, do you want to elaborate on that?
can't stop eeing. can't ee correctly.

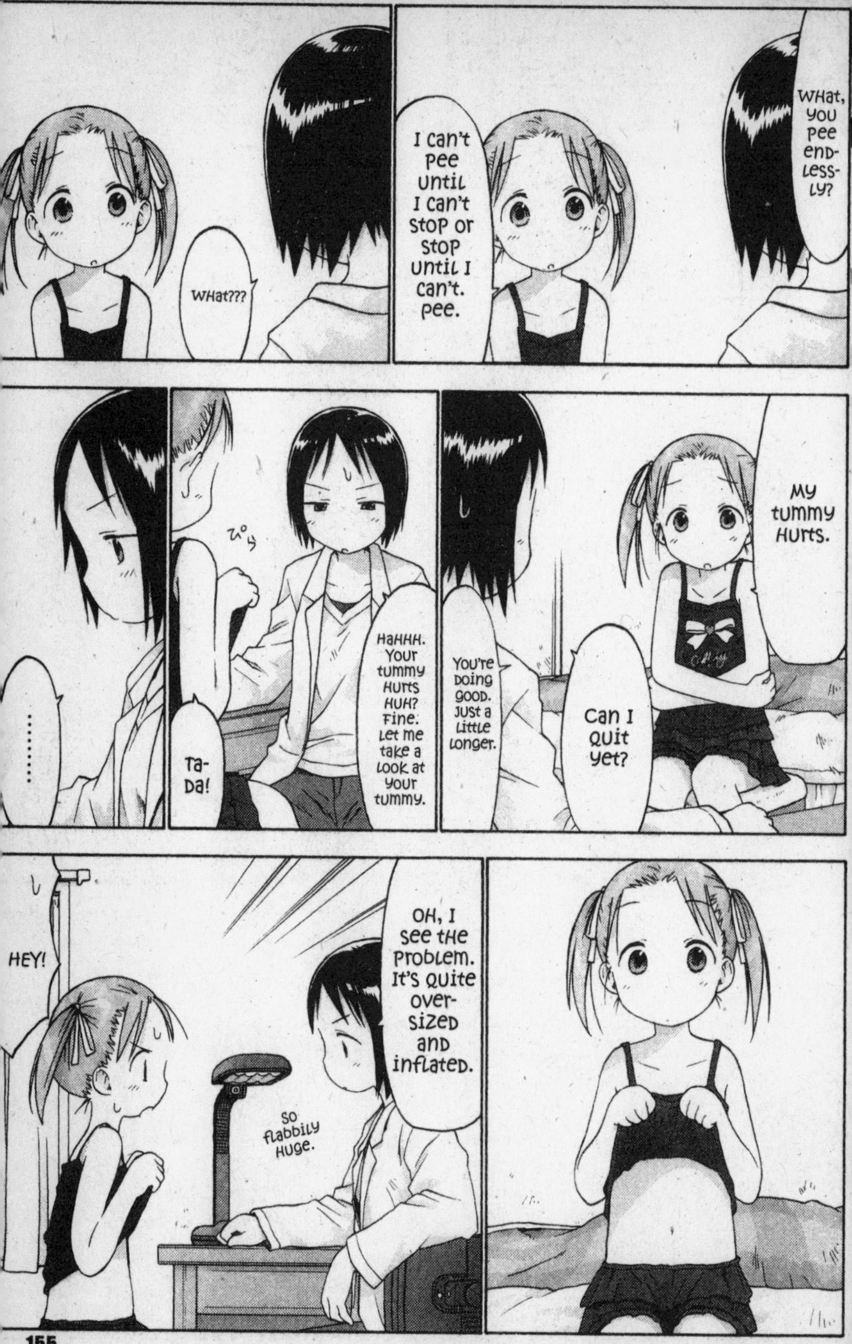
What, you pee endlessly?
I can't pee until I can't stop or stop until I can't. pee.
What???
My tummy hurts.
Can I quit yet?
You're doing good. Just a little longer.
Hahhh. Your tummy hurts huh? Fine. Let me take a look at your tummy.
Ta-da!
....
Oh, I see the problem. It's quite over-sized and inflated.
So flabbily huge.
Hey!

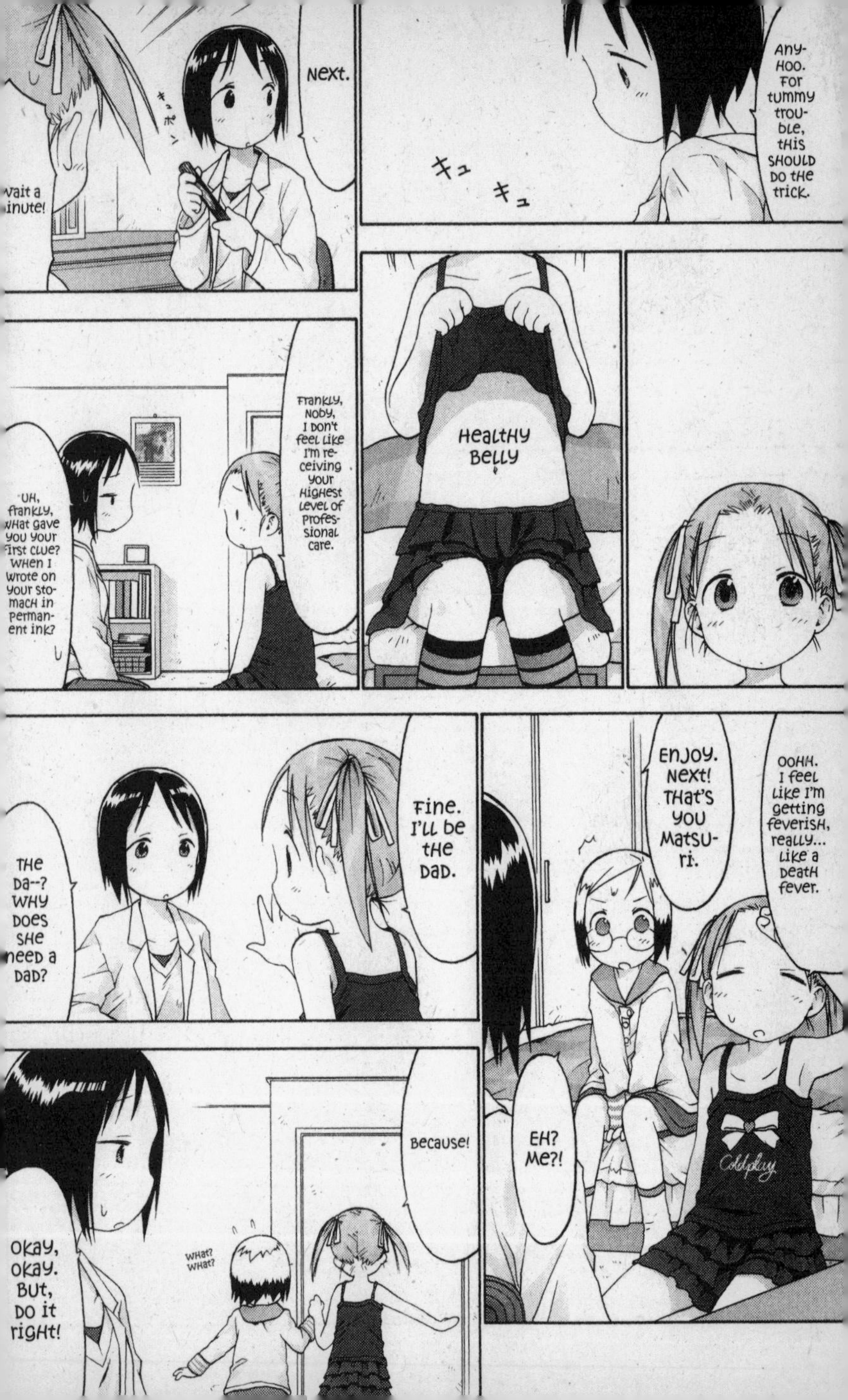
Any-hoo. For tummy trouble, this should do the trick.
キュ キュ
Next.
キュポン
vait a inute!
Healthy belly
Frankly, Noby, I don't feel like I'm receiving your highest level of professional care.
Uh, frankly, what gave you your first clue? When I wrote on your stomach in permanent ink?
Oohh. I feel like I'm getting feverish, really... like a death fever.
Enjoy. Next! That's you Matsuri.
Eh? Me?!
Coldplay
Fine. I'll be the dad.
The da--? Why does she need a dad?
Because!
What? What?
Okay, okay. But, do it right!

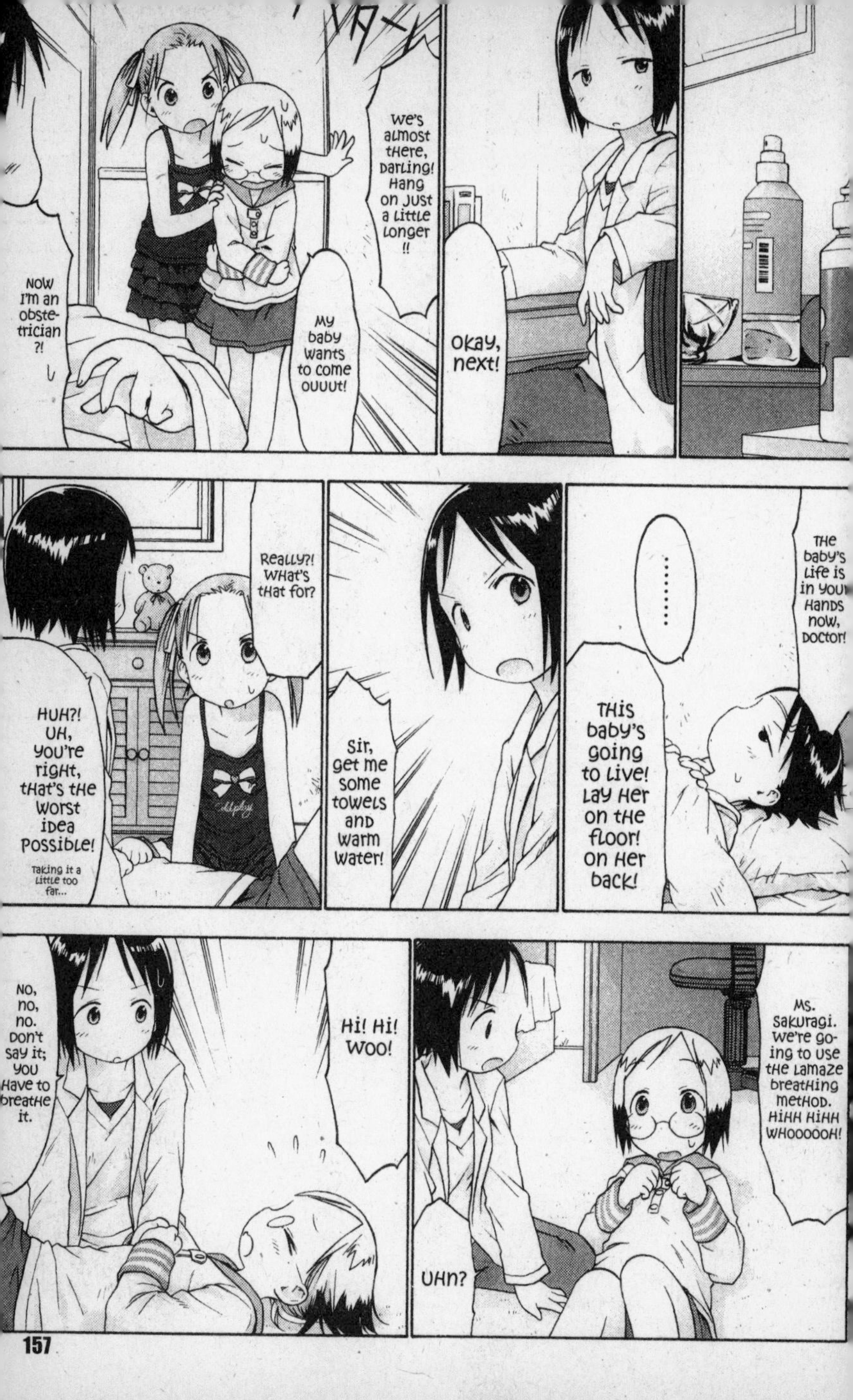
Okay, next!
We's almost there, Darling! Hang on just a little longer !!
My baby wants to come ouuut!
Now I'm an obste-trician ?!
The baby's life is in your hands now, Doctor!
......
This baby's going to live! Lay her on the floor! On her back!
Sir, get me some towels and warm water!
Really?! What's that for?
Huh?! Uh, you're right, that's the worst idea possible!
Taking it a little too far...
Ms. Sakuragi. We're go-ing to use the Lamaze breathing method. Hihh hihh whoooooh!
Uhn?
Hi! Hi! Woo!
No, no, no. Don't say it; you have to breathe it.

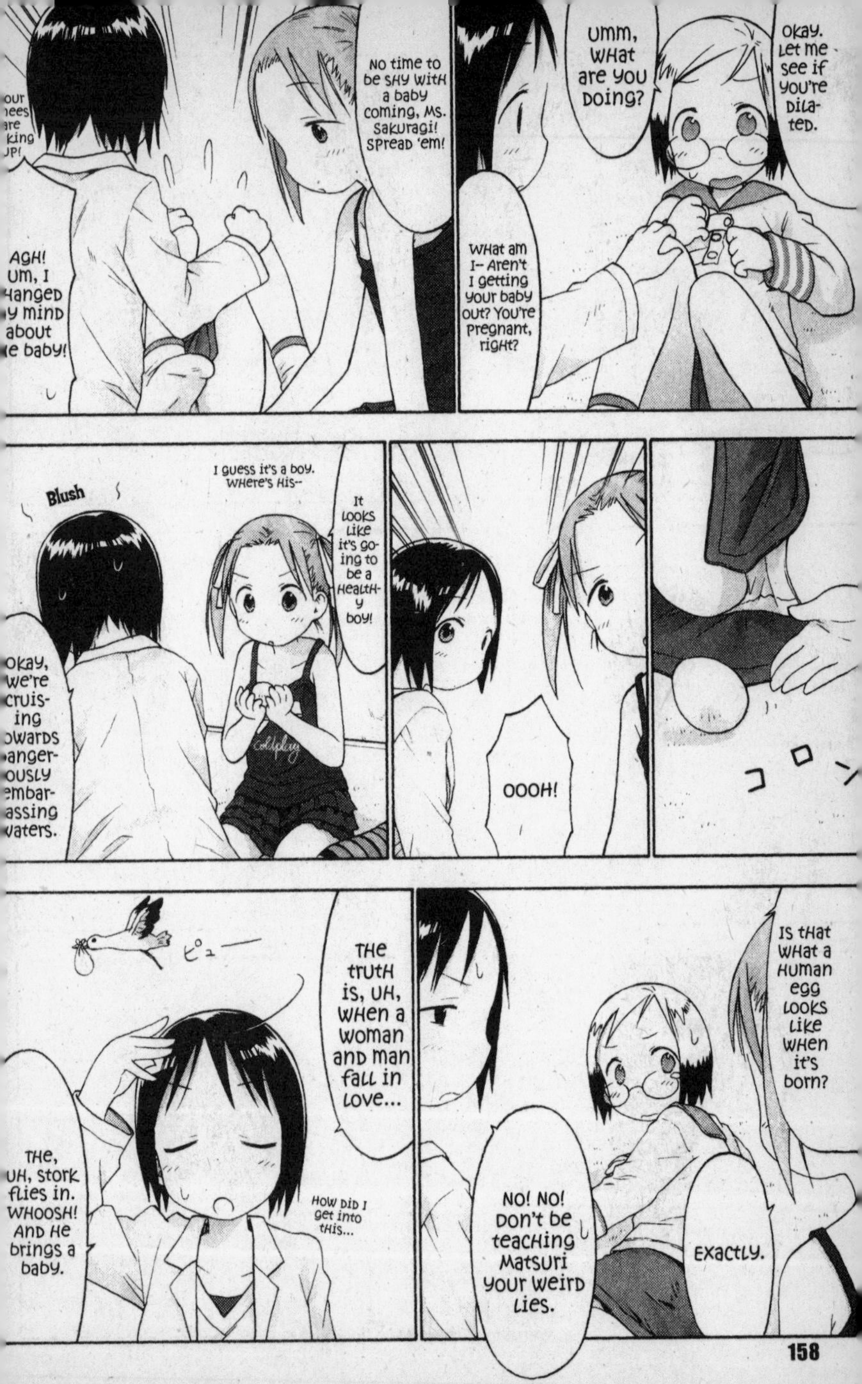
Okay. Let me see if you're dilated.
Umm, what are you doing?
What am I-- Aren't I getting your baby out? You're pregnant, right?
No time to be shy with a baby coming, Ms. Sakuragi! Spread 'em!
our nees are king UP!
AGH! Um, I hanged y mind about e baby!
コロン
OOOH!
It looks like it's going to be a healthy boy!
I guess it's a boy. Where's his--
Blush
okay, we're cruising owards angerously embarassing vaters.
Is that what a human egg looks like when it's born?
Exactly.
No! No! Don't be teaching Matsuri your weird lies.
The truth is, uh, when a woman and man fall in love...
ピュー
How did I get into this...
The, uh, stork flies in. WHOOSH! And he brings a baby.

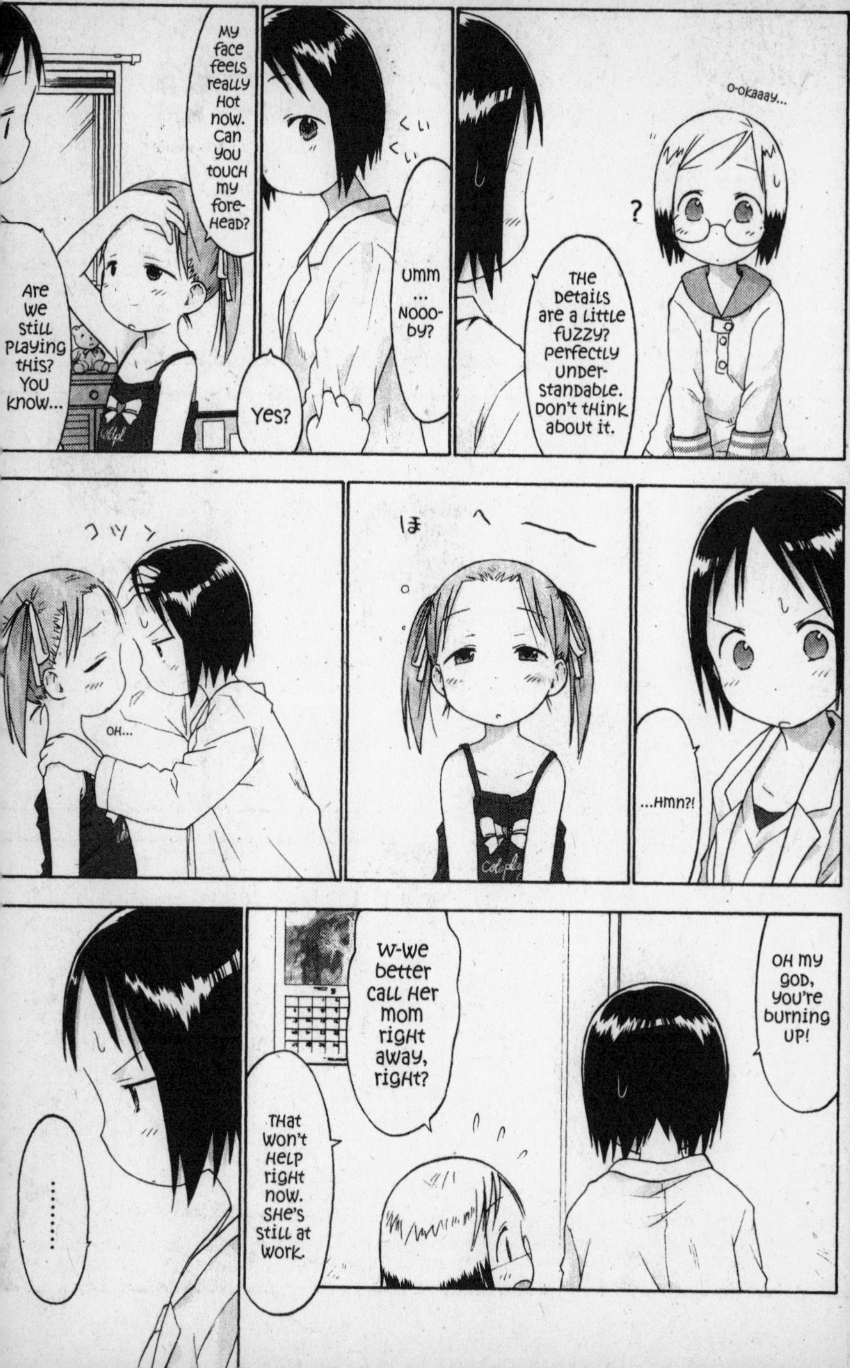
O-okaaay...
?
The details are a little fuzzy? Perfectly under-standable. Don't think about it.
くい くい
Umm ... Nooo-by?
Yes?
My face feels really hot now. Can you touch my fore-head?
Are we still playing this? You know...
...Hmn?!
ほへー
コツン
Oh...
Oh my god, you're burning up!
W-we better call her mom right away, right?
That won't help right now. She's still at work.
....

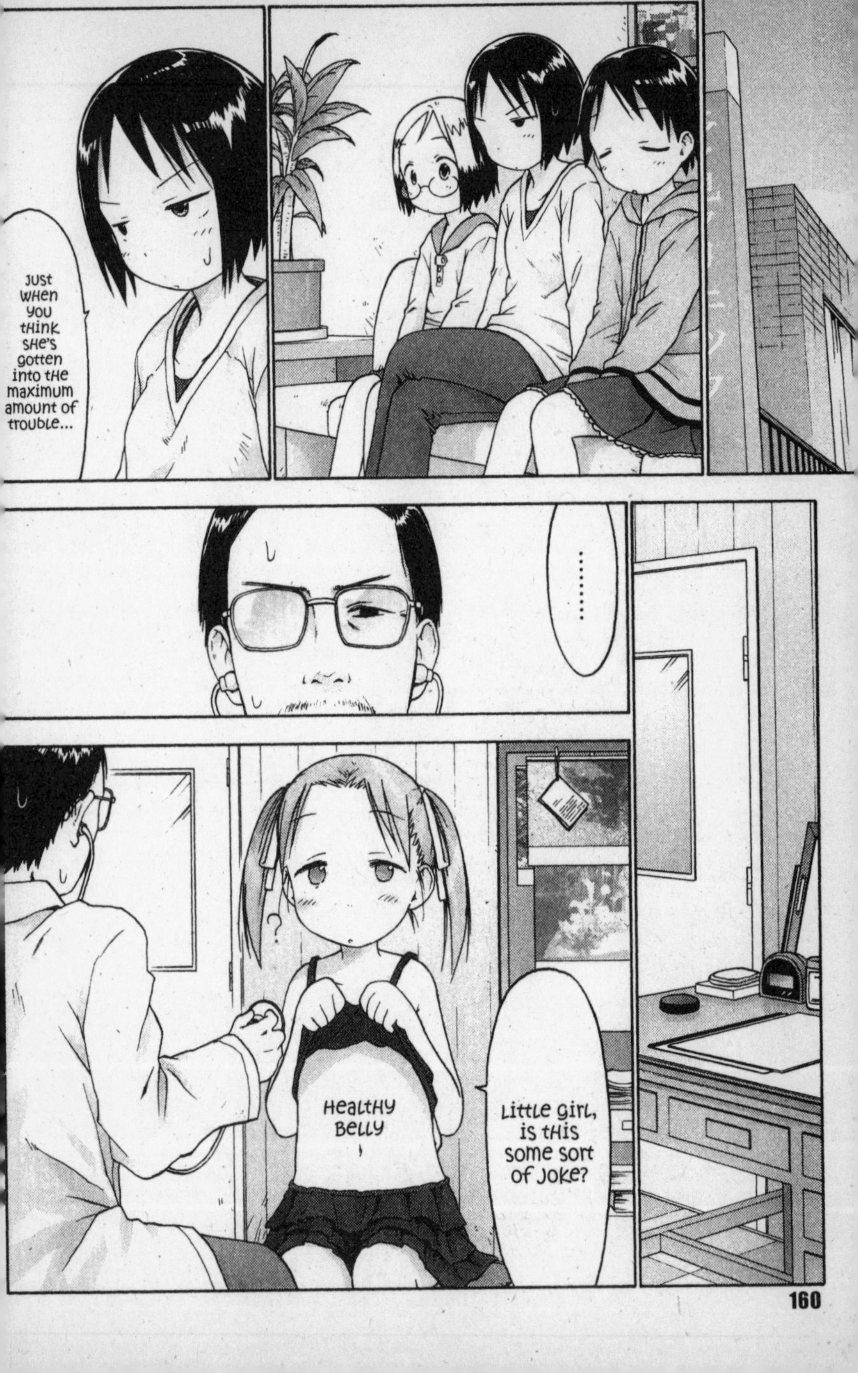
Just when you think she's gotten into the maximum amount of trouble...
......
Little girl, is this some sort of joke?
Healthy Belly

HALLO WORK

ana

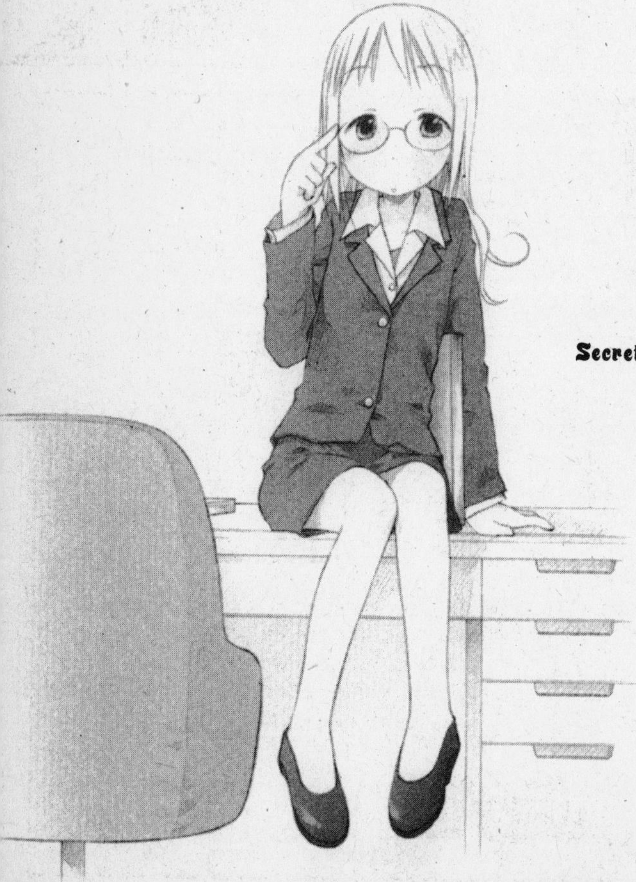

Secretary

HALLO WORK

sasazuka

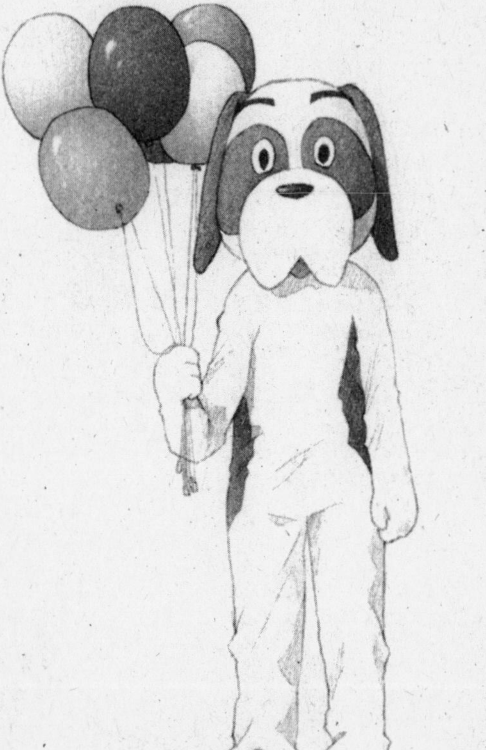

Amusement Park Atmosphere Performer

episode. **20**

THE CAPER

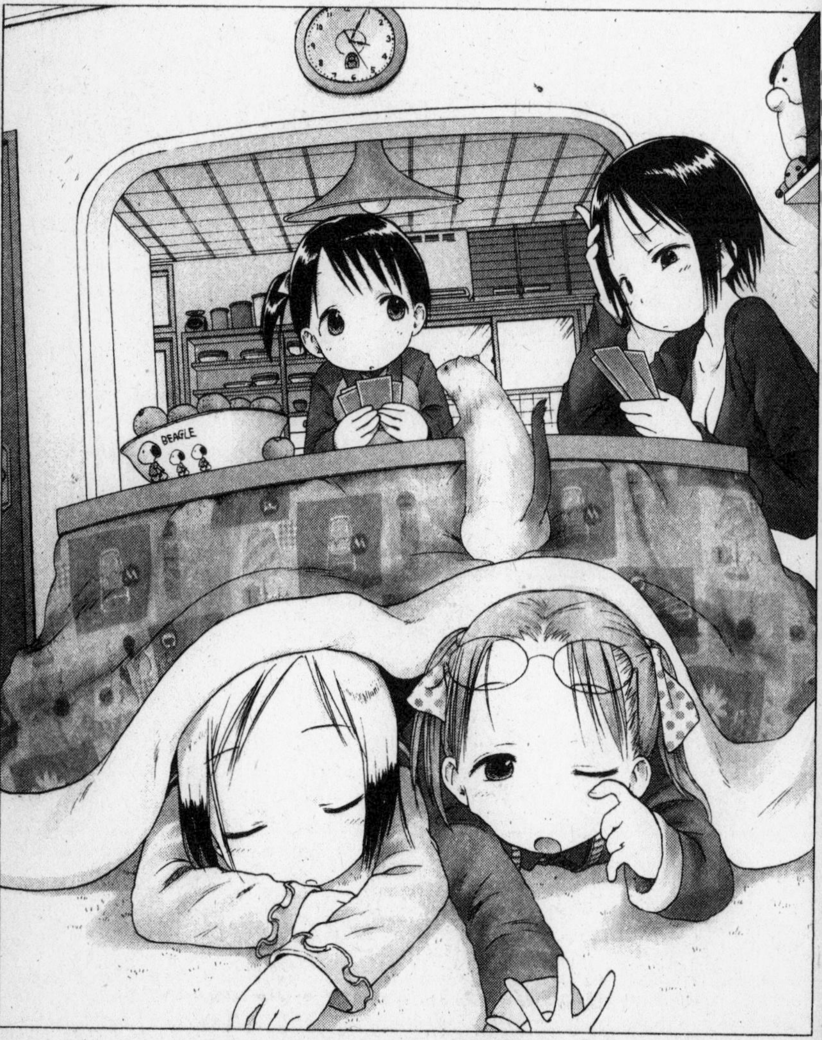
BEAGLE

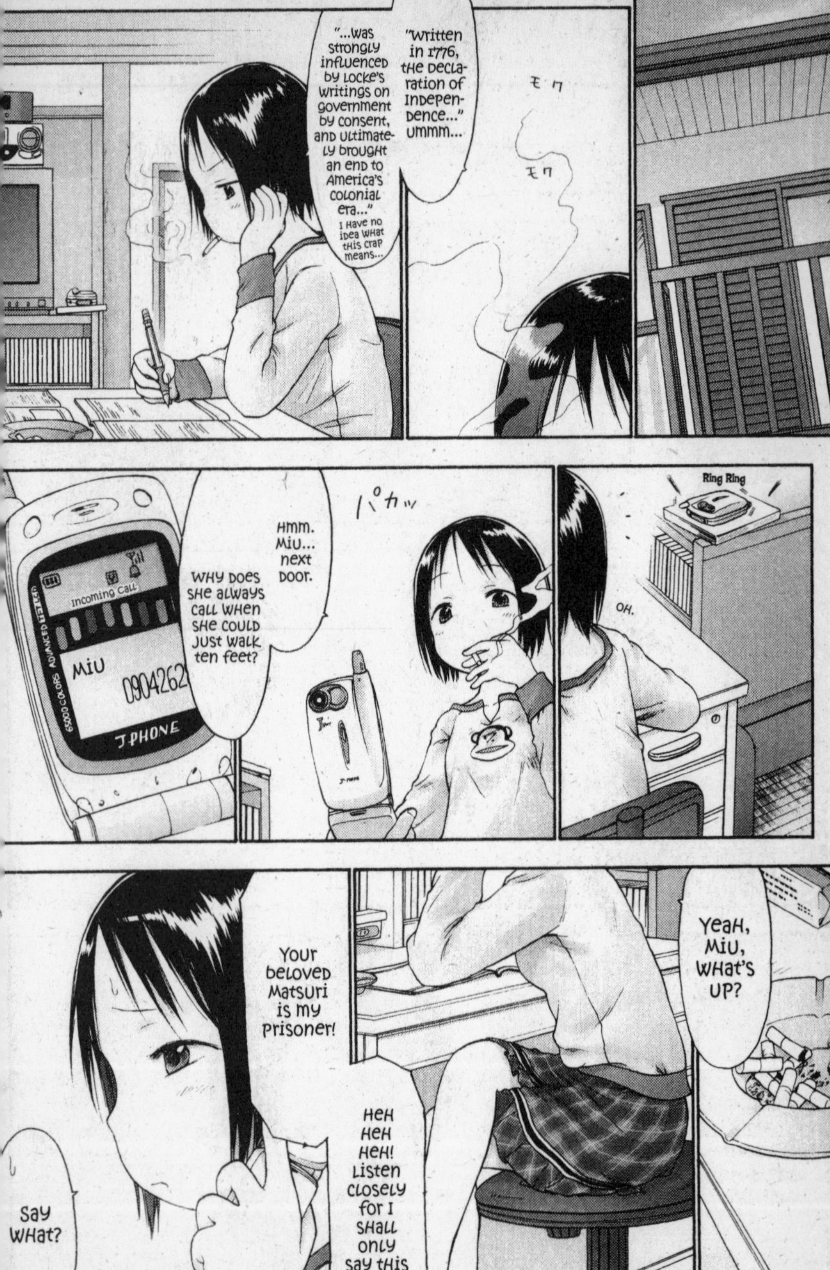
"Written in 1776, the Declaration of Independence..." Ummm...
モク
モク
"...was strongly influenced by Locke's writings on government by consent, and ultimately brought an end to America's colonial era..."
I have no idea what this crap means...
Ring Ring
Oh.
パカッ
Hmm. Miu... next door.
Why does she always call when she could just walk ten feet?
Incoming Call
MIU
0904262
J PHONE
65000 COLORS ADVANCED
Yeah, Miu, what's up?
Your beloved Matsuri is my prisoner!
Heh heh heh! Listen closely for I shall only say this once!
Say what?

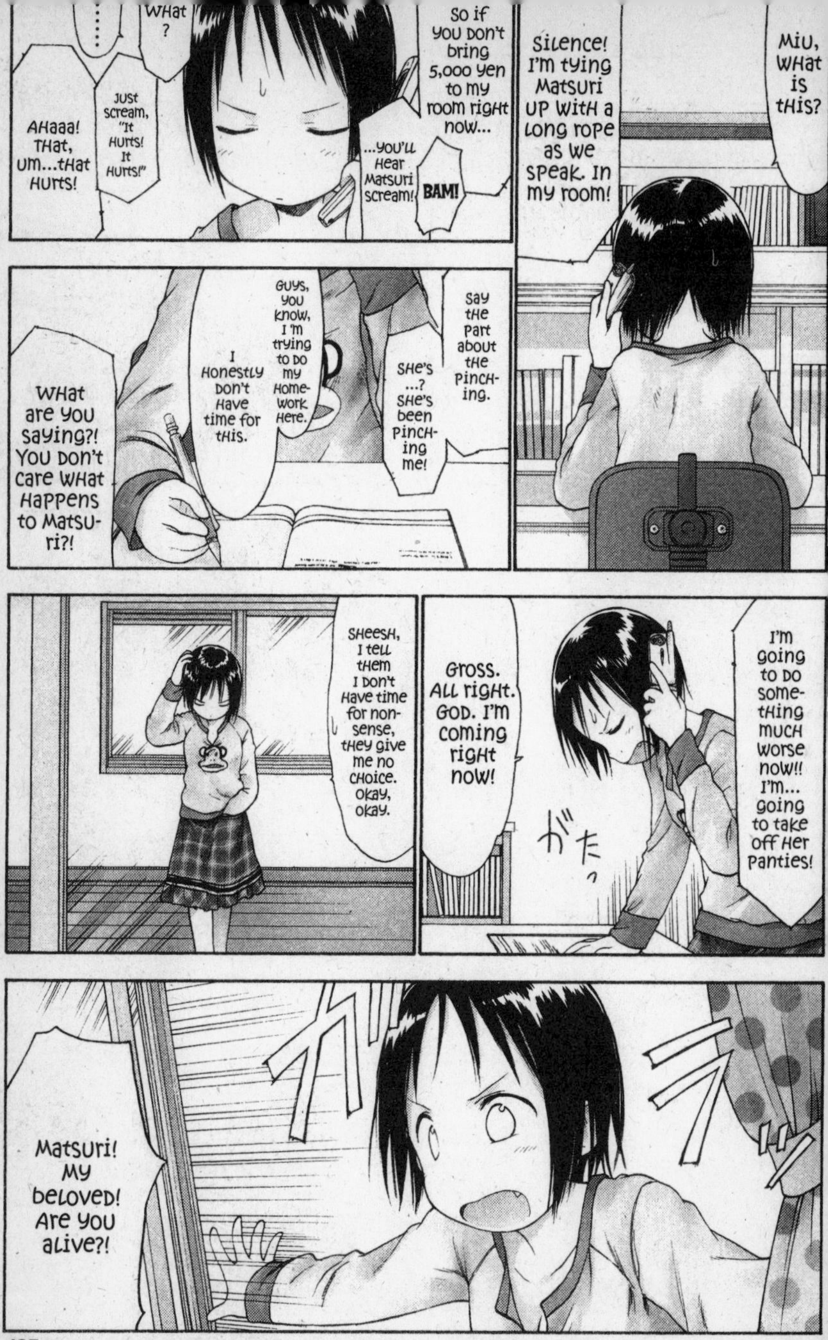
Miu, what is this?
Silence! I'm tying Matsuri up with a long rope as we speak. In my room!
So if you don't bring 5,000 yen to my room right now...
...You'll hear Matsuri scream!
BAM!
What ?
......
Just scream, "It hurts! It hurts!"
Ahaaa! That, um...that hurts!
Say the part about the pinching.
She's ...? She's been pinching me!
Guys, you know, I'm trying to do my homework here.
I honestly don't have time for this.
What are you saying?! You don't care what happens to Matsuri?!
I'm going to do something much worse now!! I'm... going to take off her panties!
がたっ
Gross. All right. God. I'm coming right now!
Sheesh, I tell them I don't have time for nonsense, they give me no choice. Okay, okay.
Matsuri! My beloved! Are you alive?!

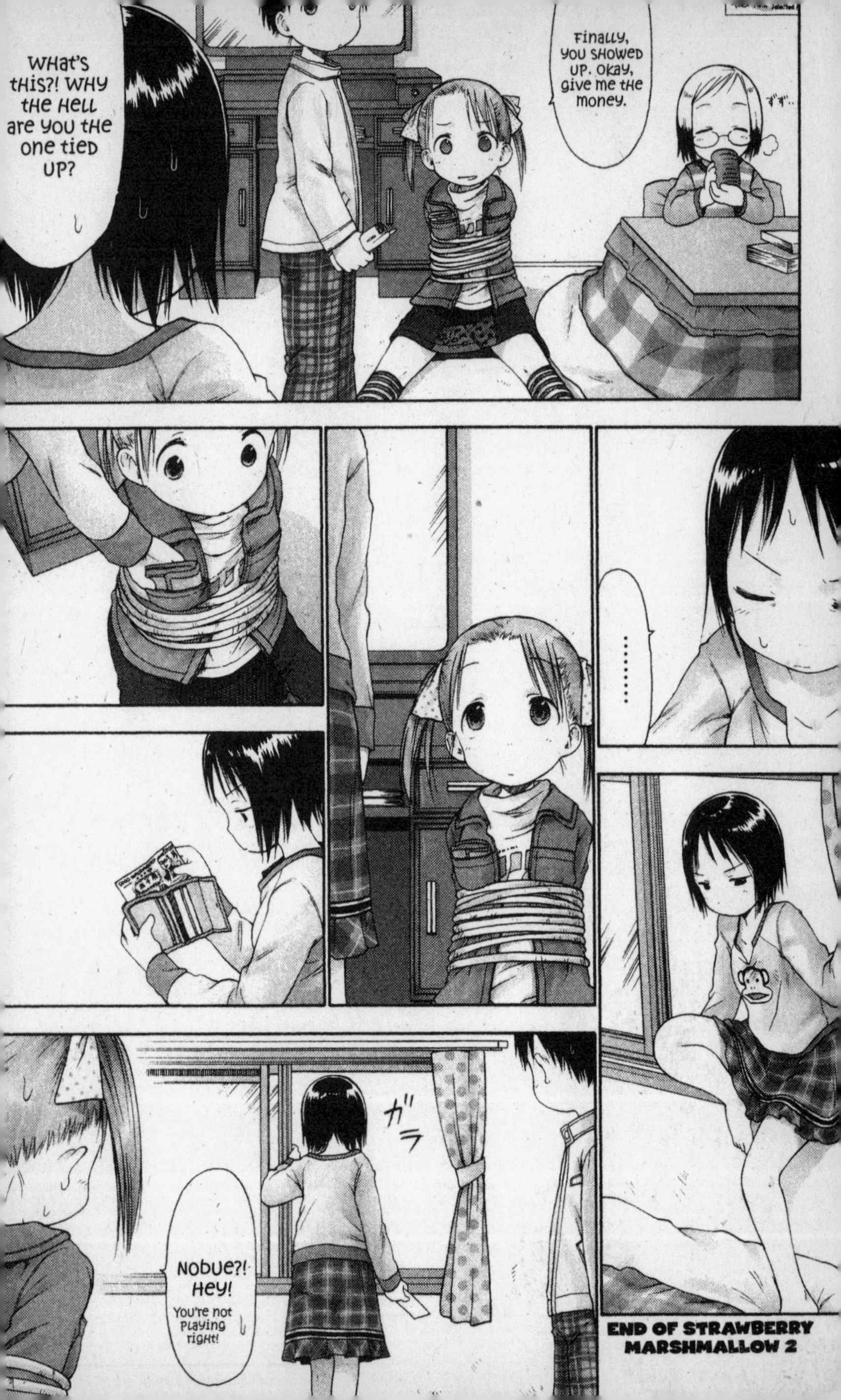
ずず..
Finally, you showed up. Okay, give me the money.
What's this?! WHY the HELL are you the one tied up?
……
ガラ
Nobue?! Hey!
You're not playing right!
END OF STRAWBERRY MARSHMALLOW 2

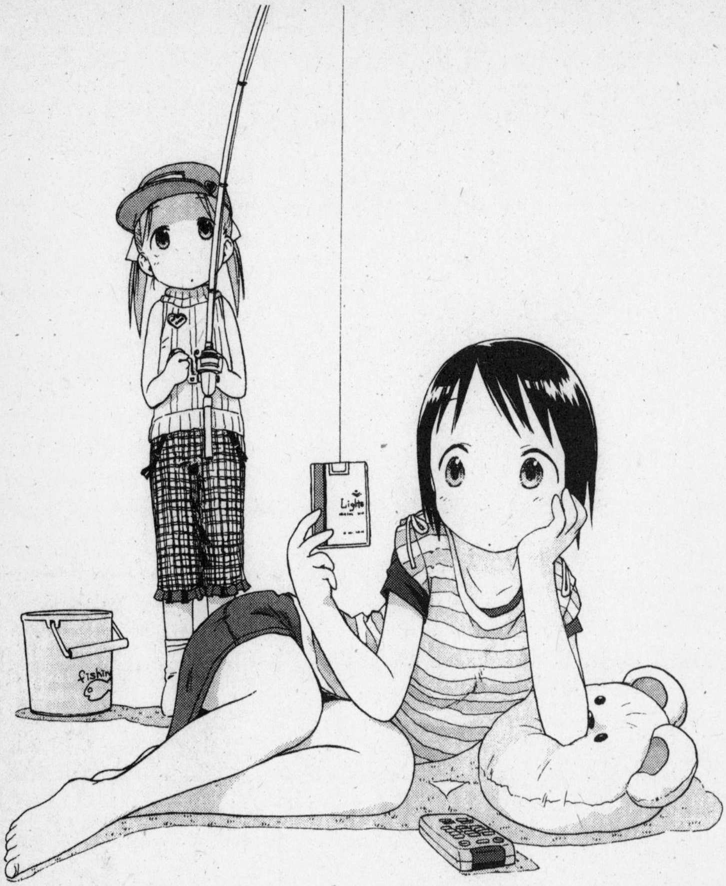
Lights

In the next volume of the always adorable *Strawberry Marshmallow*, the girls are still up to mischief every chance they get! Join in on the girls fun as they have a sleepover, play ninja, and even add a hilarious and cute twist to the classic fairytale, Cinderella...

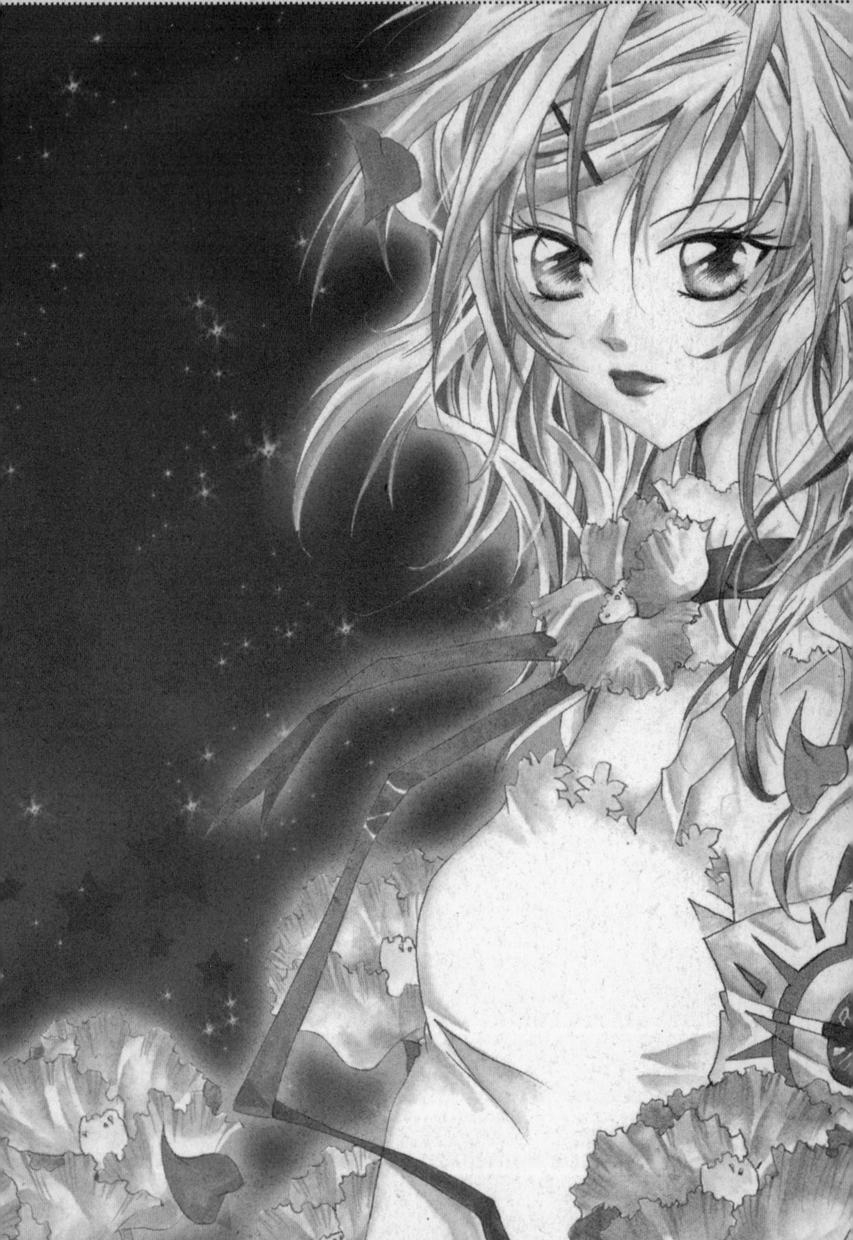

LITTLE QUEEN

Little Queen™

Jealousy, high school drama, and one cute boy!

Class rivals June and Lucia are fighting for the crown to become the Queen of Light. But will petty jealousies—and one cute boy—interfere with the Queen's duty of protecting the school from the evil King of Darkness?

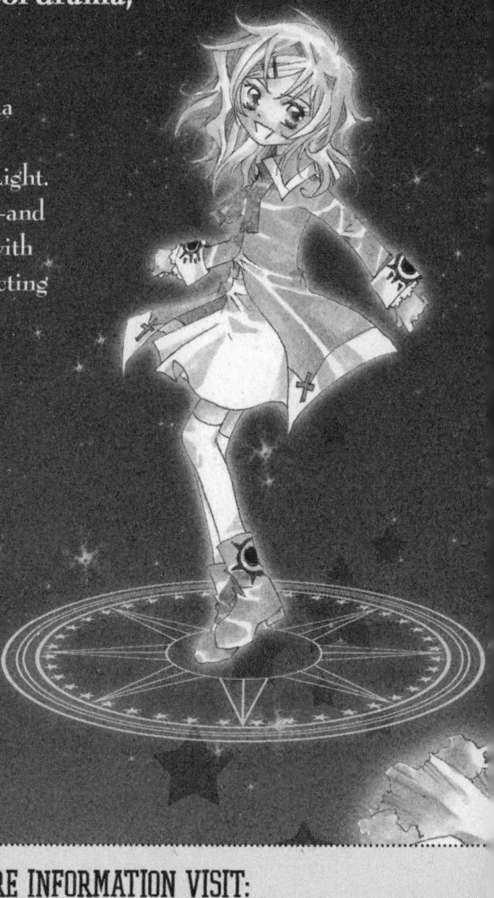

From one of Korea's best artists comes a story of angst and hilarity.

FANTASY

T TEEN AGE 13+

FOR MORE INFORMATION VISIT:

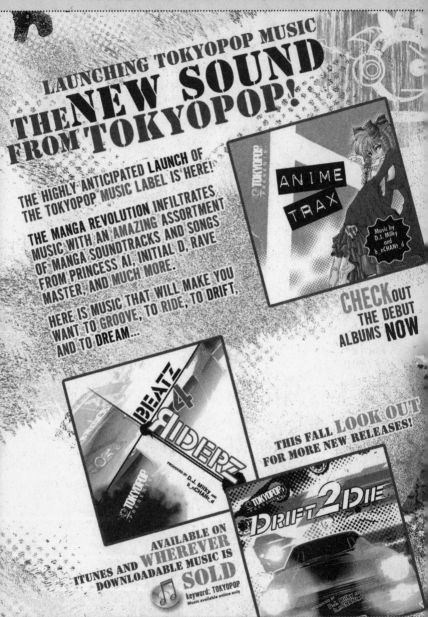

STOP!

This is the back of the book.
You wouldn't want to spoil a great ending!

This book is printed "manga-style," in the authentic Japanese right-to-left format. Since none of the artwork has been flipped or altered, readers get to experience the story just as the creator intended. You've been asking for it, so TOKYOPOP® delivered: authentic, hot-off-the-press, and far more fun!

DIRECTIONS

If this is your first time reading manga-style, here's a quick guide to help you understand how it works.

It's easy... just start in the top right panel and follow the numbers. Have fun, and look for more 100% authentic manga from TOKYOPOP®!